GUARDIANS OF THE FAITH

MARTIN ALAN FEIGENBAUM

This book is a work of fiction. Names, characters, places, and incidents either are the product of the author's imagination or are used fictitiously. Any resemblance to actual events, locales, or persons, living or dead, is entirely coincidental.

First Printing: November 2009

Library of Congress Control Number: 2009937560

ISBN: 978-0-615-32262-9

Graphic Artist: Roberto C. Suazo

SURFSIDE SIX PUBLISHING
Surfsidesixpublishing.com

Happiness is when what you think, what you say, and what you do are in harmony.

- Mohandas Karamchand Gandhi

GUARDIANS OF THE FAITH

_____

PROLOGUE

"Death to race traitors!" he yelled into the phone and hung up. He had called that new girl down at the Circle K on North Krome Avenue. They saw her in the parking lot the other day, holding hands with that big boon, like there wasn't a damn thing wrong being a white girl with a nigger boyfriend. Another one of his kind freeloading off this love-starved white trash. She worked there to make money for him so he could buy drugs and booze and want to keep hanging around. Even if she was fat and ugly and couldn't get the last white man on earth, there would be no racial mixing! It was ordained from the highest authority who gave people different colors so they didn't have to be geniuses to figure out who was their own kind. There would be no racial mixing! Death to race traitors!

Curtis Chance Thigpen stared at the only window in the small apartment, its dusty aluminum shade falling sharply to the right like a broken accordion, and made another call. When nobody answered, he hung up and squinted at the naked bulb in the center of the ceiling fan, watching the blades rotate slowly until he started getting dizzy. Just like he had done a thousand times before, he dialed another number.

"This is Reverend Sanderson." When the caller didn't say anything, after a few moments he added, "Why so early tonight?"

"Cause you're a fucking boon."

"Well, Curtis, you have a blessed night then."

Thigpen slammed the receiver down, missing the cradle and hitting the coffee table, cracking its glass top. "Son of a bitch!" Things weren't right. Nothing was right anymore.

CHAPTER ONE

The intercom buzzed shrilly like time was up to answer a question on a game show. Even after a dozen years he still winced at this loud, annoying sound. It was a dinosaur, this faded beige telephone, with its seven square buttons which popped off if you didn't push down exactly the right way. There was no line privacy, no automatic redial, and no conference-calling. This equipment was there long before the Dade State Attorney's Office had hired Rayfield Lifton, and most likely it would be there long after he was gone. At least there was a hold button. Lifton swivelled in his rickety chair, which had been listing down and to the right for a couple of months now, and gazed at the glittering skyline of downtown Miami. He shouldn't complain. Most prosecutors who worked at the Metro Justice Building didn't even have a window in their tiny offices.

It wasn't five yet, and he already was exhausted. But it wasn't from any heavy physical or mental activity. No longer did he have to rush off every day to three-hour soundings pulling a two-wheeler stacked high with bankers boxes crammed with nothing case files. Those days had been behind him for awhile. And all those hearings, defense motions to reduce bond, to suppress evidence, to compel the State of Florida to do this or do that, they too were history. And no more sentencing hearings, thank God, where the defendant's family members would cry their eyes out or scream or even pass out sometimes when the judge handed down the punishment. Rayfield Lifton was now Division Chief, Economic Crimes, and he was drained by virtue of his right to sit on his sorry ass all day and let everyone else do those things.

Extend a nice plea offer to most defendants, offer a sweet deal to these passers of bad checks and small-time thieves, he would tell his line prosecutors every day like a broken record. Give them the gift of the pretrial intervention program, if they were first-time offenders, and then *nolle prosse* their cases, as long as they agreed to spend all of four hours on a Saturday afternoon in one of the how-to-be-a-good-citizen classes. Make them pay restitution even if it had to be spread out over a ridiculous length of time. Getting a monthly check had a way of making victims stop demanding harsher treatment for the perpetrators. And, if necessary, agree with defense counsel to recommend the judge withhold adjudication so the defendant wouldn't be a convicted felon and lose his civil rights, like the right to vote, to hold public office, and to bear arms.

What else were you going to do with all these folks passing through Metro Justice, like cattle through a Midwest stockyard, even if the State really did want their hides? A federal judge recently had ruled that making hundreds of inmates sleep on cold floors in the Dade County Jail violated the Eighth Amendment's prohibition against cruel and unusual punishment. All around Florida criminals doing hard time for major crimes were being released from overcrowded prisons to make space for the next wave of newly-minted felons. It didn't make much sense to put away a small-time scam artist if it meant you had to put a recidivist child molester back on the streets two years early because there weren't enough beds behind bars.

He didn't go to court anymore because it was considered beneath the position of a Division Chief to do so unless, of course, it was a high-profile case. But it had been more than a year now since his promotion, and he was still waiting for one of those to land on his desk. Rayfield Lifton felt more like a supervisor of a widget production line than a champion for victims of economic crimes. His mood was cold and dark like a November night somewhere very far away from South Florida. The magnificent multicolored lights bathing International Place lifted his spirits for an instant until the intercom buzzed again. He already had suffered enough nothingness for the week, and he didn't want to hear one more word about another trivial third-degree felony until Monday morning. He shut his briefcase and started for the door but then retraced his steps and pushed down carefully on the flashing button.

"Yes, Moneypenny?" he moaned.

"You've got a call on line two. Alonzo Norris. I'll say you're not here."

"No, I'll take it. Go home, Moneypenny. It's late. *Adios*."

Every once in awhile Lifton would run into Alonzo "No-Time" Norris at the Metro Justice Building, in the lobby, in an elevator, or at the Pickle Barrel. The last time he had seen Norris was a few months before at the investiture of Gerald Rice, Florida's first black federal judge. "If you're offering me a full partnership, done deal. Just tell me how much I can expect to make next year."

"Well, my brother," Norris chuckled, "we may speak to that issue one of these days. So what's been going on? Things aren't so great over there? I did my time there too, you know."

"Doing time. Sounds like a prison sentence. You didn't stay around here very long."

"A year and a day to be exact."

"Now that really *does* sound like one of the prison sentences they hand out at all the time over here."

"Well, things were ripe for the picking so I picked up and left. The years have been good to me, my brother. But, you know, you're doing good too. Division Chief and all. One day we'll talk about all these things, but right now let's talk about tonight. Are you going to the Heat game?"

"I would be going except for one small problem. I seem to have misplaced my season tickets."

"Hey, my brother, I know what it's like living on a state prosecutor's salary so listen up. You're coming to the game tonight with me and my Posse. The Bulls are in town, and we're so damn close to the court you can steal the ball from Michael Jordan if you just lean forward a little. So are you in?"

"Am I in? Are you kidding, No-Time? I'm all the way in."

"Look, I'm running late. Just go to the VIP booth, west entrance, and give your name to the nice young lady there."

Lifton gazed out his ninth-floor window at the glowing dome of the Miami Arena a mile to the east and rubbed his hands. It was 1991, the Miami Heat's third season, and for the first time he was going to one of their games. And there he would get to see the great Air Jordan up close and personal.

* * *

The faded-blue Volvo 240 jumped the curb as Lifton pulled up in front of the small house on Northwest First Court. He should have cursed this beat-up old sardine can, but instead he just smiled and slid out, pushing the door shut with his knee.

"Hey, Mr. Prosecutor!" Old Lady Muir was shouting at him from the porch next door just like she did most days. Around the neighborhood Fredericka Muir was known as "Snoopy" because she constantly was sticking her nose in everybody else's business. She looked like Moms Mabley whom Lifton had seen on tv when he was a kid. Wearing a baggy housedress and floppy hat, and with her dentures removed, Moms Mabley joked about racism and sex, territory where no other black comic had dared to venture back in those days.

"Hey!" she yelled louder when he didn't say anything.

"And how *are* we today, Mrs. Muir?"

As usual Old Lady Muir's tan-and-white pit bull, Mr. T, was

tied up to her rocking chair and snarling menacingly. This mongrel was strong enough to drag Snoopy and her rocker across the porch, which was saying something, seeing as how Fredericka Muir had to be tipping the scales around two-ten.

"Pity the fool!" Lifton lunged toward his neighbor's front porch, a move which drove Mr. T bonkers, then ducked behind his sister's rusted orange Gremlin hatchback.

"Husshup, Mr. T! You're sure happy today, Mr. Prosecutor."

"Why shouldn't I be happy, Mrs. Muir?"

"Because you're always grumpy every time I see you. You probably took a bribe today or something."

"I wish I did. I could use some extra money."

"You sure got a smart mouth on you, Rayfield Lifton. Why don't you put some white people behind bars for a change? You just like locking up black folks. Hey, I'm talking to you!"

It was a close call whether Old Lady Muir had a meaner streak than her junkyard dog. Lifton pretended not to hear her and unlocked the front door. "Hey, Kim!"

"Back here," Kimberly Singletary called out from the bathroom where she was giving her daughter a bath.

"Hey, sis." Lifton bent down and gave her a kiss on an open space between two beaded cornrows.

She turned her head and looked up at him curiously. "My, my, aren't we happy today."

"What is it with everybody? Can't I be happy?"

"Of course you can. But you never are."

Lifton crouched down next to the tub. "Hey, champ," he said softly, gently stroking his niece's wet scalp.

"Will you stop calling her that!"

"Damn, Kim, I don't know why you..."

She pushed up and threw the big sponge into the hallway. "Why? *Why*? Because it's the biggest damn lie in the world!" She started sobbing and trembling, and Lifton reached out and pulled her to him while Demeka sat silently in the tub staring straight ahead as if nothing was going on around her.

"I'm sorry, sis," he whispered. "Anyway," he continued after a few moments, "to me *champ* sure sounds better than *Duh-mee-kaa*." He pushed his sister back so she could see the wild expression he was making.

She laughed hard and started coughing. "I'm sorry, Ray."

"The *thing* is making you crazy again."

She pressed a finger against his lips. "Remember. We don't talk about the *thing* in front of my little girl." She looked down at her daughter who still hadn't moved an inch. "I know she doesn't understand, but that's the rule anyway. You lawyers know about rules, right?"

"We sure do, and that *is* the rule." Lifton bent down and kissed his niece's forehead. He picked up the sponge and flung it back to his sister with a hook shot.

"Are you going out tonight or something?"

"Remember No-Time Norris?"

"Alonzo Norris? You don't hang with him."

"He called out of the blue. He said he's got a Heat ticket with my name on it. You know, Michael Jordan..."

"And the Bulls are in town. That's really great, Ray. Now I know why you're so happy tonight."

"So, Kim, now you know."

* * *

"Oh, yes, here you go, Mr. Lifton." The receptionist at the VIP booth, a pretty Hispanic girl with olive skin, long jet-black hair, and a huge smile, made him feel like a celebrity as she handed him a small envelope with his name on it. "Over there through the turnstiles and two sections down."

The announcer's voice reverberated through the Miami Arena as he introduced the starting Heat lineup, the crowd roaring after each name. Lifton bolted down the concrete passage, dodging the sea of fans, until he found the entrance to the right section. The Heat cheerleaders were on the edge of the court, strutting their stuff to M.C. Hammer's "Can't Touch This." He spotted Norris in the first row right behind the home bench. Alonzo "No-Time" Norris glittered under the Arena lights, from his clean-shaven head all the way down to his burgundy alligator boots. He was dressed to the hilt, one of his defining trademarks, a shiny long-sleeve black dress shirt with a white collar anchored by a hot-pink tie. Norris slapped Lifton on the shoulder and pumped his hand like he was jacking up a car. "You know the rest of my Posse."

Wayne Parrish, Reginald Crawford, and Donald Leeds already were on their feet, and he hugged each of his old friends. They all had grown up in the same inner-city neighborhood and attended Miami Jackson Senior High.

"What's going on, Perishable?"

"Same old. Me and No-Time doing our thing, you know, putting criminals back on the street so we can get some repeat business. And No-Time here throws me some bones with meat on them every now and then," Parrish added, and they all laughed.

Wayne Parrish wasn't a high-profile attorney like Alonzo Norris. In fact, nobody in the tri-county area was in his class. He was "No-Time" Norris because the perception was his clients would end up with no jail time if he was on their case. Alonzo Norris had a lock on the most lucrative criminal defense business in the black communities from Fort Pierce to Key West. *The Miami Herald* had christened him "glamboyant" after a surprise acquittal in an unwinnable triple-murder case. His closing arguments were legendary, sounding a lot more like he was preaching the gospel at a tent revival than summarizing the law and facts in a courtroom. He also was known to play the race card whenever it might tip jurors in favor of finding reasonable doubt. Wayne Parrish did all right too, still one of only a handful of experienced black criminal defense attorneys in South Florida. Sometimes he would sit as second chair with Norris in a murder case, especially if the State of Florida was seeking the death penalty. And whatever cases Norris didn't want, he referred to Parrish and a few other close friends.

Guardians Of The Faith

"And you, Seven? I see you in the paper all the time."

"Don't believe everything you read in the press," Crawford said with a big smile. He had earned that nickname because he had the best luck of the bunch, always winning more than anybody else when they used to roll dice after school, sitting on orange crates in the parking lot of an inner-city market. And Crawford's good luck had continued after that part of their lives was over. Instead of going on to college like the others, he got into the real-estate business. He borrowed money and bought rundown buildings in the poor neighborhoods of Overtown and Liberty City, fixing them up, and then reselling them at a nice profit, mostly to the County for public housing. When it suddenly became *chic* for upwardly-mobile professionals to live close to the glass towers where they worked, Crawford was perfectly positioned to make his biggest windfall yet. He built the first luxury condominium on Brickell Avenue on bare land he had purchased for a song a few years before. Two more high-end buildings followed with all units presold before their foundations were poured. Reginald Crawford knew how to spin straw into gold and already had made himself a small fortune.

"What's up, Doc?"

"Damn, I *knew* you were going to say that." Donald Leeds was the premier family physician for South Florida's affluent blacks. Ever since middle school he made no secret of the fact he was going to be a doctor, and he took a lot of flak for getting serious about studying way too early in his life. If he hadn't been a pretty good basketball player, Donald Leeds never would have been allowed to hang with them back then.

Lifton sat between Norris and Parrish and yelled himself hoarse before the end of the first half. He couldn't remember the last time he had enjoyed himself so much. He marveled at the gravity-defying moves of Michael Jordan and the gorgeous Heat cheerleaders strutting their stuff so close they almost gave him lap dances. He lost count of the number of rounds a leggy cocktail waitress in fishnet stockings had served him, batting her long eyelashes seductively each time she handed him his drink. These friends from his past made him feel like he still was part of the group. Lifton gazed longingly around the Miami Arena at this great spectacle. His life should have played out on *this* court, not in a court of law doing nothing cases for what had amounted to the last third of his life.

"You ever play ball anymore?" Parrish asked him as they rose to stretch after the buzzer signaled the end of the first half. "You were the greatest, Ray."

"I wasn't the greatest, Perishable."

"People still remember you, Liftoff."

"That was a long time ago, Seven."

Norris reached over and got Lifton in a headlock. "You brought fame and glory to the hood, and you don't think people are gonna remember?"

Caught off guard and under the influence, Lifton struggled to try and free himself. "Ladies and gentlemen," the announcer's resonant voice filled the Miami Arena. "Your Miami Heat are proud to have among tonight's fans.... a very special guest. One of the greatest college basketball players of all time who broke every major record while playing for the University of Miami Hurricanes. Ladies and gentlemen, please give a very warm Miami Heat welcome to *Ray...field...Lift...off...Lif...ton!*" When the spotlights began crisscrossing the area around them, Norris released him. A lot of people were on their feet now applauding and shouting out "*Three...two...one...lift...off!*" During his college basketball days this had been the chant when it looked like he was about to rush the basket to make a slam-dunk.

This surprise tribute made Lifton's eyes fill with water and, combined with the powerful spotlights now fixed on him, the court shimmered like tropical waters reflecting a blinding midday sun. He had earned the nickname "Liftoff" because he launched from ground zero like a rocket, soaring to heights never reached by other six-foot-three players, making a slam-dunk look as easy as dropping a wad of paper into a wastebasket. The national press had compared him to Don Chaney, the star guard from the Boston Celtics, even though he was two inches shorter. The Celtics had picked Chaney in the first-round of the NBA draft a few years before, and then he had gone on to be a finals champion in his rookie year. Lifton brought his forearm to his face and dabbed at the moisture. No-Time was right. People still remembered him.

He wished the second half never would end, but it seemed like it was over in a flash. The Chicago Bulls had beaten up on The Miami Heat, mainly because Air Jordan had racked up forty-two points while Glen Rice, the Heat's high scorer, only had eighteen.

"This was really great," Lifton said after they had descended the steep flight of stairs outside the Arena. "And thanks for setting up that other thing too. I know it had to be you, No-Time."

Norris stopped and cocked his head. "And just where do you think you're going?"

"I'm going home. Where else am I going?"

Norris scanned the horizon. "Right over there." When the chauffeur saw them approaching, he scrambled to open the rear doors of the shiny black Mercedes limousine. "My man Carlos floated all the way up here from Cuba on a raft. Can you dig it?" After they piled into the limo, Norris picked up the remote and aimed it at the cherry-wood console. The front panel slid to the left, revealing a mini-bar and a sound system. Parrish poured a round of Johnny Walker Black for everybody as B.B. King and Bono belted out "When Love Comes To Town" from U2's *Rattle and Hum*.

"So what really happened to you back then, Liftoff? Some people say..."

"Wayne, why don't you just let the man enjoy the moment?"

Lifton didn't like talking about the past, but he owed them. "It's alright, No-Time. It's no big mystery. My right knee got torn up bad near the end of that last season. There was no way it was going to heal right. If I was lucky, I'd be able to play at fifty-percent of what I was before. I missed the last three games, and that was the end of everything."

"I wish I'd been a doctor already back then. I would have made sure you had the best of the best."

"I did have the best of the best, Doc, and the verdict was unanimous. I was too messed up."

"Too messed up." Norris repeated, shaking his head.

"I never got drafted for the pros because everybody knew that I was damaged goods."

Back then Lifton had coined the phrase "dreambuster" to describe his career-ending injury. So he found another star to hitch himself to, law school, an internship at the Dade State Attorney's Office, and then a job there after he graduated. It was a safe way to start out and learn the ropes how to be a trial lawyer on the County's tab. He would try a lot of cases, and then after a few years he would make his fortune in private practice. A dozen years had passed now, but Lifton never had left the safety of his government job.

"You've done good, Liftoff." Crawford raised his glass and tilted it slightly in Lifton's direction.

"Done good, Seven? A man who puts a lot of his own people behind bars?"

They all laughed and raised their glasses. They were trying to make Lifton feel important, but he had given up on that idea years ago.

"Your driver went too far, No-Time. He had to turn back there on Seventeenth."

"It doesn't matter because you're not going home just yet. First, you're going to The Little Store with us."

"The Little Store? You've gotta be kidding me. In a limo?"

"We go out there sometimes and talk about the old days."

"So we never forget." Parrish lifted his glass.

"So we never forget," Crawford and Doc Leeds repeated, raising their glasses.

Guardians Of The Faith

"So we never forget who we are," Norris added, "and where we came from."

"And do you all sit on orange crates in the parking lot and drink and roll dice too?"

At the border between Overtown and Liberty City, Miami's two black ghettos, The Little Store had been around longer than anybody could remember. It had survived scores of armed robberies and even a couple of major riots. The small market smelled like someone had washed the aisles with beer, and its parking lot reeked of urine. They fished for cans of malt liquor in the big ice-filled blue plastic barrel next to the cash register. They drew lots of stares and had numerous insults hurled at them. For the junkies, winos, and derelicts who passed by the parking lot, something was all wrong with this picture, a shiny black Mercedes limousine and five well-dressed black men sipping Schlitz Malt Liquor as they leaned against it.

"How's that sister of yours?" Parrish asked. "Kimberly was one pretty lady. She married Ty Singletary, right?"

"What a piece of shit that guy was," Crawford muttered. "Hey, Ray, I'm sorry, it's just that..."

"No, Seven, you're right. Kim was married to Ty for about two years, but he was never around. He left Kim with a little girl, Demeka, but he never shows any interest. The only thing he does is pay some child support."

"So Kim's got a little girl. That's nice."

"My niece has a problem, Doc. Nobody has been able to figure it out. It came out of nowhere. She just sits around, staring off into space, some type of neurological disorder, they say. Me and Kim, we just call it 'the *thing*.'"

"Hey, man, I'm sorry," Leeds said. "Give me a call one of these days, and we'll talk about it."

They polished off a few more cans of malt liquor and watched the parade of characters going in and out of The Little Store. The sound of three gunshots rang out a few blocks away followed by the wail of a police siren.

"So can you still slam-dunk good?"

Lifton took a swig from his can of malt liquor. "Let me guess, Perishable. You guys play hoops somewhere, and you need another player."

"Guilty as charged," Parrish held up his hands.

"So tonight was a set-up, right?" He tried to sound offended but broke out laughing instead. "Well, if it was, then you all need to try and set me up more often."

"Here's the deal, Liftoff," Norris said. "We play some organized ball at the DSC. You know the place?"

Lifton had heard about the high-end Downtown Sports Club. It occupied the top two floors of the parking garage connected to Miami's tallest office building. On the lower floor of the DSC, there was a full-size basketball court.

"So you guys need another player for your team?"

Norris put his hands together and tossed his empty can of malt liquor like he was shooting a free throw. "Yes!" he shouted when it hit the rim of the dumpster and dropped in. "We've entered a team in every league there for the past two years. Right now we're five games into the winter league. We call ourselves 'The Posse.'"

"The Posse? What, you're all Jamaican now? So why do you need me?"

"Because we just lost one of our guys," said Crawford. "Leander Baldwin. You remember Lee Baldwin?"

"Yeah, he dated Kim for awhile back in high school, but he played football."

"That's true, but he's a good hoop man too. He's been doing his thing with local government, but now he's headed to Tallahassee. Governor Chiles drafted him to head up some kind of community development program."

"So we decided to draft you to play with The Posse."

"Membership in a place like that isn't in my current budget."

Guardians Of The Faith

Norris put his arm around Lifton. "You just leave all details to The Posse, *mon*."

"Other people, two of whom happen to be criminal defense attorneys, paying my way at the DSC? I don't think so, No-Time."

"You're kidding, right?" Norris stepped back, but he could tell from Lifton's expression this straight arrow wasn't bending. "Well, you clear it with your office, but do it real fast, okay, my brother? Then all you have to worry about is putting in some serious practice time with us to get ready for the next game."

After the limousine pulled up in front of Lifton's house, Carlos jumped out and opened the right rear door.

"We need you to do this, Ray."

"I'll let you know what they say, No-Time, but I always do things by the book."

"Even when some scumbag defense attorney tries to put a murderer back on the street?"

"Damn you, Seven." Parrish shoved Crawford hard against the seat.

"Hey, Perishable, I was just asking," Crawford said with a big smirk. "I wasn't necessarily referring to you or No-Time."

"Hey, Liftoff!" Norris' shiny bald head was sticking out of the open sun roof. "I'll give you a shout on Monday, okay?!" The Mercedes limousine continued silently gliding down the dark street, the bright-red glow of its taillights vanishing suddenly as it turned right at the corner.

CHAPTER TWO

The electronic scoreboard counted down the last five seconds of game four of the DSC winter-league championship. Rayfield Lifton added insult to injury when he swished a three-pointer from mid-court right before the final buzzer, giving him a total of thirty-three points for the night. Lifton had sliced and diced the opposing team, "The Golden Gavels" of Pettigrew & Shaw, the largest white-glove law firm in Florida with more than two-hundred attorneys in its Miami office alone. As he was leaving the court with the rest of his team, Chesterfield Kumble muttered something loud enough for all of them to hear, something about people like *them* being born with an unfair advantage.

"Good game, Chesterfield!" Norris shouted across the court to the six-foot-five red-haired captain of "The Golden Gavels" and the head of his firm's commercial litigation department. Fifteen years ago he had been a star forward for the University of Florida Gators. Kumble turned his head and made a sour expression, like he was sucking on a lemon, and gave them the finger, triggering a huge outburst of laughter from The Posse.

"Whitebreads like him always have first names that should be last names," said Parrish.

"That's true," Crawford agreed. "Like Burton and Kendall."

Guardians Of The Faith

"And Shelby and Chapman," Doc Leeds added.

They were still roaring with laughter as they sauntered into the locker room.

"No more excuses, Liftoff," said Norris. "You're going out with The Posse tonight. You haven't been out with us since we went to The Little Store that time. Tonight we celebrate *you*. You're the only reason we squished those fools in four straight games and won the championship." They all whined and jabbed at Lifton until he gave in.

"Alright, alright. So where exactly is it we're going?"

"Well, first, *exactly*, we're going to Joe's. Then we'll hit one of the clubs down there on South Beach."

It was only ten-minutes from the Downtown Sports Club to Joe's Stone Crab, the landmark restaurant at the southern tip of Miami Beach. The Mercedes limousine sped east on the MacArthur Causeway across Biscayne Bay, to the left dozens of brightly-lit waterfront mansions, to the right Dodge Island, the world's largest cruise port. At Joe's they feasted on plates heaped with the best stone crabs in the Southeast and polished off three bottles of very expensive Pinot Noir from California's Russian River Valley. It seemed like almost everybody in the place knew Alonzo No-Time Norris, some of them stopping by their table to shake his hand, others just calling out his name and waving.

Outside the restaurant Norris passed out Cuban *Cohibas*, and they all lit up and strolled north on Ocean Drive. They crossed Fifth Street where every night scores of exotic cars turned left and began a slow procession up Ocean Drive so their occupants could be noticed, inching north the ten blocks of that narrow street crammed with restaurants, bars, and art deco hotels. A cold December wind was blowing in hard from the Atlantic, whipping the fronds of the palm trees on the east side of the street like a thousand green banners. They stopped in front of Caribe Force, the newest club on South Beach.

"No way we're getting in soon," said Lifton, noticing the long line snaking itself around the corner. He was hoping this would convince the rest of them to call it a night.

"Never underestimate the power of The Posse." Norris whipped out his wallet and extracted a $100 bill, showed it to the stocky bouncer who grabbed it and immediately unhooked the red rope from the post so they could enter ahead of everybody else. A dozen multi-colored laser beams in sync with "Freaky Behavior," the latest song from the local hip-hop group *2 Live Crew*, sliced through the center of the club from different angles. South Beach's most famous deejay, "The Waxman," was positioned on a platform high above the gyrating mass. Norris, Leeds, and Lifton leaned against the bar and hooted and waved at Parrish and Crawford. They were making fools of themselves on the dance floor, gyrating wildly near two spandex mini-skirted girls half their age who swivelled their hips like they were twirling invisible hula hoops.

"It's a sick world, and I'm glad to be alive!" Norris had to shout even though Doc Leeds and Lifton were right next to him.

"Those girls don't even know Perishable and Seven are there," Leeds yelled back.

"Doc, I'm taking Liftoff outside. Make sure those two don't commit any felonies while we're gone!"

"We liked our music loud too, remember? But it was a big-band sound. Ike and Tina, James Brown, Wilson Pickett. You know what I'm saying?"

"Can you repeat that?" Lifton wiggled a finger in his ear like he had just suffered a sudden hearing loss.

They sat at a table outside the News Café, and Norris ordered them a round of Cardenal Mendoza.

"So how do you like hanging out with The Posse so far, Liftoff?" Norris asked as he took a sip of the Spanish brandy.

"No-Time, the past few weeks have been the best I've had in a *really* long time."

"*Damn*, there sure were some very lovely ladies back there in that club. Makes you dream, right? But I don't want to talk about

Guardians Of The Faith

the ladies. I want to talk about your future."

"I gotta tell you, No-Time, this is starting to sound a lot like that scene in *The Graduate*."

"Well, it kinda does, doesn't it?" Norris chuckled. "But I'm serious about this, Ray, about you moving on up."

"To the east side like George Jefferson?"

"This is no joke. You need to listen up, Ray, because No-Time is talking big time here." He rotated his snifter a few times before looking up. "When Don King stepped out of prison back in 1971, there wasn't one black promoter in the whole boxing business. You see, the sixties were all about getting basic civil rights for black people. And the seventies were all about taking it to the next level. When he came out of prison, Don King had the right *race*, and he picked the right *place*, a place where black men had never gone before."

"Now this is starting to sound like black *Star Trek*. Look, I don't know anything about boxing, but maybe you've got an opening for NBA coach."

Norris shook his head again. "Man, you really need to hear me out. I'm talking serious business here. The time has come for this County to have a black State Attorney." Norris fixed his eyes on Lifton while he took a sip of brandy. "You're a Division Chief, and in case you haven't checked recently, you're black. You're a natural for the job."

"You're wrong. First, this community isn't ready for that yet. Second, even if it were, I'm not high-profile. In fact, I'm nothing in my office. And if you plan on raising enough money to run a successful campaign, you've gotta be high-profile."

Norris sat back and smiled. "Who said anything about a campaign? You wouldn't have to get elected if the Governor appointed you to fill a vacancy, now would you?"

"Forget about it, No-Time. The Big Girl isn't going anywhere for a long time."

"Let me tell you something you don't know, Ray," Norris'

eyes lit up. "If a certain Democrat candidate out there wins the next presidential election, there's a good chance The Big Girl will be heading to D.C."

"Even if that happened, No-Time, to get The Big Girl's job I'd have to be a superstar. So taking into account my less-than-stellar career over there, I'd have to become an *overnight* superstar."

"Maybe not overnight but how about in a few months? What if you had a high-profile case, one where you could make a name for yourself?"

"It ain't happening, No-Time, no way, no how."

Norris savored the last few drops of his brandy. "It's a big mistake underestimating the power of The Posse."

"It ain't gonna happen, No-Time. Susan has her inner circle, and I'm not in it." He pushed back from the table and stood up.

Norris took out his wallet and placed some bills under the heavy glass ashtray. "I'm gonna go inside and call Carlos."

Lifton finished off the last of his Spanish brandy and rubbed his hands. The wind was blowing harder now, and it was a lot colder than a typical Miami Beach winter night. A few minutes later they all had piled into the Mercedes limo and were heading west across Biscayne Bay on the return trip to Miami.

"Carlos missed the exit," Lifton said, looking back as they flew past the ramp to Biscayne Boulevard.

"Don't worry about that," said Norris. "We're going to The Little Store."

"Forget about The Little Store. Man, I'm already fried."

But it was too late. The Little Store was only a few blocks away. This time Lifton didn't follow the others inside. When they returned to the limo, Doc Leeds handed him a small brown paper bag containing an ice-cold can of Colt 45.

"Drinking malt liquor in the parking lot of a ghetto market. If your patients could only see you now."

"Hey, I'll have you know I'm board-certified in internal medicine! A little alcohol is good for you."

"Donald Leeds, M.D.," Crawford reflected. "A man who never forgot his roots."

"The shit you talk, Mr. Black-ass Donald Trump." Lifton pulled back the pop-top and took a swig of the malt liquor. "You all *really* need to lose the nostalgia trip."

"Yes, sir, Mr. Prosecutor." Parrish saluted Lifton.

Lifton placed his thumb over the opening of his can, shook it hard, and directed the spray toward Parrish's face. They were still laughing hard when a few moments later a City of Miami police cruiser activated its blue-and-white lights and barreled into The Little Store's parking lot and screeched to a stop.

"*Deja vu*," Parrish mumbled.

A tall blond female officer remained next to the cruiser while the male police officer, a stocky Latin type with bulging biceps, approached them.

"You boys dealing in style tonight, huh?"

"No dealers here. No pimps. Just doctors and lawyers," Doc Leeds said calmly.

"*Yeah, right*," the officer responded. "This parking lot is a drug hole not an office building. So, tell me, what the fuck are you boys doing here?"

"You know what I think? I think you came to the hood to buy some more of those illegal steroids you use to pump yourself up with."

The officer drew his service revolver and trained it on Parrish. "Shut the fuck up!"

"C'mon, Perishable," Crawford grabbed Parrish's shoulder and pulled him back.

"I'll run you niggers in like nothing. Now, tell me, what the fuck are you boys doing here?"

"We don't have to tell you jack shit." Norris said calmly and took a swig from the can in his brown paper bag.

Just as the male cop swivelled so he could train his gun on Norris, the female officer called out, "Hey, Luis! I'm gonna need you over here a second."

The male cop retraced his steps slowly until he reached the cruiser. The female cop began speaking to him in an agitated manner, and his demeanor quickly changed from lion to lamb. The Latin officer shoved the revolver back in his holster and got into the passenger side of the front seat.

"I think the lady cop said something like `that guy's a state prosecutor.' Does she look familiar to you, Ray?"

"No, I don't recognize her, No-Time."

The lady officer got into the cruiser, turned off the flashing lights, and sped out of the parking lot.

"*Deja vu*," said Norris. "Can you believe it's the same old shit after all these years?"

"We're still just a bunch of niggers to them no matter what we accomplish in this world." Parrish crushed his empty can and threw it like a fastball across the parking lot where it hit the side of the dumpster.

"Let's get the hell out of here," Crawford mumbled.

Nobody said a word during the drive to Lifton's house. After he slid out of the limousine and started to close the door, Lifton leaned back inside. "Listen, No-Time. I am interested in what you and me were talking about tonight, alright?"

"Alright, Ray," Norris said quietly. "Alright."

* * *

Rayfield Lifton strode into the ninth floor secretarial area, briefcase in his left hand, gym bag slung over his right shoulder. "Hello, Moneypenny." He went over to Cuqui Perez' desk and gave her a peck on the cheek.

"You really are *loco* today, *señor* Bond."

"*Yesh*, I am crazy today, Moneypenny," he said, slurring his words with his pretty decent Sean Connery imitation. "*Yesh*, I am." He removed his Hurricanes baseball cap and tossed it at a coat rack in the corner, but it didn't catch on any of the hooks.

"*Señor* Bond, The Big Girl wants to see you."

It had been a long time since Lifton had spoken to Susan

Purvis. Maybe Alonzo Norris had been able to push the right buttons so that opportunity might come knocking today. He left his briefcase and gym bag next to Cuqui's desk, strode down the hallway to the fire stairwell, opened the heavy metal door, and descended to the sixth floor.

"Rayfield Lifton, right?" the secretary asked with a smile as he crossed the threshold into the Office of the Dade State Attorney. "I remember you."

"Yeah, *sure* you do," he said to himself.

"Give me a second." She pressed a button and announced his arrival.

"Yes, send him in, Nancy." Susan Purvis' deep voice had a distinctive South Florida twang. "Well, hello, Rayfield Lifton," she said, rising from behind her desk. Dade County's chief prosecutor really *was* a big girl at six-two. She had short brown hair and wore horn-rimmed glasses with thick lenses which made her eyes appear extra large.

"Sit, sit. Look at this, will you?" she said with a sweep of her hand across the huge semi-circular desk which was covered with stacks of papers and manilla folders.

"Do I hate being an administrator instead of a trial attorney? You bet I do. I miss the courtroom drama. That's what it's all about, you know. Here it's just papers and more papers and a bunch of meetings and a whole lot of blah-blah-blah. Well, I guess you should know about some of that being a Division Chief and all. Which brings me right to the point why I called you in here today.

"Ray, an opportunity, a big one, has presented itself. You probably already know we've got this new hate-crimes law. Are you familiar with it?" Before he could answer, Purvis went ahead and did it for him. "Yes. Everybody's been talking about it. Very controversial. The ACLU is screaming bloody murder it's not constitutional. Of course, we prosecutors love this new law. Here's the bottom line. We need to make a high-profile case and get a conviction so it can start making its way up the appellate pipeline. A case of first impression. If we win and get affirmed, everybody's on notice, and we move on, doing what we do best, getting the bad guys off the streets. And with this new law we can keep the worst types off the streets longer. It's ground-breaking stuff, so right for today's world, and everybody wants to be first to grab all the glory. My counterparts around the State want to beat me to the finish line, but I intend for Dade County to win this horse race."

Susan Purvis beamed at him for a few seconds. "And I've already got a case lined up. There's a Metro-Dade detective, Joel Chernin, who's been working on something. You ever had any cases with him? Let's just say he's a little out there, but he also happens to be one of the best undercover cops in the whole damn County. I told him to get together with you. Yes, Rayfield Lifton, I'm putting you in charge of our first prosecution under this new law if you want it. So do you want it?" She tapped a finger impatiently waiting for his response.

"Sure, but why me?"

Susan Purvis pulled off her thick glasses and twirled them a few times. "Why you? Why you?" She smiled and looked at him curiously. "Why even ask?"

* * *

"You've got a visitor, *jefe*. A very big one."

Joel Chernin nearly removed the door from its hinges when he flung it open. "Hail to the chief!" His head and face were shaved clean except for the light-brown chin-strip style goatee. Chernin looked more like one of the ogres from the world of professional entertainment wrestling than a law-enforcement officer. He was dressed in blue jeans and white t-shirt and had swastika tattoos on each side of his neck. Chernin noticed the miniature basketball hoop hanging on the back of the door, grabbed the nerf ball, took a couple of steps back, and flicked his wrist. "Two, two!" He barked when the ball landed in the middle of the tiny net.

"Okay, Larry Bird, have a seat."

"Don't need a seat. I've been sitting on my ass all morning

in our wonderful Miami traffic." He went over to the window and looked out. "So you got one, huh?"

"Got one what?"

"A window, dude. Consider yourself very lucky. Most prosecutors in this God-forsaken building don't have one. And none of you dudes get cellular phones. Well, nobody in my Department does either except I got one because I do undercover stuff. Anyway, you ever think of going fed? The U.S. Attorney's Office, now they know how to treat their prosecutors right. You could make more money and do big cases all the time. The feds would take you, boss, trust me, you being a local hero and all even though that was a long time ago." He smacked the big wad of gum he was chewing, rolled his head around, then jerked it rapidly from side to side. "So you ready to boogie?"

"Ready to boogie?"

"Yeah, boss, are you ready to boogie? Like KC and the Sunshine Band. You ready to boogie on the hate-crimes case?"

"Oh, yeah. Kool And The Gang."

"Groovy." He reached into his front pants pocket, pulled out a yellow sheet of paper, and unfolded it. "The Reverend, yeah, that's our case, boss man."

"The Reverend, that's our case? Well, that really *is* groovy. Let's go out and make some arrests, boss man."

Chernin strolled over to Lifton's desk. "Oh, wise guy, huh?" he said, imitating the high-pitched voice of Curly from The Three Stooges and snaking his hand close to Lifton's face. Chernin eased himself down into one of the guest chairs and took another look at the yellow sheet. "Alrighty then, some detail, governor. The Reverend Wilkie P. Sanderson is an old black preacher with a small church in Homestead. Some Klan types have been making his life miserable for awhile now. And, ah, yes, the best part. The Reverend just happens to be Commissioner Beverly Sanderson's older brother." Chernin folded the paper and stuffed it back inside his pants pocket.

Guardians Of The Faith

Beverly Sanderson was a pioneering politician, the first black female to serve on the Dade County Commission which ran the County's business with a multi-billion-dollar budget, a sum greater than the combined budgets of all six countries of Central America.

"So you think this could be a good case, Joel?"

"*Duh!* Just look at the cast of characters. You've got the victim, an African-American man of God. You've got the victim's sister, a high-profile local politician. And then you've got Thigpen. Somebody a jury would love to hate." Chernin regarded Lifton for a few moments while he smacked his gum loudly. "Any questions, *mon capitaine?*"

"*Oui, oui, mon chef.* Who's Thigpen? That name sounds familiar, but I can't place it right now."

"Yeah, Curtis Chance Thigpen. Started his career in the hate business real young. Learned everything he needed from his old man who was KKK. Papa Bear bites the big one, and young Thigpen takes over. Then remember when some civil rights group won a huge money judgment against the Klan?"

"I do remember that great moment in American history, Joel. I think the court also issued an injunction which made the Klan disband or something like that."

"Right. So all around the country the KKK was on the skids, but a lot of those fuckers weren't about to give up the cause so they just started different groups. Same old white-power shit but without the robes. The South Dade KKK disappears, and Thigpen and company start something new called the Guardians Of The Race. I've already got my people looking around the Department to see what else we've got on these fuckers."

"You said Thigpen has been making Sanderson's life miserable for awhile now. Just making somebody else's life miserable probably isn't gonna cut it. Otherwise we'd have to charge a whole lot of married folks."

"That's very funny, Lifton." Chernin stretched his arms to the side and yawned. "Look, chief, I'm sure these fuckers have committed a bunch of crimes." He got up, strolled over to the window again, and gazed out. "You're very lucky, bro. Not just a window. You've got the high floor too."

"Yeah, it's better than winning the lotto. So, Joel, what I'm hearing so far is you don't know whether Thigpen and his group have ever actually tried to harm Sanderson or committed any specific crimes against him or anybody else. Is that right?"

"Look, boss, The Big Girl brought me into this just a few days ago and told me to meet up with the Commissioner." He turned back to Lifton. "She heard about this new hate-crimes law and wanted to talk about what's been going on for awhile with her brother. These guys say threatening stuff to him like, `We're gonna kill you and all the other niggers,' excuse my French. You know, shit like that."

"Well, hey, boss, that's really super. We just might have enough right there to charge these bad guys with the major offense of saying bad words."

"Listen, chief, The Big Girl told me you wanted something like this." Chernin smacked his gum louder. "You don't, just say so. I don't have time for bullshit. This thing just got dropped into my lap. I'll go out to the church and talk to the preacher man."

"No, hold on. What I'm thinking might be better first is for you to try and..."

"Make contact with the targets in an undercover capacity and see what they're up to these days. Maybe they're into something else that might make a good case. Damn, chief, why didn't I think of that?"

"You sure are a smart-ass, aren't you, Joel?"

"You've got that right. And, please, call me JC or just Chernin. I've hated the name Joel since I was a little kid. There's a redneck bar in Florida City where these assholes hang out. As soon as I get a couple of things set up, I'll go out there and take a look around."

"Well, when they take a look at you, they'll probably offer

you a free membership."

The detective grinned, tapping the one-inch swastika tattoos on each side of his neck. "I guess you noticed these?"

"They're really not that hard to miss."

"Yeah, they've been getting me some attention, especially from my family and friends. You see, I happen to be Jewish."

* * *

Joel Chernin jerked the steering wheel hard to the right and pulled into the gravel parking lot. He would have missed it but for the small billboard at the north end of the property. Rising above the tall hedges it announced: "Skeeter's Bar And Package Liquors Last Chance For Booze Before The Keys." The background was filled with an American flag and a plea to southbound motorists: "Will The Last American To Leave Miami Please Bring The Flag?" Skeeter's was on the west side of US 1, two-hundred feet north of the entrance to Card Sound Road, the only other paved access to Key Largo. As long as US 1 wasn't backed up as a result of one of the frequent, and often fatal, traffic accidents on that narrow two-lane stretch of asphalt, Key Largo was only twenty minutes away.

Chernin was going too fast, and he had to slam down hard on the brakes of his undercover pick-up. The gravel crunched loudly, and the truck slid forward a couple of yards before coming to a rest a few inches from a concrete post. A thick cloud of dust wafted up slowly and covered the windshield. He stuck his leather wallet and badge inside the glove compartment and surveyed the area. The sun had just set, leaving behind a reddish-pink band the color of Indian River County grapefruit on the horizon. Night came before six now with Daylight Saving Time.

There were two more pick-up trucks and a pair of motorcycles in the parking lot. "Redneck happy hour must be in full swing," Chernin mumbled as he walked toward the one-storey building hidden from the road by all the thick vegetation. Painted on the wall to the left of the front door was a large skull sporting a German army helmet with the inscription: "Death Riders." To the right there was a sign: "Enter At Your Own Risk." Inside the Allman Brothers Band's signature song "Ramblin' Man" was blasting away.

Chernin pulled open the wooden door and was greeted by a curtain of cigarette smoke. To the right the package store consisted of a small room with a counter, cash register, and shelves filled with liquor bottles. Straight ahead was a long wraparound bar, and to the left next to the window was the juke box. In the middle of the main room there was a pool table where a couple of biker types were standing, chalking their cues. Two pencil-thin long-haired young men wearing baseball caps were sitting at the bar, tapping their cigarettes on a red plastic ashtray situated between them. Chernin turned to the bartender who was staring at him and had the sensation he was looking in a mirror. The ogre had a shaved head and a light-brown chin-strip just like him. But this guy was a couple inches taller and at least fifty pounds heavier. Everybody in the place was wearing the same uniform, t-shirts and blue jeans. The song ended, the others turned and briefly sized up the new arrival, then went back to their business.

"Gimme a Bud longneck," Chernin said as he sat down on one of the bar stools.

The young man sitting next to him turned and squinted. "Hey, Skeeter, check out this dude's tattoos. Kenny, take a look at this shit."

The other long-hair leaned forward. "*Damn*, dude."

Skeeter set the bottle down in front of Chernin. "I'll bet you get a lotta shit about them two things."

Chernin took a long swig from the bottle and wiped his mouth with the back of his hand. "I really don't hear much complaining about it."

"I guess not to your face you don't." Skeeter noticed Chernin already had finished his beer and pulled another one out of the cooler. "Never seen you here before."

"Never been here before." Chernin chugged down half of

the second bottle, gulped air a couple of times, then let out a loud, sustained burp. "To tell you the truth, when I first come in I thought this place was one of those gay bars, seeing as how there was a couple of faggy-looking dudes with long hair sitting over here. So I said to myself, maybe I'll just come in and kick me some queer ass." There was an uneasy silence for a few moments until Chernin belched again. "I was just kidding, you fuckers," he said, and they all laughed.

"Name is Bobby Wendt," the young long-hair sitting next to Chernin said, "and this here's Kenny Moser."

"Barbie and Ken. That's real cute. Karl Spitzer." Chernin tilted his bottle at each of them, then chugged down the rest of its contents and burped again. "And Skeeter's the owner of this place, right, Barbie?"

Wendt wasn't liking this play on his name one bit, but there was no way he was going to say something about it to this scary-looking dude. "Well, he's the owner, but that's not his real name."

"Hey, Skeeter, what's your real name?" Chernin called across the room where he was delivering two drinks.

"It's Aubrey," Wendt said. "Aubrey Swindall. But he don't like that name."

Chernin's big frame began heaving. "Did you say *Aubrey!*" he blurted out loud enough to make sure Swindall would hear him. "You *gotta* be shitting me!"

Swindall walked over to the front door and went outside. If he was checking out Chernin's pick-up, taking down the license plate number, it didn't matter. Even if one of them had a friend in law enforcement who could run the tag, it would come back registered to the name of a marina on Card Sound Road a few mile markers southeast of Alabama Jack's. A joint task force of the Bureau of Alcohol, Tobacco, and Firearms and Metro-Dade Police used that location to conduct undercover operations in South Dade, mostly reverse stings, and there were only a handful of people who even knew about it. A few years ago the property had been forfeited to the feds after its owner was convicted of smuggling several tons of marijuana from the Bahamas into the Upper Keys.

Chernin had set things up before paying his first visit to Skeeter's. Anybody on duty at the marina would confirm Karl Spitzer worked there. And a criminal history had been created for him, two cases, the files available for public viewing in the Clerk's Office at Metro Justice. One felony conviction was for battery on a law enforcement officer, "throwing a state trooper into a ditch while he was trying to arrest the subject for DUI." The other was for aggravated assault with a deadly weapon, that being a baseball bat Karl Spitzer "had used in an attack against two African-American juveniles." The files were filled with docket progress sheets, arrest forms, supplemental narratives, charging instruments, offense reports, booking photographs, and certified judgments of conviction.

"So you work around here, Karl?"

"Well, Barbie, I work on boats down on Card Sound Road. Gotta keep outta trouble for awhile."

"So you've been a bad boy?"

"That's what the niggers say."

"The boons," Wendt corrected him.

"The what?"

"The boons. You know, like baboons. That's what we call niggers around here."

Chernin cocked his head and thought about that for a moment. "Hey, Barbie and Ken, watch this. Mr. Skeeter, sir," he called over to Swindall who had just stepped back inside. "Do you all serve African-Americans here in your fine establishment?"

"Skeeter don't let no niggers hang out in here," Moser answered for him.

"Well, you know that ain't exactly true, Kenny."

"Shut up, Bobby," Moser said, knocking his elbow into Wendt's side.

"So you pussies ever done any bad shit? I beat up on a

couple of punk niggers once with a baseball bat."

"*Damn*, what happened? They jump you or something?"

"Naw, nothing like that. I just didn't like the way they was looking at me is all."

"Fucking A, man." Moser nodded and raised his hand like he wanted to high-five Chernin, but he was too far away.

"So I guess none of you boys ever done any bad shit, huh?" Chernin waited a few beats then got off his bar stool. "Well, I can see you girls ain't much fun so I'm outta here."

"We done some bad shit before."

"*Yeah, right.* I think you pussies are bull-shitting me."

"We done some bad shit before," Wendt repeated. "But it's kinda secret shit."

"Kinda secret shit like what, Barbie?"

This time instead of elbowing him, Moser shoved Wendt hard enough to tip his bar stool. "Bobby, you're drunk so just shut the fuck up."

Wendt ignored Moser and considered Chernin's question for a few moments, finally looking over at him, his eyes bloodshot and hazy from way too much alcohol and cigarette smoke. "Dude, it wouldn't be secret shit if I told you, right?"

Chernin pointed his index finger at Wendt's head like it was the barrel of a gun, then drew it in like he was pulling the trigger. "You got me there, Barbie," he said, noticing Wendt was grinning now for being a lot smarter than the next guy. Chernin took out ten dollars and handed the money to Swindall.

"It's just gonna be six dollars for the two beers."

"Keep the change. It don't look like your business is doing so good, Aubrey."

"Yeah, well, it's just a slow night."

"*Yeah, right*," Chernin smirked and headed for the front door.

CHAPTER THREE

Curtis Chance Thigpen clutched his father's hand tightly as they walked for nearly a mile down North Krome Avenue. Each Sunday morning around ten Wallace Thigpen rounded up his three sons for this journey so they "might learn something." He was the youngest of the three boys, and it wouldn't be long before his father would refuse to hold Curtis' hand, on these trips or anywhere else for that matter, because soon he would turn five-years-old. His father reminded him that after that age holding hands would make him a "sissy." Without having anybody to latch onto, those Sunday morning excursions would become so frightening sometimes Curtis would wet his pants. He was lucky his mother never complained. If she would have said anything to his father, he surely would have given Curtis a real bad whipping for being a "pissy sissy."

Curtis Thigpen loved his mother more than anything, mostly because she never said anything hurtful about him. Sometimes Mary Thigpen would just stare at him, her eyes slowly narrowing to where they almost were completely shut. And then she would blink as if she were trying to snap his image like she had a picture camera in her head. In this way she could keep him in her mind forever and shut out the great unhappiness there was almost every day in that small one-bedroom wooden house.

Guardians Of The Faith

When they finally reached the intersection at Northwest Seventh Street, Wallace Thigpen and his three sons would cross over to the southwest corner. Roy Wendt already would be there with Jimmy, his teenage son. Roy never shaved clean and was always scratching the stubble on his chin. Jimmy had a crewcut with just a little hedge of brown hair in front propped up by a dab of butch wax. His father and Roy would shake hands, then Roy would bend down and grab Curtis' shoulder, jerk him back and forth a few times, and *always* ask the same thing. "Ready to watch the nigger parade?" And then Wallace Thigpen *always* would have to correct his best friend. "The boons parade, Roy."

They would stand in the hot sun and watch the darkies walk to their church another half-block. Curtis called these people "darkies" because he didn't know what "nigger" or "boon" meant, and he couldn't very well say they were "blackies" because a lot of them were different shades of brown. For their own good they stayed on the other side of the street. Jimmy would bring a baseball bat and tap the fat end against the palm of his left hand. This was one of the real bad parts of those Sunday mornings, watching Jimmy grit his yellow teeth like a wild dog, tapping harder and harder into his sweaty palm until it made a wet slapping sound. One day Jimmy just might run across the street and swing the bat at some darky's head like he was playing little league tee-ball. Curtis trembled at the thought of the darky's head separating from his body, eyes bugging out, flying clean across the street straight at him. Most of the women darkies wore funny-looking clothes. This would make his father and Roy laugh so hard they would start coughing and end up nearly choking. Some of them had huge dresses like tents and floppy hats big as open umbrellas. And the colors were all shiny bright, tomato reds and palm greens, sunflower yellows and sky blues.

"Look at all those boons!" Roy cried out loud enough for all of Homestead to hear. "Dressed up in all their finery, *whooeee!*"

"You mean dressed up in all their *boonery*," Wallace Thigpen corrected him.

It was that Sunday morning, the last one when his father ever would hold his hand, that Curtis finally learned what his father meant by calling them "boons." It started when Curtis suddenly felt his arm being violently jerked forward. Someone had snuck up on Wallace Thigpen and touched his shoulder, making him jump forward two steps with his son still attached. When Curtis and his father looked around, there was a tall darky standing there, wearing a black suit, white shirt, and red bow-tie. He was holding a bible in his right hand, a bright purple ribbon dangling from its center. His father's eyes opened so wide Curtis thought they were going to pop right out. Roy and Jimmy stepped back a few feet to get a better view of what would happen next. Nobody said anything as the darky stood there stiffly and stared straight into Wallace Thigpen's bloodshot eyes.

"It's the nigger preacher," Roy said under his breath, taking a few more steps backward until he was able to plant one foot on the street.

"I *am* the preacher," the man acknowledged, his gaze still fixed squarely on Wallace Thigpen. "And I've seen you, Wallace Thigpen, standing over here every Sunday morning calling out names at my congregation. Ugly names."

His father released him, and Curtis inched his way over to Walter, his oldest brother, and grabbed his hand.

"The shit's really gonna fly now, you'll see," Walter mumbled as he shook free from Curtis' grasp.

"Is Jimmy gonna hit him with the bat?" Curtis asked as he shook uncontrollably.

"He won't have to," Walter answered, then leaned to the side and spat on the ground. "Pa's gonna kill him first."

By now most of the darkies realized something serious was going on. Those who were still walking in the parade froze in their tracks, and some who already had reached the church began drifting back.

Guardians Of The Faith

"I came over here to ask you one thing, Wallace Thigpen," the preacher continued calmly. "Why won't you just let us be?"

Wallace Thigpen looked around at everybody on both sides of the street, buying time while trying to figure out what to say next. After he had glanced over at his sons for the third time, he finally said, "Because you're a bunch of *boons*, that's why!"

The young preacher nodded slowly, then raised his left hand to his chin, cradling his elbow with his right hand, his expression curious. "Boons, huh?"

Across the street a young darky boy yelled out, "Somebody please call the police!"

Wallace Thigpen glanced over at Roy and Jimmy who were making faces and waving at him like he had better start doing something quick. He turned back to the preacher and blurted out with a big grin. "That's right. Boons! *Baboons!*" He scratched his chest with both hands, bobbing up and down, trying to make a monkey sound.

"Ah, yes, I see," the preacher said with a big smile. "Now I understand, Pigpen."

His father suddenly stopped and took a step closer to the tall darky. "What? What did you say?"

"I said, now I understand, *Pigpen*." The preacher's voice was loud enough so everyone on both sides of the street could hear him.

"Somebody please call the police!" the same young voice called out again.

Wallace Thigpen's silly grin evaporated, his face turned beet red, and his eyes were wild with rage. As the tall darky stepped off the curb and began crossing to the other side of the street, Wallace Thigpen ran over and grabbed the bat from Jimmy Wendt. Someone screamed out "Reverend!" But it was too late because Wallace Thigpen already had caught up to him. Curtis closed his eyes and wet his pants just as his father started to swing the bat with all his might. A few seconds later, to his surprise, Curtis heard some laughter, and he opened his right eye a tiny sliver. Roy

and Jimmy were trying to pick their father off the ground where he
lay sprawled out, flopping around like a fish out of water. It took
a couple of minutes, but they finally were able to get him to his feet.
Across the street all of the darkies were making their way quickly
toward their church.

"Fucking boon motherfuckers!" his father screamed at the
top of his lungs, sounding like a little crybaby as he kept slapping
the dirt off his bib overalls.

Later that night, when the door to his parents' bedroom
slammed shut, and he and his brothers had crawled into their
sleeping bags on the living room floor, Curtis finally got up the
courage to ask, "Walter, what happened to Pa?"

"You little pissy sissy. You didn't see nothing, did you?"

"It was *funny*," Chet started giggling and got the hiccups.

"Shut up, you little shit!" Walter reached over and gave
Chet's head a hard shove. "Don't never make fun of Pa."

The next morning on their way to school Chet answered the
question. Their father had begun huffing and puffing like The Big
Bad Wolf, building up enough steam so he could knock the darky's
head straight to Kingdom Come. But by the time he finally got
around to swinging the bat with all his might, the darky preacher
already was out of range. His momentum was so great that
Wallace Thigpen turned full circle and, as he started to unravel
back the other way, lost his balance and plunged to the ground.

"Even Roy and Jimmy was laughing at Pa," Chet said with
a giggle and a hiccup.

* * *

The pay phone on the wall between the bathrooms was
ringing as Aubrey Swindall opened the back door. "Skeeter's."

"You seen Bobby or Kenny? They ain't been by my place for
a long time. None of you fuckers have been by my place."

"Look, Curtis, do you want me to go find Bobby and Kenny
or what?"

"Yeah, I do. And you tell them to haul ass over to my place

right now so I can go out and get some stuff I need."

Swindall didn't need to look for those two very far because they were in the back parking lot washing Moser's truck. "Hey! Curtis says you gotta go over to his place so he can get his shit."

"We're not his fucking maids! Why don't *you* go help him get his shit this time, Skeeter?"

"Really, Kenny? Okay, then *you* and Bobby clean my place and pay your tab, and I'll do it." When they didn't say anything, Swindall went back inside. He returned with two six-packs and saw they already were getting ready to leave. "You give both of these to Curtis," Swindall said, handing over the beers to Wendt through the passenger window. "And I see you fuckers forgot to turn off the water again."

Moser gunned the engine and pulled away fast, covering his truck with a fresh coat of dust. They headed north on Krome Avenue to West Mowry Drive, turned left, and two blocks down parked in front of the old two-storey building. They had been going to Curtis' place about once a week until Moser decided he was sick and tired of this routine. And Wendt couldn't keep doing it on his own because he had lost his wheels after his wife kicked him out of the house and kept their pick-up registered in her name. As usual nobody was to be seen around the old apartment building. For all they knew, Curtis might be the only person living in the whole stinking place. They made their way up the creaking staircase and then down the dark hallway to Curtis' apartment. Maybe nobody else wanted to live there because it smelled like rotten eggs. Wendt knocked on the door a couple of times, but there was no answer. When he twisted the knob, he was surprised to find the door wasn't locked. Curtis always kept it locked because he stood up for white power and said some crazy boon might come over there and try and kill him.

They squinted in the bright light of the naked bulb in the middle of the ceiling fan. A few weeks ago Curtis made them remove the plastic bowl covering it so there would be more light in the room. Right now the blades were rotating slowly, but on high speed the fan would shake so violently Wendt believed one day it would fly clean off the ceiling and cut him to pieces like walking straight into an airplane propeller. Curtis was sitting in the old brown cloth recliner facing the apartment's lone window with its sagging aluminum shade.

"Guardian." When Curtis didn't respond, Wendt moved closer. "Hey, Guardian."

"Yeah, yeah, in Guard's name," Thigpen muttered. "So where you been, Bobby?"

Curtis wasn't looking so good these days, especially when he was pissed off. His freckled face got tied up in a knot, the deeply pockmarked cheeks covered with small pink patches. He wasn't shaving his head like before, and several long wisps of hair, sticky from not washing them, were plastered across his scalp. Because Curtis wasn't a particularly good sight to see even way back when, his new look made him pretty downright scary.

"Skeeter sent these over," Wendt said, holding up the two six-packs. He walked over to the refrigerator and placed them on the bottom shelf. There were only a few things inside, a nearly-empty plastic water pitcher, two bottles of Coors, and a can of Mountain Dew. Wendt shut the door and grabbed one of the grey metal folding chairs.

"You wanna go out and get your stuff now?"

"You just sit down a fucking minute, Bobby."

"I already am, Curtis."

"We've got work to do. Where's Kenny?"

"He's right over there," Wendt turned and pointed. "What work you talking about, Curtis?"

"What work you think I'm talking about? Guard's work." The pink patches on Thigpen's face were spreading to his scalp. "Are you bailing on me now? Because if you or Skeeter or anybody else wants to, you just say so, and then I'll do what I gotta do."

Wendt shifted uneasily in the metal chair, looked over at

Moser, then got up and went back to the refrigerator. "Hey, Curtis, you want one of these beers?" When he didn't answer, Wendt grabbed the two bottles of Coors because the cans they brought over weren't very cold. He handed one to Kenny, twisted off the cap, and threw back a few gulps. "Ain't nothing changed, Curtis."

"You're not bailing on me now?"

"We're here, ain't we?" Wendt glanced over at Moser who shrugged his shoulders and took a swig from his bottle.

"Call the old nigger preacher."

"Aw, c'mon, Curtis."

"Aw, c'mon, Curtis," Thigpen whined, pounding the armrest with his left hand, the pink patches starting to turn red.

Wendt flashed back to that horror flick Kenny got from the video store a few weeks ago where people's heads were exploding. "Well, what the hell you want me to say, Curtis?"

"You tell the nigger preacher he's gonna *die*, that's what."

Wendt got up and retrieved one of Skeeter's beers from the refrigerator. He sat down again, popped the top of the can, and tugged on the end of his long hair. "I ain't never said nothing like that before."

"You gonna do it, Bobby?"

"Yeah, I guess." He moved the metal folding chair closer to the coffee table and gulped down some lukewarm beer. Curtis twisted around, his face all knotted up again, ready to say something. "Okay, I'm doing it." Wendt set the can down, burped, and picked up the phone. A piece of paper stuck under the glass top of the coffee table had several telephone numbers scrawled on it in pencil, his house, Kenny's house, the pay phone at "Skeeter's." He dialed the one which had "NP" next to it and counted off five rings. He crossed his fingers nobody would answer, but right after the sixth ring someone picked up.

"This is Reverend Sanderson."

"You're a fucking boon!"

"Well, you don't sound like Curtis," Sanderson's voice was

calm, "so I wonder who you might be?"

"Say it, Bobby," Thigpen's tone was firm.

"You're gonna die."

Wendt was about to hang up, but Sanderson was speaking. "Well, I could be wrong," he continued in the same easy tone, "but is this young Bobby Wendt?"

Wendt covered the mouthpiece. "Fuck! He knows it's me."

"You still there, son?" When Wendt didn't say anything, Sanderson added, "Well, Bobby, you have a blessed night then."

"Dammit!" Wendt shouted after he heard the click on the other end. He wanted this visit to be over real soon. "C'mon, Curtis, let's go get your stuff."

"You and Kenny go. You know what I always get."

"You got money?"

"Yeah, I got money." Thigpen tried to lock the recliner's footrest in place, pushing down several times with his heels, but it kept swinging back up. "You pay with this," he said, reaching into his front pants pocket.

Wendt took the envelope and looked inside. "I can't pay with this."

"Are you just plain stupid, Bobby? It's a government check, and I already signed the back."

Thirty minutes later Wendt and Moser returned to the apartment with two brown paper bags. They put the gallon of milk, jar of mayonnaise, and packages of cheese, bologna, and ham in the refrigerator, set the two loaves of Wonder Bread on the kitchen counter, and left the rest of the money from the government check on the coffee table.

As they were leaving, Thigpen said, "You be back here Sunday morning, and you bring Skeeter too. He don't need to be at that shit-hole bar of his on a Sunday morning. You hear me?"

On the way back to Kenny's house they talked about how very messed up it was when somebody else had some really bad shit on you.

CHAPTER FOUR

Rayfield Lifton noticed it was nearly five o'clock when the intercom's annoying buzz shattered what had been a magnificent silence for the past hour. He made the mistake of pressing down too lightly on the intercom button, and it popped off, sailing across his desk like a circus performer shot from a cannon. Part of the unwritten compensation package working for government was the right to leave fashionably early on Friday afternoons. Around the office people started talking about you *only if* you stayed past three.

Lifton was groping around under his desk trying to locate the intercom button when Cuqui Perez walked into his office. "Why don't you answer your phone?"

"Why aren't you already gone?"

"*Ay, Dios mio.* You ask me the same thing every Friday afternoon, and I always tell you the same thing. 'If I leave early, maybe The Big Girl, she fires me.' And then you say, 'You don't have to worry about that because you've got twenty years here.'"

Lifton located the missing button and sat back up. "And then you always say, 'No, twenty-three years here, with you twelve.' You know, Moneypenny, it seems more like the whole damn twenty-three have been with me."

She made a fist and then extended her middle finger. "You're so funny, *jefe.*"

"Did Chernin call?"

"I wouldn't tell you if he did?" His secretary strolled out of his office grumbling, "*comemierda*," making sure she said it loud enough for him to hear.

"I *heard* that, and I know what it means!"

Cuqui Perez' wake of laughter was cut short by a fit of coughing, the result of too many years of chain-smoking. After he pressed the button back into its socket, Lifton flipped through his Rolodex until he found Chernin's numbers. When the detective didn't answer his mobile phone, Lifton left a message. He decided to wait a few more minutes to see if Chernin would call back even though he was anxious to get home and see Kimberly and Demeka who had returned from their trip to Gainesville. Two weeks ago a well-known child neurologist from Shands, the University of Florida's primary teaching hospital, had called with an offer to have his niece undergo a comprehensive evaluation. Lifton fished the nerf ball out of the miniature net hanging on the inside of his office door and returned to his desk. He leaned back in his chair and flicked his wrist, the foam ball missing the net by more than a foot. He grabbed a few sheets of copy paper, wadded them up, and tossed them toward the hoop but didn't hit the backboard even once. A pale yellow light on line three lit up, and Lifton carefully pushed the button down to answer it.

"You still in the office?" Alonzo Norris' voice was easy to identify, Barry White on too much caffeine. "You truly are a dedicated public servant."

"That's me. So what's going on, No-Time?"

"You're starting to shine, my brother. Have you seen those videos yet?"

"If you're talking about my new case, then you must know more about the damn thing than me."

"Take a look at those videos. They'll make you feel real good you've got this thing."

"Sounds like you've been talking with Joel Chernin."

"Well, you know, me and that strange white dude go way back. Yes, we have engaged in many a mighty battle me and him."

"But this time you want that strange white dude to win."

"Yes, sir, I most certainly do. This time No-Time is flipping to the side of the State of Florida. You know what I'm saying?"

"What you're saying is my detective is sharing information with you about a confidential investigation which is not a case yet."

"But it will be soon. And you don't have to worry one bit. All your secrets are safe with me. All of them, you hear me? Remember, I'm the one who wants to make you fly."

"You want me to be the new Superfly."

"That's right," Norris chuckled. "I can dig it."

"Listen, No-Time," Lifton's tone changed to serious, "I know you're the one behind me getting this new gig, and I appreciate it. I really do."

"Well, you're right for this job. All I did was give a little lift to Liftoff Lifton."

"Give a little lift to Liftoff Lifton? Can you say that ten times real fast after you've had a couple of drinks?"

"Well, my brother, I shall try that when I see you at the game tomorrow night. You in with the rest of The Posse?"

"I'm all the way in, No-Time. Pistons are in town, right?"

"It *is* the Pistons, and I've got an extra ticket so you can bring along a lady friend."

"I ain't got nobody," Lifton began belting out the Santana song, "that I can depend on, da-da-da-da, da-da-da. You know, to be grammatically correct, No-Time, it really should be 'upon whom I can depend.'"

"You don't have a lady friend to take to the game? You're a rising star now so you need to get something else *rising* too as you start moving on up."

"Moving on up," Lifton switched to the theme song from *The Jeffersons*, the most popular black tv sitcom from the seventies, "to the East Side..."

"Alright, then, Mr. George Jefferson. You know the drill. VIP Desk west entrance. Later, my brother."

"Yes," he hissed as he hung up, grabbed another sheet of paper, wadded it up, and leaned back. Lifton gracefully arched his arms and flicked the paper ball across the room. This time it landed dead center in the tiny hoop, nothing but net. He needed to get home now so he tried Chernin's number again. "How come you didn't check in with me today?"

"Hey, relax, bro. We're making progress. I'll bring you up to speed on Monday. But right now I gotta pick up my old lady and the kids. We're going to Disney World!"

"Listen, JC, there's gonna be thousands of young children there. Try not to scare too many of them, okay?"

"That's very funny. I'll wear a turtleneck to cover up my awesome tattoos."

"That would be a good thing. Otherwise Mickey and Donald might have to take you down."

"Those two pussies? I don't think so, boss. But Dumbo, now he's a player. Do you know why Minnie broke up with Mickey?"

"No, but I'm sure you'll tell me."

"Because Mickey was going around telling everybody she was fucking goofy."

"Was she really doing it with Goofy?"

"No, *man*. Mickey was just telling everybody Minnie was fucking *goofy*. You don't get it, do you? Dude, Mickey just meant Minnie was acting a little crazy is all." After there still was no response from Lifton, he added, "You still don't get it, do you?"

"I got it the first time, Chernin. I'm just messing with you."

"Well, you're a barrel of laughs today. Everything alright?"

"If you give me some good news, then you'll make me a happy camper."

"Trust me. Soon you're gonna be as happy as a camper roasting his weeny."

"That sounds pretty dangerous. Hey, JC, before you go,"

Lifton added, "Alonzo Norris told me you've got some videos."

"No-Time Norris? We call him Darth Vader. He's been our nemesis for years."

"You call him Darth Vader? You mean like that evil black dude from Star Wars? You're a racist, Chernin."

"That's very funny, chief. So Norris told you me and him have been talking, huh? I was just..."

"Forget about it, Chernin. Norris is an old friend. But, listen, we don't need to be sharing information about this investigation with everybody else, okay?"

"Fine with me. I don't want to step on anybody's toes."

"That's a very painful thought. Let me take a look at those videos when you get back in town, okay?"

"Rayfield Lifton," said Chernin reflectively, "the man with the plan."

"That's me, just like Verbal in *The Usual Suspects*."

"Dude, one of my favorite movies of all time. *Hasta la vista*, baby," Chernin said loudly and hung up.

"One of my favorite movies of all time too, *dude*," Lifton said to himself as he headed out of his office. "Only this time things better not turn out like they did in *The Usual Suspects*, where the good guys get outsmarted, and the bad guys get away."

* * *

Fredericka Muir was in her usual place, rocking back and forth, a very large human metronome, waving a paper fan. As soon as Lifton stepped out of his car, Mr. T started barking, dragging Snoopy's chair a few inches across the porch. Lifton didn't want to think about what would happen to someone caught between Mr. T's saber-tooth choppers.

"Hey, Mr. Prosecutor! Did you put any white people in jail this week?"

"No, ma'am," he said, setting his briefcase on the sidewalk, then crossing his arms like he was troubled. "You know, we really tried, Mrs. Muir, but it turned out only black folks were committing all the crimes."

Old Lady Muir rocked back and forth a few more times before his comment registered. Then she abruptly stopped, her feet hitting the wooden floor like she was slamming down on a pair of brake pedals. "What did you just say?!" she shouted with a look of disbelief. "That ain't funny one bit, Rayfield Lifton! You're a racist!" She shook her head. "He sure got a mouth on him, don't he, Mr. T?"

"Pity the fool!" Lifton yelled, lunging toward the dog, a gesture which always drove the mongrel wild. He picked up his briefcase, bolted up the steps to his house, and unlocked the front door. He found his sister standing at the kitchen counter slicing and dicing a big onion.

"Hey, Kim." When she didn't answer, he feared there was bad news. "Where's Demeka?" When she still didn't turn to face him, he gently turned her toward him. "What's going on?"

"Ray," his sister said softly, looking up at him with tears streaming down her cheeks. "I'm crying for two reasons."

"C'mon, baby," he said, wiping away a tear with his thumb. "What happened?"

"Two reasons. These damn onions. And some real hope for my little girl."

Lifton wrapped his arms around her, and they swayed back and forth. She looked up at him and asked, "Are you gonna be here for dinner? I'm making your favorite."

"I'm not going anywhere. Now will you please tell me what's going on with Demeka and Gainesville and the doctors up there and...the *thing*?" He made the quotation marks sign and scowled dramatically.

"Well, I'll tell you what," she said, tapping him on his chest. "Let me finish making this now. Demeka's already asleep. That long bus ride was hard on her. We'll talk about everything over dinner, okay, baby?"

"And then I'll know what's going on?"

"And then you'll know everything that's been going on with the *thing*."

* * *

Kimberly whistled as her brother strolled into the kitchen wearing a new shiny black shirt with a red-and-white flower pattern. "Dressed to kill!" She couldn't remember the last time he had bought any clothes. She placed her hands on her hips. "You must have a special lady friend you haven't told me about yet."

"Kim, you know I don't. I got this for tomorrow night. Just another Heat game with The Posse."

"I ain't got nobody," she started singing, kicking her leg up and strumming an imaginary electric guitar, "that I can depend on, da-da-da-da, da-da-da."

"I wish I had a dollar for every time somebody started singing a Santana song."

"Look who's talking? You do it all the time too."

"And one more thing, Kim. To be grammatically correct, you need to say 'upon whom I can depend.'"

"So why don't you write a letter to Mr. Carlos Santana?"

"I'll do that first thing tomorrow. So now will you tell me what's going on with Demeka?" With Kim acting like that after returning from Gainesville, there had to be good news.

She dipped the white plastic ladle into the big steaming pot, lifted it carefully, and took a cautious sip. "Yes," she nodded with approval. "Now I *can* get married as the Cubans say. Again."

"You'll get married again, Kim."

"*Yeah, right*. You know I won't. Read the ad. 'Divorced black woman, unemployed, young daughter with serious medical condition, currently living with brother.' No, I don't think so, Ray. I read somewhere the other day I have a lot better chance of getting hit by lightning."

"That's only because Florida is the lightning capital of the world," he stared at her with a serious expression until she broke down and started laughing. "Now here's what *I* see." He held up his hands and framed a different description. "'Very elegant black fox with great style and best daughter in the world.'"

Kimberly turned away from him, rested her hands on the counter, and was silent for a few moments. "Hey, do you want some wine or what? And you haven't even asked what I'm making for us."

"Well, it smells like spicy Cajun shrimp creole. And, yes, I will have some wine."

"Here you go," she said, handing him a glass of red wine. "*Beaujolais nouveau*. It's that time of year." She raised her glass so they could clink a toast and then kept her eyes fixed on him as she took a long sip. "Ray, I'm still nervous. And excited. Nervous and excited about what the doctor up there said. He said..." She began coughing violently after a taking a big gulp of wine which went down the wrong way.

"Hey, Kim," Lifton said, giving her a gentle pat on the back, "slow down, will you?"

"Sorry," she sputtered, waving a hand rapidly in front of her mouth. "Dr. Leo Feingold. Everybody says he's the best in child neurology at Shands, and that Shands is the best facility in Florida for this." She paused and took three small sips. "Oh, this is so good," she said and set the glass on the counter.

"Okay, so *now* are you gonna give me the bottom line on all this Gainesville greatness?"

"I'm getting there, Mr. Lawyer-Interrogator." She reached over and squeezed his arm. "I'm sorry, baby."

He pulled her close and hugged her. "We're both nervous and excited." He pushed her back a little and moved his head around like a dashboard bobblehead doll. "Excited and nervous. Which is it? Nervous and excited or excited and nervous?"

She laughed hard and started coughing again. "Ray, you're gonna make me choke."

"You were doing a pretty good job of that on your own."

"Okay, will you be quiet now? Dr. Leo Feingold. He's got

this hot-shot team, and they do heavy-duty research. Cutting-edge stuff. They're hooked up with other doctors all around the world."

"I'll drink to that. Actually, I'll drink to anything, including the fact last time I was in Gainesville we kicked serious butt against those damn Gators."

"Ray, you'll never guess who met us when we got there. Lee Baldwin and," she raised her glass so they could clink another toast, "Lawton Chiles."

"The Governor of Florida? No way, Jose."

"Yes, way, Jose. We met the Governor of Florida, yes, we did. It was great. You remember Lee Baldwin, right?"

"I remember Governor Chiles but not this Lee Baldwin."

"Oh, come on, Ray, stop it," she giggled. "You know Lee and I dated back in high school. You had to because you tried to protect me from every guy who even just looked at me. Lee, he was okay and all, but we weren't meant to be. He's been working for the Governor up in Tallahassee. And we were talking, and Lee tells me Alonzo..."

"You know, I never asked you how you got this connection. So it was No-Time, right? I should have guessed he had his hand in this too."

"Ray, does it really matter? Just be thankful my little girl has this chance to get some real hope."

"Kim, you know I am. It's just that..."

"How am I gonna pay for all this? You need to listen to the whole story first, alright? Lee introduces us to Dr. Leo who personally takes us around on a tour of the whole campus in a golf cart no less. Can you believe it? Demeka really loved that ride. I know she did. And then Dr. Leo takes us over to the hospital and introduces us to his team. And later his lady assistant sets us up in a real nice apartment which is supposed to be for VIPs like Governor Chiles."

"I don't know what those facilities are like," he frowned in mock hurt.

Kimberly giggled again and took another sip of wine. "I know how you don't like depending on the generosity of others. Well, I don't either. That's not how we were raised, but I find myself and my daughter living with you here anyway. We do what we have to do to. That's how we survive in this world. And I'm not going to deny my little girl an opportunity to survive because I'm too proud to accept help from others. Hey," she put her index finger to her lips, "let me finish. How are we gonna pay for all this Gainesville greatness? The answer is special grants. Everything they're doing for Demeka is being paid for by special grants. See, you can rest easy now because it's not charity at all." She smiled while he considered that good news. "So for the past six days the team asked me a lot of questions and did all sorts of tests on Demeka with a bunch of futuristic-looking machines."

"And how did she handle all that stuff?"

"Good," Kimberly nodded slowly with conviction. "Really good. I could feel she understood everybody there was trying to help her, and she really wanted to find a way to break out of this terrible place where she's been trapped. I prayed every day one of those machines would help her do that. And before you ask me anything else, I know you're a bottom-line guy so here's the bottom line." She emptied her glass with a few more sips and set it down. "Dr. Leo says the *thing* most likely is a form of ASD. That means autism spectrum disorders."

"I don't get it. She was fine for so long."

"She was fine when she was real little, and then all of a sudden she just changed. You remember that day when I called you because she was like frozen? You rushed right over to take me and Demeka to Jackson because Ty had split again a few days before, and I didn't even know how to reach him. I'll never forget what you said while we were waiting in the ER. You said, 'People can't change just like that.' You remember you said that, Ray?"

"Yeah, I remember. Did all those brains in Gainesville have any explanation for what's going on?"

"They say she has a disorder, the kind that's usually detected early on, mostly within the first year after birth. But it's still possible for this disorder to show up in an older child. It's rare, but it can happen."

"Did you ask them whether..."

"Yes, Ray," she cut him off, having anticipated his next question. "Yes, I asked them if she could get like that from emotional trauma. I told them about what had been going on between me and Ty for so long, all that yelling and screaming and occasional physical violence. But they said, no, not likely. All these cases they've studied, children between two and ten years, boys and girls, they believe most likely ASD is something you're born with. So as to what was going on with me and Ty, no. The answer is no, not likely."

"'No' and 'not likely' are different things."

Kimberly gave him a hard look. "You know how doctors talk. Nothing is for sure. Just like you lawyers. You're always saying stuff like, 'It's a prediction not a promise.' So you better not be inventing in your mind that Ty caused the *thing*," her voice was angry now, "because that would be total bullshit. I know you, Ray, and you'd do something really stupid and end up in jail for the rest of your life." She got up and filled two bowls with the steaming spicy Cajun shrimp creole.

"I'm thankful for what the Gainesville people are trying to do and the special grants and all that, but what about..."

"What about Demeka getting back to normal?" She handed him a spoon and sat down. "They couldn't really say anything about that right now. But they told me there are studies going on different places involving a new class of drugs, and some results from Europe already are in. Some kids are improving after only six months to a year. Not back to normal yet, but those kids are getting better. They're getting better, Ray," she repeated, her eyes moist, her voice cracking.

"Yes!" he said, raising his right hand so they could high-five.

Guardians Of The Faith

They finished off the bottle of wine and ate in silence, glancing at each other from time to time with comforting smiles. On his way to his bedroom Lifton looked in on Demeka and noticed the guardrail was in the up position to prevent her from falling off the bed. She was making a purring sound each time she exhaled. He bent down and gave her a kiss on the forehead. "Please help her be okay soon," he mouthed the words as he walked out of his niece's room, "this little girl who never did anything bad to anybody."

CHAPTER FIVE

Lifton spied Alonzo Norris and the other members of The Posse assembled on the near side of the court. They were speaking with Miami Heat stars Glen Rice and Steve Smith as the other players took their final practice shots. With his black suit, homburg, and heavy gold chain, tonight No-Time looked like Jam-Master Jay from Run-D.M.C. A five-second blast from the buzzer filled the Arena, signaling the game was about to begin, and a final flurry of basketballs were launched toward the two backboards. Norris, Parrish, Crawford, and Leeds strolled off the court and took their seats behind the Heat bench. Lifton maneuvered his way down the concrete stairs through the crush of fans trying to get to their seats before the opening tip-off.

"Hey, Liftoff." Parrish pushed his elbow into Lifton's side. "Naomi Campbell's been asking about you. You remember that cocktail waitress from the Bulls game?"

Lifton didn't have to reflect much longer on that question because she was heading straight for them. She really did look a lot like the super-model from London with her big doe eyes and puffy pillow lips.

"So what can I get for you all tonight?"

Norris leaned forward and said too loud, "Hey, Naomi! Hit

us with some *Blue* Label." He sketched out a circle with his finger. "All around."

She dropped her head slightly and batted her eyelashes. "My name is not Naomi," she said after a few beats, "and you all should know by now we don't do the Blue."

"*Ouch!*" Parrish shook his right hand rapidly like he had just touched a hot stove.

"*Um-um*. She's got *atti-tude*," Crawford smiled and nodded his approval.

"So tell us your name again, pretty lady," Doc Leeds asked.

"You don't remember?" The waitress turned and stared at Lifton like he was the only one in their group who wasn't an asshole. "Valerie."

Norris extracted a bill from his vest pocket, waved it at her like a flag of surrender, then passed it over to Lifton. "Alright, *Valer-ie*, then you can bring us all a round of the Black."

She snatched the hundred-dollar bill out of Lifton's hand like she was a hungry Venus flytrap and winked at him as she turned to go. They watched her strut her stuff until she disappeared into the corridor just as the buzzer sounded again.

"*Damn*," Parrish smacked his lips, "I'd sure like to dip into some of that sauce."

Lifton shook his head. "She sure *is* mighty fine, Perishable."

* * *

After the half-time show Norris, Parrish, and Leeds headed for the restrooms. Lifton got up to stretch, began wobbling, and nearly fell on Crawford who eased him back into his seat. "She sure *is* mighty fine." Lifton pointed to the center of the court where their cocktail waitress was speaking with some of the Heat Dancers.

"You should get her number, Ray."

"A girl like that? I don't think so."

"Why? You got something wrong with you?"

"No, Seven, I think I'm still okay in that department if that's what you mean."

Guardians Of The Faith

"So what's the problem then?"

Lifton pushed up halfway from his seat and pulled out his empty left pants pocket. "Only guys with money get girls like her."

"She likes you, Ray. I can tell. And, besides, you're on your way up."

"On my way up, huh?" Lifton sat back down and made gestures like he was climbing a ladder. "You all act like I'm gonna be the next Dade State Attorney. I'm gonna win the Lotto before that happens."

"You make your big case happen, the one No-Time has been telling us about, and everything else will fall into place."

"That big case is just an investigation right now. And there never will be any big case if No-Time keeps telling everybody about the damn thing."

"You've gotta trust No-Time. He's a mover and a shaker in what you all do."

"So just let him move and shake my life, right?"

"You know what, Ray? Maybe you haven't noticed, but we've been trying, mostly No-Time has been trying, to help you. But you've got this thing, 'I'm just a poor, overworked, underpaid public servant, going nowhere, out of my league hanging out with you all.' Man, you need to lose that tired rap real fast. I don't dig it, Ray. I really don't." He turned and put a hand on Lifton's shoulder. "Look, I'm not the smartest dude from the hood. I didn't even go to college like you all did. But, you know, I've made some good money because I understand this community. Black, white, rich, and poor. I'm pretty good at reading people and trends."

"So then, tell me, Seven. Is this the front page story?" Lifton pretended he was holding a newspaper and leaned forward to read it. "'Prosecutor gets guilty verdict in major case,'" he began, his words slurred from too much alcohol. "'Late Friday former college basketball great and veteran Assistant State Attorney Rayfield Lifton got a big win prosecuting the first case brought under the State's new hate-crimes law. Word on the street is Lifton will be the County's next top cop, the first African-American to hold that position, taking over from Susan Purvis, the legendary Dade State Attorney, who is heading to Washington."

"As much as you might want to doubt it, that's pretty much it, Ray."

Lifton held up his hand so they could do the brother's handshake. "Well, you know something, Seven, that does sound pretty damn good to me."

Lifton felt a tap on his neck and started to turn around. "Hey, quiet man," a soft voice whispered in his ear. "Are you ever gonna ask me out or what?"

* * *

Norris instructed his chauffeur to drive to the north end of the Arena and park near the loading dock. Arena employees were streaming through an open door, smiling and laughing, glad they were on their way home, and that the Heat had beaten the Pistons.

"I know you're nervous, Ray, so the doctor has prescribed some medication." Leeds dropped a couple of ice cubes into the highball glass and poured a generous amount of Johnny Walker Black into it. "Take this now and repeat every thirty minutes."

"Hey, I'm nervous too," said Parrish.

"You can get your own drink, Perishable."

"Well, excuse my poor black ass, Donald Leeds, M.D." Parrish scooted over and knocked into him.

"Cut it out, Perishable! You're gonna make me spill No-Time's expensive booze all over his nice leather seats."

"Hey, will you all behave now? I see Liftoff's lady has just walked out the door."

The leggy cocktail waitress no longer was wearing a black mini-skirt, fishnet stockings, and high-heels. Now she was dressed in blue jeans, orange halter top, and sneakers. Slung over her shoulder was a black leather gym bag with the Miami Heat logo. Even in sneakers she had to be at least five-ten.

"*Val-er-ie!*" Norris exclaimed.

Guardians Of The Faith

"*Val-er-ie!*" the others began chanting.

"Hey!" Lifton shouted over them waving his hand. "Don't blow it for me."

"Actually," Crawford said, "we were hoping Valerie would take care of that for you." Even Lifton had to join in their outburst of laughter which ended abruptly when Carlos stepped out so he could guide Valerie over to the limo.

"No worries," Norris said, as he followed the others who were leaving through the right rear door. He stuck his head back inside and tipped his homburg. "My limo is your limo tonight."

The left rear door opened, and Valerie ducked inside. "Well, quiet man, I hope *you're* not leaving too."

"So, *amigos*, where are you going?" the chauffeur asked them after putting Valerie's gym bag in the trunk.

"I have no idea, Carlos. Valerie?" He shouldn't have left it up to her. It might turn out to be a very expensive night.

"Hmmm," she mused. "Well, let's see. We've got a Cuban chauffeur. And I'm starving. Sounds like a Cuban food night."

"That's good," Lifton thought, a lot of food and a small check. "I can dig it. Carlos, take us to Versailles."

"This is something else, isn't it?" Valerie's eyes lit up as she took in the interior of the eight-pack limousine and ran her hand along its plush leather wrap-around seat. "What's that?" she said, pointing at the elegant cherry-wood console planted in the middle of the passenger compartment.

"I'll show you." Lifton picked up the remote and aimed it at the console. A panel slid to the left, revealing the mini-bar and sound system.

"*Very nice.*" She slid over close to him. "Please tell me you're not gonna put on a Barry White song."

"No Barry White. I was thinking more like Run-D.M.C., Heavy D & The Boyz, or 2 Live Crew."

"Aren't you a little old for rap music, Mr. Prosecutor?"

"I'm not that old, and how do you know what I do?"

Guardians Of The Faith

"I've been asking your friends about you. They come to a lot of games, but I only saw you that one time when the Bulls were in town. Your friends think they're God's gift to women."

"If I get you drunk, will you tell me everything they said about me?"

"Well, not right now because we're getting pretty close to Versailles. But, if you want, you might give it a try later," she smiled coyly, "and then maybe I'll agree to submit to one of your harsh interrogations."

Carlos twisted around and gave Lifton a thumbs up.

"Okay, Carlos, you can go ahead and put the glass up now."

The smoked-glass pane rose slowly, sealing off the passenger compartment. They spent the rest of the ride playing eye games, trying to make each other laugh, as the limousine headed west on *Calle Ocho*, the main artery of Little Havana. Lifton spied the long line of people waiting for a table at Miami's most famous Cuban eatery. Those who only wanted Cuban coffee or pastries didn't have to go inside the restaurant because there was a big walk-up counter on the other side of the building. Every day scores of Cubans congregated at the walk-up counter, sipping *café cubano* and talking exile politics in loud voices, like how it was a certainty Fidel Castro's communist regime soon would fall. Trouble was people had been making that very same prediction at that very same spot since 1971 when Felipe Valls transformed Versailles, a small florist shop, into a beautifully-appointed Cuban restaurant.

"Don't worry," the chauffeur told them after he parked the limo. A few moments later he exited the restaurant with his arm around a young girl. Carlos pointed at the limo, she nodded approvingly, he kissed her on the forehead, and then gave a thumbs up. Insults in Spanish were hurled at them as they breezed by the dozens of people waiting in line. As soon as they stepped inside the hostess Carlos had sweet-talked grabbed two menus and guided them to a table in the rear section of the restaurant.

"Don't you just love all these fancy mirrors?"

"I thought you were going to say you loved this place because of the big portions of Cuban food."

"Well, I *am* a lover of big sizes." She looked down at his waist and then stared at him to see if she could make him laugh first. "If you know what I mean."

Lifton met her challenge, his face a blank page. "Did you see in the news where one of the presidential hopefuls came here the other day?"

"Oh, you," she sputtered, "did you even hear what I said?"

"Of course I did. And I just won another round. You keep forgetting I'm a seasoned trial attorney. You don't understand who you're up against. Damn, I just gave you another straight line."

"I was *not* about to say I'd like to be up against you." She was able to maintain a serious face only for a few seconds before bursting into laughter.

"*Buenas noches.*" A stocky older waitress in a beehive hairdo and too much makeup arrived with a pitcher of water, a basket of toasted Cuban bread with garlic, and two huge laminated menus. She pulled out a pad from one of the pockets of her dark-green uniform and switched to English. "You know what you want?"

"A *media noche* sandwich, please, black bean soup with extra onions, avocado salad, and fried plantains, the round ones."

The waitress rolled her eyes at the thought of that explosive combination. She repeated his order in Spanish as she jotted it down. Valerie was still flipping through the pages of the big bilingual menu. The waitress turned over two glasses and filled them with water. "You know what you want?"

"What are those plantains he ordered?"

"*Tostones.* Plantains smashed," the waitress said, making a hammering gesture. "Not sweet plantains which are *maduros.* If you order a dinner, you get three sides. It can be *tostones, maduros, yuca, moros,* black beans, white rice, or yellow rice. *Moros,* that's white rice and black beans mixed together."

"This one, please." Valerie pointed to a spot on the menu.

"With black beans and white rice, but separately, sweet plantains, and a bottle of Perrier. So what's with the long face?" Valerie asked after the waitress had collected their menus and strolled off toward the kitchen."

"Perrier? What's wrong with just good plain old tap water?" He regarded her coldly. "What, you think I'm made of money?"

She reached across the table and gave him a shove. "I'm not doing the staring thing anymore tonight because your serious face is too funny. You look like a cross between Michael Jordan and Chevy Chase. So who was it you said was here the other day?"

"Bill Clinton. And Ross Perot and Pat Buchanan also were here not so long ago. All these politicians come to this place for the photo opportunities, drinking Cuban coffee and talking politics with the exile community here in the heart of Little Havana. Cubans have a lot of political clout. They say if you want to get your party's nomination, you need to win the Florida primary. And to carry Florida, you need the Cuban vote."

"Politics suck." Valerie reached for a piece of Cuban bread. "I'm gonna have garlic breath, but I'm starving."

"Go for it." Lifton pushed the plastic basket closer to her. "You deserve to pig out. You burned a few thousand calories tonight making all those trips getting drinks for us."

"Tell me about it. I'm seriously thinking about buying stock in the Johnny Walker company after seeing how much you guys spend on that stuff."

"You mean how much No-Time spends."

"That's true. He always picks up the tab, and he tips good too. Your friend is really something else, huh?"

"People say he's 'glamboyant,' glamorous *and* flamboyant."

"I like that word. There's only one problem with him. He's in love with himself."

"Well, No-Time has earned some bragging rights. Over the years he's walked a lot of defendants on tough cases. That's how he got the name 'No-Time.' In the courtroom he can be like a revival preacher, all fire and brimstone. The man is heavy-duty."

"So I guess he doesn't make you prosecutors very happy."

"You know, everybody is pretty much alright with No-Time. He's a people person. He knows how to work a crowd, and that includes the opposition. May the best man win, all's fair in love and war, and all that jazz. But he's known to play the race card too, and that does piss off the powers that be in our office."

"So, do you drink Cuban coffee?"

"You mean the rocket fuel? Every chance I get. And you?"

"You better believe it."

"Addicted," they both said at the same time and laughed.

Their orders came quickly, and they ate in silence. Before he had finished his *media noche*, Valerie already had wolfed down her entire plate of shredded beef, black beans, white rice, and sweet plantains. Lifton was amazed how she could put away all that food so effortlessly. They finished off their meal with *café cubano* and coconut *flan*.

"This is *so* good," Valerie said, closing her eyes, savoring the last spoonfuls of the rich dessert, chasing them each time with small sips of the strong *espresso*.

The waitress shuffled over to their table, flipped through her pad until she located their check, tore it off, and handed it to Lifton. He pulled out his wallet, gave her a ten and a five, and told her to keep the change.

"You let her keep the change from those fifteen dollars? Wow!" Valerie rolled her shoulders like an exotic dancer. "Hey, big spender."

"And there's more where that came from. That is, if you'll give me a lap dance in the back of the limo." She reached out like she was going to slap him, but he caught her hand. "I think I better go and see what Carlos is up to." He released her and pushed away from the table.

"Changing the conversation again?" She sat back and tried to look upset but started snickering instead.

Guardians Of The Faith

Lifton spied Carlos at the walk-up window, drinking a *café cubano* and puffing on a big, thick cigar while engaged in animated conversation with some old-timers.

"We still got our ride?"

"Yeah, Carlos is outside talking with some of his Cuban *compadres*. Let's give him a few more minutes."

After he sat down Valerie looked deep into his eyes. "So, Rayfield Lifton, what's *your* thing? Most people have one. I can see by that face you're making you want me to explain. Okay, your *thing* is what moves you. What you love to do. For me it's taking acting classes at Miami-Dade. It's perfect for me because the downtown campus is just a few blocks from the Arena. I want to be in movies or tv. Like Olivia Brown, you know, Detective Trudy Joplin on *Miami Vice*. I met her at a game once. She was sitting with Phillip Michael Thomas."

"Detective Ricardo 'Rico' Tubbs," they said at the same time and laughed.

"Now you know *my* thing."

"So what name should I be looking for on the big screen? Valerie what?"

"Well, my first name isn't Valerie. It's Bernice." She opened her mouth and jerked her index finger near it like she was trying to make herself vomit. "My full name is Bernice Valerie Witherspoon. So, *ta-da!*" she said with a flourish of her hands, "I gave myself a stage name. Valerie Swann. That's Swann with two 'n's."

"Well, that's sure a lot better than Bernice whatever you just said you name was. In fact, I can see the cover of *People* magazine already." Lifton raised his hands and made an imaginary frame. "'The Valerie Swann Story. Ugly duckling transforms into elegant swan. And, folks, that's Swann with two 'n's.'"

"Hey, ding-a-ling, I'll have you know I wasn't ugly even when I was little."

"Well, Naomi, you sure aren't now either judging by all the looks you've been getting here. So maybe I'll see you on an episode of *Miami Vice* pretty soon."

"Uh, *no*, I don't think so. *Miami Vice* ended three years ago. And I *don't* look like Naomi Campbell."

"You're right. You're *much* better looking."

"You are *such* a liar!" She leaned forward and pushed his shoulder. "I'll bet what you do everyday *is* like *Miami Vice*."

"Uh, *no*, I don't think so. It's more like *Night Court*. Listen, my job *definitely* is not my thing."

"Alright, so if your job is not your thing, then what is?"

"I don't have one."

"Well, then, you need to get one."

"Really? So who died and made you boss?"

"Oh, wow, that line is *so original*."

"You know what, Valerie? I don't need a *thing* because somebody really close to me already has one. And that *thing* is enough for her, me, and a whole lot of other people."

"And just what the hell is that supposed to mean?"

"What it means is..."

When he didn't finish the thought, Valerie grabbed his arm. "Hey, you can't just stop like that."

Lifton gently pulled her hand off his arm. "It's a long story." At that moment Carlos appeared at the big window next to their table. "Let's go." He got up and headed for the door, then turned around and saw Valerie still sitting at the table with her arms crossed and wearing a big frown. He shrugged his shoulders like "what's up?" When she didn't react, he returned to the table.

"I'm not leaving until you finish what you started to say."

"You don't want to know."

"I'll be the judge of that."

A few minutes later they walked out of the restaurant, and Lifton told the chauffeur to drive them to his house in Overtown.

"You sure you want to do this?"

She slid across the seat and cuddled up to him. "You should have realized by now I'm interested in everything that's going on with you, Mr. Rayfield Liftoff Lifton. Even if you do make a lot of stupid jokes."

"My place isn't anything to shout about."

"I already heard enough shouting at the game tonight."

"And my sister probably is asleep already."

"Will you just shut up for awhile?" She locked her arms around his waist and squeezed hard. "You're supposed to be the quiet type, remember?"

Lifton closed his eyes and dropped his head back against the soft leather. Valerie's sweet perfume filled his nostrils, and he reached down and gently massaged her right earlobe between his thumb and index finger.

"*Mmmm*, that feels good," she purred and squeezed him harder. "Will you promise to take me out after every Heat game, quiet man?"

CHAPTER SIX

Rayfield Lifton found Joel Chernin in one of the small windowless conference rooms on the ninth-floor of Metro-Justice. "So how was Disney World?"

"Well, I didn't traumatize any young children if that's what you're asking. I wore a turtleneck and covered up my swastika tattoos. The only problem, boss, was I had to take down the Seven Dwarfs because they started hitting on my old lady." Chernin described how the seven midgets were scurrying around making lewd comments about his wife and diving under her dress, and how he had tossed each one like a horseshoe into the moat at Cinderella's Castle.

The door opened, and a short, wiry maintenance man pushed a metal cart carrying a large tv and a VCR into the conference room. He plugged the electrical cord into a socket and made sure everything was working. "My pleasure," he said after Lifton thanked him.

"Man, you guys are really cruel. That old guy's bent over at a forty-five degree angle. The dude can barely walk."

"You're a laugh riot, Chernin. Vernon has been working in this building since the day it opened. He loves his job. We'd be really cruel to terminate him."

Guardians Of The Faith

"Well, then, if you did terminate him, he'd say, '*I'll be back.*'"

"I hate to burst your bubble, Chernin, but you're not getting *Ah-nuld*'s part in the next *Terminator* sequel."

"You don't want me to get *Ah-nuld*'s part because you know I'm gonna make you rich and famous."

"Rich and famous, huh? Well, I won't bet the farm yet just in case you're wrong."

"Well, ain't that special? Don't worry. I'll get us where we need to go."

"We haven't gone anywhere unless I'm missing something."

"I said don't worry. We gotta do things right. Aren't you the one who keeps telling me that, *mon capitaine?*"

"*Oui, oui, mon chef.* So are we going to the movies today?"

Chernin unzipped his black leather satchel and pulled out two plastic cases. "Okay, let's see here. We've got 'Interview' and 'Rally.' Let's do 'Rally' first." He pressed the power button, fed the videocassette into the VCR, and hit the play button. There was snow and loud hissing for a few seconds until a bright blue background and a white-letter caption appeared: "July 4, 1987, Guardians Of The Race Independence Day Rally, Fasulo Park, Florida City."

"One of our undercover guys went to this shindig."

"They do this every Fourth of July?"

"Don't know the answer to that. We've got some tapes of a couple more things like it, but they're older than this one."

"Why did your people send a UC out there?"

"I asked around, but nobody knows. The guy who made this moved out of state. I could try and track him down."

"Yeah, do that. Maybe he's got some information we might be able to use."

Chernin pressed the fast-forward button. "Here they're just bringing coolers and setting up their stuff in this structure." He pointed at the picnic shelter, a big concrete slab covered by an asphalt-shingle roof and four long aluminum tables. Someone turned on a boom box, and they could hear a loud-mouthed pitch for a "marathon sales event this July Fourth weekend" at the Homestead Ford dealership.

"Nobody hassled your UC when he took this video?"

"Naw, he must have blended in okay with this type of crowd." Chernin pressed the fast-forward button again, and the video showed more people arriving, women holding babies, children running around, and dozens of men swigging bottles and cans of beer. "Okay, here we go."

The camera panned to the right, and four men dressed in jeans and white t-shirts entered the shelter. The first was short and stocky and looked older than the other three. He was followed by a hulking, shaved-head, three-hundred-pound ogre waving a big handgun and two younger skinny long-haired men carrying a large banner affixed to two poles. Their arrival prompted a smattering of cheers and whistles.

Chernin pressed the pause button. "That real big dude is Aubrey Swindall a/k/a Skeeter. He's the one who owns that redneck bar out there in Florida City where the Guardians meet up, and that's a .44 magnum he's holding."

"The most powerful handgun in the world." Lifton's Clint Eastwood imitation was pretty bad.

"Dirty Harry's weapon of choice. A real hand cannon. The young dudes with the banner are Bobby Wendt and Kenny Moser."

"So the other one has to be Thigpen."

"Yeah, Curtis Chance Thigpen. Leader of the Guardians Of The Race."

"He sure is an ugly one. Have you met him yet?"

"Not yet. Hold on a second." Chernin pressed the play button again, and the four men continued striding through the shelter. The camera zoomed in on Thigpen as Wendt and Moser set up the banner behind him, the American flag, with a swastika in the canton where fifty white five-pointed stars should have been, and the words "In Guard We Trust." Thigpen's freckled face was heavily pockmarked as the result of a particularly severe case of teenage acne. He had jug ears, a gap-toothed smile, and his left eye was set lower than the right one. "Is it just me, or does he look a little like that dude from *Mad Magazine?*"

"You mean Alfred E. Neuman? Yeah, he does. A lot."

Thigpen raised his right arm slowly, then jerked it all the way up, and Swindall shouted "Guardian!"

"In Guard's name!" Wendt and Moser barked in response, their right arms also shooting upward.

"Guardian!" Swindall shouted again.

"In Guard's name!" This time there were others who joined in the response.

Thigpen folded his arms and surveyed the crowd with a crooked defiant smile while the timer at the bottom right of the screen advanced more than a minute before he started speaking again. "Independence Day?!" His voice was a high-pitched whine. "This ain't no Independence Day! Not for white Christian America it sure as hell ain't! The niggers, kikes, and spics have been hijacking the country. And all you gotta do is drive thirty minutes north to see what I'm talking about."

"Fuck Miami!" a woman's voice cried out.

Lifton put his elbows on the conference table, rested his chin in his hands, and watched intently as Thigpen continued speaking, interrupted by occasional cheers and applause.

The end of the Civil War marked the beginning of a terrible time of oppression for white citizens in the Southern states. So back then six men of honor, just and decent men, came together to try and save the white race from renegade Negroes and the country from disaster. Now, history was repeating itself, America being destroyed by this same type of treason. And it wasn't just in the South anymore. It was throughout the entire Nation. Newspapers and television and Hollywood promoted anti-white, anti-Christian thinking. There should be no mistake about those gathered there today for the rally. They were proud to stand up and say America was a white man's country and should be run by white men. The Guardians Of The Race, they weren't the Ku Klux Klan, but they still had a duty to fight for white supremacy. And any white person who polluted the white race was a race traitor. The Guardians Of The Race had a duty to expose what was *really* going on so white American Christians could take back their government from the hands of the niggers, kikes, and spics.

"How much longer?"

Chernin pressed the pause button. "A couple of minutes. Is there a problem?"

"Do I really need to see any more of this right now?"

"It might make you feel good about our case."

"I'm already there. If I see any more right now, I might want to puke."

"There's a bathroom right next door." Chernin grinned, chomped his gum, and pressed the play button.

"Now, I don't advocate violence," Thigpen said, his beady eyes narrowing, his crooked smile expanding, "but some people just plain *need* hanging." Swindall waved the .44 magnum over his head, Wendt and Moser made fists and shook them fiercely high in the air, and there were shouts of "yeah!" and "that's right!" "Now I don't want any of you good people going around blowing up buildings or burning down churches. But, if that ever happens," Thigpen paused for dramatic effect, "I sure hope there's a lot of dead..." The cheering and applause were so loud Thigpen's last word was drowned out, but Lifton didn't have any trouble filling in the blank. "Death to race traitors!" Thigpen's hand shot up. "Death to race traitors!" he yelled.

Chernin pressed the stop button, ejected the videocassette, and put it back in its case. "The other tape is a Thigpen interview with that really hot tv reporter what's-her-name. You want to check it out now?"

Lifton pushed back from the conference table and stood up. "Chernin, the only thing I want to do right now is check the *hell* out

Guardians Of The Faith

of here so I can go and puke."

* * *

Aubrey Swindall cursed under his breath and pushed down hard on the accelerator of his Ford F-150 pickup as he headed north on Krome Avenue. His buddy, Ted Tatum, who owned a small marina on the bay side just south of Key Largo, had called a little after seven that morning and invited him to go bottom-fishing. It was going to be a perfect day for that, a clear February Sunday, high of sixty-five, seas one-to-two feet. Swindall didn't have anything to stop him from having the time of his life that day except for the fact he had to go and pick up Bobby and Kenny and meet up with Curtis. And so he had been *very* pissed off when he had to tell Ted that, *no*, he couldn't go out bottom fishing with him because something had come up.

Swindall daydreamed about how it could have been for him that day, gliding along the glass-top ocean in Tatum's Boston Whaler, a twenty-foot open fisherman, cutting through the brilliant turquoise water like a steak knife on warm butter, heading toward one of their favorite fishing spots. Even a couple of miles offshore, at Molasses Reef and Grecian Rocks and Carysfort Lighthouse, the water was so crystal clear you could see the bottom fifty feet below, craggy rocks and elkhorn coral formations, like a mural of the Grand Canyon painted on the ocean floor.

After they picked their spot and dropped anchor, they'd thread small pieces of squid on hooks tied to the fishing lines wrapped around plastic yo-yos, and they were ready for action. Those morsels of squid twirling around, a couple of feet above the ocean floor, would hypnotize the intended victims. And on a day like today they could haul in two dozen snappers, groupers, or grunts per hour, *no problem*. Hook, line, sinker, and a little red-and-white plastic bobbin, the yo-yo was the simplest of all fishing methods unless you counted bare hands. Swindall would sit there, line between his thumb and index finger, waiting for that most pleasurable of sensations, a quick, sharp tug as a fish picked at the bait. And then, at exactly the right moment, he'd jerk the line up at a forty-five-degree angle to try and hook his prey. Swindall ranked this experience right up there with good sex. And, of course, while they were bottom-fishing, he and Ted would have to put away a couple of six-packs, bottles iced down so cold they were full of little slivers of ice.

Swindall wasn't paying attention as he thought about all the great fun he *wasn't* going to have that day. He overshot the intersection at Krome and Northwest Sixth Street and had to jam on the brakes and peel rubber in reverse until he was able to make the left turn. He honked twice as he pulled up to Moser's tiny concrete block house on the western fringe of Homestead. Bobby Wendt had been staying there for nearly six months now after his wife had kicked his ass out of his own place. The front door opened, two pit bulls ran out, followed by a chubby plain-jane girl in a faded floral housecoat. The baby she was holding started wailing after she shouted, "Hey, Kenny, Skeeter's here!"

"Here comes Three Dog Night," he muttered as Moser and Wendt exited the house.

"Hey, Skeeter, what's going on?"

"I'll tell you what's *not* going on, Bobby. Me fishing with Ted Tatum, that's what."

"The guy with the marina down around mile marker 89?"

"Yeah, Bobby, that's right. Ted calls me up this morning to go out bottom-fishing. But, *no*, I can't go out fucking bottom-fishing with Ted today because I've gotta meet up with you two peckerwoods and go over to fucking Curtis' place."

"Whoa, dude," Wendt said. "You think *we* wanna do this?"

"Hell, *no*, we don't!" Moser confirmed.

"Then why the fuck are we going over there?"

"Like I told you before Skeeter. We just gotta."

Swindall didn't say anything else during the ten minutes it took to get to Thigpen's place on West Mowry Drive. He bit down on his lower lip, angry at himself for having agreed to waste time for no good reason.

"Let me go up first, Skeeter," Wendt said after they parked.

"I'm not waiting around. I'll tell Curtis right now I'm not wasting my time on any bullshit."

"Skeeter, listen up. Right now is not a good time to be making Curtis mad at us."

"Now, tomorrow, what the fuck is the difference, Bobby?" He noticed Wendt and Moser trading glances. "If you two got something to say, just spit it out."

They trudged up the stairs, which creaked heavily under Swindall's weight, then filed down the dark second-floor hallway to Thigpen's apartment at the far end.

"Damn if this place don't stink a lot worse than before."

"Old sheets my dogs sleep on smell better."

Wendt tapped lightly on the door, then turned the knob. "Guardian." Thigpen was sitting in the old brown recliner facing the only window in the apartment.

"In Guard's name," Thigpen muttered as he pushed up and twisted around. "Where's Skeeter?"

"You don't see me, Curtis?"

Thigpen's eyes narrowed. "You still remember where I live, Skeeter, or did Bobby have to show you?"

"Well, I don't see you coming by my place no more."

"Maybe I don't like sitting around with a bunch of Miami faggots. You all let anybody drink in that shit-hole of yours." Thigpen got up and made his way slowly over to the couch, knocking into the coffee table as he eased himself down.

Swindall was ready to get into his ugly face and tell him, "You don't like my shit-hole now? Then why don't you pay up for all the free drinks you and all the fucking Guardians got over the years?!" But he held back because he wanted to find out first why this wasn't a good time to get Curtis mad at them. Swindall grabbed one of the metal folding chairs and sat down directly facing Thigpen. It had been a few months since he had seen him, and Curtis was looking a lot uglier than before which was saying something. Several patches of unwashed carrot-colored hairs were pasted across his shiny scalp, and his freckled, pockmarked face had a lot more red splotches than before.

"You don't wanna be part of this anymore, Skeeter, you just let me know." Thigpen was squinting so hard there were only two slits where his misaligned eyes were supposed to be. "Same for anybody else. And then I'll just do what I gotta do."

"You'll do what you gotta do? And just what the *fuck* do you mean when you say that shit, Curtis?"

"Well, Skeeter," Thigpen answered calmly, "you've been a Guardian since we started. And you swore an oath to do Guard's work. But now I guess you don't remember so good about what we done."

"You know what, Curtis? We ain't really never done shit. None of us. *Never.* Unless you wanna count rolling queers on South Beach. So what the *fuck* are you talking about? If I say one day, *fuck* the Guardians, you're gonna do exactly what? Keep on playing with yourself?"

"C'mon, man," Wendt said under his breath, tapping his elbow against Swindall's bicep.

Thigpen's thin lips split into a crooked smile like he was enjoying being provoked. "Well, I guess maybe you just don't remember so good."

"I remember sitting around all the time like a bunch of pussies and getting drunk and talking about all the shit we were gonna do which we never did."

This time Moser knocked into Swindall from the other side. Getting elbowed by these two little shits was too much to take. He turned and shoved Moser so hard he fell off his metal chair. "I'm outta here," Swindall announced as he stood up.

"Wait up!" Wendt shouted as Swindall lumbered down the dark hallway. "Skeeter, wait up!"

"C'mon, Skeeter!" Wendt was tapping on the driver-side

Guardians Of The Faith

window as Swindall turned the ignition key.

"You two fuckers can get your own ride back," Swindall told him after he rolled down the window.

"C'mon, Skeeter! Man, can you just hold up a second?"

"Hey, Skeeter!" Moser had just arrived huffing and puffing. "We *really* gotta talk."

Swindall looked at both of them and decided there probably was something he needed to know, and now they were ready to tell him. "Alright, get in, you peckerwoods. But this better be good."

* * *

They got the booth all the way in the back on the small side of the restaurant which had a view of the parking lot.

"What the hell's wrong with you, Skeeter?"

"You've gotta be shitting me, Bobby."

"You don't want to be pissing off Curtis right now."

"*Really*, Kenny? Well, then one of you better tell me why real quick because I'm not putting up with any more bullshit."

Wendt made sure they were out of earshot of everybody else. "If we don't do what Curtis wants, we're all gonna be in trouble, Skeeter. Real big trouble."

"Real big trouble," Moser repeated.

Swindall leaned forward, reached across the table, and flicked the back of his right hand against Moser's chest. "You shut the fuck up, Kenny, okay? Why are *we* gonna be in real big trouble because I ain't never done shit." Swindall crossed his arms, and leaned back. "Go ahead, Bobby, just spit it out."

"Well, we, maybe not exactly you, but Curtis and us, mostly Curtis, we done some bad shit, man."

Moser was about to add something, but he remembered Skeeter had just swatted him like a fly for butting in.

"Oh, *really*? Maybe not *exactly* me? And just what the *fuck* does that mean?"

"Well, basically, it was Curtis and me and Kenny."

"Welcome to Denny's." A heavy-set older waitress in a beige

uniform had arrived at their table with a water pitcher. "You all ready to order?"

Swindall figured he was going to be stuck there for awhile so he ordered coffee, three fried eggs over easy, hash browns, biscuits with gravy, and sides of bacon and sausage. Wendt and Moser ordered cokes and french fries.

The whole thing started at Skeeter's late one afternoon three years ago, a few days after Christmas, the time of year when it turned pitch black by six. Being situated at the southernmost limit of Florida City, Skeeter's was the last place you could stop for liquor before getting on the desolate twenty-mile stretch of US 1 to Key Largo. That's why Swindall had put up that billboard on his property, to remind everybody heading south it was their "last chance" for liquor before the Keys. So people would stop off there with the idea of having a few drinks for the road, but most ended up just buying some booze from the package store after they entered the poorly-lit main room, thick with cigarette smoke, and got a look at the regulars drinking at the bar or playing pool. Some tourists went inside to ask questions, like how far was it to this or that location, where were the best places to stay for fishing or scuba diving or just plain old partying, and was it really worth making the one-hundred-twenty mile drive all the way down to Key West.

There was that mixed couple who showed up in the early evening, having escaped from a big New York City snowstorm, the fancy boon in the flower shirt and the real pretty blond white girl with the big knockers, wearing a bright-yellow halter top and cut-off jeans, like she was Daisy Duke or something, and driving them all fucking crazy. They wanted to know stuff about Key West, like if it really was a good place to party hard on New Year's Eve, and then, being the heavy-duty party people they were, deciding to hang out there for awhile and have some drinks before heading on down south. And they were all over each other, that mixed couple, tossing back tequila shots, the pretty blond girl now *really* driving them fucking nuts.

Guardians Of The Faith

"You all need anything else?" the waitress asked as she delivered their orders.

Swindall was lost in thought, trying to recall something as outstanding as a very hot blond girl with big boobs. He figured too much alcohol over the years was making him forget important things like that. And not that many niggers ever wandered into his place, *especially* with a white girl, what with the extremely large "Death Riders" helmet and "Enter At Your Own Risk" sign on the side of the building and the pick-ups and bikes parked out front.

"You all need anything else?" the waitress asked louder, getting closer to Swindall's face. "Anybody home?"

Swindall looked up with a blank expression, and the waitress shook her head and shuffled away. He picked up the dark-green mug, took a sip, and set it down. "Yeah, yeah, I remember now. The hot blond who got real drunk and did a table top on the bar? But, man, that was a long time ago."

"Remember how she flashed those big titties while she was dancing, Skeeter?"

"She finally passed out, right, Bobby?"

"Yeah, she sure did, Skeeter," Moser said. When Swindall didn't reach out to swat him, he continued, "It was me and Bobby had to carry her to the back where the fancy boon parked his big-ass rental car. And you and Curtis went out back there too."

Swindall brought the coffee mug to his mouth and took another sip. "Alright, go on, so what happened?"

After they set the girl down on the back seat of the Lincoln Continental, the fancy boon thanked them, and said they needed to get going, because they were heading down to Key West, to the La Concha Hotel on Duval Street where they had a reservation. So then Curtis tells the dude, it's already pretty late, and Key West is still like a three-hour drive, so don't he want to take the fastest route possible to get down there? And the fancy boon says, sure, so Curtis tells him, then don't take US 1 because that's the big mistake everybody makes. It's better to go the other way, just turn left about a hundred feet ahead where the sign says Card Sound Road. It's the only other way to get to Key Largo, but it's quicker because you don't have to worry about the drawbridge being up at Jewfish Creek where you might get stuck for an hour or more behind a long line of cars. So the boon says "dy-no-mite," thanks them all again, even wants to shake their hands.

"He said `dy-no-mite,'" Moser snickered, "just like that skinny boon on the tv show. What's his name, Bobby?"

"Jimmy Walker," Wendt answered in a low voice, like Moser shouldn't be interrupting him right now.

Swindall was starting to see where this was going. You didn't take Card Sound Road even if you were from around here. If you ran out of gas or broke down late at night out there, the chances of somebody driving by anytime soon were slim to none. And even if they did, no way they were stopping to help you out. The mixed couple takes off, and Curtis tells Bobby and Kenny to jump in his pick-up. They're thinking, Curtis is gonna follow them, come up alongside and yell stuff, just get them good and scared out there in the middle of nowhere in the pitch-black night. They pulled out of Skeeter's fast enough to catch sight of the rental car turning left off US 1 onto Card Sound Road. They don't do nothing for awhile, keeping a good distance from the other car until after the toll booth just past Alabama Jack's. Now there's nothing on either side of the narrow two-lane road except the mangroves. Then it starts raining a little, and that's when Curtis decides to floor his truck all the way. They get even with the Lincoln Continental, Curtis starts honking like crazy, the fancy boon looks over, and you can tell he's freaking. He slows down, Curtis slows down. He floors it, Curtis does the same. But the fancy boon drives good, holds his own. So Curtis pulls way ahead, then jams on the brakes, but the fancy boon just swerves to the left and *passes them*.

Now Curtis is *really* pissed off and tries to knock the dude off the road. They're yelling at Curtis, him and Kenny, that he better slow down. Everybody knows the road gets real slick when it's just

Guardians Of The Faith

a little wet, a thin greasy film making you hydroplane. But Curtis starts screaming at them, they're a couple of chickenshits and stuff like that. And they're shouting back they're gonna run off the road into the mangroves and all get drowned. But right then, a few hundred feet ahead, the rental car hits something in the middle of the road, a big piece of truck tire most likely, swerves out of control, and crashes into a thick clump of brush off the road to the right. The fancy boon must be okay because he's gunning the engine, trying to back up out of the gooey muck, tires smoking like a metal-shop grinding wheel, but the rear end just keeps bobbing up and down in the same spot.

Swindall lifted his coffee mug but set it down right away because he didn't want these two ding-dongs to notice his hand was trembling.

"Hey, Skeeter, aren't you gonna eat your food?" Moser asked. He grabbed the plastic ketchup container and turned it upside down, shaking and squeezing it over his plate until a thick red pool covered what was left of his french fries.

Reaching across the front seat, Curtis pops open the glove compartment and realizes he doesn't have his pistol. They all get out, and Curtis goes around to the back of the truck to see what he's got there, but he doesn't have his tire iron or baseball bat either. So he just starts walking slowly toward the car, they're following right behind him, the fancy boon is still gunning the engine, but the car hadn't moved an inch. And as they're walking over there, Curtis turns back to them, his hand shoots up, and he yells "Guardian!" And so they shout back "In Guard's name!" because they figure this is part of spooking the mixed couple. Then Curtis shouts "Death to race traitors!" But they don't say anything so Curtis turns around and shouts again "Death to race traitors!" And they go along with it and holler back "Death to race traitors!" And right then something happens that was pretty scary because, even though it only had been sprinkling a little up to that point, a big lightning bolt hits close by, booming thunder makes the ground

Guardians Of The Faith

tremble like there was an earthquake, and it really starts pouring.

The driver's door is locked, and the dude won't even look over at Curtis who's screaming for him to get the fuck out of the car. Curtis tells them to go find something to break the window, and Kenny sees a few feet away next to the water's edge there's some concrete blocks people sit on while they're fishing. He brings one back and gives it to Curtis who raises it over his head. The fancy boon, he slides real quick over to the other side of the front seat before Curtis crashes the block into the window. Now the lady lying down in the back seat sits up, looks around, she's all messed up, trying to figure out what the *hell* is going on. Curtis pulls up the driver's door lock, the others pop up too, and he tells them to go and grab the dude. So he and Kenny do just that, open the passenger door, each grabs one of his arms, and they pull him out and drag him behind the rental car. Meanwhile the girl is twisting and turning in the back seat, trying to see what the *hell* is going on, and then she starts screaming. There's a lot more heavy-duty lightning and thunder, and they're all getting soaked.

The fancy boon is lying on his back in the gooey muck, looking up at them, eyes bugging out, not fighting back, not saying or doing anything. Curtis goes over to them, raises his left foot, plants it in the middle of the dude's chest, calls him a "fucking boon" and tells him he's "under arrest for aiding and abetting a race traitor." Now they start thinking this is going a lot further than just scaring the living shit out of the mixed couple because Curtis is talking crazy like he's some kind of police officer. *"He's under arrest?"* What the hell is that shit? Curtis keeps pressing his foot on the dude's chest, the girl is screaming at the top of her lungs and pounding on the rear windshield, the lightning is striking nearby, the ground is moving back and forth like it wants to swallow them up, and they're completely soaked through and starting to shiver from the cold.

Curtis tells Kenny to get the concrete block so Kenny lets go of the dude's arm who figures now is his chance to make a run for it. He's got the one arm free and latches onto Curtis' ankle and uses the tight hold on his other arm to pull himself up which causes Curtis to lose his balance and fall to the ground. He breaks free and starts to take off, but they catch up and tackle him. They drag him back over to the car and give him a couple of swift kicks in the ribs and back. So now they look over at Curtis and, man, if you could've seen the crazy look on his face right after he got up, patting the back of his head a few times, checking his palm to see if he's bleeding, what with the lightning flashes and thunder, he looks like a fucking monster in one of those old horror flicks. He walks over real slow, gives the fancy boon three good kicks in the side, and says again he's "under arrest for aiding and abetting a race traitor." And then he says that he's "adding another charge, assault and battery on a white Christian officer of the Guardians Of The Race."

Now what with the lightning and thunder and rain coming down harder, and the dude being kicked pretty hard a few times and charged with two offenses, Kenny says, "Well, we sure showed them." And Bobby says, "Yeah, we sure did so let's get the fuck outta here now." But Curtis still has that crazy look, "Death to race traitors," he says again. That's when Kenny decides he's already had enough and releases the dude's arm and starts walking back to the truck, and Curtis calls him a "chickenshit." This whole thing, it's getting way out of hand, so Bobby says to Curtis, "Kenny's right. We done enough." And Curtis says, "Go ahead, Bobby. Go over there with your girlfriend, you couple of pussies." And Bobby does just that, walks back to the truck and gets inside with Kenny. They sit there, trying to see what's going on, but the rain is coming down so hard they can't see jack-shit. The rain lets up a little, there's a lightning flash, and they catch sight of Curtis standing over the fancy boon with the concrete block. And Curtis lifts it higher so he can crash it down on the dude's head.

Swindall started to raise his coffee mug again but quickly set it down, his hand now trembling out of control. "So did he do it? Did Curtis do it?"

Guardians Of The Faith

Wendt looked over at Moser who shrugged his shoulders like "go ahead." "Yeah, Skeeter, he did. Curtis bashed the dude's head in with that damn concrete block."

Swindall tugged on his chin-strip and bit his lower lip hard. "And what happened to the girl?"

"Well, what we saw is Curtis, he goes over to the car and drags the lady out. And she's fighting pretty hard, scratching and punching and kicking. And she kicks him in the balls so Curtis belts her a good one in the head, and she goes down right next to her boyfriend. With all that rain and whatnot we couldn't see much after that. Curtis gets back in the truck, and we take off."

"That's it? Nothing else happened to the girl?"

Wendt looked down and took a long draw on his straw until it made a wet sucking sound in the bottom of the plastic tumbler. "Well, I guess something did. While we was driving back to your place, Curtis says the blond lady, the fact her being a race traitor and all, well, he just had to put her out of her misery too."

Wendt and Moser finished up the last of their french fries, dragging them through the big red pools of ketchup on their plates. Swindall wedged his way out of the booth, pulled out his wallet, and placed some bills under the ashtray.

"Hey, big guy!" The waitress called out to Swindall as he lumbered toward the main entrance. "You don't want your food or some change?"

CHAPTER SEVEN

"I'm going downstairs, *jefe*. You want some *café cubano*?"

"Moneypenny, you know I'm always ready for some rocket fuel." Lifton got up from his desk so he could pull out his wallet.

"No, no," she waved her hand, "I'm buying today."

"Well, I guess miracles do happen. A *cortadito* then." Lifton pointed to the large square envelope his secretary was holding. "Is that for me?"

"Oh, yeah, I forgot." She handed it to him and, lowering her already deep voice, said, "*I'll be back.*"

"Damn that *Ah-nuld*! He has no idea the harm he's caused."

"Well, I love him. Did you already see *Terminator 2?*"

"I bet you'd love *Ah-nuld* even more if he went to Cuba and terminated Fidel."

"Yes!" She made a fist, shook it hard, and looked up. "My dream come true."

"Too bad your *Ah-nuld*'s not in politics so he could try and do something about the situation down there, but we all know that's never gonna happen."

Lifton stood in the doorway and watched her leave the secretarial area, recalling his first day on the job a dozen years ago when he learned she had been assigned to work for him. They had traded stories about their pasts, and how each had ended up

Guardians Of The Faith

working for the Dade State Attorney's Office. Like hundreds of thousands of Cuban refugees, Cuqui Perez left behind close family members whom she never would see again. Her parents chose to remain in Cuba when she emigrated because her two older brothers were of military-service age and couldn't get permission to leave the Island. For nearly thirty years now she never had returned for a visit. It was her belief, like most in the exile community, that traveling to Cuba, or even just sending a few dollars now and then to family there, helped keep the failing communist regime in power with much-needed hard currency.

Last year Cuqui Perez received a letter from one of her brothers advising their mother and father had passed away within a few days of each other. She hadn't seen her parents in nearly three decades even though there were fewer miles between Miami and Havana than Miami and Orlando. When Lifton got the news, he told his secretary to take the rest of the day off, but she refused. She had been wrong all those years, she confided in him. She should have returned to Cuba *at least once* to see her parents before they died. He convinced her to leave the office with him, and they drove aimlessly for several hours, north to the Broward County line, then south on A1A and Collins Avenue to the southern tip of Miami Beach. She did almost all the talking, first recalling with sporadic laughter the happy memories from her childhood. And then, when she relived the bad times, she sobbed uncontrollably. By the time they turned around and were heading across the MacArthur Causeway back to Metro Justice, Cuqui Perez was doing a lot better, as if she had wrung dry a towel saturated with all the tears of those unhappy times.

Lifton returned to his desk and opened the square envelope. Inside was a card which read: "You are cordially invited to attend the Annual Reception Honoring Members of the Federal Judiciary in the Southern District of Florida. Tuesday, February 11, 1992, 5:00-8:00 p.m. Intercontinental Hotel, 100 Chopin Place, Miami, Florida. $35.00 per person. Complimentary hors d'oeuvres, fine wines, and premium spirits with price of admission." He picked up the phone and called his house. "Hey, Kim, what's going on?"

"We're good, Ray. What's going on with you?"

"You have school tomorrow night, right?"

Last month his sister had signed up for two classes at the downtown campus of Dade Community College. She was only taking a few credits, but it would get her back on track to earn her associate degree.

"No, I don't. Why?"

"I thought you had classes on Tuesdays. You still owe me three dollars for baby-sitting the last time you went to class."

"Put it on my tab," she laughed. "After getting back from Gainesville I started thinking they could call any day, and then who knows how long we'd have to stay up there next time. So for me to be in school right now doesn't make any sense." When he began to say something, she cut him off. "Now, don't start, Ray. I'm gonna finish college one day, but at this point in my life it's still all about the *thing*, okay?"

"Are you sure, baby sister?"

"Yes, I'm sure, *older* brother. So, Mr. Popularity, are you stepping out with your girlfriend on a weeknight? Sounds like it's getting pretty heavy between you two, huh?"

"So what do you think about Val-er-ie?"

"She's great, Ray. Really great. I'm very happy for you. So where are you two lovebirds going tomorrow night?"

"I got invited to a judicial reception. Federal."

"Federal? Sounds important. How did you swing that?"

"I don't know. Only problem is it's thirty-five bucks."

"Well, it's *federal* so you best spend the money and go. Are you gonna be home regular time?"

"Yeah, why? Are you cooking up a storm?"

"Matter of fact I am. Your favorite. And I mean your real, real favorite."

"Spicy Cajun shrimp creole?"

"*Oh, yeah.* And, yes, we've got plenty of hot sauce. Bye!"

He reached out for his Rolodex and spun it to "N." One

afternoon a few years back Lifton had noticed Alonzo Norris in the Metro Justice lobby with a big contraption pressed against his ear which looked a lot like a World War II walkie-talkie. It turned out to be one of the first cellular telephones on the market, a Motorola DynaTAC 8000X, nicknamed the "brick" due to its shape. Now Norris had a brand-new mobile telephone, one-third the length and width of his first one, a second generation cellular with digital signaling, the current status symbol. "One day when I grow up, I'll have one of those cellular telephones too," Lifton said to himself as he dialed the number.

"Talk to me."

"Wait, this sounds like Barry White. I'm sorry, Mr. Barry White. I was trying to reach glamboyant Alonzo No-Time Norris."

"My main man Liftoff."

"Are you going to that federal judicial reception tomorrow?

"Sure thing. I do federal sometimes so I gotta go."

"Well, I don't do federal, but I got an invitation anyway."

"So you gotta go. All the movers and shakers will be there."

"Well, that confirms whoever sent it to me definitely made a mistake."

"Man, that damn attitude you get, Ray. You *really* need to lose it. You know what your only problem is?"

"I've only got one?"

"Did you hear what you just said? *That's* your problem. It's *you* who always pulls *you* down. But lots of people are counting on you now so let me ask you a question. Do you feel good about doing this new case?"

Lifton flashed back to the Guardians videotape. "Actually, No-Time, I'm feeling pretty damn righteous about it."

"Well, that's *damn* good, Ray. In this life you've gotta feel good about what you do. Am I right, or am I right?"

"You're always right, No-Time."

"Not all the time," Norris chuckled, "but my batting average has been pretty good. I'm sending the limo to pick you and Val-erie up at your place tomorrow around five."

Guardians Of The Faith

"I'm not planning on taking her. That would put me in the hole seventy-bucks."

"Well, being in the hole with Val-er-rie would not be such a bad thing. You know what I'm saying?" Norris laughed. "But, listen, what it's gonna cost you is nothing because I've already got you two covered. The Heat are away so you go ahead and bring that very *be-you-tee-ful* young lady with you. Gotta run now."

The Big Girl had cleared him for the gift of a one-year membership at the DSC, but this was another freebie on top of the Heat tickets. There were no conflicts with Norris or Parrish because he didn't have any cases with them, and nobody in The Posse had asked him for any favors except to score a lot of points for their team. He picked up the phone and made another call.

"This better be Rayfield Lifton."

"Do you say that every time you answer the phone? What if it was one of your better-looking boyfriends on the other end?"

"Better-looking boyfriends? First, for your information, I don't have any other boyfriends. Second, you're..."

"Tall, dark, and handsome?"

"Well, you got two out of three right."

"Tall and handsome?"

"No, silly. Tall and the other one."

"I think I look more *mulatto*."

"*Café con leche*, you're not, Ray. You or Wesley Snipes."

"You know, Val-er-ie, the other day I was thinking about your *thing*. Acting in movies and on tv. So to help launch your career, you might want to consider doing some commercials first. I was thinking maybe some Kingsford commercials."

"Kingsford? What's Kingsford?"

"C'mon, Val-er-ie. Kingsford. The company that makes charcoal. You know, barbecue charcoal."

"*Oooh*, you," she said with mock anger. Lifton pictured her shaking her fist with a big smile. "You're *really* gonna get it the next time I see you."

"Well, I hope I really *do* get it the next time I see you."

"*Oh, wow!* Everybody's a comedian now."

"No, I'm just naturally funny."

"I don't think so. Truth be told, your mood usually is so very dark like..."

"My skin?"

"Exactly right. And thanks for stealing my punch line. And you know what else, Rayfield Lifton? I think you're just a lot of talk and no action."

"Are you free tomorrow night?"

"There you go again changing the subject. Why am I not surprised? Tomorrow night? Well, the Heat are out of town, but since you hardly ever call me anymore, I'm not sure if I really want to see you that much."

"Are you kidding me? We talk practically every day."

"Yeah, that's right, except I'm the one who has to call *you*."

"And it should be like that. Makes me feel important."

"You're actually getting to be very funny. You must be on something illegal."

"So is that a `yes' or a `no'?"

"Depends on where you're taking me."

"I thought you just said being with me was good enough."

"I didn't say that. But you know what, baby?" Her voice changed to a soft purr, "That would be true."

He jerked the phone away from his ear and covered the mouthpiece. "*Damn*," he mumbled, "this is *very* good."

"Are you still there, Rayfield Lifton?"

"Yes, Val-er-ie. It's a meet-and-greet with federal judges."

"Well, it sounds pretty boring. But then again, I'll be with you, right?"

"Kool and the Gang."

"You are *such* a seventies kind of guy."

"That's me. The dark-black disco king."

"So what should I wear? Being with a bunch of prosecutors and judges, I don't want to get charged with a fashion crime."

"You mean like indecent exposure?"

Guardians Of The Faith

"Baby, I promise you I'll only commit that kind of crime in your presence."

"Well, I'm wearing my one good suit if that gives you an idea. No-Time's sending the limo over to my place around five."

"Okay, then, but most likely I'll be there before that. Me and Kimberly have some things to catch up on."

"Some things to catch up on?"

"Yeah, girl talk, if that's alright with you, or is that a crime now too?"

"That depends what you two say about me."

"You're never gonna find out so it doesn't really matter."

"Well, what if I've got the house bugged?"

"Well, what if I've got a video camera hidden somewhere in my bedroom?"

"You always have to have the last word."

"I see you're finally getting to know me."

"Bernice Valerie Witherspoon, you're a real trip."

"I love you, Rayfield Lifton." It was the first time she had ever told him that.

"Take care," he said. It was the only thing he could think to say before he hung up.

* * *

Like during most of the drive from Metro Justice to his house, Rayfield Lifton wasn't paying attention as he turned into his street and pulled up to the curb. Instead, his thoughts were elsewhere, in bed with Bernice Valerie Witherspoon, his arms wrapped tightly around her, soaking up in her special sweet smell. A loud explosion shattered his daydream as he struck his neighbor's big aluminum garbage can which took off rolling down the street, leaving a wake of trash behind.

"Hey, Mr. Prosecutor!"

As he got out of his car, Lifton glanced over at the front porch where Old Lady Muir was huffing and puffing, struggling to get up from her rocker. Mr. T was barking wildly, pulling the rocker another couple of inches each time he lunged forward. This jerky movement forced Snoopy back down twice before she finally was able to maintain her balance and slowly straighten all the way up.

"Sweet Jesus!" She shouted like she was at a church revival. "What the *hell* is wrong with you? Mr. T, will you husshup!"

"Sorry about that, Mrs. Muir." Lifton got back inside his car, pulled twenty feet forward, and parked. "I'll go and get your garbage can right now," he called out to her as he headed down the street, glancing back a few times to make sure Mr. T was still chained to the rocker. One day Old Lady Muir might decide to unleash her vicious beast on somebody who made her really mad.

The garbage can had come to a curbside rest halfway down the block. As he made his way back, Lifton picked up the papers, bottles, and cans which had spilled out. The array of trash confirmed Fredericka Muir still consumed large quantities of Twinkies, Ring Dings, and Cheetos and was still getting her news from *The National Enquirer*. Every once in awhile Lifton would discover Snoopy's garbage can on its side, its contents partially spilled out, most likely the result of kids knocking it over. If you wanted to learn a lot about a person, you didn't need to hire a private investigator. All you had to do was take an inventory of their trash. Lifton picked up the lid, which had landed on his driveway, and set the container down next to the curb in front of Fredericka Muir's house. She had one hand above her eyes to help her focus better, and she was chomping hard on her gums which meant her dentures were somewhere other than in her mouth.

"You better hope you didn't break my can, or I'm gonna sue your black ass!"

"Your can looks fine to me, Mrs. Muir."

"I can't see so good this time of day, but I'm sure gonna check tomorrow."

Lifton returned to his car and grabbed his briefcase off the back seat. Taking a quick look at the front end of his car, he noticed some fresh damage. It didn't matter because over the years it had collected dozens of dings and dents. In South Florida you didn't drive a Volvo 240 to look like a player but rather to protect yourself

Guardians Of The Faith

from the greatest concentration of the world's worst drivers.

"Hey, Kim." Lifton set his briefcase down on one of the kitchen chairs and came up behind his sister. She was standing in front of the stove, the air thick with the smell of shrimp, onions, tomatoes, green peppers, and garlic.

"Hey, Ray," she said, turning to greet him with a big hug.

He stood back and pretended like he was playing a guitar. "Strumming my six string, on my front porch swing, smell of the shrimp they're beginning to boil," he sang, trying to imitate Jimmy Buffet's voice in "Margaritaville," his most famous song and the unofficial national anthem of "The Conch Republic," also known as Key West, Florida. "Wasting away..."

"In Overtown!" Kimberly joined in, substituting the name of their inner-city neighborhood for "Margaritaville." "Searching for my lost shaker of salt," she continued.

Lifton made a face, like he was upset she had interrupted his solo performance, and then finished the chorus with her. "Alright, so what did I do to deserve my real, real favorite dinner tonight?"

She looked up at him and smiled. "Everything."

"Everything, huh? I hate it when you give too much detail."

"Ray, you've done everything for me and Demeka. If we didn't have you, I don't know what..." Her voice cracked, and her eyes started to water.

"Hey, hey." He touched the bottom of her chin. "You don't have to keep saying that. I just wish I could do more for you two."

She reached over to the counter, tore a paper towel off the roll, and pressed it lightly against her eyes.

"Any word from that hot-shot doctor in Gainesville?"

"Dr. Feingold? No, nothing yet," she said, turning her head to the side. "But I know something good is coming soon. I just know it. I can feel it." She dabbed the paper towel at one eye, then the other. "The food is almost ready."

"Okay, then, I'm gonna jump in the shower." He picked up his briefcase and turned to go. "Is the VCR still working okay?"

"As far as I know it is. Why? Did you pick up some movies

from Blockbuster?"

"No, I've got a video from that new case I'm working on."

"Well, it's not a Hollywood film, but I still could go ahead and make us some popcorn."

"It's probably gonna be pretty damn boring, but you can watch it with me if you want."

"Hmmm. Dinner and a movie," she said reflectively, the back of her hand propping her chin. "With my brother. At his house. Now *that's* what I call a *very* romantic evening."

He pointed a scolding finger at her. "Kim, it could be worse, you know."

"This is true," she laughed.

He paused by the door to his niece's bedroom. Demeka was sitting on the floor, dressed in *Sesame Street* pajamas, a Big Bird doll from that show lying on the blue shag carpet in front of her. She wasn't playing with the doll. She wasn't moving. She wasn't doing anything except staring straight ahead at nothing.

* * *

After they ate Kimberly helped Demeka into bed, gave her a kiss on the forehead, and pulled up the guardrail.

"Does she really still need that contraption?"

"I took it off a few days ago, but last night she must have fallen off the bed and ended up across the room. I almost hit her when I opened the door this morning."

Lifton finished off his third bowl of spicy Cajun shrimp creole while Kimberly cleaned up in the kitchen.

"You're gonna o.d. on hot sauce," she said, watching him shake the last few drops out of a small bottle which had been half-full before dinner.

"It's good for you. They say Mexicans don't have stomach problems. I guess those jalapeño peppers and other hot things they eat down south kill off all the bad stuff."

"They should put a warning label on those bottles, 'shake at your own risk.'"

"You're getting very funny these days, sis."

"That's exactly what Valerie says about you. But don't worry. I'm sure she doesn't tell me *everything* that goes on between you two." Kimberly turned her head and winked at him slyly. "Ray, do you know why we're both getting funnier?" She shut off the faucet, reached for her glass of wine, and turned to face him. "Because we're doing better. Your career is on the move. You've got a drop-dead gorgeous girlfriend. And, most important, I just know Demeka is gonna be fine again real soon."

Lifton finished the rest of his wine, then looked down and stirred his spoon slowly around in the half-empty bowl.

"The *thing* will be history real soon, Ray. I just know it. I can feel it."

* * *

Lifton squinted at the buttons on the VCR. It had been awhile since the last time he had used it. Every week he would get three or four movies from the Blockbuster on Biscayne Boulevard. But that routine had stopped when things started getting very busy for him, basketball at the DSC and spending a lot of time with Bernice Valerie Witherspoon. His dance card was pretty full now, and he was feeling a little guilty about not being at home more with his sister, watching movies and munching on microwave popcorn on a lot of lonely nights.

"Okay, here we go," Lifton said, feeding the videocassette into the machine as Kimberly set a big plastic bowl on the coffee table and plopped down on the couch. "What the hell's wrong with this?" The screen still showed the three contestants pondering the final question on *Jeopardy*. Lifton pressed the eject button, and the cassette slowly receded.

"You don't remember? You have to put the tv on channel 3."

"Damn, that's right." Lifton pushed the cassette back in, switched channels, and the screen turned dark blue.

"Whew," Kimberly sighed. "I ate way too much to have popcorn now, and I shouldn't have had that third glass of wine. I'll probably be asleep in two minutes."

White lettering appeared on the screen: "July 11, 1987

Guardians Of The Faith

Reporter: Kara Mello TV 5 Interview: Curtis Chance Thigpen, Guardians Of The Race."

"She's a good reporter that Kara Mello."

"I see her snooping around Metro Justice now and then."

"So maybe she's related to Snoopy next door."

"Kim, I'm taking you to the eye doctor first thing tomorrow."

The title page slowly dissolved, replaced by the image of the tall, voluptuous, raven-haired reporter wearing a black dress with a plunging neckline. She was standing in front of the same picnic shelter Lifton had seen on the other videotape.

"I'm here in Florida City," she began, "at Fasulo Park where one week ago a group calling itself Guardians of the Race held a Fourth of July rally. Here are some highlights from that rally." The screen changed, showing Thigpen inside the picnic shelter, a big banner behind him, the American flag, with a swastika in the canton where fifty white five-pointed stars should have been, and the motto: "In Guard We Trust." The camera zoomed in on Thigpen, shaved head, heavily-pockmarked face, uneven beady eyes, and a crooked smile of defiance. He slowly raised his right arm to forty-five degrees, and then a big ogre behind him yelled "Guardian!" Two skinny long-haired men on each side of Thigpen, their right arms shooting up, responded "In Guard's Name!" "Guardian!" The hulking ogre shouted again, but this time the response "In Guard's Name!" was louder because others joined in.

"The big dude is Aubrey Swindall, they call him Skeeter, and those two young punks are Bobby Wendt and Kenny Moser."

"The niggers, kikes, and spics have been hijacking the country. And all you gotta do is drive thirty minutes north to see what I'm talking about." There was a bleeping sound where Lifton recalled a woman had shouted "Fuck Miami!" There were other short clips from his speech where Thigpen talked about the media and Hollywood promoting anti-white, anti-Christian thinking, and that America was a white man's country and should be run by white men. The Guardians had a duty to fight for white supremacy and to take back the government from the niggers, kikes, and spics.

Guardians Of The Faith

"Now, I don't advocate violence," Thigpen said with a crooked smile, "but some people just plain *need* hanging." The final clip panned the cheering crowd and showed Swindall waving a big handgun over his head and Wendt and Moser shaking their fists high in the air.

Lifton glanced over at his sister who hadn't said a word. She was frozen, her eyes fixed on the screen, her expression one of disbelief.

"That was one week ago," Kara Mello said. "We were able to track down Curtis Chance Thigpen, the leader of the Guardians Of The Race, who agreed to be interviewed on camera as long as our crew came out here to Florida City." The cameraman followed the reporter to a spot where Thigpen was standing a few feet away. "Mr. Thigpen, thank you for agreeing to speak with me today. You call yourselves the Guardians of the Race. What exactly is your group all about?"

Thigpen folded his arms. "What we're all about is, what do you call them other groups? Yeah, we're just like one of them conservation groups."

"Mr. Thigpen, really," the reporter said with a frown. "I saw a video of your rally last week right here at this very same place. You gave a speech where you..."

"Listen, here now," Thigpen interrupted her. "You've got all these groups, save the whales, save this and save that stupid-ass bird. Well, our group is out to save the white Christian race. It's the *real* endangered species."

"Mr. Thigpen, you can't be serious when..."

"You people in the media's just part of it like the rest of them, spreading the big lie that's destroying America."

"And just what is this big lie that's destroying America?" She turned her head slightly and winked at the camera.

Her gesture wasn't lost on Thigpen. "You can make fun of what we do out here all you want. But you, like all good white Christians, you need to find out what's really going on, and maybe then you'd want to fight back like we do."

Guardians Of The Faith

"And you think I'm a good white Christian?"

"Well, you told me you ain't no spic or kike. Otherwise I wouldn't have talked to you. And you sure ain't no nigger."

The reporter's expression telegraphed she regretted stepping into that one. "And so tell us, Mr. Thigpen, what is this big lie that's destroying America?"

"The big lie," Thigpen answered impatiently, like he was having trouble teaching something simple to a difficult child, "is that America ain't a white Christian country, to be run by white Christians, which is God's chosen people."

"And who spreads this lie?"

"The niggers and the kikes. And you all in the media help them do it."

"Mr. Thigpen, you must be aware the Ku Klux Klan lost a huge lawsuit in federal court just a few years ago and, as a result, it had to declare bankruptcy. The court also ordered the Klan to disband. My question to you is, your group here in South Florida, the Guardians Of The Race, isn't it just the Ku Klux Klan with a different name?

"What's the Ku Klux Klan?"

"Mr. Thigpen, last week at the rally you talked about blowing up buildings and burning down churches. Does your group advocate such violent acts?"

"You got it wrong, lady. I didn't say for nobody to do none of those things."

"But at the end of your speech, you said 'death to race traitors.' So what exactly did you mean by those words?"

"Listen, lady, it's real simple. It's against God's law for the races to mix. That's why we've got different colored skins so you don't have to be a genius to figure out who's your own kind. And if you break God's law, or you help somebody do it, then you're guilty and have to be punished, just like everybody else who breaks the law. And God's law is the highest. Higher even than the nigger and kike laws like we got now."

"So tell me then, Mr. Thigpen," Kara Mello said, shaking her head, "do you believe violence is..."

"Listen, lady, I believe we've gotta save the white race any way we can."

"If you'd let me finish, Mr. Thigpen, I'd..."

"Aw, this is all a bunch of..." An editor had bleeped out Thigpen's final words as he started walking away. "Mr. Thigpen, just a few more questions," the reporter called out as she and the cameraman followed, but Thigpen put his hand up for them to back off. Swindall approached, covered the camera lens with one of his meaty hands, and the screen went dark.

"We were unable to ask Curtis Chance Thigpen anything else about the Guardians Of The Race," Kara Mello said, standing again in front of the picnic shelter. "However, it is our intention to follow up until we get the answers we know our viewers are looking for about this elusive group. Are they just a small number of isolated hate-mongers, or do they represent a growing phenomenon, a clear and present danger of violence against minorities here and in other parts of the country? One unnamed source recently told me that's a question law enforcement officials would like to have answered sooner than later. Reporting live from Florida City, I'm Kara Mello, special investigative reporter, Channel 5 News."

There was a hissing sound as snow filled the screen. Lifton got up and pressed the stop button. "So what do you think, Kim?" Lifton glanced over at his sister who remained frozen in the same position as before, a look of disbelief still etched on her face. "Kim? So what do you think?"

After a few moments she finally began thawing out, shaking her head slowly. "That Thigpen guy and the other ones. Are they gonna be the defendants in your new case?"

"Well, so far it's just an investigation, but, yeah, they might be. And, Kim," he added, "nobody's even supposed to know about this investigation except me and the detective who's working it."

"Ray, you don't have to worry about me telling anybody." She pushed up from the couch. "So what do I think? I think you better get these bad guys. I don't know what they've done. I really don't even want to know. Just go out and get them, all of them, and put them away for as long as you can. Because God help us all one day if you don't."

CHAPTER EIGHT

"You want some more coffee?" The big oaf must have gotten stood up by his girlfriend. She already had served him three cups during the forty-five minutes he had been sitting there alone. That last booth on the small side of the restaurant was the one people picked when they needed some privacy, people cheating on their spouses, for example. The waitresses had an inside joke, calling it "the kissing booth" like the attraction county fairs used to have back in the good old days.

She remembered this big guy as the customer she had waited on the other day, the one who never touched any of the big breakfast he ordered and didn't want it for take-out either. It wasn't easy to forget all three-hundred pounds of him or his massive bald head, sitting there with those two skinny long-haired freaks, talking low and nervous-looking. They probably were doing some kind of drug deal but, of course, that wouldn't be unusual around these parts. There were smugglers bringing in loads of cocaine and marijuana all the time where Dade County ended and the Keys began. She was sure it had to be something like that because no way this big guy was gay although the other two did look like they might be three-dollar bills.

Aubrey Swindall was starting to feel the effects of his caffeine

Guardians Of The Faith

overdose. His heart was beating real fast now, and he was shifting his legs every few seconds. He decided to take another look at the letter he had received from the lawyer while he waited for the dude from up north to arrive. "Dear Mr. Swindall. This will confirm our recent telephone conversation wherein you expressed interest in selling property in Florida City consisting of a three-acre lot and free-standing building zoned for commercial use. As we discussed, my clients, Stewart and Karen Malman of White Plains, New York, advised me they may be interested in purchasing said property including the current liquor license. This also will confirm Stewart Malman anticipates traveling to South Florida in the next few days to view a number of properties, including yours. Upon receipt of this letter, please contact me to schedule an appointment with Mr. Malman if you still are interested in such a potential sale."

Swindall figured this couple had to be Jewish, being from New York and all and having a Miami Beach lawyer with a name like Tannenbaum. He was surprised people like that would be interested in buying a redneck bar and package store at the far-south end of Dade County instead of one of those delicatessens in Miami Beach. Swindall slowly traced his index finger over the raised letterhead with the attorney's name, address, and telephone number. He called Aaron Tannenbaum, Esq. right away after he got the letter, telling him, sure, he was interested in selling his place and would be glad to meet with one of the potential buyers. A few days later Tannenbaum called and said Stewart Malman was traveling to South Florida this weekend and could meet with him on Sunday morning. That was a good time because Swindall didn't want to be explaining to anybody what he was doing hanging out with some strange-looking Hebe from up north. After what Bobby and Kenny had told him about what went down three years ago, when a cement block had crushed the skulls of that mixed couple, all bets were off.

Swindall told the Miami Beach lawyer he would meet up with Stewart Malman at the Denny's restaurant on US 1 just north of East Palm Drive in Florida City. If it turned out there was going to be serious money involved, then he'd go ahead and take the Hebe over to his place himself and hope those two long-haired peckerwoods didn't show up, like they did sometimes on Sundays, to drink beer and use the hose in the back to wash Moser's truck. Swindall glanced out at the parking lot and saw a black Lincoln Continental pull into a space. It had a Hertz bumper sticker so there was a good chance this was his visitor from New York. When the driver's door opened, Swindall was expecting a short, fat bearded guy in heavy black clothing to step out. Instead, it was a trim young man over six feet with rugged features and a crewcut, wearing a white t-shirt and blue jeans and dark wrap-around sunglasses. "Wrong dude," he realized. But after the man entered the restaurant and started looking around for somebody, Swindall raised his hand.

"Aubrey? Stewart Malman," the man introduced himself and extended his hand after he removed his sunglasses.

"Thought you'd look different."

"Oh, really?" The man smiled and tapped his head like he understood. "Well, it's true the old crewcut hasn't been in style for awhile now."

"Good thing he didn't get what I was thinking," Swindall said to himself.

"A lot of guys now, well, like you, Aubrey, are doing a Marine kinda thing, you know, completely shaving their heads. But I've had this since Desert Storm." Malman pointed up at the half-inch row of light-brown hair at the front of his scalp standing at attention with the help of some butch wax.

"Desert Storm, huh? That damn thing is over now, right?"

"Yeah, Aubrey. It's been awhile already. We launched the first air strikes mid-January of last year, and the ground assault started about a month later. Less than a week after that Saddam Hussein caved. So, I guess, it's been over about a year now."

"So what did you do over there?"

"Army Ranger. Well, it's true more people have heard about the Green Berets," Malman added after he noticed Swindall's puzzled expression. "What we Rangers do is come in airborne and seize and secure strategic targets, like an airfield for example. But we do a lot of other things too, direct-fire battles, close combat, stuff like that."

The waitress arrived with a pot of coffee and checked out the clean-cut arrival, concluding he probably was a pilot from Homestead Air Force Base, and wondering what the hell he was doing at the same table with meathead. "You all ready to order?"

"Yes, Frances. I'll just have a cup of black coffee, please."

She turned to Swindall and asked, "You want another refill?"

"Yes, ma'am, if you could, please," he mumbled.

"Maybe the big oaf is gay after all," she pondered as she walked away from their table. He was being real polite, and he had a silly schoolgirl grin instead of a sourpuss now that the slim handsome young man had joined him in the "kissing booth."

"Army Rangers, huh? Gunfights and kung-fu shit. Sounds like the kinda stuff I'd like to do."

"Well, Aubrey," Malman pointed at Swindall's gut, "first you'd have to lose that thing. To get into the Rangers you've gotta be able to do things like run five miles at eight-minutes or better per mile."

"Well, I'm probably too old now anyway."

"Yeah, I didn't want to say anything about that part," Malman grinned, picking up his mug of steaming coffee.

"So you been out of the army only about a year," Swindall cocked his head," and you already made some good money?"

"I'm not sure what you mean by good money, Aubrey, but enough to be able to buy some property down here. I've been able to sock away some bucks because end of last year we got bought out, a little software company me and my partner started back in our college days. We were supposed to have completed the sale sooner, but things got sidetracked when my unit got called up for Desert Storm." Malman took another sip of his coffee. "Well, you know what they say, Aubrey, 'shit happens.'"

"Man, ain't that the truth," Swindall agreed.

Guardians Of The Faith

Malman and his wife were planning on buying a residence in South Florida now that he didn't have to work anymore if he didn't want to. They hadn't decided yet if they wanted to do the beach-condo thing or be more adventurous and buy something down in the Keys. On prior trips they had checked out high-end buildings on Miami Beach and Key Biscayne and also had taken a look at some water-front residences in the Upper Keys. But wherever they finally chose to make their new home, they also were planning on buying a small business. And that was because the Malmans knew they would get bored very quickly if they retired at their young age. "We'll start rusting away if we don't have the challenge of running some kind of a business down here," Malman said, tossing back the last of his coffee. "That's why we're interested in your place."

"You mean you and your wife would consider running a redneck bar?"

"No, Aubrey, of course not. And you know what else?" Malman's friendly smile suddenly became a blank page. "We also gave up on the idea of opening one of them kosher delis or bagel places out yonder here."

Swindall quickly diverted his eyes to the parking lot. "*Shit*, the dude *did* pick up on it when I said 'thought you'd look different,' and now he's letting me know."

"So, Aubrey, if we did end up buying your property," Malman continued, "we'd turn it into something else, maybe a tourist shop. You know, souvenirs, postcards, tropical clothing, things like that." Malman explained Skeeter's was the last chance to buy booze before heading out on the barren stretch of US 1 to Key Largo, but there wasn't a single place selling tourist stuff in Florida City. And you probably could snare lots of first-time visitors going south who didn't know just twenty-minutes away in Key Largo, and throughout the rest of the three-hour drive to Key West, they would find scores of tourist shops. And you could get them returning north too, those who realized this was going to be their last opportunity to buy tourist stuff they should have picked up while they were still down in the Keys.

"What I'm saying, Aubrey, is we could get them coming and going, if you know what I mean. But I don't want to say anything else." Malman's smile had returned, and he winked at Swindall. "I'm already pumping up your place too much."

"Oh, you don't have to worry about that." Swindall was glad Malman wasn't going anywhere else with the 'thought you'd look different' thing. "I already know I got something real good, but I ain't no hog neither." He raised his cup and took a sip, trying to pretend the cold coffee didn't taste like crap now. "So, Stewart, you got any idea how much my place is worth?"

"Well, I really can't say yet. I've driven by a couple of times. I'll need to take a good look inside to get an idea whether your building can be renovated, or whether it has to be torn down. Then, if we go to the next stage, we'd have to get estimates for the work. There's still a bunch of things we'd have to check out before we could start talking final price." Malman signaled their waitress he needed the check. "So, Aubrey, if you have the time, I'd really like to go over to your place right now."

"Yeah, sure, Stewart." It wouldn't matter who saw them together out there because this New York Hebe looked like *he* should be a Guardian.

"Thanks, Frances." Malman handed the waitress a ten-dollar bill. "You keep the change and have a good day." She watched the two men leave together and get into Swindall's pick-up. She overheard cutie-pie telling meathead he'd really like to go over to his place right now. She looked again at the bill she was holding to make sure it really was a ten when the check for two coffees with free refills was only two-fifty. And crewcut was real nice because he had called her by her first name which hardly anybody had the courtesy to do anymore. "If their kind are real gentlemen and tip like this all the time," she said to herself, "we seriously should think about turning this place into a gay restaurant."

* * *

"I don't know, Aubrey." Malman was shaking his head as he

made more notes on a yellow legal pad. They were standing in the middle of Skeeter's front parking lot after a twenty-minute inspection inside the building. "Your place needs a lot more work than I had anticipated. The fixtures pretty much are shot to hell. How old is the roof?"

"It's pretty damn new," he lied. "And it's never had a leak. Not even one."

"But then again you've never had a bad hurricane out here since you bought this place, right?"

"A bad hurricane? Well, I don't remember a real bad one or nothing, but we get storms every year."

Malman made some more notes and then clicked his pen shut. "Oh, yeah, Aubrey, just one more thing. What types of coverages do you have on your place?"

Swindall cursed under his breath. With each of these damn questions he figured this New York sharpie was looking for another way to jew him down on the price. "You mean insurance? I really don't know. Emily, my wife, she takes care of all the paperwork. I can find out and get back to you. But let me ask you something, Stewart. Does that have anything to do with the price?"

"No, Aubrey," Malman laughed, "not at all. It's just that, if we end up buying your place, we need to know what coverages we've got for things like floods or whatever."

Swindall was relieved to hear the insurance didn't have anything to do with the price. "Well, you don't have to worry about getting any floods around here, Stewart."

"That may be, Aubrey, but we still need this information before we could seal the deal. And the next thing after that would be to get a general contractor out here and have him tell me more or less what it would cost to knock down and rebuild."

"So you don't think you could just fix up my place?" Malman turned toward the building and took another look. He was focusing too much again on all the wrong things, like the image on the wall next to the front door, the large skull wearing a German army helmet and the "Death Riders" inscription painted below it. Malman turned again and faced the billboard at the south end of the lot with its big American flag and the inscription beneath it: "Will The Last American To Leave Miami Please Bring The Flag?" Malman glanced over at Swindall and shook his head "no."

After they pulled into the same parking spot back at Denny's, before he opened the passenger door, Malman said, "Look, Aubrey, I want you to know you haven't wasted your time today. I can tell you this. You get me the insurance information I need and, in the meantime, this is my thinking." Malman pulled the pen off the collar of his t-shirt, clicked it open, flipped to a clean page of his yellow legal pad, and jotted something down. "I'm thinking and, of course, don't hold me to this, but we're probably looking at a number around something like this to buy your property."

Swindall leaned down and over to his right to see what Malman had written on the pad. At that moment their waitress was serving coffee to one of her kissing-booth regulars, a pudgy middle-aged man, who was sitting with a skanky stripper from one of the naked bars in Cutler Ridge. She glanced out at the parking lot and noticed meathead's pick-up truck had returned to its parking space. And then she did a double-take and winced when she saw him going down on cutie-pie right there in the front passenger seat. She started feeling nauseous when the big oaf sat back up wearing a huge shit-eating grin. In the meantime she had overfilled the stripper's mug. "For crying out loud," she mumbled, soaking up the small puddle of burning-hot coffee before it reached the end of the table, "you two should get a room."

"What?!" the middle-aged man snapped, thinking she was talking about them.

"All he does is watch me dance, lady."

"Oh, I wasn't talking about you two," the waitress said, dabbing at the last few drops of coffee with the thick white rag.

Aubrey Swindall gripped the steering wheel hard. Seven-hundred-fifty-thousand dollars? That was nearly one million dollars! And he didn't owe anything on his place except for this year's property taxes which were probably less than three-thousand dollars.

"So, Aubrey? Are we in the ballpark?"

Swindall tried to look like he was lost in thought instead of ready to shout "deal!" He bit his lower lip. "You know, Stewart, I really can't say for sure right now. I have to talk to my old lady because she's an owner too."

"Okay, Aubrey." Malman opened the passenger door and stepped down. "Get me the insurance information I need, speak with your wife, and give my attorney a call if you're still interested. I'd buy you lunch, but I've got another appointment to go to now."

As the door slammed shut, Swindall felt like he was going to have a panic attack. What if Malman decided to buy the next property he looked at? Swindall thought about jumping out and trying to stop him before he drove away. Instead, he bit into his lower lip again, but much harder this time. "Don't hold me to this," Malman had told him, meaning the big number he had thrown out wasn't for sure. He did the right thing by not saying anything about that number being in the ballpark because otherwise he might look too desperate. Then for sure those New Yorkers would try and jew him down on the price after they got some contractor to jack up the estimates to fix or rebuild his place. He needed to stop worrying. Malman would be back and offer to pay that serious money. Nobody had a location as good as Skeeter's, the one and only last chance piece of commercial real estate before the long and lonely stretch down US 1 to Key Largo.

Swindall waited until the rental car was out of sight and then grinned wide again like a kid just given the keys to the candy store. As he started to twist around to make sure nobody was behind him, Swindall noticed their waitress at the big window, shaking her head with a look of disgust. "What the fuck is your problem?" he muttered and threw his truck into reverse. As he pulled out of the restaurant parking lot, Aubrey Swindall realized he now was a man on a mission. And, just like one of those Army Rangers, there were a couple of strategic targets he would have to take care of so he could make this deal happen and get rich quick and far away

Guardians Of The Faith

from South Florida.

* * *

One of the doormen, dressed like he was going on safari, stepped forward and opened the Mercedes limousine's right-rear door. "Hey, honey!" a woman exclaimed as she handed a ticket to one of the parking attendants. "Isn't that supermodel what's-her-name?" A very sunburned older man with a flowery shirt and Indiana Jones fedora lifted his camera and snapped a picture of Bernice Valerie Witherspoon as she straightened her black-and-ivory one-shoulder cocktail dress. After Lifton climbed out, she raised her left arm so he could lock his right one inside it, and they climbed the dozen marble steps. Another hotel employee pulled open one of the glass doors, and they entered the lobby. A sign on a metal stand read: "Federal Judicial Reception Grand Ballroom Second Floor."

"So you must be very happy," Lifton said as they stepped onto the escalator.

"Yeah?" She looked back at him. "And why is that?"

"'Hey, honey, isn't that supermodel what's-her-name?'" Lifton raised his hands like he was holding a camera. "Oh, my God, it's Naomi Campbell! Click, click."

She shoved him so hard he had to grab the rail to keep from falling backward. "You're just jealous because nobody compared you to anybody famous."

"You just wait awhile, and you'll see. I get Clint Eastwood a lot. Well, a young Clint Eastwood that is."

"*Yeah, right.*" Valerie shook her head and laughed.

They stepped off the escalator and spied a table halfway down the long corridor where they checked in and were given name tags. Several hundred people were milling around in the Grand Ballroom, mostly men in dark suits, a good number sporting the ever-popular yellow power tie. Lifton didn't see many familiar faces. "Let's go that way," he said, tilting his head toward a group assembled at the far end of the ballroom next to one of the open bars. "They're the only black people I see around here except for the chefs slicing roast beef at the buffet tables. "If No-Time's here, he's gotta be over there."

Norris had called earlier that afternoon and said he had an afternoon hearing in federal court and would walk over to the hotel. Carlos had arrived late at Lifton's house because the limo had been in the shop. Valerie didn't mind the delay at all, enjoying another opportunity to gossip with Kimberly. Lifton spent time with his niece in her room, talking to her or, more accurately, talking at her, trying to get her to play with her toys. He could swear he saw Demeka's chronic troubled expression soften slightly when he started cheering for Big Bird, calling him "Big Larry Bird" instead, moving the plastic figure rapidly like it was the legendary Boston Celtics forward bolting down an imaginary court, jumping high, and making slam-dunks.

Lifton saw Gerald Rice, the first black judge in the Southern District of Florida, flanked by Norris and Parrish and a half-dozen young black attorneys Lifton didn't know. Commissioner Beverly Sanderson was there too. From what he knew about her, Lifton was surprised Judge Rice still appeared to have command of the conversation. Norris spied him and Valerie and motioned for them to join the group.

"So, unfortunately, that's why I think there may be a problem when it makes its way to the appellate courts. But do I like it? Oh, yes. Just like that song from Crosby, Stills, & Nash, this new hate-crimes law, it's been a long, long time coming."

Norris put his arm around Gerald Rice. "Are you admitting you used to listen to that white-bread rock and roll instead of soul music from the brothers like James Brown and Wilson Pickett?"

"And The Righteous Brothers," Parrish added.

One of the young black attorneys with very thick glasses raised his hand and said, "I'm pretty sure The Righteous Brothers were white."

"He's just making a joke, Todd," Judge Rice explained. "The Righteous Brothers were white, *and* they were one of my favorite groups too. Those were the good old days, weren't they? Marvin

Gaye, Ike and Tina, The Temptations, The Four Tops. By the time I went to law school, the music you heard around campus was called acid rock."

Norris pointed a finger at Gerald Rice and nodded approvingly. "You see, everybody, he's too modest to mention the name of the school he went to was Yale Law School. And he studied there with another brother, Clarence Thomas, who is the newest member of our United States Supreme Court."

"People, we're getting off the subject," said Beverly Sanderson, her tone like a teacher scolding inattentive students.

"And what subject is that, Beverly?" Norris asked, bending down, imitating Groucho Marx rolling his eyes and tapping an imaginary cigar.

"You can't be serious for two minutes, can you, Alonzo?" Sanderson folded her arms and gave Norris a cold stare. "Judge Rice was talking serious business here about this new hate-crimes law before you so rudely interrupted. So, Gerald, tell me again what's this constitutional mustard you were talking about?" Norris and Parrish burst out laughing, and there was loud snickering among the young lawyers. "Now what did I just say that's so damn funny?"

"What I was talking about was whether this new hate-crimes law would pass 'constitutional *muster.*' That's a legal term, Beverly, as to whether a law can survive judicial scrutiny in light of fundamental constitutional guarantees."

"Well, I don't see how any judge could say this law doesn't deserve to survive. It's supposed to punish racists and bigots, isn't it? If you look at history, and I mean just take our history right here in Florida, you'll see that..."

Judge Rice raised his hand. "Now, finishing the thought, Commissioner, we'll have to wait and see whether the appellate courts will hold this new law doesn't violate certain rights each citizen enjoys. But, quite honestly, since it's a new state law, and I sit on the federal bench, I haven't really..."

"Well, don't trouble yourself any further, Your Honor," said

Norris, putting his arm around the Judge again and pointing at Lifton, "because our own legal expert on this particular subject is in the house."

"Is that Rayfield Lifton I see over there?"

"Sure is, Judge," Norris said like a proud father. "Ray, come on over here and introduce your *be-yoo-tee-ful* lady to everybody."

"Hey, Ray, it's good to see you," Gerald Rice said, pumping his hand warmly. "Thanks again for attending my investiture."

"It was great being there, Judge."

"So are you two going to have a private chit-chat now, or is the expert here going to explain this new hate-crimes law that has me all confused?"

"Now, just hold on awhile, Commissioner," Norris said, handing a glass of white wine to Valerie and a scotch on the rocks to Lifton. "Let these folks catch up on things."

"No, it's alright," Lifton said, clinking glasses with Rice, Norris, and Valerie, then taking a sip of his drink. "But there's not a whole lot to say about this brand-new law yet because, that's just it, it's a brand-new law. You can find it on the books at Section 775.085, Florida Statutes, and it has a title something like 'Evidencing Prejudice While Committing An Offense.' What this statute does is reclassify the penalty portion of other criminal statutes if a defendant shows prejudice as a motivation to act against the victim. And the prejudice can be based on the victim's race, religion, sexual orientation, national origin, advanced age, and probably a couple of other things which I can't recall right now."

"What's that mean, 'reclassify the penalty'?"

"Why don't you let the man finish?"

"Oh, shut up, Alonzo." Beverly Sanderson gave Norris a hard shove causing part of his drink to splatter onto his bright yellow-and-violet Hermes tie. Norris swore under his breath and began dabbing at the wet spots with a paper napkin.

"Well, Commissioner, basically what it means is that, upon conviction, the defendant's offense is kicked up a notch. A first-degree misdemeanor becomes a third-degree felony. A second-degree felony a first-degree, and a first-degree felony a life felony. A misdemeanor is a crime for which the maximum term of imprisonment is one year. So, for example, let's say somebody committed a misdemeanor battery, and the crime evidenced racial prejudice. Upon conviction the defendant could be imprisoned more than one year, up to five years, the maximum for a third-degree felony. You see how it works?"

"I do see. Yes, I do." Beverly Sanderson's head bobbed approvingly. "But I don't understand why Gerald here says there might be a big problem with this new law."

"Because, like I said, Commissioner, it's brand-new, and the appellate courts haven't had an opportunity to review it yet. The first time one of the appellate courts has that opportunity, it will be known as a 'case of first impression.' Sometime soon a trial court will have a case where this new law will be an issue. If the defendant goes to trial, loses, and receives enhanced punishment, as a matter of right he can appeal to the next higher court. For a case from Dade County that would be our Third District Court of Appeal, and it would decide whether the enhanced punishment was constitutional. If it says it was, the defendant could seek review in the Supreme Court of Florida and, if he loses there, he could file a petition for a writ of *certiorari* in the United States Supreme Court."

"What did you just say? A petition for sushi?"

After another round of loud snickering, Judge Rice said, "The word is pronounced *sir-sho-raw-ree*, Beverly. That's a request you file to try and get the United States Supreme Court to review your case. It's the court of last resort for everybody in the country. So even if the Supreme Court of Florida says this hate-crimes law is okay, the United States Supreme Court still could take the case and decide whether this Florida law violates a defendant's rights under the United States Constitution."

"Oh, well, this is all over my head anyway. All I'm saying, Gerald, is I don't understand how on earth giving harsher punishment to bigots and racists can't be legal."

"Well, Commissioner, let's just say this area of the law is going to present some interesting challenges for the legal eagles among us. Ray, any more thoughts?"

Before Lifton could say anything, Norris jumped in. "This is all very interesting, but why don't we talk about some more important things going on right now." Norris handed his drink to Parrish, made fists, and started swinging like a prize fighter. "You all heard the news, right? A jury just convicted Mike Tyson of raping that girl."

"Oh, *please*, Alonzo. That animal deserved it. I say lock him up and throw away the key for good."

"Well, just wait up awhile, Beverly. Anybody else here think Iron Mike really raped that girl, what's her name?"

"Desiree Washington," one of the young lawyers chimed in, "from the Miss Black America beauty pageant."

"Oh, *please*, Alonzo," Sanderson repeated.

"I'm *serious*, Beverly. The man is innocent." Norris got his drink back from Parrish. "Commissioner, Judge," he raised his glass and bowed slightly. "I'll catch up with you all later. Wayne, what say we go mingle for awhile?"

"I'll look for you later, Alonzo," Judge Rice said. "I really would like to talk with you about the Tyson case."

Valerie gave Lifton a peck on the cheek. "Baby, I'll be back in a few," she said, and began strutting away like a runway model.

"Well, I'm going to try some of that delicious-looking roast beef," said Beverly Sanderson. "I'm really starving after all this heavy legal talk. Rayfield Lifton, you and me need to chat about some things tonight."

"She's a trip, isn't she?" Lifton said after the Commissioner was out of earshot.

"A very long and tortuous one."

"But you have to give her credit. First black female on the Dade County Commission. And she's done a lot of good for the community over the years."

The Judge smiled and nodded in agreement. "Oh, without

a doubt. And I hear she even may take a run at County Mayor. If she can pull that one off, it will be another milestone. Her only problem is she comes off a little too self-important, but then again I guess most politicians do. Let's just hope our elected officials do the right thing like in the title of that Spike Lee movie."

"The other day I saw something about Spike's new flick. Isn't it amazing how they can make Denzel Washington look so much like Malcolm X. They say Denzel might even be up for best actor this year."

"And maybe he'll even win the Oscar. You know, Ray, these days anything is possible. We're busting out all over which is a subject I'd like to discuss with you."

"Let me guess," Lifton gestured with his hands like he was climbing a ladder, "vertical career move?"

"Vertical is a lot better than horizontal, Ray. You really should hear me out."

"Well, you're a federal judge now so I guess I don't have much choice."

"You can always appeal to a higher court if you don't agree with my reasoning," he chuckled. "My wife loves to dance," he nodded to his left where four musicians were setting up next to the parquet floor. "So I say let's get another drink and hide out for awhile before the music starts."

As they neared the Grand Ballroom entrance, Lifton spied Norris talking excitedly, most likely about the Tyson case, to a large group of people. Valerie was there too, and she waved at him with a big smile which said, "Don't worry. I'm having a good time."

"Ray, I understand you've taken on a case involving this new hate-crimes law," Gerald Rice said as they headed down the thickly-carpeted corridor.

"Well, it's still only an investigation right now, but it seems like almost everybody around town already knows about it. It won't be long before the bad guys hear about it too and head for the hills."

"Alonzo and Wayne told me some things, but you shouldn't

be concerned. Now let's just try and be serious for a moment. Oh, my Lord." Judge Rice scratched his chin. "I'm starting to sound like Commissioner Sanderson now, and that's a very scary thought." He took a long sip of his drink. "Listen, Ray, your investigation will become a case, and it's going to be a very good thing for your career. An African-American in charge of the first prosecution your office brings under this new law, and some real bad guys, neo-Klan types, as I understand it. And, you know, it's a very good thing for others too, kids with dreams who want to make this world a better place, like those young attorneys you met a few minutes ago."

"You mean the stars of *Revenge Of The Black Nerds*?"

"That describes them pretty well, doesn't it?" Rice chuckled. "But, you know, what? At the same time it has to bring tears to your eyes. What's right with this picture? Not so long ago you wouldn't find a single black attorney at a federal judicial reception like this one."

Lifton reflected on how there had been only a small number of black lawyers in South Florida until the recent past. And even now Alonzo Norris really was the only one with widespread name recognition. "The Girl From Ipanema" began wafting down the corridor as the quartet struck up its first song.

"Well, there's the signal I better go look for my better half. How she *loves* to dance." Rice finished off his drink with one big gulp. "I just want to say one more thing, Ray. You need to make this case happen. Play it out with the same passion you used to play basketball. That, my friend, truly was a work of art." He handed Lifton his glass, leaned forward, and pretended he was dribbling a basketball, waiting for the right moment to make a break toward an imaginary basket. "3, 2, 1, Liftoff!"

Valerie and Judge Rice's wife were swaying to the *bossa nova* beat with Norris and Parrish. The two women broke away from their partners and pulled Lifton and the Judge over to the parquet floor. The quartet began playing a fast *samba*, and there were cheers and applause as Judge Rice shuffled his feet quickly, showing everybody he actually knew what he was doing. The next song was "The Macarena Dance." Lifton tried to walk away, but Valerie latched onto his arm and forced him to stay on the dance floor and learn the routine. Norris and Parrish joined them with two white girls, and they all ended up dancing three more songs until the musicians took their first break.

Lifton steered Valerie in the direction of one of the buffet tables. "I want food!"

"You need to try some of the roast beef, baby. The end cut is delicious. I'm gonna make you a plate. Your friends are sitting over there."

Lifton felt a heavy hand on his shoulder. "Rayfield Lifton, I'm not letting you out of my sight again until we talk."

"I was just getting ready to have some food."

"Well, I always talk and eat at the same time, and you can too. Your lady friend can bring your food over to my table. Now you just follow me."

Beverly Sanderson eased her big frame down into one of the chairs and picked up a small pastry covered with a light-brown, gooey substance. "These are so good," she said, admiring it for a moment like a precious stone before popping it into her mouth. "I want to know what's going on with my brother's case. It's already been awhile since Susan gave it to you."

"Well, Commissioner, there's no case yet. It's still just a confidential investigation."

Sanderson frowned and shifted in her chair, then prevented an audible belch by making a fist and tapping her mouth a few times. "Well, it might be confidential for everybody else but not for me. Just in case you don't know, I'm the one who got you this big career opportunity in the first place."

Lifton folded his arms and leaned back in his chair. "Really?"

Beverly Sanderson didn't pick up on the sarcasm in his voice and reached out for another pastry. "Yes, really. You see, I'm very tight with all the powers that be in this community, like your boss, Susan, and Alonzo. I've known Alonzo Norris since he was just a child. When I heard about this new hate-crimes law, I started mixing things up. And I can tell you this. If it weren't for me, you wouldn't be *in* the mix."

Valerie arrived at the table bearing a plate heaped with food and immediately picked up on the situation. "I'm gonna need you over at my table right now, baby. You've already left me alone too much tonight, and I'm not real happy about that."

"He'll be over in a minute, honey."

"Please don't keep him long, Commissioner." Valerie's expression told him she was sorry her rescue mission had failed.

"So what has Wilkie told you about what's been going on way out south there where he's at?"

"I haven't spoken with him yet, Commissioner. I've got a Metro-Dade detective working on this investigation."

"Well, what did Wilkie tell him?"

"He hasn't spoken with him either."

Sanderson raised her eyebrows. "What? Nobody's been out to see Wilkie yet? My Lord, he's the damn victim."

"We're doing things a certain way to try and maximize the chances we can make a good case against the bad guys."

Sanderson surveyed the remaining items on her plate, picked up another pastry, and took a big bite. "Not speaking to the victim after all this time has passed? That doesn't sound right to me. Susan told me she would make things happen real fast so you people could grab all the fame and glory before anybody else did with this new law."

"Commissioner," Lifton said as he got up from the table, "I really appreciate you getting me involved."

"Well, you should, young man. You're on your way now to bigger and better places because of me. Did you know I had a hand in getting Gerald Rice nominated for federal judge?" She gestured for him to sit back down. "If we win the election this year," she leaned close to him, "there's talk Susan may be heading for Washington."

"That would be good for her."

Sanderson looked at him like he didn't understand. "And it would be good for you too. Alonzo says if Susan leaves there's a chance you could get her job. First black State Attorney? How does that sound to you? You could be famous again like when you were a basketball star way back when. Except this time you might have something to show for it."

Lifton stood up again, anxious to leave before something flew out of his mouth he later would regret. "Well, you have a nice evening, Commissioner Sanderson."

"We gave you all the cards you need, Rayfield Lifton. This could be your last chance to make it big."

As he headed over to the table where Valerie was sitting with Norris, Parrish, and some other attorneys, he noticed Susan Purvis speaking with Gerald Rice and a couple of other federal judges.

"I know you tried, Val-er-ie. And I truly appreciate your efforts to save me from Jabba The Commissioner." He sat down and began attacking his plate of food.

"So, Alonzo," said Kirby Chappelow, an attorney from Satterfield & Sawyer. "Let's make a trade. We'll give you three of our guys for Liftoff Lifton here."

"Well, we *might* be able to do it for three of your players," Norris said loudly, "*plus* three million cash," he added, and everybody laughed.

Lifton polished off a second plate of food and a glass of red wine, and then he and Valerie returned to the dance floor. As they held each other close, swaying to Nat King Cole's "Unforgettable," Norris sauntered over to tell them something.

"Me and Perishable are leaving now. I don't need the limo. My man Carlos is parked right out in front, and he'll take you whenever and wherever."

Lifton noticed the two white girls Norris and Parrish had been dancing with earlier were leaving with them. "Looks like my homeboys got a booty call tonight."

"Poor baby." Valerie stroked the side of his cheek with the back of her hand.

Guardians Of The Faith

"They have all the luck. No booty for me tonight."

"You know what, Mr. Prosecutor?" She put her arm around his neck and pulled him close to her. "Even you can be wrong sometimes," she whispered in his ear.

CHAPTER NINE

"*Damn*, if this ain't real good!" Aubrey Swindall snapped his head triumphantly like a pitcher who had just thrown a blazing fastball to win the final game of the World Series. As he turned the ignition key in his F-150, he added, "*Yes, sir!*" Twisting around to pull out of the driveway, he gently eased the pickup down the steep incline so he wouldn't scrape the undercarriage. Once he completed this delicate maneuver, he paused for a moment. The day would come pretty soon when he could leave behind for good that stupid little dollhouse where he and his wife had lived for the past dozen years. At least, as he frequently had to remind himself, it was a lot better than all of those rundown shacks where migrant workers stayed out there in South Dade.

As the pickup rolled slowly forward, Swindall caught sight of Emily staring at him through the half-opened jalousie windows. Those windows weren't worth a shit, with their little panes of glass which *never* closed all the way, letting in hot air and mosquitos, no matter how much you tightened the flimsy crank at the bottom. But there was no way he was going to spend one more cent to fix up this dopey little cottage. He constantly thought about the day they'd be able to move up north far away from South Florida. He waved at Emily before he gunned the engine, and the F-150 took off with a muffled roar.

He had been telling himself he was doing this thing for Emily, but he really wanted it even more for himself. "Let's get the hell outta Dodge, dude!" he whooped it up as he sped down Southwest Second Street. Since the day he met Stewart Malman that phrase had been bouncing around in his head at all hours of the day and night, and he started worrying if he might be losing his marbles. He pressed down on the gas pedal as the pickup neared the slight uphill grade before the railroad crossing, something he never had done on purpose. The truck launched a few inches off the ground as it hit the first rail, providing the sensation he was hoping for, sitting on a bull just out of the chute. These days he needed some reassurance he still was willing to do macho shit like this because he also was concerned he was turning into some type of pussy. Like when he was looking at his wife a few moments ago, he had been thinking, "She sure does look real sweet framed behind those windows, her hair let down all wild, her mouth fixed in a sexy pout, after their big roll in the hay, like one they hadn't had in so many years."

"Are we really gonna do it, Brey?" she asked softly as they lay in bed, the sheets soaked with sweat from their prolonged love-making. "Brey," that's what Emily called him sometimes, but he didn't let her use that nickname around anybody else after he saw *Klute*, the movie where Jane Fonda played a prostitute named Bree Daniels. "Yes, ma'am," he proudly confirmed as he gently passed the back of his hand over her cheek like he used to do years ago. "Like I told you, honey, I could have said yes right then and there to that Jewish guy from up north. But, you know, I played it real cool so we could hold out for more money."

Emily never liked the Guardians thing, and she didn't allow him using words like "nigger" or "kike." She had reminded him enough times about when she was a little girl in elementary school in Pensacola one her best friends was Jewish, the daughter of a military man stationed at Eglin Air Force Base. And then there was Webster, a Negro, her father's right-hand man who worked in his small repair business which serviced the airbase, and that Webster was one of the nicest persons she had ever known. She would recall that one evening, after her father and Webster had finished building an extension to their back porch, when her mom had asked him to stay for dinner. Webster gazed over at the dining room table with longing, all that great-smelling food, meat loaf and mashed potatoes and sweet corn on the cob slathered with butter. But, of course, back when she was little, Emily didn't understand Negroes and whites didn't mix like that, having meals together and all. Webster thanked her mother and politely declined the offer, chuckling and scratching his head as he strolled out of their house. So Swindall kept the Guardians stuff to himself except to remind his wife every so often Skeeter's still needed their business even though he knew that hadn't been true for awhile.

After he met Stewart Malman, he started thinking, that *jew* looks like the way people were *supposed* to look, not like Curtis Chance Thigpen who was looking more and more like some kind of subhuman reject. And this added to Swindall's fear he was turning into a pussy or, worse, some type of queer. But that couldn't be right because for the first time since he could remember he was performing in bed like a steam-snorting bull again which had to be proof positive he wasn't becoming a fag. It was very strange, all this stuff going on recently, but he couldn't think about it much. Instead, he needed to stay focused on other things right now like getting the insurance information Stewart Malman needed so they could sign the papers and close this deal real soon.

Once everything was on track he and Emily would take a drive up to The Panhandle and visit with her sister, Kaye, and her husband, Cecil, who owned a real-estate business. He had spoken to Cecil Hornby a few days ago, and it was incredible how you could buy a mansion in that part of Florida for less than a hundred grand, and that was property just a few blocks off the best beaches in the whole State of Florida. And if you wanted a place right on the sugar-white powdery sand, all you'd have to do was spend another fifty grand. Even shelling out that kind of bread, he still would have big bucks left over to get a new truck and a nice little Boston Whaler open fisherman. And it got better. Cecil was going to let him invest in a new business he was starting up, buying vacant land and building houses for all those folks from up north coming down to The Panhandle to retire. With the big real-estate boom just starting to kick in, very soon they'd both be multi-millionaires. Being in the real-estate business and all for so long, Cecil had the inside track on the best land deals and knew general contractors who'd work fast and cheap. It would be what they called a *no risk* investment. "Damn if this all ain't too fucking good to be true!" he shouted out as he barreled north along South Dixie Highway toward Cutler Ridge. He was on his way to The Newcastle Insurance Agency in a little strip mall which had a Dunkin' Donuts and a Big Daddy's liquor store.

A few minutes later Swindall was sitting in front of Charlie Newcastle who, just like every time Swindall had seen him, was wearing a white short-sleeve dress shirt with a button-down collar and a wide tie, this one kelly green, which fell only halfway to his waist. Newcastle had paper-white skin and thinning red hair and sported a chronic South Florida sunburn. He had a stocky build which suggested fifty years ago he had played high-school football or was on the wrestling team.

"Can you believe it, Aubrey?" Newcastle leaned back and cushioned his head with his hands. "You and me have been doing business for more than a dozen years now."

"Sounds about right, Charlie. Course you weighed around a hundred pounds less back then."

"Oh, this," Newcastle said, moving his hands to his pot belly. "Yeah, I'm due next month," he chuckled.

"Looks like twins."

"You should talk, Aubrey. You're starting to look more like the Pillsbury Dough Boy than the Jolly Green Giant."

"Ho, ho, ho!" Swindall squeezed his love handles. "It's bad being in the beer business down here, Charlie. Damn heat makes you drink up your own inventory."

"I'm sure it does." Newcastle pulled his glasses off and began cleaning the lenses with a tissue. "By the way, how's Emily doing? She's such a sweet girl."

"Emily is doing great, Charlie. Love that girl to death."

"You all never have asked me about any health insurance so I'm guessing Emily has pretty good coverage at work. She used to be with K-Mart if I remember right."

"Yep, she's still there. They take a little out of her paychecks, but she gets all these benefits, and I'm covered too."

"That's good, Aubrey." Newcastle made a ball out of the tissue, tossed it into a wastebasket, and repositioned his glasses. "I could never beat that kind of deal anyway, but I sure hope you'll continue renewing the policies you have with me. You always get the best rates. I don't think you've ever had any claims as far as I can remember."

"We've never had any type of claim, Charlie. I guess I could have tried to get a few bucks a couple of times with different things that happened. But, hell, my premiums would go up then, right? Listen, Charlie, the main reason I came over to see you is to find out what types of coverages we've got."

"For which policy?"

"Well, I pretty much know what we've got on the house and truck. But damn if I know what we've got on my business. Emily does all the paperwork, writes the checks, and whatnot. The other day she was looking at some of the insurance papers, but she wasn't sure how to read the coverages."

"Alright, then, mister ho-ho-ho," Newcastle said, swivelling his chair so he could open one of the drawers of the grey metal file cabinet behind him. He pulled out a manilla folder and turned back to his desk. "Let's see here," he said, flipping through the pages. "This is the property on US 1 near Card Sound Road, right? Okay, good. Swindall's Bar & Package Store, Inc. doing business as 'Skeeter's.' Well, you've got flood insurance with the federal program, the National Flood thing, and you've got a very nice commercial package which covers just about everything else."

Guardians Of The Faith

"What's that, Charlie, a very nice commercial package?"

"Well, let's take a look-see at the declarations page which lists the specific coverages. You've got your structure, $500,000, and you've got your contents, $250,000. You've got your general liability, $100,000 per person, $300,000 per incident. So you've got your place fully covered, Jolly Green, just like the full coverage on your truck. You total your truck or somebody else does, or you injure somebody real bad, you're fully covered. It's the same with your commercial package. Somebody gets hurt on your property, slips and falls, breaks their neck, whatever, your policy pays their medical bills and pain and suffering, all those kinds of damages. And the policy also provides you with a legal defense so you don't have to worry about hiring a lawyer or paying any legal fees."

"So what you're saying is, my building goes up in flames or whatever, the insurance company is gonna pay me $500,000?

"For a total loss of your business? No." Newcastle smiled when he saw Swindall's worried expression. "No, Aubrey, they're gonna pay you $750,000 because you've got your contents covered up to $250,000."

Swindall tugged on his chin-strip. "That's close to like a million dollars more or less."

"This would be true. You have the same amounts on your federal flood policy as well. In a word, you're covered from A to Z, my friend."

Swindall shook his head approvingly. "That's great, Charlie. You know, I really should write some of this stuff down."

"Naw, you don't need to do that. I'll just make copies of the declarations pages. They lay out everything important you need to know about your policies, and Emily can keep them in a file for handy reference."

Newcastle leafed through the folder again, found the pages he needed, and went over to the small photocopier. He turned the machine on, tapping his foot impatiently until a bright green light finally appeared under the glass copying surface. The machine was very old and slow, and the whole process took nearly five minutes.

Guardians Of The Faith

Newcastle returned to his desk and handed Swindall the copies.

"I'll bet we must be paying through the nose for all these great insurance coverages."

"I wish that were true," Newcastle laughed, "so I'd make more commissions, and then I could buy one of those fancy new Xerox copiers they keep trying to sell me. But, man alive, are they expensive! So I'll just hold onto that dinosaur over there," he nodded in the direction of the photocopier, "as long as I can. Okay, now hold on a second," Newcastle mumbled as he rummaged through the loose papers. "Last check your wife wrote to cover this year's premium for the commercial package," he held up a photocopy so Swindall could see, "was just under twelve-hundred. And your federal flood premium," he held up another photocopy, "was around seven-hundred. And I see Emily has paid both of the premiums so the policies are in full force through the end of the year. And that's a very good thing because hurricane season is just around the corner, and it won't be over until the end of November. Did you know insurance companies won't write any new policies, or even renew old ones if they're not paid up, once the National Weather Service gives a name to a tropical storm that's out there?"

"Well, looks like I'm in real good shape then. And your prices seem pretty damn cheap with all these coverages I've got on my property. I really appreciate it, Charlie."

"I told you we always get you the best rates." Newcastle closed the manilla folder. "All you need to do is stay claims-free and keep paying your premiums on time. Here," he added, "help yourself to a couple of these logo pens and our 1993 desk calendar. Can you believe they're out already? Now you give one of each to Emily with my regards."

"Will do, Charlie." He shook Newcastle's hand, took his gifts, and turned to go.

"Oh, Aubrey, there's one more thing," Newcastle said as he wedged the manilla folder back into the file cabinet drawer. "I've only been out to your place the one time back when we first wrote your policies. Have you altered your property in any major way since then? If you have, we need to update your information to make sure you have enough coverage. Of course, the more value you insure, the more your policy will cost you."

"Naw, Charlie, it's still the same exact piece of crap you saw way back when. The amount you got us covered for is plenty enough. But I gotta tell you," Swindall quickly added, just in case he had created any doubt about the value of his property, "we always keep the place in real good shape. I mean it, Charlie."

"Not to worry," Newcastle chuckled. "Hey, Jolly Green," he called out as Swindall opened the front door, "it's been awhile since I've seen anybody from that group of yours in the news. Are you all still doing the white power thing out there in Florida City? What is it you call yourselves, the Keepers Of The Race, or something like that?"

Swindall suddenly felt a rush of heat to his face, and he knew he was turning red. He glanced around the small office for no good reason because there wasn't a soul around except for Charlie Newcastle. "The Guardians Of The Race."

"Yeah, that's the one. The Guardians of the Race."

Swindall rubbed his nose rapidly a few times with his index finger and snorted.

"Not so much into that kind of stuff anymore, are you?" Newcastle answered for him. Swindall nodded sheepishly and snorted again. "Well, good for you, Aubrey," Newcastle added with a wink and smile. "Good for you. Then I'll see you again whenever, Aubrey, I mean Jolly Green."

* * *

"Can I speak to Stewart, please?" Swindall guessed it was Malman's wife who had answered the phone. "Hey, Stewart? It's me, Aubrey, down here in Florida."

"Hey there, Aubrey. How are you doing?"

"Great, Stewart. Listen, I got the information you need about the insurance coverages."

"Fantastic. Let me get something to write with." He could hear the sound of footsteps walking away from the phone.

Malman probably had a big house with one of those real expensive wood floors. Swindall took a swig from the ice-cold Budweiser longneck he opened right before he called Malman. A dog started barking, a baby was crying, and the same woman's voice said something before Malman returned to the phone. "Okay, shoot."

After Swindall described the policies and limits of coverage, Malman said, "Okay, that's great. Would you mind it if I speak with your insurance agent directly in case I need more information? Maybe I could use him for my other stuff too, you know, like our cars and residence, once we get situated down there."

"Oh, yes, things are looking real good," Swindall thought to himself. "You go right ahead and do that, Stewart. Charlie always has the best rates on everything." Swindall was glad now he and Charlie had that little talk about the Guardians.

"The Newcastle Insurance Agency, Charlie Newcastle," Malman repeated as he jotted down the information. "That's November, echo, whiskey, charlie, alpha, sierra, tango, lima, echo. Okay, thanks, big guy."

"So, Stewart, when do you think you'll be heading down this way again?"

"Well, Aubrey, it probably won't be long. I checked out everything else we needed to on this last trip so we're probably ready to go ahead and do something pretty quick. It'll be up to the lawyers after that to prepare the paperwork. Do you have a particular attorney you use?"

"Are you saying you're ready to buy my place?"

"Well, I'll be honest with you. Yours is not the only property we've been considering, but you're definitely in the running. And, you know what?" Malman lowered his voice like he didn't want anybody else to hear. "Personally, I'm leaning toward your place, and I like to think I'm still pretty much the boss around here. Are you there, Aubrey?"

"Hold on, Stewart," Swindall took another big gulp from the ice-cold bottle, but it went down the wrong way, and he started coughing violently.

"You ought to do something about that cough, Aubrey. I didn't think you guys down there got bad colds like we do up here in the north."

"Well," Swindall started to answer between hiccups, "it's all the damn going in and out of air-conditioning when I'm sweaty."

"Anyway, like I said, the next thing is you might be hearing from our attorney, Aaron Tannenbaum, pretty soon. And he'll probably ask you for the name of your lawyer so the two of them can start doing whatever it is lawyers do."

Swindall bit his lip, but he couldn't stop himself from asking the next question. "So, are we still talking the same price range?"

"You mean around seven-hundred-fifty? Yeah, I think that's what I said before. I hope I'm not bidding against myself."

"No, no, that's what you said before, Stewart."

"Quite honestly, Aubrey, there's two other places in the Upper Keys for less money, one in Key Largo, the other one in Tavernier. But, you know, I still like my idea about how to get them both ways, coming *and* going."

"Yeah, and that's why my location is the best. You get them coming *and* going."

"Anyway, listen, I need get out of these wet clothes before I start sounding like you. I was out walking the dog and got soaked in a cold rain. Can you believe this time of year it's still in the low fifties up here? That's why I'm looking forward to moving down to your neck of the woods. Take care, Aubrey."

"One down and one to go," Swindall said to himself as he hung up the phone.

* * *

As he swivelled to the right Rayfield Lifton had to grab the edge of his desk to keep from falling because his chair had taken a deep plunge, the springs groaning like they were being tortured. "*Yesh*, Moneypenny," he said, noticing his secretary at the door.

"The Big Girl wants to see you. And don't forget you have the interns coming at twelve." She frowned when she noticed his blank expression. "You don't remember? *Ay, Dios mio.* Your girlfriend is making you crazy. You want some *café cubano*?"

"The Big Girl, huh? Better get me a quarter *colada*."

"You're going for extra-hyper this morning?" As she turned to leave, she added, "*I'll be back*," lowering her bass voice another full octave.

"Somebody *really* needs to put a stop to this Terminator thing. *Ah-nuld* has no idea what he's started, Moneypenny."

"Look who's talking." Cuqui's laugh was followed by her chronic cigarette cough. "You do the same thing all the time, *jefe*."

Every semester the State Attorney's Office hired a dozen third-year law students to work as "certified legal interns." They spent most of their time doing legal research, drafting motions and memoranda of law, and interviewing victims and witnesses. A few days ago Lifton pressed into service two of them he found in the law library and assigned them the job of researching hate-crimes laws. Because there was no precedent yet in the State of Florida under the brand-new statute, they were going to have to try and find decisions from courts in other states with similar laws. The pages from Lifton's 1992 looseleaf desk calendar were disappearing rapidly, and he still hadn't filed a case against Thigpen or any other members of the Guardians of the Race. And, most likely, this was the reason why Susan Purvis wanted to see him.

When Cuqui returned from the cafeteria, Lifton finished off the quarter *colada* while reviewing old telephone messages wedged in the metal holder on his secretary's desk. "Okay, *hasta la vista*, baby," he said, dropping the styrofoam cup into the wastebasket. "And please don't forget to tell Vernon the springs in my chair are shot on both sides now. If he can't fix it, tell him to try and find me another chair."

Susan Purvis was handing some papers to her secretary when Lifton entered the Office of the Dade State Attorney. "Oh, there you are, Rayfield Lifton. Nancy, don't forget to call the U.S. Attorney's Office. Remember I have to cancel tomorrow's meeting about that new joint task force. Reschedule it for sometime next week. Just tell them something big came up." Purvis motioned for

Guardians Of The Faith

Lifton to follow her into her office. "Sit, sit. Will you look at this? Papers and more papers. Here in my office the only thing I get to fight are these," she said with a sweep of her hand, "letters, memos, papers, and more papers. I sure miss the courtroom action. You want some coffee?"

"No, thanks," Lifton said, his hand shooting up like a school crossing guard. "I just had too much Cuban coffee."

"Too much rocket fuel, huh?" Purvis pressed the intercom button. "Nancy, make some fresh coffee and bring it to me in my big green-and-orange mug. You know, Ray, I've been drinking too much of the stuff myself these days, but I've got a lot on my plate. Do you know what a clipping service is? I pay for it out of my own pocket so everything is above board, and I can tell you it isn't cheap either. Here's some stuff from the *Washington Post* and *New York Magazine*," she held up several pages of photocopies, "both talking about how the largely unknown Governor from Arkansas is advancing rapidly in the race for the nomination. For example, this article says 'the whole picture has changed since the Governor of New York, Mario Cuomo, announced right before Christmas he's dropping out of the race.'" She leaned forward and lowered her voice, "I'll tell you something if you promise you won't let it go any further than here. See, there's talk I might be headed for D.C. if the Democrats win the election. And if the Governor from Arkansas is our next President, well, I've been told it's almost a sure thing."

Lifton was about to ask if she had any idea what she might be doing in Washington, but just as his mouth opened she said, "I really don't know what I'd be doing there. Something in the Department of Justice I imagine. Attorney General maybe? That sure would be a huge leap for me, but I could handle it. The point is, if I leave for D.C., somebody has to take over here. My Chief Deputy initially would be in charge but only until the Governor appoints someone to finish out my term. And Madeline? Well, she may not be able to take the job. Something about her hubby wanting to relocate to Montana or Wyoming or some really cold place like that. Pretty far cry from living in paradise, right?

Anyway, whoever takes over eventually will have to run for reelection, but that would be something like three years down the road. So if I end up leaving for Washington, whoever the Governor picks is going to be sitting right here at this desk for a good while without having to worry about winning an election. Plenty of time to make a name for himself. We all know the drill. Be an innovator, grab the headlines, and all that jazz. And, of course, if you're a minority these days? Well, I shouldn't have to tell you, Rayfield Lifton. There's no way to go but up."

"I'm a minority?" He asked, pointing at himself. Purvis didn't appear to appreciate his attempt to inject some humor into her monologue. "Are you saying I might be the one sitting in your chair by the end of the year?"

"I don't think so, Ray." Purvis regarded him like he had just made another stupid comment. "That wouldn't be until the end of January of *next* year *after* the inauguration." She grinned widely, letting him know she too was capable of a little humor. "Your high-school friend, Leander Baldwin, is your man in Tallahassee. I understand he has Governor Chiles' ear anytime he wants. If things go according to plan for you, you'll be right there at the top of the list for next Dade State Attorney. Did you know there's never ever been an African-American State Attorney in Florida?"

The secretary tapped on the door, entered, and carefully transferred a big steaming cup of coffee to her boss. "I'm sure you recognize this little fellow." Purvis pointed at the tropical bird, The Ibis, which adorned the mug. "Ray, did I ever tell you how much I used to love to watch you play?" Lifton shook his head. "Are you sure? Not even when you became a Division Chief? I'm very surprised because I always make it a point to have a chat with everyone who gets promoted to Division Chief." She took a cautious sip of her coffee. "I'll bet you're wondering if I played basketball too. Well, is the Pope Catholic? But, you know, back then it was just for fun. These days a girl can get a full scholarship at a lot of schools. But let's get back to the business at hand. A few ships have to come in before you can start thinking about sitting in this chair. The reason I called you in today was to talk about the most important one for right now. At the judicial reception the other night Commissioner Sanderson said she spoke to you, and you told her nothing was happening in the case. Well, I'm sure you didn't say it just like that. Coincidentally, the next day I got the news the Hillsborough County State Attorney is ready to file his first case under the new hate-crime law. But, you know what? I really don't care. Filing a case doesn't mean anything. It's all about who gets the first conviction. So if the Commissioner is wrong about what you said, and you're getting close to wrapping things up, then all we need to do is just beat those Tampa cupcakes to the finish line." Purvis took another sip of coffee while peering at him over the rim of her glasses. "So where are we at, Ray?"

"Chernin has been doing his undercover thing down south, but so far he hasn't come up with anything of value to make a case. I've got a couple of interns doing research on hate-crimes laws to make sure we understand the type of threshold we need to meet."

Susan Purvis frowned and set down her mug. "That's really not the answer I was expecting from you this far into the game." She removed her thick glasses and began twirling them around. "Ray, Ray, Ray. You can't win a race if you never push off the starting block. And you all need to push off the starting block like it was yesterday. I put my complete faith and trust in you when I approved you for this job. So please don't prove me wrong, okay?"

CHAPTER TEN

Aubrey Swindall constantly had to keep jerking the steering wheel left and right to avoid hitting dozens of potholes on Northwest Sixth Street as he drove out to Kenny Moser's place. He might as well be driving through a battlefield full of land mines. It was going to be *so nice* to get the hell out of shit-hole Dade County with all its third-worlders washing up on its shores, making a big stinking mess of what used to be a pretty decent part of the State of Florida. *Oh, yeah, so nice.* His mind drifted to a sugar-white beach in The Panhandle. There was only him and Emily and Kaye and Cecil and a few other people out there. And everybody was Anglo, and little kids were building sand castles right next to the glittering turquoise water. Miami Beach wasn't even in the same league as up there around Destin and Fort Walton Beach. No *fucking* way.

There was an explosion as the right-front tire dropped into a huge pothole, but Swindall could only smile. At that moment he was picturing Emily sitting on a blanket, leaning back, propped on her elbows, eyes closed, head tilted slightly upward, her smile warmer than the bright sun she was soaking up. He was lying on his stomach next to her, his chin resting on his hands, alternating his view between her and his brand-new two-storey house right there next to the water, elevated sixteen feet to protect it from a hurricane's tidal surge. On the big concrete slab beneath it were two more of his loves, a brand-new shiny cherry-red-sparkle pick-up and a twenty-one-foot Boston Whaler open fisherman perched atop its trailer. *Oh, yeah, so nice.* Fuck Miami Beach and everybody else in South Florida!

Moser and Wendt hadn't shown up yesterday at his place like they always did after work, the one time out of a million he really wanted to talk to them. So he had called Moser's house, and Lizbeth told him Kenny and Bobby hadn't come home yet, thinking they had gone over to Skeeter's right from work like they always did. So now he was going to pay those two little peckerwoods an early-morning visit. Moser's truck was parked in front of his place which was no surprise because that lazy piece of shit still would be sleeping at this hour like the other loser, overstayed house-guest Bobby Wendt. As he approached the front door of the small concrete-block structure, Swindall heard a baby crying and Moser and his wife arguing. He knocked hard several times, and there was an abrupt silence followed by the sound of Moser's pit bulls rushing toward the door.

"It's Skeeter." Swindall heard Moser tell his wife to shut up, and the dogs started barking. "C'mon, open up!"

"Hey, Skeeter." Moser said with a big yawn as he pushed open the front door.

Wendt was standing right behind Moser, shirtless and in his underwear, just like Moser. "Hey, Skeeter."

"I need to talk to you two right now."

Moser twisted around and looked at Wendt, then turned back to Swindall. "You mean like right now?"

"No, Kenny, I mean like next year. Now will you two get the hell out here so we can talk in peace." Swindall stuck his foot out when Moser started to pull the door shut. "And hurry up."

As they headed toward the Denny's on US 1, Swindall asked, "So where were you two yesterday? I'll bet you were at the house when I called." When neither of them answered, he added, "I need to know what's going on with Curtis."

"You know what, Skeeter? You don't have to talk to me and Kenny like we're some stupid-ass little kids."

"Oh, *really*, Barbie?" Swindall whined.

"Yeah, *really*, Skeeter. And you know what else? It's funny you're asking where we were because, for your information, we just happened to be over at Curtis' place."

"Oh, *really*, Barbie?"

"Yeah, *really*, Skeeter."

"Here we go again," Frances mumbled, as President Reagan used to say, noticing the real big homely gay guy entering the restaurant with those two tutti-frutti long-hairs, heading toward, where else, the kissing booth. Too bad today meathead wasn't with that military guy who was a really good tipper.

"Alright, Barbie, give me the latest bullshit with Curtis."

Before Wendt could answer the waitress arrived at their booth and passed out the laminated menus. "So are you all ready to order now?"

"Give us a few, okay?" Swindall muttered without looking up at her like he was upset she had interrupted their conversation.

"No problem." She shrugged and walked away, wanting to say something just loud enough for him to hear like he was a big fat inconsiderate homo.

"Well, Skeeter, you know me and Kenny, we've been going over to see Curtis pretty regular since the last time you was there. And he's still *real* pissed off at you, and..."

"*Really*, Barbie? So what else is new?"

"Man, you need to listen up, dude," Moser jumped in. "Curtis is talking serious about what happened three years ago with the fancy boon and the blond lady. What Curtis has been saying every time we go over there to his place now, what he says he'll do, is go to the police if we don't..." Moser turned to Wendt for some help.

"Would you two stop looking at each other like a couple of Miami Beach queers? Okay, Curtis is talking serious about what happened to that mixed couple, and he's going to the police if you don't do something. I have no idea what the *fuck* you're saying. So just spit it out, Kenny." He sat back and folded his arms, the veins in his neck throbbing. He couldn't afford to put up with any more bullshit at this important point in his life.

Moser checked to see if anybody was within earshot. "If we don't kill a nigger."

Swindall inhaled deeply, then shook his head like a wet dog trying to dry off. "*What?!*" he blurted out loudly.

As the waitress approached the booth she could see fat ass was *really* upset now. Maybe he didn't want those two ding-dongs acting so flaky, seeing as how they were meeting up in a regular place. Most likely meathead was leading a double life, and he was worried somebody from the straight world might see him there sitting with those two fruitcakes.

"Alright, what can I get you ladies?" The waitress took a step back, that last word having flown out of her mouth like an involuntary muscle contraction. She expected the big guy to say something real nasty but, instead, he just looked up at her blankly and ordered coffee, the other two, fries and cokes.

"Here's the deal, Skeeter," Wendt said after the waitress was gone. "It's not just any nigger he wants us to kill. It's gotta be that old Reverend dude. 'He's gotta die. He's gotta die.' That's what Curtis keeps saying all the time now."

"We were hoping he'd just forget about it, but he's real hung up on that shit."

"So what you're saying is Curtis is even fucking crazier now than before."

"That's right," Wendt and Moser said at the same time.

"What I don't get is why you two don't just tell him nobody is killing nobody."

"Well, yeah, Skeeter, we said something like that to him, and he says, 'So you all are worried about picking up a murder charge? Well, you already got blood on your hands because of what happened to the fancy boon and the blond lady.' He says we're already guilty, *all of us,* of a double murder."

"Wow, *all* of us are guilty of a double murder! Is that what Curtis said, Barbie? Well, you know what? It sounds to me like it's you two who've got a real big problem. There's no damn way I've got the same problem because I wasn't there when all that shit went down. I don't even know nothing about it."

Wendt glanced over at Moser. "Well, Skeeter, that's not the way Curtis sees it."

"Oh, *really?*" Swindall stopped talking because the waitress had returned and was handing out their orders. He lifted his mug but then set it down right away because his hand was shaking.

"Yeah, see, it's like this," Wendt continued after the waitress left. "Curtis says you've got the same problem as us because you were there when the whole thing started at your place. The blond lady getting drunk, doing a table top for everybody, passing out, me and Kenny taking her out back to the rental car, and then us running them two down out there on Card Sound Road, and..."

"Now just hold on a second. It's *real* simple. There's no way I'm involved because I wasn't there with you and Kenny and Curtis when all the bad shit happened."

"Well, Skeeter, according to Curtis, in the law it don't work like that. Because, see, you're a Guardian, and it was Guardians killed those two."

Swindall leaned back and put his hands behind his head. "Well, he's wrong then because I personally didn't do nothing."

"Well, that's what we said to Curtis too because we didn't do nothing really bad neither. But that's not the way Curtis sees it. He says he talked to some lawyer about all this shit, and there's some kind of law called conspiracy, and it was Guardians killed them two so all Guardians are guilty."

Swindall stared out at the parking lot while Wendt and Moser attacked their plates of fries. "I'll be back," Swindall said as he worked his way out of the booth.

"*I'll be back,*" Moser repeated, trying his best to sound like the Terminator, but his voice was way too high.

Swindall lumbered over to the front entrance where there was a pay phone on the wall between the two bathrooms. He pulled out his wallet and fished for the business card the attorney had included with his letter. Maybe he'd get lucky and catch him in his office this early. He popped in a quarter and dialed the lawyer's number.

"Aaron Tannenbaum," a boyish voice answered crisply.

"Hey, Mr. Tannenbaum. This is Aubrey Swindall."

"Aubrey Swindall, Aubrey Swindall. Oh, yeah, the guy from way down south in Florida City with the commercial property for sale, right?"

"Yes, sir, that's me. Any news from Mr. Malman?"

"Not recently. Hasn't he been in touch with you directly?"

"Yes, sir, he has. Actually, I'm not calling you about my property. It's something different. And since you're a lawyer and all, I thought you might be able to give me some legal information."

"Well, I'll give it a shot. But just keep in mind, and I tell everybody the same thing, my practice is limited to dirt and dead people. You know, real estate and probate."

"Well, sir, the situation is this. I've got this cousin up there in North Florida, and he says he possibly might have some kind of a criminal problem and..."

"Whoa there, pardner!" Tannenbaum cut him off. "You're saying this is a criminal law problem? That's something I *definitely* do not handle. That would be like a podiatrist trying to give advice about how to do brain surgery."

Swindall wasn't sure what the lawyer meant by that, but he wasn't going to waste time finding out. "Well, it's not really like advice or nothing I need for my cousin. I just want to ask you a question about some legal word. Please, sir, right now I don't have anybody else I can talk to about it."

"Well, alright then, Aubrey, I'll give it a shot."

"See my cousin up north says he heard about some kind of crime called conspiracy, but he doesn't know what it means."

"Has your cousin already been arrested? Because if he has,

he needs to consult with defense counsel right away. If he can't afford to hire an attorney, the court will appoint one for him. That's been the law since the United States Supreme Court decided *Gideon v. Wainwright*, which started out as a state criminal case many moons ago right here in the State of Florida. Every person charged with a crime has a fundamental constitutional right to counsel. Well, actually, I think it has to be a felony but, you know, I'm not really sure. Anyway, you've seen the cops give the *Miranda* warnings in the movies and on tv, right? And so, whether your cousin gets private counsel, or the court appoints a lawyer for him, that's the person your cousin needs to speak with about his case."

"No, see, Mr. Tannenbaum, that's the thing. There's just talk going around about him *maybe* having a problem, but nothing has happened yet."

"Oh, okay, now that's a little different. Let me think about this." There was a brief silence as the attorney mulled over Swindall's question. "You know, you're making me go way back to my law school days. And you know what else? It's funny, actually, because I think we had an essay question about criminal law and conspiracy and that kind of stuff on my bar exam, but that was like seven years ago."

"You don't have to be exactly right, sir. Just whatever you remember is fine."

"You know, Aubrey, please understand that you and your cousin can't rely on anything I tell you. I'm not a criminal defense attorney. Like I said before, my practice is limited to dirt and dead people. You know, real estate and probate. That would be like a dentist trying to give advice about how to do a heart transplant."

"You don't have to worry, Mr. Tannenbaum. I'm not gonna tell my cousin or anybody else who gave me the information."

"Okay, then, as long as we understand each other. And by the way, will you please call me, Aaron? And remember again, whatever I tell you is just some information and is not to be considered legal advice."

"*Jesus K. Christ*," Swindall thought, as he tapped his foot impatiently, "this fucking loud-mouth lawyer!" Now somebody else was waiting to use the phone, a young lady with two rowdy kids whining and tugging at her skirt.

"No, sir, I understand. I'm won't be telling anybody that we even talked."

"Alright, Aubrey, then as long as we understand each other. Well, if I remember correctly, a conspiracy is an agreement between two or more persons to commit a crime. And it's the making of the agreement which is the crime, like an agreement to rob a bank or to possess with the intent to distribute a controlled substance like marijuana or cocaine or heroin."

"So if a person doesn't do nothing, like actually rob the bank or sell drugs, then he can't be guilty of conspiracy, right?"

"No, I don't think you're hearing me, Aubrey. Listen, if two or more people *agree* to commit a crime, like robbing a bank or selling drugs, they're guilty of the crime of conspiracy. It doesn't matter whether they actually commit the crime because it's the *agreement* to violate the law which is a crime all by itself. Now the particular crime the defendants agree to commit is called the *object* of the conspiracy, like robbing a bank or selling drugs. If they carry out of the object of the conspiracy, they're guilty of a *separate* offense called a *substantive* crime. I think there's even another crime which is called an 'attempt' if the defendants took at least one important step to carry out the substantive crime but didn't complete it. You know, I'm a little hazy on that last one. But, anyway, do you understand what I'm saying, Aubrey?"

Swindall took the receiver away from his ear and frowned at it like it wasn't working right. "I heard everything you said, Mr. Tannenbaum, but this is what I don't get. How can you be guilty of a crime if you don't actually do anything?"

"You're *still* missing the point, Aubrey. You see, you *are* doing something. When you get involved in a conspiracy, you make an agreement with others to violate the law, and that agreement is illegal, a separate crime all by itself. And each person who joins in the making of that agreement is called a coconspirator.

And each coconspirator is like a partner in crime with all the other members of the conspiracy. And *each* coconspirator is criminally liable for *all* of the reasonably foreseeable acts of the other members of the conspiracy."

"Okay, I think I get it now. Thanks, Mr. Tannenbaum."

"You're very welcome, Aubrey. And please call me Aaron. And if I hear anything from Stewart, I'll be sure and let you know. But right now I have to scoot. I've got a nine-thirty closing in Coral Gables, and the traffic is horrible this time of day."

"That sure was a long piss you took, Skeeter," said Moser.

Swindall squeezed back into the booth and tugged for a moment on his chin-strip. "So, Bobby, what else did Curtis say about this conspiracy shit?"

The way Curtis saw it was, if you were a Guardian, then you agreed with things like "death to race traitors," and that's exactly what the blond lady was, a race traitor, and the fancy boon was in on it. So *all* Guardians agreed those two had to be punished because they were guilty of race treason. And even though nobody, except Curtis, crushed their skulls in, all Guardians shared the same beliefs which meant they agreed with the sentence Curtis handed down that night. And so all of them were guilty of the crime of conspiracy because they should have known something real bad might go down like it did. Swindall had seen Wendt and Moser carry the blond lady to the back lot and put her in the rear seat of the rental car. And he was there when they took off in Curtis' truck to go after the mixed couple out on Card Sound Road. But he didn't do anything to try and stop them which, according to Curtis, was the *same thing* as agreeing with what happened.

"No. No *fucking* way. I didn't know what you all were going to do that night. This is the biggest crock of shit." Swindall leaned forward, put his elbows on the table, and massaged his scalp for a few moments. "So Curtis wants us to kill the old preacher, or he's gonna get us all charged with conspiracy? Is that what you're saying, Bobby?"

"Yeah, that's about the size of it, Skeeter. And if we get

convicted, he says we're all gonna have a date with Old Sparky."

"Oh, *really*? We're all gonna fry in the electric chair? Is that what Curtis said?" Swindall pushed back against the green vinyl padding and shook his head slowly. "And I guess you two just believe all the shit he tells you, right?"

"Thing is, Skeeter, me and Kenny, we're pretty scared."

Swindall's head was starting to pound with a king-size headache. "Why don't we just kill Curtis?"

Wendt looked over at Moser. "Well, Skeeter, we thought about that too."

"We sure did, Skeeter," Moser added.

Swindall shook his head like he was punch drunk. "Are you both fucking crazy?! Nobody is killing nobody, you got that?!"

"We don't have much time, Skeeter."

"What the *hell*," Swindall said slowly, "are you talking about *now*, Bobby?"

"Curtis has been saying we don't have much time to take care of this business with the preacher."

"Did you hear what I just said, or are you both fucking deaf!? Nobody is gonna kill the old preacher *or* Curtis because nobody is killing nobody, understand!?"

"So you're just gonna let Curtis go ahead and send us all to the electric chair?"

"Nobody is gonna get fried either, Kenny. What's wrong with you two? *Jesus K. Christ!*"

They sat in silence for a few minutes. Swindall crossed his arms and stared out at the parking lot while Wendt and Moser finished off their Cokes, each making wet sucking sounds with their straws when there was nothing left in their glasses except little slivers of ice.

Swindall reached out and pulled the two brown plastic tumblers away from them. "We need to buy time while we think this through."

"How about this, Skeeter? What if somebody else, not us but somebody else, did what Curtis wants? That way we don't get involved in that shit, and then Curtis just might leave us be."

"Oh, yeah, Bobby? Somebody else like who?"

"Well, Skeeter, that's what me and Kenny's been thinking about ever since we left Curtis' place last night."

CHAPTER ELEVEN

"I'm going to lunch now," Cuqui Perez announced as she stood at the door to Lifton's office.

"Those interns should be here soon, right?"

His secretary extended her left arm, closed one eye, and checked her watch. "*Sí, señor* Bond. So you want me to bring you back something?"

"No, thanks, Moneypenny. I'll take the interns downstairs for some lunch."

"Taking them to lunch at the Pickle Barrel, huh? Hey, big spender. Make sure you order some Pepto Bismol for dessert."

"Did you reach Chernin yet?"

"He'll be here around four."

"And what about Vernon?"

"The *viejo* says he's coming by later. And, *señor* Bond, you better call your girlfriend. She sounds pretty mad. If you don't call her back soon, for sure you're not getting any."

"Hey, Val-er-ie, it's me. Val-er-ie, are you there?"

"Yeah, I'm here," she finally responded in a cold monotone.

"Look, I'm sorry I haven't called."

"You sound a little upset. I hope it's not with me."

"No, baby, you don't have to worry about that. I had a

meeting with The Big Girl this morning. She read me the riot act."

"You mean about your big case?"

"Yeah, long story. Let's just say the heat is on."

"Hey, baby, I know that tune," she said, her voice warming. "I just want you to heat things up for me."

Lifton flashed back to the last time they were together. Things had gotten off to a very good start at her apartment when Valerie told him to call Kimberly and tell her not to worry if he didn't make it back that night. She put on some Brazilian jazz, lit two scented candles, and retrieved a bottle of Johnny Walker Blue Label and two shot glasses from the kitchen. Then she told him to make himself comfortable, because that's exactly what she was going to do, and then disappeared into the bedroom. He drank two shots of Blue Label before she returned dressed in a white negligee over white bra and panties.

"Victoria's Secret?" His voice cracked as he averted his gaze. "Or maybe Ebony and Ivory," he said to himself and smiled.

"What's the matter, Liftoff Lifton? You never seen a girl like this?" He looked down at the coffee table and poured himself another drink. "And what about me? I don't get a drink? Did you know a bottle of that Blue Label you're drinking costs around one-hundred-fifty dollars?"

"I won't ask what you had to do to get it. Anyway, I'll still need to see some i.d."

"Well, I don't know where I put it so I guess you'll have to search me." She raised her arms and twirled around. "A full body-cavity search. Hey, why don't you look over here at me, Mr. Prosecutor? What's the matter, cat got your tongue? Well, you best try and get it back. You might be needing it in a little while."

The anaesthetic effects of the strong liquor had kicked in, and he was feeling light and relaxed as he sized her up.

"Alright, tell me. What's with the stupid grin?"

"Like the Invisible Woman," he sputtered, then realized he had just made a huge mistake. "No, no, forget about it," he added, trying to hold back the spasms of laughter.

Guardians Of The Faith

"You can't do that! You *know* you can't do that with me, Rayfield Lifton! You tell me right now why you just said 'like the Invisible Woman.'"

Valerie hadn't budged an inch so he figured he better get this over with. "It's just because it's a little dark in here," he started laughing, "and you've got those white things on, and, you know, you're very....so it was like you were..."

She rushed the couch, flattened him on his back, and sat down on top of him. "Rayfield Lifton," she said, shaking a finger at him, "I'm gonna kick your ass."

"The Invisible Woman or a black ghost."

"Oh, you!" she whined, swinging her fists and jabbing him in the ribs. "You *really* must not want to get any tonight."

"Now, you just chill, Naomi." Lifton pulled her down, and they kissed for a long time, something akin to a tongue fencing match. After they drank some Blue Label, Valerie led him to the bedroom where they made love until the early morning hours.

"Earth to Lifton. Earth to Lifton. You there?"

"Yeah, yeah, sorry."

"I guess you really must have a lot on your mind."

"I was remembering something. Anyway, Val-er-ie, maybe we can get together tomorrow night. Are the Heat in town?"

"Yeah, but that's never stopped us before. Call me tomorrow before noon, okay, baby? And try not to work so hard."

* * *

After the two legal interns, Jennifer Trazenfeld and Timothy Melton, arrived at his office, Lifton grabbed a pen and a yellow legal pad and invited them to a working lunch in the cafeteria on the first-floor of the Metro Justice Building.

"Any luck so far?" Lifton asked them as he took the first bite of his cheeseburger.

"Well, some, Mr. Lifton," Trazenfeld said, pulling out a stack of papers from a brown accordion file. "You want the long or short version of what we found?"

"Judging by the number of fries on my plate, I can go with

the long, but you two legal-eagles eat first."

"No, we're good. Tim and I can alternate." She took a sip of her *café con leche* before continuing. "Okay, this whole thing about hate crimes started back in eighty-one when the Anti-Defamation League proposed some model legislation, the core of which would be penalty enhancement. Of course, mere expressions of hate, protected by the First Amendment, would not be criminalized."

"But to qualify for the imposition of a greater penalty," Melton took over, "the prosecution would have to prove beyond a reasonable doubt the perpetrator *intentionally* selected his victim based upon *his* perception of the victim's race, religion, national origin, and so forth."

"Let me see if I understand this. Tim, you're black, right? So the defendant would have to perceive you as being black."

Melton hesitated, not sure if Lifton was pulling his leg. "Yes, sir, that definitely would be a requirement under the hate-crimes laws. The perpetrator would have to perceive me as being black."

"As opposed to perceiving you as being white like her?" Lifton inclined his head toward Trazenfeld.

Both interns looked at him with puzzled expressions. "I'm just messing with you two. So did you find any cases from other states with hate-crimes statutes?"

"Well, sir, it's still pretty much uncharted waters in terms of reported decisions. As you know, it takes awhile for new laws to work their way through the appellate courts. But, to give you a couple of examples, there are laws on the books like this in Minnesota and Wisconsin. I've got a copy here of a case called *R.A.V. versus City of St. Paul*, where the Minnesota Supreme Court upheld as constitutional a local ordinance prohibiting the display of a symbol known to arouse anger, alarm, or resentment in others on the basis of race, color, creed, religion, or gender. The court said it could be narrowly interpreted to prohibit only expressive conduct amounting to fighting words or imminent lawless action. And, again, that conduct has to fall outside the protections of the First Amendment. The expressive conduct there was burning a cross on a black family's lawn. *R.A.V.* currently is pending in the U.S. Supreme Court which should be deciding that case this term."

"And what do you think the Supremes will do with *R.A.V.?*"

"Well, the Court heard oral argument on December 4," Trazenfeld continued. "I was able to get a sense how things went and, quite frankly, it doesn't look too good for the home team. Justice Scalia had a lot of tough questions for the State of Minnesota. He'll probably be able to win over a majority and write the opinion. Most of the other Justices didn't seem too thrilled with the arguments Minnesota advanced in favor of upholding that hate-crimes law."

"What's going on is this," said Melton. "It very well might be that on its face the law will be held unconstitutional because it imposes special prohibitions on speakers expressing *unpopular* views on subjects like race, color, creed, and religion. Nobody is thinking about passing a law prohibiting people from saying they're ready to fight *for* racial tolerance and equality and all that good stuff. So on the flip side, under the First Amendment, it wouldn't be fair then to have a law prohibiting people from saying they're ready to fight *for* intolerance and inequality and any of the bad stuff."

"So what you're saying is a hate-crimes law can't punish a person's viewpoint."

"Right," both interns said at the same time.

"And that's what I predict the Supreme Court is going to hold later this year when it decides *R.A.V.*"

"Tim, I understand the First Amendment issue about a person's viewpoint, but what's the bottom line about enhanced punishment for actual conduct? A real crime where a victim is selected under one of the prohibited factors."

"Well, we found another case," Trazenfeld said, pulling a set of stapled pages from the stack of papers. "Okay, this is *Wisconsin versus Mitchell.* In *Mitchell*, the Wisconsin appellate court held its hate-crimes law was constitutional. A group of black men watched the movie *Mississippi Burning*. Defendant Mitchell incited the group to assault a young white man. He said, 'Do you all feel hyped up to move on some white people? You all want to fuck somebody up? There goes a white boy. Go get him.'"

"So in that case it looks a lot better for the home team," Melton explained, "because the bias motivation was tied to specific criminal conduct, that is, aggravated battery and theft."

"I think I get it," Lifton said. "If the law penalizes not just bigoted ideas but actual criminal conduct connected to those ideas, like beating the shit out of somebody targeted because of his race, then enhanced punishment is constitutional."

"That would appear to be the case," said Trazenfeld.

"What's the posture of *Mitchell* right now?"

"Well, in June of last year the Wisconsin Court of Appeals found the law was constitutional. The Wisconsin Supreme Court granted further review and recently heard oral argument. From what I could gather speaking with several of the lawyers involved, the chances are pretty good for an affirmance. Actually, the decision could be any day now."

"Do you think the Supremes will take the case if the Wisconsin Supreme Court upholds the law?"

"Oh, without a doubt," Melton answered. "These hate-crimes laws are the flavor of the month."

"*R.A.V.* probably won't fly," Trazenfeld said, "but I think that *Mitchell* very well could. They're just so different on the facts."

"You guys are good," Lifton nodded approvingly, as he made a few more notes on his legal pad. "Ebony and Ivory."

As the elevator doors parted on the sixth floor where the interns were getting off, Trazenfeld turned to Lifton with a look of concern. "Mr. Lifton, I'm sorry, but could I ask what you meant when you said 'Ebony and Ivory?'"

"Ebony and Ivory?"

"In the cafeteria after we finished discussing the cases, you looked at us and said, 'You guys are good. Ebony and Ivory.'"

Lifton smiled and held the doors open as the two interns stepped out. "'Ebony and Ivory' was a song by Paul McCartney and Stevie Wonder. It came out when you guys probably were about ten. Good song. You should check it out."

* * *

"Hey, Kim, what's going on?"

"Everything's fine, Ray. We just got back from Publix. You know, our regular weekly food-shopping adventure. I checked the messages on the machine, and one of them was from Dr. Feingold's secretary, for me to give her a call back. It's probably about scheduling our next trip up there."

"How did she sound?"

"How did she *sound*? It was a message on the answering machine. She *sounded* like she wanted me to call her back."

"I know I *sound* pretty stupid, but I'm just worried."

"I'm sorry, Ray. I know you are, and you've got a right to be. You've been part of the *thing* for a long time now. Hey, are you coming home regular time?"

"Yeah, no hot date for me tonight."

"Well, I'll just have to give Val-er-rie a call then and try and find out what's wrong with you two lovebirds."

"No, Kim, you don't have to do that. Everything is fine between us."

"I'll give her a call anyway just in case there's a problem you don't know about yet. That's what sisters are for, aren't they? Love you, Ray."

"Love you too, Kim," he said, but she already had hung up.

"Mr. Lifton?" Vernon Castleberry, the maintenance man, was standing at the door carrying a yellow plastic toolbox.

"Come right on in, Vernon. I've got major problems with my chair here."

"I remember when I braced one side of that damn chair for you awhile back."

"Can you take a look at it?"

"My pleasure." The maintenance man advanced slowly, twisting from side to side, his upper body stiff as a board.

Lifton left his office and reviewed the telephone messages

stuck in the metal holder on Cuqui's desk, mostly requests from junior prosecutors seeking his approval for plea bargains. He wished he could dispose of this rubber-stamp ritual by advising all of the Assistant State Attorneys in his Division that, unless a particular economic crime involved murder or mayhem, which it never did, they didn't need his blessing to close out a case. Of course, such a blanket authorization never would be approved by the powers that be on the sixth floor. And, as he reminded himself from time to time, if such a proposal were approved, there would be little need for his continued supervisory services at the State Attorney's Office.

"Hey, boss man." Dressed in his undercover uniform, white t-shirt and blue jeans, Joel Chernin's hulking figure came barreling toward him.

"My main man, Chernin." Lifton started gyrating like John Travolta in *Saturday Night Fever*. "You ready to boogie?"

"That's *my* line, chief. You must have hit the Cuban coffee pretty hard today, or maybe you finally got some nookie last night, huh, captain?"

"No such luck, JC. I'm just high on life."

"Kool and the Gang." The detective began writhing like he was doing The Twist. "You know, I've gotta be honest with you. Now that I've seen your dance moves, bro, disco definitely is not a black thing."

"And, Chernin, now that I've seen your moves, bro, *any* type of dancing definitely is not a white thing."

"Mr. Lifton? Sorry for interrupting, but do you want your chair real tight or with a little play?"

"I'll go with real tight, Vernon. A little play a few minutes ago almost caused me substantial bodily harm."

"My pleasure," Castleberry said as he turned to go back inside Lifton's office.

"Man, you guys around here really are cruel. Can't you see the old man is in pain every time he takes a step? Why can't you find it in your hearts to give him a little pension and let him retire?"

"I'm sorry, JC, before we can do that we just want to watch him suffer a few more years. Now do you want to go downstairs and get some Cuban coffee or what?"

"I think you'll be fine for awhile," Castleberry said when they returned from the Pickle Barrel.

"How long is awhile, Vernon?"

"I'd rather not commit, Mr. Lifton. Let's just say you might do well to get Ms. Purvis to buy you a new chair sooner than later."

"Don't want to commit? You sound like a lawyer, Vernon."

"Well, maybe that's because I've been around you lawyer types for so many years."

The chair was so rigid now Lifton no longer could make it swivel at all. He grabbed the armrests, lifted it a few inches, and set it down in a different position.

"So, boss man, how's that really hot girlfriend of yours? The one who looks like Naomi Campbell."

"You know about her? You must be tailing me."

"I don't think so, chief. That would be too damn boring."

"Forget about Naomi Campbell for awhile. Just tell me about all the great progress you've been making on our big case."

"Starting to get heat from The Big Girl, huh? Well, you know I've been working it. We talk all the time you and me."

"You and me talking won't cut it anymore, JC. We've gotta make the case happen. The Big Girl told me Hillsborough County is ready to file a hate-crimes case."

"Tampa, huh? What kinda case they got?"

"I don't know, and it doesn't matter. If they get the first conviction under the new law, they'll grab all the headlines."

Chernin stood up and rolled his neck around. "I haven't been sitting on my ass, you know. I've been out to Skeeter's a bunch of times, but so far Thigpen never has showed up. They'll mention his name every now and then but don't say much about him. He's like the man behind the curtain. At least when I'm there all these Guardians do is talk a good hate game. And they hate *everybody*, except their own types, of course, and it makes you just want to puke up all the beer you've been drinking with them."

"So that's it? That's what we've got so far?"

"That's what we've got so far, boss."

"Today I met with two of our legal-eagle interns, and they gave me the bottom line on hate-crimes laws. And bad guys who make you want to puke with their bigoted ideas just won't cut it. What we'd have to prove beyond a reasonable doubt is, *one*, the bad guys committed an actual crime, and *two*, they selected the victim based on his race, religion, or membership in some other protected class."

"Well, then, chief, as things stand right now I'd say we're pretty much screwed."

"You haven't talked to Sanderson yet, right?"

"We agreed I wasn't supposed to do that until you gave me the green light."

"The undercover thing was a better way to approach this, but it hasn't worked out. So now the light just turned green. We need to talk to Sanderson and find out if there's anything else he's got besides just a bunch of bad words being thrown at him."

"And if he can't help us seal the deal, then what are we gonna do?"

"We don't need to worry about that right now. Let's see if The Reverend can tell us about any specific incidents which could turn into a case. It's too bad your Guardian buddies didn't get you involved in something they're planning or just tell you about something they've already done. And having some audio and video on them would have been a whole lot better yet."

"I'll tell you what." Chernin tugged on his chin-strip. "Let me go out and see those fuckers one more time. It's been awhile since my last trip out to Skeeter's. I've been tied up working a joint task force with the feds, a reverse-sting home-invasion drug-ripoff thing. If I still come up dry at Skeeter's next time, I'll get Sanderson down here for a meet."

"Alright, JC. And one last thing. Is there anything else going on out there you know about that might fly?"

"You mean another hate-crimes case? Sorry, Charlie. If I still come up dry after my next trip to Skeeter's, and there's nothing there with The Reverend, we're shit out of luck."

* * *

As he made his way up the stairs to his house, Lifton noticed Old Lady Muir wasn't rocking away on the front porch like she usually did this time of day. She probably was at Publix stocking up on Cheetos, Twinkies, and Eskimo Pies.

"Hey, Kim." Lifton set his briefcase on a kitchen chair and went over to the sink. "What's wrong?"

"Mr. T bit the mailman today," she said softly without turning to face him.

"I *knew* that was going to happen sooner or later. How bad was it?"

"An ambulance came for Mr. Greer, and the police sent for animal control, and they took Mr. T away."

"Kim, look, what happened to Harold is not a good thing, but Mr. T getting busted is. That dog is a menace to society. I was worried one day he was going to hurt you or Demeka. Kim?" Lifton put his hand on Kimberly's shoulder and gently turned her toward him. His sister's face was bathed in tears, and he realized something else was going on.

Kimberly had spoken with Dr. Feingold that afternoon. He had been trying to reach her to cushion the blow of some papers she would be receiving by mail. Harold Greer delivered the big manilla envelope a few minutes after the doctor had given Kimberly the bad news. She picked up the envelope on the counter and held it out for him to take. Lifton grabbed a beer and headed for the living room.

The manilla envelope contained a cover letter and a narrative report. Lifton flipped quickly through the report until he reached a section entitled "Conclusions re: Potential for Administration of Experimental Therapies." The medical team had hoped several new drug therapies would be able to help Demeka. Those therapies had produced promising results in several recent

Guardians Of The Faith

European clinical trials. However, to be a candidate for those drugs, Demeka's condition would have to fall within the range of "autism spectrum disorders or ASD." Early on the team had determined she didn't meet the specific criteria for an ASD pervasive development disorder or a PDD. Yet, they had hoped further testing would show she qualified for the new therapies as long as her condition involved an alternative "not otherwise specified or NOS" class of ASD. "Based upon the most extensive and comprehensive battery of physical and mental testing available to our team, we conclude, within a reasonable degree of medical probability, this patient does not suffer from a form of ASD classified as either PDD or PDD-NOS. Consequently, the above-mentioned experimental treatments are not indicated and cannot be recommended for administration to this patient."

Lifton put the report on the coffee table, sat back, and drank the rest of his beer. He picked up the report and read the "Final Diagnostic Impression" on the last page. "This patient appears to suffer from a severe and relatively rare form of ASD, known as Rett Syndrome, affecting almost exclusively females. Its frequency in the population is in the range of one out of 10,000 to 15,000. Its symptoms usually appear between the ages of six and eighteen months, generally after a period of normal development, and include, but are not limited to, regression of mental and social development, cessation of speech, lack of control of limb function, and wringing of hands. Some of the problems associated with Rett Syndrome can be treated with physical, occupational, and speech therapy. However, if this intervention begins too late, due to failure to early diagnose this condition, the prognosis for improving the quality of life of the patient is greatly diminished."

Lifton flung the report across the living room, and the pages fluttered to a landing fifteen feet away. He returned to the kitchen where Kim was still standing next to the sink. She raised her hand so he wouldn't say anything.

"You're gonna ask me if I called back Dr. Feingold after I read the report, right? No, I didn't. Why? The bad news is right there in black and white. And he already said he was very sorry about the way things had turned out. You know, everybody on the team *loves* Demeka and all that stuff. So what now? That's your next question, right?" Kimberly Singletary looked at her brother with an unhappy smirk. "What now? *Nothing* right now." Before Lifton could get his next words out, she added, "And, no, Dr. Feingold didn't have any advice about what to do except to start with some of the traditional therapies mentioned in the report."

Lifton went to his bedroom and changed clothes. "I'm going jogging," he shouted as he slammed the front door. His pace was faster than usual as he headed along Biscayne Boulevard toward downtown Miami. If he didn't make this ten-mile round-trip right now, Lifton knew he might end up doing something stupid. The big metal plates on the Miami River drawbridge bounced under his weight, making a sound like rolling thunder. He needed to feel the physical pain a long run would bring to his old knee injury to neutralize the dark thoughts overtaking him.

At the south end of Brickell Avenue, Lifton crossed over to the Rickenbacker Causeway. After he passed the toll booths, he glanced back at Villa Vizcaya, the stunning Italian Renaissance palace surrounded by ten acres of tropical gardens. To his right scores of windsurfers manipulated their multicolor sails as they glided across a plate-glass Biscayne Bay. When he reached the base of the big fixed bridge, Lifton stopped and stretched for a few moments. He gazed across the water at the bright-white buildings of the Miami Seaquarium complex, and he wondered if his niece ever would be able to enjoy that wonderful place like other children. "Bad guys keep living large," he thought, "and a little girl who never did anything to anybody suffers every day."

CHAPTER TWELVE

"I know you got his number, Skeeter." Bobby Wendt lit up a Marlboro and handed the red plastic lighter back to Kenny Moser. "You don't remember?"

"I told you I don't have it." Swindall reached out and took back the two unopened beers he had just set down in front of them. "And, you know what else, Barbie and Ken? You two haven't paid down your bar tab in awhile."

"When the dude was here last time I seen you write his number down. You don't remember?" Moser extracted a cigarette from the flip-top box and popped it in his mouth. "You know, Skeeter, I think you're getting too old to remember a lot of shit." He looked over at Wendt, and they both started snickering.

"You two bitches think you're so damn funny." Swindall set the bottles back on the bar. "I already said I'm the one gonna talk to him about our situation. I told you again I don't have his number, and I ain't waiting any longer to see if he shows up here. So, you finish your beers, and then you go out and find the *fucking* dude at the *fucking* place he works on Card Sound Road!"

"*Oooo*," Moser howled, raising his hands and wiggling his fingers in mock fright.

"If you weren't drunk, Kenny," Swindall said, "you wouldn't

be acting like such a smart-ass. You might remember the other day you and Barbie here were like two fraidy-cat schoolgirls about this situation we got."

"Skeeter, I told you I don't like you calling me Barbie."

"Well, you know, that name just stuck with me after Karl gave it to you." Swindall pulled a Budweiser longneck out of the cooler, twisted off the top, and took a swig. "I'll forget about what you owe me for right now, but you two gotta go out and find Karl whatever the hell his name is."

"Speltzer, Spritzer," Moser mumbled, "some shit like that."

"You tell him we got something real interesting to talk about, but you *don't* tell him nothing in particular, you understand? So do we all agree now what we're gonna do?"

Wendt knocked his elbow into Moser's side. "Well, Skeeter, thing is if we all *agree* to do something together, then we'd be making one of those conspiracies."

Swindall silently suffered another round of snickering from these two little shits. "Man, I will be so fucking glad when this part of my life is over," he thought as he watched Wendt and Moser slowly get off their bar stools and take their sweet time picking up their cigarettes, lighters, keys, and two more beers for the road.

* * *

Moser slowed his pick-up as they approached Alabama Jack's. "I need toll money."

"Why do I gotta pay every damn time?" Wendt arched up, fishing for a dollar bill in the right front pocket of his blue jeans.

"Dude, I'm the one paying for the damn gas. And you know what else, Bobby? You've been freeloading off me and Lizbeth for about a year now."

"It's only been like six months, dude!"

"It was six months back first of the year. Whatever." The truck rolled to a stop next to the toll booth. "You got the bread?"

"I don't think that damn place is gonna be open even if we find it." Wendt slapped the dollar bill into Moser's hand.

Moser gave Wendt a dirty look for hitting him so hard.

Guardians Of The Faith

"Whatever. Skeeter said go out and find the dude so that's what we're doing it. It's better than paying down the damn bar tab."

"I'm sure glad I'm drunk, Kenny, because being out here right now, that night is starting to come back, dude."

"You don't need to talk about that shit, Bobby."

"It was like the scariest fucking night of my life."

"Dude, you're totally wasted so just *shut up*."

"Funny how things turn out."

"How is it *funny*, Bobby?"

"It's like we never did anything real bad, right? And, Skeeter, well, he didn't do nothing at all. But now we all gotta do something *real* bad so we don't get in trouble for *not* doing something real bad. You know what I'm saying, Kenny?"

Moser released the steering wheel for a couple of seconds and tugged on his long hair. Even though Bobby was more drunk than he was, he had hit the nail right on the head. Now they were about to get themselves involved in a *real* bad thing just to save themselves from something they never meant to happen. They didn't deserve sitting on death row for how things had turned out. His beer buzz wasn't making him feel good at all now. For an instant Moser thought about gunning the truck and throwing the steering wheel to the right, the truck would fly off the road and into the mangroves, and this whole damn mess they had gotten themselves into would end once and for all tonight. Moser's hands started trembling, causing the pick-up to cross back and forth over the center line.

"Why did we have to become fucking Guardians anyway?"

"Well, you always liked it, Kenny."

"Liked what, Bobby?"

"Being a Guardian, asshole, what else are we talking about?"

The back of Moser's right hand shot out striking Wendt in the middle of the chest. "Don't call me an asshole, *asshole*."

Wendt grabbed Moser's hand and flung it back at him. "Hey! What the hell's wrong with you tonight, Kenny?!"

"What's wrong with me?! What's wrong is you getting me

into this Guardian shit."

"Oh, yeah, right, like somebody forced you all this time." After a few moments, Wendt said calmly, "You know what, Kenny? When I think back about my dad and my grandad, I don't feel so bad I was in the Guardians."

Neither of them said anything for awhile as the truck rumbled along, behind them the last splashes of orange, pink, and blue dissolving into the black of night.

"How are we gonna find this place?"

"It's gotta be up here before Crocodile Lake. Hey, I see some lights over there!"

Moser gently pressed on the brake pedal so they wouldn't skid off the road. He threw the truck into reverse and backed up a hundred feet.

"I told you it was gonna be closed," Wendt said, after they jumped down from the pick-up and went over to the big steel shed.

"Well, this place ain't locked up yet." Moser pulled the big sliding door to the right, and it groaned heavily as it rolled along its rusty track. Inside there was a forklift, a workbench with a partially-disassembled outboard motor lying on it, a big red multi-drawer tool box, and a small refrigerator.

"You think they got some cold ones in there?"

"Hey, are you looking for something?"

Wendt squinted up at the loft. "Yeah, we're looking for a dude named Karl."

"He went out to the naked bars tonight."

"We need to talk to him."

A phone started ringing, and the man answered it. "No, nothing, but there's a couple of guys here looking for you. I have no fucking idea. Hey, Karl wants to know who's looking for him."

"Just say it's Skeeter wants to talk to him."

"Some guy named Skeeter and some other guy."

"Tell him to go by Skeeter's tomorrow night around eight."

"Well, that was pretty damn lucky," Chernin thought, Swindall and somebody else tracking him down at the undercover marina wanting to talk to him. Maybe he and his asshole buddies finally were ready to let him in on something he could use to make a case just when he almost had given up on them.

* * *

Lifton told Chernin to hold on a minute as Cuqui handed him the tiny plastic cup slightly larger than a thimble. She pinched the top of the styrofoam container to form a spout, then carefully poured him a shot of *café cubano*. "So what happened last night?"

"Nothing happened, boss man. I never went to Skeeter's, but don't get your shorts all in a knot. I called the undercover marina just before heading over to Skeeter's yesterday, and guess what? Swindall and somebody else were out there looking for me. I'm supposed to meet up with them tonight. Maybe these dudes finally want to get me involved in something."

"Well, keep in mind just sitting around talking racist bullshit doesn't cut it."

"You made that very clear the other day, chief."

"Are you gonna wear a wire?"

Lifton could hear Chernin smacking his gum. "I hate to admit it was your idea, boss, but I like it. I'll call Andy Medina and tell him to get what we need."

Later that day Medina fitted Chernin with a tiny microphone which transmitted up to a quarter mile. "I'll be right across the road," Medina told him. "Just make sure you're not sitting too close to that damn jukebox you told me about."

* * *

"I think you two peckerwoods are lying," Aubrey Swindall said as he set the bottles on the bar. "I'll bet you these two beers you pussies never even found the damn place." Swindall went to the other side of the bar where the only other customer was nursing his third gin and tonic. Across from Skeeter's, in a small clearing on the east side US 1, Metro-Dade Detective Antelmo Medina sat in a grey Dodge Caravan. He checked again to make sure the recording equipment on the passenger seat was working properly, then reached under the driver's seat to confirm his Glock 9mm was handy in case there was a problem. A few minutes later Chernin pulled into Skeeter's. He glanced at the three vehicles in the lot, two pick-up trucks, owned by Swindall and Moser, and a faded-blue Jeep Wagoneer with simulated woodgrain side panels which belonged to a gin-drinking old codger.

"Do you read me, Andy?" Chernin asked as he looked in the rear-view mirror. A single flash of headlights across the road told Chernin he was good to go. Medina picked up his camera and twisted the telephoto lens. When he got out of his pick-up, Chernin turned around and waited a few moments, giving Medina time to take a couple of shots, and then Medina flashed his headlights again. Before he went inside Chernin looked down one more time to make sure the tiny device taped on the left side of his chest didn't make an outline under his t-shirt.

Medina was able to make out the figure of a long-haired subject standing next to the window on Chernin's right, looking down at what probably was the jukebox. He snapped two photos thinking this kid reminded him of Cory Wells, the lead singer in one of his favorite groups from the sixties and seventies. "Will you have whiskey with your water or sugar with your tea?" Medina began singing Three Dog Night's "Mama Told Me Not To Come." "What are these crazy questions that you're asking me? This is the wildest party that there ever could be. Oh, don't turn on the lights cause I don't want to see."

The Georgia Satellites' signature song "Keep Your Hands To Yourself" started up as Chernin entered the bar. He saw Moser standing next to the jukebox and went over to him. "Hey, Kenny. Somebody said Skeeter came looking for me last night."

"Naw, Karl, that was me and Bobby, but Skeeter wants to talk to you."

Chernin walked over to the bar, and Swindall's eyes lit up as soon as he saw him. "Hey, Karl. You got the message, huh?"

"No, I hear voices." Chernin sat down on a stool next to Wendt. "How's it hanging, Barbie?"

"I haven't seen you around here in awhile." Swindall pulled

Guardians Of The Faith

out a Budweiser longneck from the cooler. "On the house."

Chernin gulped down half the bottle, belched loudly, and then said, "Man, this fucking place? I got tired of just talking bullshit which is the only thing you fuckers do around here. And no broads. Stripper music and no broads. Ain't that great?" He finished off the beer, set the empty bottle on its side, and began spinning it. "So I been checking out some of the naked bars down in Cutler Ridge and whatnot."

Swindall leaned forward. "You know, Karl, sometimes we don't just talk bullshit around here." He tilted his head and gestured for Chernin to follow him. "Hey, Barbie, watch the place for me, okay?"

"Watch the place for me?" Chernin muttered under his breath. The only other people in the whole damn place were the old gin-drinking regular and Moser.

Swindall picked a table halfway between the jukebox and the pool table. "Kenny sure loves that song. He'll play it all night."

They sat down, and Swindall regarded Chernin curiously for awhile, like he was making up his mind whether to go ahead and tell him something important. The song ended, and suddenly the bar became very quiet.

"So you're tired of just talking bullshit, is that right, Karl?"

"I just said that two minutes ago."

"Yeah, baby!" Medina shouted. Without that stripper music he could hear their voices clearly now. He glanced over at the tape recorder to make sure the red record light was on and the reels were turning.

* * *

As Joel Chernin pulled out of Skeeter's and turned right, he noticed Medina's Dodge Caravan crossing US 1 to the southbound lane. When he got back to the marina, Chernin called Lifton's home number. "Hey, boss man, sorry I'm calling you so late, but I've got something for you."

Lifton squinted at the red numbers on the radio-alarm clock. A sharp pain flashed through his right knee as he sat up in bed. It

Guardians Of The Faith

was the second straight day he had done the Key Biscayne jog, and he was paying a heavy price. "What's up, JC?"

"This is just too damn good. These dudes want Reverend Sanderson dead."

"What!? Hold on a second." Lifton set the phone down on the night stand, stood up, stretched, and then sat back down. "Say that again."

"These dudes. They want Reverend Sanderson dead. I just got back from Skeeter's. Medina had me wired up. He was across the road recording everything." Chernin heard the groan of the metal door below. "Hey, Andy! Bring your stuff up here. I got the prosecutor on the line."

Lifton reached over and turned on the lamp. "Are you on your mobile? Let me call you back in a few." He hobbled to the kitchen, cursing his stupidity for jogging ten miles two days in a row. He poured himself some orange juice, squeezed half a lime into the glass, and took two aspirins. He unplugged the kitchen phone and took it to the living room where there was another jack. "Okay, JC, talk to me."

"Alright, chief, listen up." There was silence for a few seconds and then a familiar rock song with the lyrics, "My honey, my baby, don't put my love on no shelf. She don't hand me no lies and keep your hands to yourself." Lifton could hear the voices of two men, but the music was so loud he couldn't make out what they were saying. When the song ended two minutes later, Lifton heard one of the voices say, "So you're tired of just talking bullshit, is that right, Karl?"

"Stop the tape, Andy. Did you hear that, boss? That's Swindall talking. Hold on. Andy, start it up again."

"I just said that two minutes ago."

"Well, we're thinking about doing something."

"Who's we?"

"The Guardians, man. The Guardians Of The Race."

"What's that shit?"

There was silence for a few beats. "It's white power, man.

Just like you got tattooed on your neck. The same shit we talk about all the times you been here."

"You mean you pussies actually do something? I thought you was all just talk."

"We ain't all just talk, Karl. And we know you ain't either."

"Oh, really? And how's that?"

"We checked you out. You really done what you said."

"Hey, Kenny!" a different voice called out. "Put on a different fucking tune!"

"So what is it you girls have in mind? Because if it ain't real I'm heading down the road seeing as how nobody here's gonna give me a lap dance."

"Well, see," Swindall's voice got lower, "there's this old nigger preacher and..."

At that moment the jukebox started blasting out another song, and the voices of Chernin and Swindall were muffled by AC/DC's "T.N.T." Lifton thought he heard Swindall use the word "kill" a couple of times, but he wasn't sure.

"Stop the tape. Dammit! That last song sure screwed things up. Andy, we have people who can do something about that background noise, right? Hey, Lifton, remember that first day when we talked about The Reverend? You said we didn't have a case because all we had was these assholes saying bad words. So we decided I'd do the undercover thing and try and come up with something else that might turn into a case. Well, you can stop worrying now because it turns out these dudes want to do a *real* crime. They want The Reverend dead, and they want *me* to kill him. A real crime *and* Sanderson is the victim. Can you believe that shit? They even gave me their stupid little secret Guardians greeting. I'm telling you we've hit the mother-lode. This is a grand slam, boss. Andy, play our nice prosecutor some more of the tape."

* * *

"Hey, yo, Chesterfield!" Norris shouted at The Golden Gavels' captain as he stomped off the court. "I thought people like that," he tilted his head in the direction of the newest addition to

Pettigrew & Shaw's team, "are born with an unfair advantage."

Chesterfield Kumble turned to face Norris, made a fist with his right hand, and extended the middle finger. The Posse had just beaten The Golden Gavels in the final game of the playoffs to win the DSC summer-league championship. Lifton scored thirty-four points and had bottled up the other team's new six-foot-five center, Leon Rolle, holding him to only ten points.

"They thought they'd get cute when they hired that big dude as a summer clerk," Doc Leeds said as The Posse headed toward the locker room.

"I hear it's the first time that white-glove firm ever recruited a brother from the University of Miami. And we all know they're not going to offer him a permanent job. They only like to hire from Harvard or Yale or big-name schools like that."

"You're forgetting something, Perishable. The University of Miami is well-known as the Harvard-by-the-beach."

Parrish laughed and gave Lifton a hard shove. "You sure did good tonight."

"Wayne, you be careful with my star player." Norris said, shaking a finger at him. "We've won three in a row now, and I'm gonna need Liftoff here in one piece for the fall league. We win that one, it's a clean sweep, and we break the DSC record."

"Winter, spring, summer, and fall, you know, just like that James Taylor song."

"Damn, Ray, you still listen to that white-bread music from the sixties?"

"Yeah, I do, Seven, and there's even a song from back then called 'No Time' by Guess Who."

"I give up. Who?"

"No, Seven, that's the name of the group. You know, if you'd just chill once in awhile by listening to some James Taylor, Cat Stevens, and Jim Croce, maybe you could shed your *Boyz n the Hood* image."

"He doesn't have that problem anymore, Ray," said Doc Leeds. "Everybody knows he magically transformed himself into

Mr. Black-ass Donald Trump."

"I'm taking you all out tonight, but don't count on going to Joe's Stone Crab or any fancy place like that. We shall celebrate our latest victory the way it should be done. Yes, that's right, my Posse, I'm taking you back to our roots, that is, to the Little Store to partake of some fine Schlitz Malt Liquor or maybe some vintage Colt 45."

Norris stopped and held up a hand as they reached the locker room. "Now, hold on a second, Liftoff. You can forget about The Little Store tonight. That's not the right place to go after a big victory like this. And Joe's is still closed until October so I say we all head over to The Forge."

"That's a real big ticket place for somebody on a state prosecutor's salary."

"Don't worry about that, Liftoff," said Parrish, nodding his head toward Crawford. "Mr. Black-ass Donald Trump here will loan you some of his big bucks."

"We're taking *you* out, Ray," said Crawford. "Without you that big brother would have kicked our butts tonight."

"That's right, Seven," said Norris. "This matter is settled so I say let's all haul ass over to Miami Beach where we can take in some of that fine wildlife grazing around over there. Tonight ladies drink free."

* * *

The Forge was buzzing with young urban professionals and South Beach models. The hostess led them to a table near the small stage where two musicians were setting up.

"There's sure a lot of fine ladies here tonight but none more beautiful than Val-er-rie."

"You better be careful, Ray," said Doc Leeds. "Mr. Black-ass Donald Trump is a very dangerous man with all those big bucks he's got."

"Yeah, Seven, don't get any ideas about moving in on my girl, okay?"

"You don't have to worry about me, Liftoff. Your lady is too much to handle even for me. And, besides, she lets everybody know she's really into you." Crawford waited while he made sure everybody was listening. "And so we all hope you're really *into* her too. You know what I'm saying?"

Lifton shook his head disapprovingly but couldn't help laughing along with the rest of them. A waitress took their drink orders, and they sat in silence for awhile observing the dynamic of this high-end looking-for-love crowd.

"So, my Posse," Norris said, "have you been following what's going on with the nomination? But before I say anything else, I think there might be a secret Republican spy among us, and it's probably Doc because we're ABA and he's AMA. And that means he wants tort reform and an end to medical malpractice suits. But, then again, it could be Seven because he's big business now so he hangs with all those banker types."

"But, hold on a second, No-Time." Crawford said. "It could be somebody else within the ranks of The Posse. C'mon, who is it? You'll feel better once you confess whoever you are. You know, I really think it might be you, No-Time."

"Okay, I confess," Norris said, lifting his highball glass. "So I say four more years for President George Herbert Walker Bush!" When none of the others joined in the toast, Norris took a sip of his drink and set the glass down. "Well, how about that? Not one damn vote of support! I have no choice then, my Posse, but to announce my return to the ranks of the Democratic Party."

"Praise The Lord!" Parrish exclaimed, raising his drink. "Our leader has just renounced the dark side of The Force."

"Alright, now that I'm back on the side of truth, justice, and the American way, let's talk turkey now. Can you believe it looks like Clinton's pretty much got the nomination wrapped up?"

They ordered another round of drinks and talked about the Presidential race. The Democratic National Convention was scheduled to start July 13 in New York City. The only two high-profile Democratic candidates, Governor Mario Cuomo and Congressman Richard Gephardt, long ago had dropped out of the race. None of the remaining seven candidates were well-known beyond their home states, and so the press had been referring to them as the "Seven Dwarfs." Early in the primaries Bill Clinton had been dogged by several sex scandals and had dropped to single-digit support. However, he had emerged as the "comeback kid" after finishing a strong second to Massachusetts Senator Paul Tsongas in the New Hampshire primary. After Clinton won a major victory in the crucial Illinois contest, most of the remaining primaries fell like dominos into his column.

"The way things are going right now," said Doc Leeds, "most of the people in the know don't believe the Democrats can take the White House. Let's face it. President Bush still is riding high after the Gulf War. And it doesn't seem to matter the economy is doing bad and the deficit is out of control."

"You may be right about all that, Doc," said Crawford, "but I gotta tell you. That Clinton, he's got street smarts. Bush is sixty-eight, and his thing is experience and trust. Clinton is forty-six, and his thing is youth and change. And who knows? It just might work again like it did for JFK back in 1960."

"You all heard last night Clinton picked Al Gore as his running mate, right?"

"You see, Doc, that's exactly what I'm saying," Crawford continued. "You've got Clinton, Yale law school and governor of a Southern state for a dozen years, coming off as a real smart centrist New Democrat. And now he's bringing to the table a United States Senator, another young Southerner, who just happens to be Congress' poster boy for protecting the environment. Clinton is positioning himself to win over Southern states and young voters who want to save the planet."

"I think you're all forgetting there's a guy in the mix named Ross Perot."

"Aha! Rayfield Lifton, our resident pessimist, has just weighed in."

"Well, No-Time, you can say what you want about me, but you all gotta admit that feisty little Texan has a lot of unhappy citizens rooting for him. He's a successful billionaire businessman, and people are asking, why not put a guy like him in the White House? He might not know much about politics, but he sure could fix the economy better than anybody else."

"Look, Ray, Perot's got zero chance of winning. If anything, he's gonna draw votes from Republicans and end up hurting Bush's chance of getting reelected."

"Seven's right," said Parrish. "Just like when Ralph Nader takes votes away from Democrats every time he runs except he's not running in this election."

"I don't think anybody should be betting the farm on this one," said Doc Leeds. "But I'd be willing to put some good money on Clinton and Gore taking this thing."

"Well, my Posse, we'll just have to wait and see, won't we? So, Ray, I'll bet you never thought one day your future would be tied to a Presidential election. I told you awhile back, 'Never underestimate the power of The Posse,' and you laughed at me. But now you see things are happening just like we planned. Am I right, or am I right?"

"Oh, Poppa Bear," Parrish said in a squeaky childlike voice, "will you please tell us the story again? Please!"

"Okay, my children." Norris leaned forward. "Once upon a time, William Jefferson Clinton got the Democratic Presidential nomination. And then he got elected President of the United States of America and went off to live in the *be-yoo-tee-ful* White House. And then he asked The Big Girl to join his administration, and she went off to D.C. Meanwhile, back in the land of Florida, Rayfield Liftoff Lifton was making headlines with his big hate-crimes case. And then our man in Tallahassee, Leander Baldwin, whispered in Governor Lawton Chiles' ear, and the Governor appointed our man in Miami as the next Dade State Attorney. And that's how Rayfield Liftoff Lifton got the keys to the castle, and everybody lived happily ever after."

"To the keys to the castle!" Parrish blurted out and raised his glass. Norris, Crawford, and Leeds echoed his toast, and they all clinked glasses.

"What's wrong, Liftoff?" Norris asked when he noticed Lifton hadn't joined in. "Is there a problem with your big case?"

"I was wondering when the damn subject would come up." Lifton looked down and shook his head sadly. "You all haven't talked to Chernin lately, have you?"

"It's been awhile," said Perishable. "Damn, Ray, please don't say there's a problem with your big case."

Lifton hesitated to make sure he had them going. "Gotcha!" He made some moves like he was boxing and landed a left hook on Parrish's shoulder. "Yes, my Posse, I am pleased to announce something should be going down real soon. Why else would I be inviting you all out tonight?"

"Liftoff, if this election and your case go according to plan, your fortunes will be rising real fast. Am I right, or am I right?" The musicians struck up their first piece, and Norris added, "I don't feel like having the fancy food they serve here. What say we go down the road and try and get us some good barbecue?"

* * *

Norris gave his chauffeur instructions to drive north on Collins Avenue, the only road on Miami Beach stretching its entire nine-mile length. When they reached 95th Street, Norris told Carlos to turn left over to Harding Avenue and park. The Town of Surfside had a two-block business district which looked like the movie set of a small-town right out of the fifties, including a corner drug store with a soda fountain.

"Are we going to Big Daddy's liquor store?" Lifton asked as they piled out of the limousine. "Damn, No-Time, we could have gone to the Little Store like I wanted."

"No, man," Norris chuckled, "you're looking the wrong way. See, Big Daddy Joe Flanigan has a barbecue joint right over there that's pretty damn good."

They sat at a table next to one of the sliding-glass doors which opened to the sidewalk and ordered draft beers and large racks of pork ribs.

Guardians Of The Faith

"So what's going on with your big case, Ray?"

"Well, Seven, I might as well spill the beans because No-Time finds out everything from my detective anyway."

"Ah, the mighty Joel Chernin, our worthy adversary, right Perishable? The dude is a little whacked out, but the son-of-a-bitch is a pretty damn good undercover cop."

Lifton described what happened on Chernin's last trip out to Skeeter's. Aubrey Swindall took Chernin aside and told him the leader of the Guardians Of The Race, Curtis Chance Thigpen, had ordered the murder of The Reverend Wilkie P. Sanderson. And it got better. Swindall had asked *Chernin* to kill Sanderson. At this point it looked like there were four individuals who could be charged with murder conspiracy, Thigpen, Swindall, and two other Guardians, Bobby Wendt and Kenny Moser.

"How about an attempted murder charge?" Parrish asked. "Some jurors don't like conspiracy. It's easier for them to convict on an attempt because they see the defendants were actually doing something to try and carry out the crime, not just talking about it."

"The problem with that is so far we don't have evidence of both elements needed to prove up an attempt charge. We have evidence of the first one, knowing and willful intent. And so far we have the Guardians trying to recruit Chernin to kill Sanderson which probably would qualify as the overt act we need to support a conspiracy charge. But I don't feel real warm and fuzzy about that same fact satisfying the second element of an attempt charge. For that we would need proof beyond a reasonable doubt the defendants took a substantial step toward the commission of the crime which strongly corroborates their criminal intent."

"I saw something in the paper the other day about a hate-crimes case going on in Orlando or someplace like that."

"You're talking about that case in Tampa involving a beating outside a gay bar. But, Doc, that's nothing compared to what Liftoff has here. He's got a real blockbuster movie." Norris made a v-shape with his hands and clapped them together. "Take one. Neo-Klan group *busted* for planning murder of elderly black minister. You know what I'm saying?"

"Have you got anything to back up what Swindall has said to Chernin?"

"We've got Swindall on audiotape. Chernin was wired."

"*Oh, baby.* I can see JC writing up the A-forms as we speak."

"No, Perishable. We decided to charge by way of indictment. Once this thing starts up the ACLU or somebody else will be jumping on the publicity bandwagon. Under the enhanced penalty provision of this new law, the murder conspiracy will move up from a first-degree to a life felony, a non-bondable offense. The defendants will be entitled to an *Arthur* hearing where I'd have to convince the judge that proof of guilt is evident or the presumption of it is great. If I can't make that showing, the court will set a bond. I'm not so concerned about the defendants getting out on bond and fleeing. The problem with an *Arthur* hearing is the defense attorneys would get an early shot to try and trip up our witnesses and punch some holes in the case. But if we charge by way of indictment, a grand jury will hear testimony from our key witnesses, find probable cause, and no defense attorneys will be in that grand jury room. Then at the *Arthur* hearing we can meet our burden by just relying on the transcript of the testimony from the grand jury proceedings."

Parrish raised his mug. "I'll drink to that, Mr. Prosecutor."

"But wouldn't the defense attorneys still have the right to question your key witnesses at that *Arthur* hearing?"

"Well, first, Doc, those witnesses would have to be there. And there just might be some reason they're not available at the time." Parrish glanced at Norris and Lifton, and the three of them smiled at the inside joke.

Norris raised his beer mug. "My Posse, so far this year it's been all about Mike Tyson and John Gotti. But our main man Liftoff here has a case which is gonna be right up there making big headlines too. To victory!"

"To victory!" they all repeated loudly.

CHAPTER THIRTEEN

Rayfield Lifton carefully took the plastic thimble of *café cubano* Cuqui was transferring to him. "My favorite detective isn't answering his mobile phone. I need you to track him down and tell him to get over here this afternoon with all his stuff. And I also need to make sure those interns, Jennifer Trazenfeld and Timothy Melton, are coming."

"Well, some lady called a little while ago." Cuqui pinched the top of the styrofoam cup to form a spout before she poured herself a shot of Cuban coffee. "She said Ebony and Ivory were on their way. I asked who's that, and she said you already know."

"*Yesh*, Moneypenny, I do," Lifton smiled, "so just reach out to Chernin, and we're cooking with gas." He picked up the phone and carefully pushed a button for an outside line, punched the keypad with the number he was calling, and looked up at his secretary. "It's a private call."

"Well, *excuse* me." She made a sour expression. "You better call your girlfriend," she added as she turned to go, "or you won't be getting any for awhile."

"You know I call Valerie all the time because you're always listening in on my private business. But just for your information, I'm not calling her right now. I'm calling my sister." Lifton flicked his wrist, shooing his secretary away. "Hey, Kim. It's me."

"Hey! You don't recognize my voice?"

"Val-er-ie? What are you doing at my house?"

"*Hello.* Like I never come over here to see Kim and Demeka."

"Yeah, I'm a little messed up today."

"Why? You got problems over there at *Miami Vice?*"

"Actually, things are going really good. Too good in fact. Everything okay with my sister and my little niece?"

"They're fine. By the way, I heard you're real close to launch time in your big case, Liftoff Lifton. Am I right, or am I right?"

"You're *always* right, Val-er-ie."

"You're just saying that so you can take advantage of me because you guessed I was inviting you over to my place tonight."

"Luck be a lady tonight?"

"Wow, you really *are* old. Sinatra was *way* before my time."

"Just don't let your song be 'U Can't Touch This.'"

"I don't know about that. It sure worked for M.C. Hammer. *People Magazine* said he made thirty million on that song. And he lives in a twelve-million dollar mansion in Freemont, California, has seventeen luxury cars, and a really big staff."

"Well, Val-er-ie, you should know by now I have a really big staff too."

"*Oh, my!* You're really getting to be such a funny and naughty little boy."

"You've only got yourself to blame for the naughty. And one more thing, Va-ler-ie. Don't call me boy. Now, can you *please* put my sister on the phone?"

"What *did* you say to that girl, Ray?"

"I'm sure she'll tell you after I hang up. Anyway, sis, remember how you got that night while we were watching that Guardians video?"

"Yes, I sure do. I was like frozen."

"Well, I never forgot what you said to me that night."

"What did I say? I don't remember."

"You said, 'Ray, you better get these bad guys. I don't know what they've done. I really don't even want to know. Just go out and get them, all of them, and put them away for as long as you can. Because God help us all one day if you don't.'"

"You remember all that? I'm impressed."

"When you tell me something important, Kim, I always remember. I just wanted to let you know I'm finally getting ready to do what you told me to do."

* * *

"Can we come in?" Timothy Melton poked his head around the half-open door.

"Yes! My favorite interns are in the house!"

"Does that mean you're going to offer us jobs here when we graduate, Mr. Lifton?"

Jennifer Trazenfeld jabbed Timothy Melton in the ribs with her elbow. "Don't ask him something like that now, Tim."

"Rough out there in the old job market, huh?"

"Yes, unfortunately it is," Trazenfeld answered. "There's too many attorneys, especially here in South Florida."

"Well, we can blame *L.A. Law* for that situation because it made being a lawyer look so glamorous and easy. But I guess we can still pretend it's like that."

"Then I'll be Blair Underwood."

"Sorry, Tim, but I look a lot more like Blair Underwood than you. Seriously, kids, people don't realize most lawyers work at least sixty hours a week and hardly ever attain fame and fortune. And if you divide what lawyers make by the hours they put in, it's pretty damn low wages."

"Unless you went to Harvard or Yale and get a job with one of the big law firms."

"Well, you know what, Jennifer? Then it's going to be more hours than that because young associates end up taking a lot of their work home. They don't have a life. If you do the math, you'll see big law firms are nothing more than glorified sweat shops."

"So why are you still a lawyer?"

"Why do I still work here at the State Attorney's Office?"

Lifton stood up and stretched. "To get the bad guys, of course."

* * *

Timothy Melton strode over to their table and set down the dark-brown plastic tray. "Okay, here's a *cortadito* for Mr. Blair Underwood, a *café con leche* for Miss Susan Dey, and a shot of espresso for me, Ah-nuld."

Lifton swatted the table with the copy of *R.A.V. versus St. Paul, Minnesota* which Trazenfeld had just handed him. "Okay, that's it. I've had it with the Schwarzenegger imitations. I can't take it anymore! My secretary, my sister, my girlfriend, and now you, Tim. Go on, get the hell out of here. You're fired!"

When Lifton didn't lose his serious look, Melton asked, "You're kidding, right?"

"Okay, Tim, I'm putting you back on the team. Otherwise, I'd be a hypocrite because I do *Ah-nuld* imitations all the time myself. Everybody does. It's part of the new world order along with *L.A. Law* and *Miami Vice*."

"The *Miami Vice* television series ended three years ago," Trazenfeld said, taking a small sip of her *café con leche*.

"Yeah, I already heard that from somebody else, Jennifer. Anyway, getting back to the business at hand, *R.A.V.* is one of the cases we talked about before, right?"

"Yes, it is. The Supreme Court heard oral argument on it in December of last year. The opinion finally came out June 22 right before the Court adjourned for the summer."

"It looks pretty long so why don't one of you legal eagles summarize it for me."

"Well, it's just like I predicted when we last met, Mr. Lifton, including the fact that Justice Scalia would be the one writing the majority opinion. There are some separate concurring opinions, but there was no dissent. In a nutshell, Scalia held St. Paul's 'Bias Motivated Crime Ordinance' was facially unconstitutional."

Melton reminded Lifton the city's ordinance prohibited the display of a symbol which was designed to "arouse anger, alarm, or resentment in others on the basis of race, color, creed, religion, or gender." A group of white juveniles had been involved in a series of cross burnings, including one on a black family's front lawn. The Supreme Court held the ordinance was unconstitutional because it prohibited speech on the basis of the *subjects* it addressed. Some categories of speech were not immune from regulation, such as obscenity, defamation, and fighting words. However, government could not impose special prohibitions on speakers who simply express *politically-incorrect* views on subjects like race, color, creed, religion, or gender. St. Paul's motivation was to make it the city's official policy that it didn't condone "group hatred." Although it had a noble objective, as Justice Scalia pointed out, the city could not punish protected speech no matter *how* offensive. Instead, it could only punish "group hatred" *if* it manifested itself through criminal acts such as trespassing, arson, vandalism, or terrorism.

"What about that other case you guys told me about?"

"*Wisconsin versus Mitchell*? If the Supremes grant *certiorari*, the earliest that case will be heard would be the Court's next term."

"Isn't that the case where the Wisconsin appellate court upheld the hate-crimes law, the one where a group of black youths attacked a white boy after seeing the movie *Mississippi Burning*? You said the Wisconsin Supreme Court was going to affirm that case because there was a real crime, aggravated battery or something like that."

"Jennifer called that one wrong."

"Thanks a lot, Tim. I'd poke you in the ribs again, but I don't want to spill my coffee."

"Sorry, Jen. The truth is we both called that one wrong."

"When we last spoke to you about the *Mitchell* case, the Wisconsin Court of Appeals had affirmed imposition of enhanced punishment. The trial judge doubled the defendant's two-year sentence for aggravated battery because he selected the victim based on his race. We told you the Wisconsin Supreme Court had granted further review and, well, that court ended up reversing the intermediate appellate court, finding the law violated the defendant's free speech rights. It said the trial court could not give Mitchell extra punishment because of his personal views even if they were prejudiced ones. In so doing, the Wisconsin Supreme Court relied heavily on *R.A.V. versus St. Paul*."

"The Wisconsin Supreme Court has made really bad law with that decision," Melton added. "This poor white kid, who was fourteen-years-old, was severely beaten. He was in a coma for four days and suffered permanent brain damage."

Lifton considered what the interns had told him as he finished the last of his *cortadito*. "Well, here's my problem. I'm finally getting ready to indict some people, and it's going to be the first time we're filing under Section 775.085. And now you're telling me the United States Supreme Court has struck down a Minnesota hate-crimes law, and the Wisconsin Supreme Court another hate-crimes law. I can understand the decision in *R.A.V.* because that case was about a person's right to display symbols, even racist ones, under a First Amendment free-speech rationale. But I'm very troubled by this *Mitchell* case because it involved a real and very bad underlying crime. It doesn't look like any of these laws are going to fly."

"Well, I'm more optimistic. To get up to speed to discuss these developments with you, I went ahead and spoke with one of the lawyers who argued *Mitchell* for the State of Wisconsin. They've already drafted their *cert* petition." Trazenfeld flipped to one of the pages of her yellow legal pad. "Their main point for the Supremes likely is going to be enhancements only apply to criminal acts, not speech, symbols, or beliefs, and that judges always have had the power to consider a number of factors for sentencing, including a defendant's motives to commit the crime. Finally, they'll argue eliminating criminal behavior based upon prejudice is a 'compelling governmental interest' and, therefore, should be held constitutional. I think these are winning arguments. This is a law and order case, and I'm predicting Chief Justice Rehnquist, along with a majority of the Supremes, will be willing to uphold the Wisconsin law."

"And just to cover all the bases for you," said Melton, "I called one of the Wisconsin defense attorneys and pretended to be from the Public Defenders Office down here. If the Supremes agree to take the case, their main argument is going to be that selecting a victim is a mental process protected by the First Amendment. They're also going to argue a judge can consider a broad range of factors when handing down a sentence, but no law should require him to *automatically* increase punishment based on a defendant's personal views, no matter how offensive they might be to most people. They're also going to raise equal protection and argue hate-crimes laws treat criminals motivated by prejudice differently from those not so motivated even though the crimes they commit are identical and the impact on the victims the same."

"I don't know," Lifton shook his head. "It doesn't look too good for the home team. And, Tim, you shouldn't be deceiving people about who you are. That's not a good way to start your legal career."

"I'm sorry, sir. I guess I wasn't thinking."

"Okay, the way I see it is I can charge somebody under 775.085, get a conviction, the defendant will appeal, and then we'll have to wait and see what the Supremes do in *Mitchell*. If they reverse it, then a conviction in our case likely is going to stick. But if they affirm, we lose. If the Supremes find penalty enhancements for crimes motivated by prejudice are unconstitutional, that will be it for hate-crimes laws. And you say we're going to have to wait until next summer to find out what's going to happen in *Mitchell*?"

"At least until next year, Mr. Lifton, and that's only if the Supremes grant the *cert* petition."

"Well, many thanks for all your hard work on this project. And a special thanks to Tim for taking on the risks associated with going undercover." Lifton gave Melton a pat on the back as he got up to leave.

"Before you go, Mr. Lifton," Trazenfeld said, "Tim and I wanted to give you something." She reached into her purse and rustled its contents searching for something. "Here." She pulled out a small plastic case and handed it to him. "This is for you."

"We found it at a store on South Dixie Highway across from the UM campus. They sell old tapes and records there."

"Oldies but goodies. I know the place. This is great. Let's see here, the label on the back says 'Paul McCartney's *Tug Of War* album, including number one hit song 'Ebony and Ivory' released in 1982.'"

"We wanted you to have something to remember us by."

"Just in case Tim and I end up applying for jobs here at the State Attorney's Office, maybe you could put in a couple of good words for us."

"Well, if we're successful with the case I'm getting ready to file," said Lifton, dropping the cassette into his shirt pocket, "and it turns out you're right about what the Supremes will do in *Mitchell*, I just might be in a position to help you two out."

* * *

Joel Chernin ambled into Lifton's office and set his black leather satchel on the floor. "I kept telling you not to worry."

"Only thing I'm worried about is you dislocating my wrist."

"Ooops!" Chernin stopped his rapid pumping of Lifton's hand. "Sorry, chief," he added, noticing Lifton was still grimacing. "I didn't hurt you, did I?"

"If we do any more cases together, I'm putting in a request for body armor."

"I'll rent you mine for a small price. I've still got some left over from my days on the S.W.A.T. team."

"Weren't you supposed to return it to the Department?"

"No way, general. I still use it sometimes when we're out doing a raid, or when I'm on a gig where I might get whacked."

"Groovy. So now I'm no longer your boss, chief, captain, or governor? I'm a general now?"

"Well, now that you've made your big case, you're going to be moving up the ranks aren't you?"

"Made the case? I don't think we're there just yet."

"Dude, you really need to take that course on the power of

positive thinking. Let's go and get some Cuban coffee."

"I guess you're not hyper enough yet, huh?"

"I need a caffeine boost to kick things up a notch."

They went downstairs to the Pickle Barrel and ordered a *colada*. After Lifton poured himself two plastic thimbles, Chernin drank the rest of it like it was a glass of water.

"Damn, Chernin. Nobody drinks a whole *colada* like that. You're gonna be wired like a nuclear power plant."

"Well, bro, you know what? Don't knock it till you try it. It might help when you're not performing up to speed with Miss Naomi Campbell."

"I haven't had that problem so far."

"Really? Got any pictures of you two doing it?"

"You don't have enough money to buy them, and you probably wouldn't understand what you were looking at anyway."

When they returned to Lifton's office, Chernin unzipped his satchel and took out a brown accordion file containing an audiotape, a transcript of the incriminating conversation, some photographs Andy Medina had taken of Chernin's last visit to Skeeter's, and videos of the Fourth of July Guardians rally and the Channel 5 Thigpen interview.

"Were your people able to enhance the sound?"

"Yeah, a little. At least it's better than the original version."

"So you think the transcriber was able to get it all down?"

"Well, you know how those transcribers are, always inserting words in brackets like 'inaudible' or 'unintelligible' when they're not sure what somebody said. And there was too much of that shit in the first draft I got back from the service we use. Like where we plan how I'm gonna kill Sanderson. So I said, forget about it, and tracked down a court reporter I know real well who agreed to do this job for me. So me and her sat down and redid the whole transcript without all those 'inaudibles' and 'unintelligibles.'"

Lifton tried to lean back in his chair, but it was as rigid as a concrete utility pole. "So you just told her what to put down."

"Oh, please. How many years have you been here now?

Cops do this all the time with transcribers until they get it right. You know, I shouldn't have said anything about it, and then we'd never be having this conversation. Look, general, I didn't make up anything. What's on the transcript is what really went down."

Lifton was silent for a few moments while he stared at the transcript, tapes, and photographs on his desk. "Make extra copies of the original tape."

Chernin smiled and smacked his gum after he saw Lifton had decided to drop the transcript issue. "Man, that is a copy. The original tape and two more copies already are safely locked away in a place where the sun don't shine."

Lifton told Chernin he would be calling him and Andy Medina to testify before the grand jury where he would seek the return of a single-count indictment charging Thigpen, Swindall, Wendt, and Moser with conspiracy murder. "Bring twenty-five copies of the transcript with you so we'll have enough for the grand jurors to follow along while you're playing the tape. And bring any rap sheets and booking photos you've got on these defendants." Lifton made some more notes on a yellow legal pad and then looked up at Chernin. "So what am I forgetting?"

"Why don't you call that really hot reporter chick who did the Thigpen interview?"

"Kara Mello from Channel 5?"

"Yeah, her. That chick is hotter than a witch's tit. We should bring her into the loop now so she'll be ready to break the big story. The guy who got me these videos out of archives said she's called a few times asking about the Guardians."

"*No way*, JC. The last thing we need right now is the media screwing things up for us. When the time is right maybe we'll let her run with the story."

"I hereby nominate myself to be the one to have contact with her. If you know what I mean, *mon capitaine*."

"*Mon capitaine*? I thought I was a general now. And I do know what you mean, Chernin. And you having contact with Kara Mello is a very scary thought."

Guardians Of The Faith

"So when do we bring Sanderson in on this?"

"He won't be able to help us with the grand jury, but we'll get him in here soon and let him know what's going on."

"You know, general, down the road I'm seeing book deal and sale of movie rights." Chernin made the quotation marks sign. "The incredible true story of one courageous detective who risks his life going undercover with a violent white-power group to save the life of an elderly African-American minister."

"Well, you can stop fantasizing for right now, Chernin. By the way, you would have told me if there were any chance these Guardians might go ahead and do this thing without you, right? If there's any risk that could happen before we've got these dudes in custody, we need to take steps now to protect Sanderson."

"No worries, general. These fuckers want me to do this thing, and I've got them hooked into believing I will. It must be like some kind of initiation or some shit like that. But now you're making me a little nervous. I told Swindall I'd meet him tomorrow to nail things down. I'll make sure this is gonna be my thing so we can rest easy."

"Okay, then. If everything goes according to plan, these bad guys should be off the streets pretty soon."

* * *

Valerie Witherspoon lifted the bottle of Blue Label from the coffee table, filled one of the two shot glasses, and handed it to him. "What's wrong, baby? You're so quiet tonight."

"You're not joining me?"

"Yes, I will. I had a rough day too so I sure could use a stiff one tonight." She smiled provocatively at him and ran her tongue around her lips, trying to make him laugh first so she could win this round of the eye game.

"Sorry, but you lose again, Val-er-ie," he said after she started sputtering.

"Well, you won easy enough because something made you get all serious on me. So what's wrong, baby?" She filled the other shot glass and took a sip. "When we talked earlier today you said everything was good. I think you said *too good* so something must have happened after that."

"Well, the thing is, I'm finally getting ready to file *the* case. So I called in my legal-eagle interns who have been doing research on hate-crimes laws to get an update on what's going on in other states. And they told me the Supreme Court recently found that a Minnesota hate-crimes law was unconstitutional, and the Supremes may decide another hate-crimes case from Wisconsin next year which could go either way."

Valerie stared at him as he finished the rest of his Blue Label. "I know you pretty well by now, Rayfield Lifton. And because you're getting real close to making it big again, you've started drifting back into that dark place where you like to hide out with your insecurities. So I think you best relax and do something to get your mind off work." She reached for her glass, stood up, grabbed his hand, and led him to the bedroom. She used her free hand to push hard against his chest, making him fall back onto the bed. "Now you stay put right there, okay?" A few moments after she had disappeared into the bathroom, the lights went out, and the bedroom turned pitch black except for the faint-red glow emanating from the digital radio-alarm clock on the night stand.

"I can't see you. Are you wearing *black* Victoria's Secret?"

"*Oh, you!*" she shouted and pounced on him. "Will you just shut up for awhile?" she whispered, pressing her lips against his and reaching down to unbuckle his belt. "You just let me do all the talking tonight."

"You usually do."

"I thought I told you to shut up, Mr. Prosecutor." She removed his shoes and threw them across the room, peeled off his pants and underwear, then unbuttoned his shirt and pulled it back. "Now that's more like it." She scooted to the edge of the bed, unhooked her bra, and slipped out of her panties.

"Hey, are you gonna just lay there like a big lump of coal?"

"You know, Val-er-ie, at the office it's the Terminator stuff all the time, and with you it's the black-skin thing. I've gotta be honest with you. That's getting to be such a turnoff I don't know if I'm gonna be able to perform tonight."

"You're the one who started the whole black-skin thing, or have you already forgotten you had me starring in those Kingsford charcoal commercials?"

"Well, at least there's no black Terminator jokes."

"You don't think so? Well, how about this," she lowered her voice, *"I'll be bla-aaa-ck."*

"Okay, that's it! That's the last straw, a black Terminator joke. Now I'm definitely gonna be impotent tonight."

"You really think so?" She dug her chin into his chest and slowly began sliding down. "I seriously doubt that. *Oh, yes,"* she purred as she reached his waist. "Remember I said I sure could use a stiff one tonight? Well, it looks like I'm already getting my wish."

CHAPTER FOURTEEN

Aubrey Swindall pulled his F-150 pick-up over to the curb on Northeast Third Road just south of the Homestead bus station and switched off the ignition. Emily had opened the passenger door halfway when she noticed her husband was staring ahead with a blank expression, his hands still on the steering wheel. She reached over and gently turned his head. "What's wrong, Brey? C'mon now, honey, what is it?"

He looked over at her, and his eyes started to water. After all those years of being so incredibly dumb and fat, he didn't deserve such a smart and loving person like Emily. This thing he was doing, it was for her too, and he couldn't even tell her about it. Of course, if it went bad, she would find out real fast.

"It's nothing, honey," his voice was weak.

"Now, don't tell me that. After all these years together I *always* know when there's something wrong. And I'm not leaving here until you tell me what it is, Brey."

"It's nothing, babe." He glanced at his watch. "You're gonna miss your bus."

"Well, I don't believe you," she crossed her arms, "and I'm not going anywhere until you tell me what's wrong."

He had messed things up with this involuntary show of emotion and needed to think of something to say real quick. "I'm just sorry you have to take a damn bus all the way up to The Panhandle."

"Well, why would you be bothered by that?"

He reached over, wrapped his meaty right hand around her left upper arm, and squeezed it gently. "Because you deserve better, Emily."

"What?" she asked with a curious smile.

"Yeah," he continued the white lie. "It takes like fifteen or twenty hours to get there on the damn bus. You should be flying up there."

"Oh, you silly goose. It was like nine-hundred dollars round-trip on an airplane. We checked, remember? And that's crazy because it only costs like three-hundred round-trip to New York. And it's just because hardly anybody flies to The Panhandle from down here, but a lot of people go to New York, and they always fill up those big planes."

Swindall bit his lip. "Well, babe, I'm still sorry you have to go all that way up there on a Greyhound bus."

"I don't mind one bit going all that way up there on the bus. I've got my magazines and my crossword puzzle books and my food." She reached down and picked up two plastic bags bearing the K-Mart logo. "See? I'm gonna be fine. We don't need to be spending any of that big money you say we're getting before we get it, okay, Brey?"

"Alright, honey," he said looking down with a childish grin.

"Now help me with my stuff because I see people getting on a bus over there."

Swindall grabbed the beat-up grey Samsonite hard-shell suitcase from the back of the truck and followed Emily over to the ticket window.

"Are you sure you don't want me to get a round-trip ticket?"

"No, babe. Just get the one-way. This deal is gonna wrap up real soon, and then I'll be heading up north."

"After these two weeks of vacation I'll have to let the store manager know if I'm not coming back to work."

Guardians Of The Faith

"You'll know something by then, honey," he said, biting his lower lip again.

They strolled over to the bus, its diesel engine idling, gurgling like a big pot of boiling water. Emily handed her ticket to the tall black driver standing next to the open door. He tore the stub off, grabbed her suitcase, slid it into the belly of the bus with the rest of the luggage, and shut the compartment.

Emily wrapped her arms around her husband's waist and gave him a squeeze. "So, I'll call you when I get up there, okay, babe? Did you hear me?" She stepped back and looked up at him. "You know you're gonna draw blood."

"I'm gonna do what?!"

"You don't need to shout, babe. I just meant if you keep biting your lip so hard, you're gonna start bleeding."

"I'm sorry, honey." Swindall let out a big sigh and shook his head. "I'm just...."

"Gonna be missing me too much, I know," she smiled. "You sure you'll be okay here all by yourself?"

When he didn't say anything, Emily took a step forward, stood on her toes, and gave him a peck on the cheek. "Well, if things are taking longer than you expect, Brey, then as soon as that baby's born," she lowered her voice, "*I'll be back.*"

"No, honey," Swindall said in the most convincing tone he could muster, his meaty hands planted firmly on her shoulders. "You just stay up there and help Kaye with the baby. You know how Cecil is. He's not gonna be hanging around the house changing diapers and whatnot. He's gonna be out there hustling and making deals, and your sister is gonna need all the help she can get."

"Well, as soon as the baby's born we'll see what's what." She gave him another hug and then climbed up into the bus.

As the driver backed up so he could make a wide turn to exit the small terminal, Emily waved and blew kisses his way. Swindall walked alongside the bus and waved back, and he saw Emily's smile widen as he tried his best to keep up. He got back in his truck, closed his eyes, and rested his forehead on the steering wheel. "Lord, I've never talked to you since I was a little boy. Please forgive me for everything I've done and for what I have to do now."

As he drove back to Florida City, Swindall recalled what Emily had said. "You're gonna draw blood." At that moment he had been lost in thought about what still needed to be done, and it was like she had been able to get inside his head. He felt bad about shouting at her, but her words had jolted him like an electric shock. His nerves were shot, his emotions riding a roller-coaster. He wondered whether soon his dreams would come true, or whether for all practical purposes his life would be over.

* * *

Kimberly Singletary entered the living room carrying a large blue plastic bowl of microwave buttered popcorn, paper plates, and a roll of paper towels. "Anything interesting going on yet?"

"Not so far, but it's almost time for the keynote address."

"Barbara Jordan, right?" She tilted the plastic bowl, filling a paper plate with a small mountain of popcorn.

"You're wrong. Michael Jordan." Lifton grabbed a handful of popcorn, dropped it on his plate, and sat back on the sofa.

"You're so funny, just like the Governor from Georgia."

"Zell Miller? 'Not all of us can be born rich, handsome, and lucky, and that's why we have a Democratic Party,' and, 'Our Commander-in-Chief talks like Dirty Harry but acts like Barney Fife.' That guy?"

"Yeah, that guy. Okay, here she comes so be quiet now."

Wearing a short-sleeve white jacket and a bright-pink blouse, former Texas Representative Barbara Jordan made her way to the lectern, the delegates rising and cheering wildly. She raised her outstretched arms, and the sound became a deafening roar.

"Did you know she was the first black Congresswoman from the deep South?"

"I do know that, and she also was the first black law student at Boston University. But, sis, that's not important now. She really needs to do something about that hair. She looks like a Negro Harpo Marx."

"That's not funny, Ray."

"Then why are you giggling like a silly schoolgirl?"

"Will you just eat your popcorn and be quiet now?"

A silence fell over Madison Square Garden as Barbara Jordan began to speak. "It was at this time. It was at this place. It was at this event sixteen years ago I presented a keynote address to the Democratic National Convention. With modesty, I remind you that that year, 1976, we *won* the presidency. Why not *repeat* that performance in 1992? We can do it. We can do it."

As the scene shifted from the lectern to a panning of the convention floor, they heard a series of loud knocks. Valerie was at the front door, her Heat logo gym bag slung over her shoulder. "Hey, baby." She stepped inside, let the bag drop to the floor, and they hugged and kissed. "Heat Dancer tryouts started tonight."

"You're going for Heat Dancer?"

"I'm thinking about it. The tryouts last a couple of weeks, and it's a good workout anyway. I was close by so I thought I'd catch the end of the convention with you guys."

"Hey, Val. You got here just at the right time. It's starting to get really interesting. Look, Ray," Kim pointed at the screen, "there's your boss, see?"

Susan Purvis was sitting in an aisle seat next to the sign designating the members of the Florida delegation. To her right was Bob Graham, the former Governor who now was a United States Senator serving his first term.

"We are one, we Americans," Barbara Jordan said. "We're one, and we reject any intruder who seeks to divide us on the basis of race and color. We honor cultural identity. We always have, we always will. But separatism is not allowed. Separatism is *not* the American way. We must not allow ideas like political correctness to *divide* us and cause us to reverse hard-won achievements in human rights and civil rights."

"Is she good or what? Here, Val, have some popcorn."

"Well, I guess I could have some. I burned a whole lot of calories tonight."

"Hey, Kim, did you know she's going for Heat Dancer? She likes strutting her stuff and shaking her booty any chance she gets."

"Ray, will you please be quiet now?" Kimberly passed him the plastic bowl. "I want to hear this."

"We seek to unite people, not divide them. As we seek to unite people, we reject both white racism *and* black racism. This party will not tolerate bigotry under any guise." Barbara Jordan spoke about the strength of the country being rooted in its diversity and the harm budget deficits would cause for future generations. Then she talked about equality for women, and how a nineteenth-century visitor from France, Alexis de Tocqueville, had observed, "'If I were asked to what singular substance do I mainly attribute the prosperity and growing strength of the American people, I should reply, to the superiority of their women.'" Jordan waited for the applause to subside before she continued. "I can only say the twentieth century will not close without the presence of women being keenly felt."

"Yes!" Kimberly turned so she could high-five Valerie who then twisted to her right so she could do the same with Lifton.

"*No thanks.*" Lifton grabbed a handful of popcorn instead.

"Dumb ass," Valerie said, dropping her hand and giving him a shove.

"Now look what you did, Val-er-ie." Lifton reached down and started picking up the pieces of popcorn which had been knocked off his plate.

Barbara Jordan was nearing the end of her speech. She recalled what Franklin Roosevelt had said during his 1933 inaugural address. "'In every dark hour of our national life a leadership of frankness and vigor has met with that understanding and support of the people themselves which is essential to victory.' Given the ingredients of today's national environment, maybe, maybe, just maybe, we Americans are poised for a second 'Rendezvous with Destiny.'"

Guardians Of The Faith

The Democratic National Convention officially was over a few minutes later with a downpour of thousands of colored balloons and the blaring of Fleetwood Mac's "Don't Stop," Bill Clinton's Presidential campaign theme song. Clinton and Gore returned to the stage, shook hands and embraced, and the stage filled with their close family members.

"It's already late, Val. Why don't you stay here tonight?"

"No way, sis. We'll never be able to get any sleep. She snores like an ox."

"You can stay with Mr. Sunshine in his room, or I can make up the sofa."

"*No thanks*, Kim. Your brother is a male chauvinist pig at heart so he's in the dog house now." She got up and went to Demeka's room and planted a soft kiss on the child's forehead.

"You know I was just kidding about you being in the dog house with me," Valerie said as she leaned against her Honda Civic. She put her arms around Lifton, pulled him toward her, and squeezed hard. "I think you've already lost a few pounds from all that jogging you've been doing lately."

"Just call me buns of steel."

She lowered her hands and squeezed his buttocks. "*Mmm*, they do feel mighty fine. Hey, you," she said, looking up. "Things are going really good, aren't they?" When he didn't answer, her tight hold relaxed. "Damn you, Ray. You don't want things to go really good, do you?"

"Everything is just *groo-vy*, Val-er-ie."

"I never can tell when you're serious. I wish you could be more like that damn campaign song. 'Don't stop thinking about tomorrow,'" she sang softly. "'Don't stop, it'll soon be here. It'll be here better than before. Yesterday's gone, yesterday's gone.'"

"You might just want to stick with acting and dancing."

"Can't you ever be serious? Don't you ever think about tomorrow for us?"

Kimberly already had gone to bed but had left the television on. Peter Jennings was interviewing Democratic Party Chairman

Guardians Of The Faith

Ron Brown. Lifton picked up the plastic bowl and was finishing off the few remaining pieces of popcorn when the phone rang. He raced to the kitchen cursing whoever was calling so late.

"Is that you, Rayfield Lifton?" The distinctive South Florida twang told him it was Susan Purvis. "I took your home number with me before I left for New York. Did you watch any of the convention tonight?"

"Yes, I did. As a matter of fact I saw you during Barbara Jordan's speech."

"My Lord, wasn't she great? Listen, I only have a minute. Everything we've talked about, well, it all seems to be coming together. In fact, I have to stay up here a few more days. Clinton and Gore want to talk to me in more detail about where I might fit in if they take the election. So do you have any good news for me?"

"Yes, I do, actually. We're ready now to present the case to the grand jury."

"So you're charging by way of an indictment, huh? This isn't a capital case, is it? Well, I'm sure you all must have weighed the pros and cons of whatever you're doing. I'm sorry, Ray, but I have to run now to one of those after-parties."

On the way to his bedroom Lifton checked in on Demeka. If he became the next Dade State Attorney, not only would he make a lot more money, he would have access to the best connections for anything he needed. And then whatever humanly possible could be done for her, he would find a way to help his little niece.

* * *

"You ready to rock and roll, my friend?"

When those were the first words out of Aaron Tannenbaum's mouth when he had called a few days ago, Aubrey Swindall knew it had to be all good. "I guess so," he replied, trying not to sound too anxious.

"I'm telling you this, my friend, because it looks like the Malmans want to go ahead and buy your property."

"Looks like, Mr. Tannenbaum?" He suddenly felt his legs go weak and had to lean against the wall next to the payphone.

Guardians Of The Faith

"Hey, call me Aaron. What I'm saying, buddy, is you came in first place. Now it's just about doing the paperwork, and after that it will be a done deal."

Swindall felt the sweat coating his hand, and he had to clear his throat before he could speak again. "Well, you see, they're getting..." The receiver slipped out of his hand and dangled by its metal-encased cord. "You still there, sir? I was just saying they're getting a good deal."

"Well, Aubrey, you don't have to convince me," he chuckled. "I'm sure it's a good deal for everybody. Stewart and Karen are flying down here in a couple of days so I'm thinking we should try and meet Thursday to go over the contract."

"So then you want me to go to your office this Thursday, Mr. Tannenbaum?"

"Man, Aubrey, you're making me feel old. Just call me Aaron, okay? Yes. The answer is yes, but I don't know what time yet. You can bring your attorney so he can take a look at the paperwork and make sure you're protected. My office is in Miami Beach. I'm in the last building at the east end of Lincoln Road. You know, that real old building with the digital display, time and temperature, and right now it's reading ninety-eight degrees. You could fry an egg on the sidewalk, my friend."

"So after we sign the papers how long will it be before I get my money?"

"Well, Aubrey, executing the purchase-sale contract just starts the process. Then there's the title search, inspections, you know, all that good stuff."

"Yeah, all that legal bullshit," Swindall thought. That's how lawyers got big money, making simple things complicated. Why couldn't he get his big check when he signed the papers so he could get the hell outta Dodge? "Well, when is it I do get my money?"

"If everybody signs off on the deal when we meet, and if everything goes smoothly after that then, let's see," the lawyer flipped through the pages of his desk calendar, "I'd say we probably could schedule the closing sometime around the third week of August."

"Such bullshit," Swindall cursed under his breath, but he was smart enough not to ask for it to be sooner because this fucking lawyer then would tell the Malmans he was sounding desperate. And then for sure those sharp New Yorkers would try and jew him down on the price.

"Hey, Aubrey, are you still there?"

"Yes, sir. Just one last thing. Does my wife have to sign any of those papers?"

"Well, if she's on the title to the property, yes. But your lawyer can draw up a specific power-of-attorney for her to sign. You bring that with you, and then you can sign any papers relating to this transaction on her behalf. But, look, I shouldn't be giving you legal advice because I represent the Malmans. I'm sure you've heard the phrase 'conflict-of-interest,' right? And, you know, I'm glad to explain that concept to you if you like."

"This *fucking* lawyer," Swindall thought. "No, that's okay. So you'll give me a call, Mr. Tannenbaum, and let me know at what time I gotta be at your place Thursday, right?"

"Yes, and please don't forget to call me Aaron. Have a great day, Aubrey."

After he heard the click of the lawyer hanging up, Swindall slammed the receiver back in its cradle. "Man, all this *fucking* bullshit!" He went over to the bar and pulled out a Budweiser longneck from the cooler. He sat down at one of the tables and thought about what still had to be done. That's when he decided it would be better for Emily to head up north now. Kaye was ready to give birth to her third child soon, and for awhile they had been talking about Emily helping her out. He had called his wife at the store and convinced her to go ahead and ask her boss if she could start her vacation a few weeks early. Because she had been such a good employee for so long, and things were slow in the summer anyway, her boss granted the request. After he got off the phone with Emily, Swindall called Charlie Newcastle.

"Aubrey, you don't need a lawyer for a power-of-attorney,"

Charlie advised him. "I've got the darn forms right here in my office. Just swing by today anytime you want between two and five. And you won't have to pay me any of those big attorney's fees," he chuckled. "There's no charge for you, Jolly Green."

When Swindall arrived at The Newcastle Insurance Agency, Charlie invited him to go over to Dunkin' Donuts at the other end of the strip mall.

"Damn, this one sure is good," Swindall said, licking the chocolate icing off his thumb before popping the rest of the cream-filled eclair into his mouth.

"You know, ever since I was a little kid I've loved these sprinkles." Newcastle pointed to the multi-colored flecks on the white icing of his donut. He noticed some of them had fallen on his white short-sleeve dress shirt and burgundy tie and brushed them off. "So you need a specific power-of-attorney for Emily for the sale of your commercial property, right? Why the long face, big guy?" Newcastle flicked his hand like it was no big deal. "I already know you're selling your business because the buyer from New York, Mr. Mailman or Mr. Mormon, whatever his name is, called yesterday for me to verify your coverages. He said you authorized release of the information."

"Yeah, I told him to go ahead and give you a call, Charlie."

"I figured as much, or how else would he know to call me? Anyway, don't worry about anything. He seemed very satisfied with the information I gave him."

"That's good, Charlie. Thanks for doing that."

"Well, why the long face then, my friend? I hope you're not embarrassed about me finding out you're selling your place. I'm not upset about losing your business. I've got plenty of customers to keep me in moccasins for a long time. And you know what else, Aubrey? If I could get a decent price for this agency, hell, I'd unload it in a flash."

"You would, Charlie? And then what would you do?"

"Well, I'll tell you." Newcastle cleaned his hands on a paper napkin, brushed off a few more sprinkles from his shirt and tie,

Guardians Of The Faith

then folded his arms. "I'd probably move down to Key West, me and the wife, and buy one of those beautiful old wood houses, three storeys, with a big wrap-around porch on the first floor and balconies on the other two. Then me and the wife could sit around in a couple of those big wicker rocking chairs, like the ones they have at Cracker Barrel, and watch all the locals and tourists strolling by. Let me tell you, that can be pretty darn entertaining if you've ever been down to Key West. And I'd also get me a small boat, fifteen, seventeen feet, would do just fine. Boston Whaler is the best brand in my opinion. Did you know you can cut one of their boats in half, and both pieces will still float? And that would be a good thing for somebody already up there in years like me. And I'd keep it at a marina close by. Well, really everything is close by in Key West because it's only four-miles square. And you know what, Aubrey?" Newcastle continued after being lost in thought for a few moments, "I've gotta tell you I'm a little jealous because you've already got the jump on me. So what are you planning on doing after you sell your business?"

"Pretty much the same, Charlie, but up in The Panhandle."

"Except you're not an old coot yet like me. You and Emily have a lot more years ahead of you before you're ready for rocking chairs. You know," Newcastle said as he took a bite from his remaining donut, "I always forget to ask if you have any children?"

"We don't, Charlie. We've never been blessed like that."

"Well, I had a total of seven little rug rats," Newcastle said, raising his eyebrows. "Of course, they're all grown up now. In fact, my oldest just turned thirty-seven, and my youngest will be twenty next month."

"You've sure had your hands full." Swindall shook his head and frowned. "Me and Emily, we pretty much gave up on having kids about five years ago."

"Well, you be sure and give my best to your lovely wife, will you? Okay, let's head back to the office now and get that specific power-of-attorney you need. After that I've gotta finish up some paperwork on a couple of auto accidents and send it out to the insurance companies today."

Newcastle helped him fill out the form and showed him where Emily needed to sign it in front of a notary public. "I'm a notary too, but I'd have to see Emily sign in person before I'd be allowed to put my seal on it. I'm a real stickler about that kinda stuff, but Emily can just go to any bank. They all have a notary right there on the premises."

When Swindall asked Newcastle if he knew a lawyer who wouldn't charge too much to represent him with the sale of his business, Newcastle laughed. "Most people don't know this, but you really don't need a lawyer if you're the seller. I mean, all you're really interested in is how much money you're getting for your property unless, of course, you're giving back a purchase money mortgage. So if you're financing all or part of the purchase price for the buyer, then there's things like the promissory note, the mortgage, the interest rate you're charging, the amortization schedule, stuff like that. And then, yes, it's probably a good idea to hire an attorney to make sure those things are done properly just in case one day you have to file a foreclosure action if there's a default on payment of the balance of money you're still owed."

"No, I'm not financing nothing, Charlie. I want all my money up front."

"Alright, then, so here it's the buyers who need an attorney to make sure they don't inherit any problems after this deal closes. You know, like finding out there's a judgment lien, or worse, it turns out you and Emily weren't the real legal owners of the property. That's why the buyers have a lawyer or a title company do a search of the county records to make sure your property is free and clear of any claims or encumbrances. Otherwise, the buyers won't be able to get a title policy. And then there's stuff like inspections to see if there's any major problems with the structure or fixtures. But, again, those are things the buyers need to be concerned about."

Swindall shook his head. "You sure know a lot about this kinda stuff, Charlie. I'm going over to Big Daddy's so I can buy you a bottle for all the help you're giving me."

"Well, I do like to tip a few," Newcastle laughed, "but you hold on to your money. It's cheaper to give me a bottle from your own inventory where you paid wholesale. I like a good rum so next time you're down this way you can drop off a bottle if you want. But there's really no need even to do that. You've given me your business all these years, and that's thanks enough. And, anyway, you already gave me a nice present not so long ago."

Swindall squinted, trying to remember what the insurance agent was talking about. "What was that, Charlie?"

"Well, Aubrey, last time you were here you told me you weren't into that white-power group anymore."

Swindall rubbed his nose rapidly with his index finger and snorted. "Well, yeah, I'm not no more, Charlie."

"Well, good for you," Newcastle said with a wink and a nod. "Good for you, Aubrey. I mean, Jolly Green."

If Charlie Newcastle only knew about the terrible mess he had gotten himself into, looking to kill the old preacher, he wouldn't keep saying "good for you."

CHAPTER FIFTEEN

Lifton stopped massaging the back of his neck and looked up. "How could this happen, Moneypenny?"

"Don't get mad at me, *jefe*. I have nothing to do with that."

Due to a clerical error the grand jury summonses had been sent out with a report date of August 7 instead of July 31. This afternoon the grand jury foreperson should have been signing the indictment which lay on Lifton's desk next to the four arrest warrants and the motion to seal the court file until all defendants had been taken into custody.

"I'm going downstairs. You want some *café cubano*?"

"I need to talk to Chernin. And the way things are going so far today I feel like drinking a whole *colada*."

"I don't think so," she shook her head at this really dangerous idea.

"Why not? Chernin does it all the time."

"I rest my case." Cuqui went back to her desk, reached Chernin, and transferred the call to Lifton.

After Lifton told him about the one-week delay there would be to present the case to the grand jury, Chernin said, "Well, boss, shit happens, but this is definitely not good news. Those dudes want this thing done soon. We should go with Plan B. You know, we go out and arrest these fuckers on an A-form, and you charge by way of an information."

"We've already been over this, JC. We don't need a bunch of headline-grabbing defense attorneys using an *Arthur* hearing to screw up our case a few days after it's filed. There's no defense cross when you and Medina testify before the grand jury. It's a one-way street going only our way. And then we can rely on the transcript of the grand jury proceedings at an *Arthur* hearing without you or Medina having to be there."

"Fine. I understand all that, but you'd still have a couple of weeks after we make the arrests to get an indictment before the arraignment deadline."

"Yeah, I'm aware of that, Chernin. I've been doing this for awhile, you know. But, just like today, shit happens so there's always a chance the *Arthur* hearing could be held before we're able to present the case to the grand jury."

Lifton could hear Chernin smacking his gum. "Well, maybe this dark cloud has a silver lining in it or however that saying goes. While I'm trying to keep these dudes at bay for another week, I could try and get some better audio. That way you won't have to keep agonizing over what I did with that court reporter. I know you let it ride, but you didn't like it. So you want me to do that, try and get some more evidence, something real crisp and clear so you'll be able to sleep good at night?"

Lifton tried to push back in his chair, but it was as rigid as a concrete utility pole. "Look, JC, right now we've got a nice little presentation for the grand jury. I don't want you to do anything which could mess things up."

"Mess things up like how? These Guardians already have incriminated themselves. It can only get better."

"Are you sure about that? Have you ever heard of a defense to a conspiracy charge called early withdrawal?"

"What is this, a police academy pop quiz? Yeah, I'm familiar with early withdrawal but only in relation to sexual intercourse."

"That's very funny, Chernin. Early withdrawal is a defense

to a conspiracy charge where the defendant claims he withdrew from the conspiracy before he gets arrested."

"That sounds too easy, boss man. Otherwise, defendants would be using it all the time, and I would have heard about that defense by now."

"Well, the truth is it's not that easy. A defendant has to do more than just show he stopped participating in the conspiracy before he gets busted. He also has to show he took affirmative action to disavow or defeat the purpose of the conspiracy before any of its members committed an overt act in furtherance of it."

"And for those reasons I'm guessing that defense hardly ever comes up."

"It comes up once in a blue moon, but it's still out there."

"So what you're saying is, if these dudes suspect we might be conducting a sting operation, and they tell me they never really intended to harm Sanderson, that they were just testing me or some shit like that, then that could screw up the case."

"Not just screw up the case, JC, they would be disavowing the conspiracy before any overt act was committed, and then we'd have no case."

"Well, that sure would suck big time. But just hold on here a second. I thought you told me the fact they recruited me to kill Sanderson was an overt act we could use to prove up the conspiracy charge."

"I told you it *probably* would qualify as an overt act."

"Well, you know something, general? I don't like the way *probably* sounds at this point in time. You shouldn't be so worried about me doing something which might screw up the case and that early withdrawal defense. You should be a lot more concerned about leaving things the way they are if what we've got so far isn't enough to make this case a lock."

* * *

It had been awhile since Aubrey Swindall had made the trip to Miami Beach because for a long time now they hadn't been doing any more shit like they used to down there. The last time was one real hot summer night after he closed up Skeeter's. They piled into Curtis' truck, Swindall riding shotgun, Larry Gentry and Bill Tipton in the back. They brought along a case of beer and polished it off before they arrived in Miami Beach.

It was easy enough to find some wrong to do down there on South Beach. You could take your pick. There were the *marielitos* thick as flies who had arrived in South Florida on hundreds of small boats after Fidel Castro temporarily opened the floodgates a few years before. And many of the worst from that bunch, hardened criminals and looney-tunes crazies, had decided to make their permanent residence in an area bordered by 1ˢᵗ and 5ᵗʰ Streets and Ocean Drive and Alton Road, transforming a good chunk of the southern end of Miami Beach into a no-man's land more dangerous than Overtown or Liberty City where most of the niggers lived. Then up the road just a little further you had your regular American fruitcakes, exotic man-birds flitting and fluttering in and out of dimly-lit clubs in the basements of old hotels. And in the middle of that very fucked-up mix, there were a lot of *really* old Jews sunk down in plastic chairs at all hours of the day and night, crammed like sardines on the front porches of crumbling small art deco hotels and apartment buildings, their skin like somebody had applied a coat of walnut stain to it, the result of soaking up too much of the relentless South Florida sun.

That night Curtis decided to park his truck a little further north at 17ᵗʰ Street and Washington Avenue. They walked back to 11ᵗʰ Street and Ocean Drive where an old hotel called "Sweet Suites" was situated. It was still early by GST, Gay Standard Time, a very fucking funny name Curtis had made up on one of their trips to Miami Beach, so they looked for something else to do for awhile. They bought four six-packs at a little Spanish market and hung out in Lummus Park, drinking beer and watching the non-stop parade of human crap along Ocean Drive. An hour later they crossed the street and descended into Sweet Suites' basement where the fag bar was located. The air was thick with dust, and pieces of drywall were piled almost to the ceiling.

"Well, there ain't no queers coming here." Swindall pointed at the paper taped to the front door stating the bar would be closed temporarily starting that night due to construction.

"Unless they don't know it's closed," Curtis said, looking behind an opaque plastic curtain across from the entrance to the bar. "You all get inside this room," he said, holding the curtain open for them. "Skeeter, you go turn off those lights down there."

Swindall found a grimy rag and twisted the two bare light bulbs until they went off, a sliver of light from the area of the stairs faintly illuminating spirals of dust lazily wafting through the corridor. A few minutes later they heard footsteps descending to the basement and then stop suddenly in front of them.

"Ain't no fucking faggots here tonight," Curtis blurted out as they all emerged from behind the plastic curtain and confronted a tall, slender young man dressed in blue jeans and white t-shirt, the same clothes they were wearing. "Only us girls."

The young man tried to bolt for the stairs, but Swindall already had grabbed one of his arms. Gentry and Tipton punched him in the stomach and back a few times, and he crumpled to the sawdust-covered concrete floor, laying there doubled up in fetal position, coughing violently.

Thigpen raised the two-foot level he had found in the space behind the plastic curtain. "You see this, you fucking faggot? Now I'm gonna level your head."

"No, please don't," the man begged in a sissy voice.

Curtis rocked his arm back and forth a few times, then turned and flung the level down the corridor where it made a loud pinging sound when it hit the floor. "Larry, you and Billy take care of this pansy. I'm too fucking drunk for this shit."

"What'd you end up doing to the fag?" Swindall asked Gentry and Tipton after they caught up with them down the street.

"We just gave him a good kicking is all."

They swaggered down Ocean Drive, figuring they had a few minutes before the police would be called to Sweet Suites. They took in the spectacle of the *marielitos*, men dressed in flowery shirts and hats like people wore back in the forties, big chains hanging around their olive-skin necks, their women painted with heavy make-up and wearing cheap stretch pants so they could show off their big spic asses.

"Our work is done," Curtis said after they had walked a few more blocks. "Let's get the hell out of here. This place makes me want to puke up my guts."

Now years later Swindall was returning alone to South Beach for his meeting with the Malmans who had told their lawyer they were ready to sign the contract to buy his place. As he made his way along Biscayne Boulevard in downtown Miami, to his left were big office buildings and scores of towering royal palms, to his right the Miamarina and Bayside Marketplace. He finally spotted the sign for I-395 and the MacArthur Causeway and gunned his truck as it began climbing the entrance ramp. The blazing noonday sun pierced Biscayne Bay all the way to its sandy bottom, making its waters sparkle a half-dozen shades of blue and green.

Swindall glanced in his rearview mirror and took another look at the glittering skyscrapers he was leaving behind. Then he marveled at the two enormous cruise ships docked at Dodge Island to his right and dozens of magnificent water-front mansions on Palm and Star Islands to his left. It was like he had traveled a thousand miles to a different *country* instead of only forty miles within the same *county*. Big fishing boats with tall tuna towers, cigarette racers, and jet skis were plowing the waters of Government Cut as Swindall made the two-mile trip to the southern tip of Miami Beach. At the end of the causeway Swindall drove a few more blocks east on 5th Street to Washington Avenue, then a mile north to the building with a big digital display at the top. In that part of Miami Beach it was the only structure more than a couple storeys high. He found a metered parking space on a side street and grabbed a handful of change from the plastic seat caddy. He looked at his watch and saw he was more than an hour early for his 2:00 p.m. appointment. And he was feeling way too anxious, like a little kid at the front gate of Disney World. It definitely wasn't a good idea to go to the lawyer's office now, especially if the Malmans already were there. He'd look too desperate, and then for sure those sharp New Yorkers would try and jew him down on the price.

Swindall decided to kill some time by taking a walk down memory lane. He headed over to Collins Avenue, then down to 15th Street where he crossed over to Ocean Drive. *"What the hell?!"* This couldn't be the same place he had been a few years back. The street was flooded with a lot of really decent-looking people, pearl-white tourists wearing straw hats, sporting flamingo-pink sunburns, and talking in foreign languages, and lanky models in tiny string bikinis whizzing by on rollerblades. There wasn't one damn *marielito* or any other type of trash in sight. All the buildings he remembered were gone, either demolished and replaced with new construction or so completely renovated you'd never know they had former lives as sleazy hotels. *"What the hell?!"* Swindall said again as he reached 11th Street. Where "Sweet Suites" once stood there now was an elegant white mansion enclosed by a massive wrought-iron fence.

"Here, sir." A very pretty young girl with long blond hair dressed in white hot pants and a bright-yellow halter top handed him a sheet of paper.

Swindall was about to ask her to explain what this was all about but decided to read the paper instead. Gianni Versace, the legendary Italian clothes designer, had purchased this property to use as his residence. The original 1930 structure, called Casa Casuarina, was modeled after the *Alcazar de Colon* which Christopher Columbus' son had built in Santo Domingo 1510, the oldest existing house in the western hemisphere. After receiving permission from the City of Miami Beach, Versace also acquired the building next door, which Swindall knew used to be "Sweet Suites," demolished it, and made a two-storey 6,100 square foot addition to Casa Casuarina.

"We're having the grand opening of our new Versace South Beach store today," the pretty blond advised Swindall as he was admiring the structure's balconies and red Spanish barrel-tile roof. She took the sheet of paper from Swindall and flipped it over. "Here's the address of our new store if you're interested in attending the event. And Mr. Versace himself is going to be there from six to eight."

As he continued his trek down Ocean Drive, Swindall wondered how all this could have changed so fast. It was as if somebody had waved a magic wand over these ten blocks on Ocean Drive, making its crumbling buildings and undesirable inhabitants disappear, replacing them with a whole lot of cool bars and restaurants and hot young broads and goofy-looking tourists.

"*Damn*, if this ain't good," Swindall mumbled as he reached the corner at 8th Street and sat down at a small table shaded by a big dark-green umbrella. The Eagles' "Peaceful Easy Feeling" was pouring out of the open doors of the restaurant.

"Hi, there!" said a perky little brunette with a ponytail. "Welcome to the News Café. Can I get you something to drink?"

"When did this place open up?"

"Well, I wasn't working here back then, but I believe it was at the end of 1988 or something like that. They tell me it started off pretty small, just a newsstand or something like that, and they only served little sandwiches and small salads and things like that. But now they've got a separate bar, a full-service kitchen, and, as you can see, a lot of sidewalk and courtyard seating, and even some retail space over there." The waitress half-turned in the direction of a shop next door. "Oh, I'm sorry. Way too much information, right? So would you like to start off with something to drink first?"

"I'll just have some coffee."

"Okay, would you like a *caffe latte*, a cappuccino, one of our flavored coffees, or just a regular espresso?" After Swindall didn't say anything, she added, "Too many choices, right? Doesn't look like you're from around here. I'll bet you're from the Midwest. Me too. Let me help you out. Espresso is coffee brewed by forcing steam through finely ground, darkly roasted coffee beans. *Caffe latte* is espresso mixed with hot or steamed milk. Cappuccino is one-third espresso, one-third steamed milk, and one-third *frothed* milk, and then they sprinkle powdered cinnamon on top as a garnish. And then we've got decafs for all of the above. Why do I sound like I know all this stuff so good? It's because I worked in a place called Starbucks in Chicago. That's where I'm from. And I can tell you they sure have a lot of different types of coffees. I started working in their first store in Chicago back in 1987. I think Starbucks is out of Seattle, but I'm not sure. Anyway, by the time I came down here in 1989, Starbucks already had something like *fifty* stores in different states. Incredible, right? But I'll bet you must be thinking, *way* too much information, right? Maybe I'm like this because I've already had *way* too many espressos today."

Swindall pushed back from the table and stood up. His head was swimming from the waitress' rapid-fire chatter and the uninterrupted flow of people clogging the sidewalk only inches away in front of him. A few blocks further south he realized he better turn around and start heading back to the building on Lincoln Road. When he got there, the digital display showed it was only 1:43 p.m., still too early to show his face at the lawyer's office. He decided to go looking for a cheap t-shirt to buy so he could ditch the sweat-soaked one he was wearing. He strolled along Lincoln Road until he reached the middle of the next block, stopping at a silver metal cart shaded by a small faded beige umbrella. "You got anything cold to drink?" Swindall asked the skinny shirtless guy wearing raggedy jean shorts and flip-flops, his salt-and-pepper ponytail sticking out of the back of his New York Yankees cap.

"Is the Pope catholic?" The aging hippie turned around and opened a huge white ice chest just like the one Ted Tatum always took out on his Boston Whaler when they went bottom fishing. "I recommend a *really* cold one on a day like this. You could fry an egg on the street right now."

"Well, it's still a little early for me."

"Maybe to fry an egg, but it's *never* too early for a really cold one. Well, okay, then I guess I'll just have to drink alone." The man reached down and took out a can of Budweiser, popped the top, and took a loud sip. "Damn, that sure is cold!" The man bent down again and fished out another can. "Here, dude. You look like you definitely can use one of these right now."

"I just gotta go to a lawyer's office is all."

"Well, that usually is never a good thing. I could tell something was bothering you. So, okay, then all the more reason to have a really cold one, my friend." The man shoved the freezing can into Swindall's meaty hand. "On the house. So I'm guessing you're going to that big building on the corner down there on the next block, the one with the time and temperature, right? That place is crawling with lawyers."

Swindall nodded as he gulped down half the can and wiped his mouth with the back of his hand. They each drank another beer and made small talk as they watched the odd mix of pedestrians passing by them, good-looking girls in bikinis on their way to the beach and dozens of bearded men in long black coats and wide-brimmed hats engaged in animated conversation.

"Fucking weirdos," Swindall mumbled.

"You mean those orthodox Jews?" He handed Swindall his third can of beer.

"Exactly. Dressed in those heavy clothes on a hot fucking day like this. Those people don't belong here."

The street vendor raised his beer like he was about to make a toast, and Swindall did the same. "L'chaim!"

Swindall repeated whatever the man had said, thinking it probably was some kind of hippie guru shit. He took another big gulp of the freezing-cold beer and let out a huge belch. "So what the fuck did I just say?"

"You said 'l'chaim' which means 'to life' in Hebrew. It's the standard toast. You know, like 'cheers.'"

Swindall had to think about that one for a few moments. "So, what's the deal? You Jewish or something?"

"You got it. Mickey Kaplan," he said, lifting his can again, "guilty as charged."

Swindall suddenly felt streams of sweat ooze out of his forehead and cheeks. He should have realized the baseball cap was a giveaway. He looked down at the cart and saw it had a small red and blue banner with yellow lettering which read "Hebrew National Beef Franks." "Well, I didn't mean nothing bad about your people."

"No harm, no foul. Look, I'm not religious or anything, but I gotta ask you something now that we're drinking buddies. Would you have said the same thing if I had told you those folks were the Amish from Ohio down here on a visit to Miami Beach?"

Swindall reached for his wallet, but Mickey Kaplan grabbed his arm and squeezed it. "Next time, my friend. I said 'on the house,' remember?" He opened the ice chest and took out another can of beer. "And this one is for the road. Having to go to a lawyer's office usually is a real bummer."

Swindall sat on the edge of a broken water fountain and drank his fourth beer. When the digital display on the office building read 2:10 p.m., he walked over to the entrance, pushed through the revolving doors, checked the tenant directory, and rode the elevator to the fourth floor. He needed to take a major leak and found the men's bathroom in the middle of the hallway. He had made a really dumb-ass mistake, the mixture of all those ice-cold beers and burning midday sun now making him sway as he relieved himself at the urinal. On this day, one of the most important in his entire life, he needed a clear head to make sure he didn't get screwed. He had been so stupid for not asking Charlie Newscastle to come down here with him today! He zipped up, splashed some water on his face, and pulled out a fistful of paper towels from the wall dispenser.

"Hey, there, big guy," said a young man who entered the small bathroom which had only one urinal and one toilet. He was short and wiry with jet-black hair and was wearing a white shirt with blue pin-stripes, bright-yellow power tie, and burgundy suspenders. "I'll bet you're Aubrey. Am I right, big guy? Aaron Tannenbaum. We were starting to wonder where you were. I hope you didn't have a problem finding a parking spot."

"No, sir." Swindall began wiping his face with the wad of paper towels.

"Call me Aaron," Tannenbaum said as he entered the stall. "Hey, where's your attorney?" he asked after latching the door.

"My attorney? Oh, he couldn't make it today. He had court or something."

"Aubrey, now would be a good time to get out of here." The toilet seat dropped and made a dull thud as it hit the bowl. "If you know what I mean."

"Leave? Why? My lawyer already told me I could go ahead and sign the papers without him having to be here."

"No, Aubrey," Tannenbaum chuckled. "I meant I'm just about ready to let rip a really big one."

Swindall grabbed another handful of paper towels and pulled the door open.

"Hey, Aubrey, my office is the last one on your left."

The reception area had just enough space for a small black leather couch, two chairs, and a coffee table piled high with magazines, *People*, *U.S. News & World Report*, and *Time*. Swindall tapped the bell on the ledge in front of the frosted sliding-glass window. A few moments later the interior office door opened, and Stewart Malman stood there dressed in jean shorts, khaki t-shirt, and sandals.

"Hey, Aubrey," Malman said, extending his hand.

"Sorry, Mr. Malman, but I'm real sweaty."

"Aubrey, on a day like this we all are. And, please, call me Stewart, okay?"

He followed Malman into a small conference room where a very pretty blond lady was seated. Swindall did a double-take because she looked a lot like Sharon Stone in *Basic Instinct*, a movie he and Emily had seen a few months ago at the theater down in Cutler Ridge.

"Aubrey, this is, Karen. Karen, this is Aubrey Swindall."

"Sorry, ma'am, but I'm real sweaty."

"Oh, don't worry about that, Aubrey," she said, continuing to hold out her hand so they could shake. Swindall peeled off a couple of unused paper towels and handed them to her. "Thank you, Aubrey."

"So grab a seat, Aubrey. Is your attorney coming?"

"Naw, he said he's got court today or something." Swindall avoided looking at the Malmans and, instead, gazed aimlessly around the conference room. The beer buzz was gone, replaced by a very bad headache growing stronger by the minute. Worse than that, he knew he must be smelling pretty bad, being soaked with so much sweat and all, and having forgotten to buy a new t-shirt.

"So everybody ready to rock and roll?" Tannenbaum asked as he breezed into the conference room and sat down.

"We're ready, Aaron. Aubrey?"

Swindall nodded, reaching into his right front pocket for the envelope with the paper Emily had signed at their bank the day she left for The Panhandle.

"Alright, let's see what you've got there," Tannenbaum said as he took the paper from Swindall. "Okay, specific power-of-attorney, and your wife's signature is duly notarized." He put the paper on the table and sat back in his chair. "Aubrey, before we go forward, I want to make sure we're clear about one thing. You're here today without assistance of counsel. Now this isn't a closing or anything like that, but signing an agreement for the sale of real property still is serious business."

"Just cut the bullshit and give me my fucking payday," Swindall said to himself. His head was starting to throb now, and he needed to get the hell out of this big-mouth lawyer's office as soon as possible.

"I just want to make sure you know you have the right to have an attorney to assist you before you sign any papers."

Before he left for the trip to Miami Beach, Swindall had checked to make sure he had one of Charlie Newcastle's business cards in his wallet. "Yes, I understand. My attorney said I could call him if I have any questions while I'm here."

"Excellent," Tannenbaum nodded approvingly, "then let's get started." He passed out copies of the purchase-sale contract and went over its terms and conditions. Parties to the transaction, legal description of the property, sales price $750,000, title insurance, prorations, hazard insurance, closing costs, default provisions, seller's warranties, condition of property, $25,000 earnest money now, $50,000 more in ten days, closing date September 4. "Alright, that's about it. Everybody clear on all that stuff? First, Stewart and Karen."

"Yes, Aaron," the Malmans said at the same time.

"And now you, Aubrey."

"I do most of it, sir, but if you don't mind, I've got a couple of questions."

Tannenbaum leaned forward and folded his hands on the table. " Okay, Aubrey, shoot."

"This earnest money thing, that's more or less like a down payment, right?"

"Exactly right, Aubrey. That's what earnest money is. And under this contract there's two such payments the Malmans are required to make. One today and one in ten days, total $75,000, amounting to ten-percent of the purchase price."

"And if they decide they don't want to go through with the deal, then I get to keep that money, right?"

"That's exactly right, Aubrey. But that's not going to happen. They want your place. Am I right, Malmans? And, unlike most people who want to purchase real estate, these folks have all the cash they need to close this deal. There's no financing involved. Do you know what I'm saying, Aubrey?"

"So then my other question is why the September 4 closing date? You told me it was going to be the third week of August."

"I might have said that. To tell you the truth I really don't remember what I said before. Listen, if everything goes smoothly, we still might be able to close that week. Let me put it another way. September 4 is more like a deadline. It gives the Malmans a little extra time to make sure everything is kosher before they pay you the big bucks. As their attorney I'm obligated to protect their legal and financial interests in this transaction, just like your attorney is doing for you. Do you know what I'm saying, Aubrey?"

"A little extra time to make sure everything is what?"

"That everything is kosher." Tannenbaum glanced over at his clients with a grin. "That just means to make sure everything is in order, like the title search, insurance coverages, inspections, all that good stuff."

"This is the biggest crock of shit," Swindall said to himself. They must be trying to screw him in some way he couldn't figure out right then. "Stewart knows I've got good insurance. Hell, he already talked to my agent, Charlie Newcastle."

"Aubrey's right. I did speak with his insurance agent."

"Whoa!" Tannenbaum held up his hand and shook his head. "Stewart, you and Karen hired me to protect your legal and financial interests in this transaction. I'm very sorry, clients, but that's what I'm trying to do here today. So why don't you two let me do the talking, okay?" He turned toward Swindall. "Aubrey, the reason for the September 4 date is because shit happens, excuse my French. Look, nobody here is trying to take advantage of anybody, right?"

"Yeah, I'll bet," Swindall thought. "Okay, so where do I sign on these papers?"

"Are you sure you understand everything okay, Aubrey? Please feel free to call your attorney and ask him anything you want before you sign."

"No, that's alright. Just show me where to sign."

Tannenbaum pulled a thick silver ballpoint pen out of his shirt pocket and handed it to Swindall. "Initials go here," the lawyer said as he turned each page. "And on the bottom of this last page, you sign here, print your name, and put the date. Okay, people, I believe we're done. Let me make some photocopies of the executed contract for you."

"Aubrey, if everything goes according to plan," Malman said after Tannenbaum left the conference room, "we'll see if we can close earlier than September 4."

"I'd very much appreciate that, Stewart. Me and the wife are moving up north."

"Oh, really, Aubrey?" Karen Malman swivelled in her chair and gave him a big smile as she slowly crossed her legs. For a moment Swindall thought she might flash him like Sharon Stone did for the cops during her interrogation in *Basic Instinct*. "So where are you and your wife moving?"

"The Panhandle, ma'am. The area around Fort Walton Beach most likely."

"That's great. Some of the best beaches in the world are in The Panhandle."

"Karen's right. A few years back I was at Eglin Air Force Base for some training, and we had time to check out the area. Honey, where was it we went a few times that we liked so much?"

"Well, actually it was pretty close to Fort Walton Beach. We also liked the beaches around Panama City. Did you know, Aubrey, that in some areas of The Panhandle the pure white sand is made up of finely-ground quartz crystals which washed down from the Appalachian Mountains thousands of years ago? Anyway," Karen Malman continued, her smile turning into a guilty grin, "we made a couple of trips to the St. Vincent Wildlife Refuge, but I don't know if Stewart really wants me to talk about that."

"Oh, I don't care. In fact, I'll tell Aubrey myself. Have you ever been there? It's a barrier island about twenty-two miles southwest of Apalachicola. You can only get there by boat. Twelve-thousand acres of lakes and marshes and pines. Bald eagles, sea turtles, even red wolves. But for some people I happen to know," Malman looked slyly over at his wife, "those things really aren't the main attraction. Because it's so isolated, some visitors like to bathe out there in their birthday suits."

"Which happens to include you, Mr. Nude Eco-tourist."

"Guilty as charged." Stewart Malman held up his hands. "Anyway, Aubrey, it's very beautiful in The Panhandle but probably a little too quiet for us."

"That's the whole fucking idea," Swindall said to himself. His head *really* was throbbing now from all this chatter.

"Okay, people, here's your copies." Tannenbaum handed them manilla envelopes. "It was very nice meeting you, Aubrey. Stewart and Karen, you can stay as long as you like, use the phone, whatever. Just make sure the front door is locked when you leave."

"Thanks, Aaron, but we're going to have to scoot too," Karen Malman said. "He doesn't know it yet," she jabbed an elbow into her husband's side, "but Mr. Hey-Big-Spender here is taking me to Bal Harbour for some therapeutic shopping."

"I am?" Malman looked over at Swindall and winced like he was in pain.

"Oh, isn't that *real* cute," Swindall thought, his head pounding like someone was driving a nail into his skull. "This rich New Yorker, with his trophy wife, going shopping at some fancy place Swindall had never even heard about. Could you all just stop yapping for awhile and pay up quick so I can get the hell outta fucking Dodge?!"

Swindall hoisted himself up from the conference table. "You all take care." He was praying they wouldn't walk with him down the hallway. Swindall pressed the down button, and the elevator doors snapped open. He was relieved to see the Malmans were still talking to their lawyer next to the front door of his office.

"Hey, Aubrey!" Tannenbaum called out just as Swindall stepped forward. "I forgot to ask you. Whatever happened with your cousin?"

"What the *hell* is this asshole lawyer yapping about now?" he cursed under his breath, holding the elevator doors open. "What, Mr. Tannenbaum?"

"Your cousin from up north with the criminal case. You asked me about the law of conspiracy awhile back."

"Oh, yeah. Well, everything is okay. Thanks for asking."

"My pleasure, Aubrey."

"Such bullshit!" Swindall blurted out after the elevator had started to descend.

Guardians Of The Faith

Swindall started feeling better after he was on the MacArthur Causeway heading back to Miami. He glanced over at the big manilla envelope sitting on the passenger seat and reached out to touch it to make sure it really was there. To his right, across the sparkling turquoise waters, stood the mansions of Star and Palm Islands. He tossed the manilla envelope on the floor, rolled the windows down all the way, and drew in a deep breath. He closed his eyes for an instant, picturing the nice house he'd get up north. It wouldn't be a big mansion, but his place would be better, situated on an isolated beach in The Panhandle, where the sand wasn't sand but finely-ground quartz crystals washed down from the Appalachian Mountains hundreds of miles away. Man, how cool was that?! The wind was whipping sharply through the cab, and Swindall pretended his pick-up was an open fisherman, cutting through the waters off Fort Walton Beach like a steak knife on hot butter. But when he noticed the sign for the exit to I-95 south, his bright mood suddenly turned dark as he started thinking about the bad situation there was at the other end of Dade County.

CHAPTER SIXTEEN

"Hey, babe," Emily said softly. "You up yet?"

"Yeah, honey." The blazing early-morning sun was filtering through the thin white curtains, and Swindall grabbed a pillow to cover his eyes.

"I know it's pretty early, Brey, but I wanted to talk to you." She waited a few seconds and then squealed with delight. "Kaye just had the baby. It's a boy! Nine pounds seven ounces. I'm calling you from over here at the hospital."

"Well, Cecil must be happy as shit since he's already got the two girls." It felt like he had a piece of sandpaper in his mouth, rubbing against his throat with each word he said. He was dehydrated from the six-pack he never should have drunk so late last night. "Put that cracker on so I can talk to him."

"Well, Cecil's not here right now. We didn't think this would happen for a few more days, but then Kaye's water broke around midnight. Cecil went over to Pensacola yesterday afternoon to meet with some big-shot developers. You know Cecil, wheeling and dealing at all hours. So we had to call a taxi to bring us over here to the hospital. Kaye was in labor the whole night."

"So is everything okay then?"

"Everything is great. The baby is *so* beautiful, Brey. They've got this machine they hooked Kaye up to as soon as we got here. You can watch the baby's heartbeat and everything. They tell you if there's a certain number of beats per minute, then it's probably a boy. Baby-boy heartbeats are slower than little-girl heartbeats. Me and Kaye watched that darn machine all night like a couple of hawks, and it turned out it was right, Brey!"

"Well, you give Kaye my love."

"I sure will. So, babe, how are you doing? You sound tired."

"I already signed the papers to sell the place."

"For real, Brey? Oh, that is *so great*! You know, I've been telling Cecil he's not the only wheeler-dealer in Florida."

"Well, I guess you'd be right about that then."

"Do you think we're really gonna move up here? Kaye and Cecil want us to so much. Everything is new and clean and cheap. And Cecil keeps saying if you don't get up here pretty soon, he's gonna be too big for you to get into business with him."

"Well, you tell that crazy cracker he'll just have to wait a few more weeks. Tell him if he don't, next time I see him I'm gonna kick his ass all the way back to Alabama."

"A few more weeks, Brey? Well, if it's gonna take that long, then I'm coming back home."

"No, babe, that don't make no sense, not for just a few more weeks. You stay up there and keep helping your sister out. And you can go ahead and start looking for a place for us to buy, but it's gotta be on the water. And it's gotta be real big too, not like this stupid dollhouse we've been living in all these years."

"Oh, I wish you'd stop saying that about our nice little house. I've always been very happy there with you, Brey. Now, are you sure you don't want me to come back and help you out? What about packing up all our things?"

"Naw, babe. I'm gonna rent one of those U-Hauls. And I'll get one of those real estate agents to sell the house, and that money will just be icing on the cake with what we're making on Skeeter's."

"Oh, Brey," Emily sighed. "All this is happening so fast."

"Don't worry about anything, honey." He needed to get off

the phone so he could go look for some aspirin. "It's all good," he lied as he pushed up from the bed.

* * *

"You have a new girlfriend, *jefe*?" Cuqui Perez asked over the intercom.

"What is it *now*?"

"You know, you're becoming a real *viejo* way too soon."

"Sorry, Moneypenny. I've got a lot going on."

"So does everybody. There's a lady on line three with a very sexy voice, and it's not your *negrita*."

"Vicky Vale, ace lady reporter here in Gotham City. I hope I sound like a lady."

"You *really* don't have to worry about that one."

"Well, that's a relief. So, Batman, I hear you've been doing the prosecutor thing for awhile, but I've never run into you before."

"Maybe that's because I'm not a high-profile kind of guy."

"Do you want to be a high-profile kind of guy? A not-so-little bird told me you've got a big case for me to scoop."

"That might be true, but there's timing issues."

"You should know by now your colleagues try and get me into the mix early on. They know I put together a nice package."

"Well, I checked mine out while I was taking a shower this morning, and I'm still pretty much okay with it."

"That's very funny, *Liftoff* Lifton. Yes, I remember you. I'm not as young as I look. I used to love watching you play way back when. You know, good basketball is like good ballet. Actually, it can be a lot better if you're sitting close to the court. Then it's good ballet with that funky men's locker-room smell." When Lifton didn't say anything, she added, "What's the matter, Liftoff? Cat got your tongue?"

"Look," he said, clearing his throat, "when the time is right, I won't have a problem speaking with you."

"How do you know the right time isn't now?"

"Because things haven't happened yet."

"Maybe that's the best reason you should talk to me now."

"I don't think so."

"You don't want to know right now what I already know?"

"Not really. It's just going to piss me off at whoever told you about the case, that not-so-little bird you mentioned."

"I never reveal my sources. And before you hang up on me, are you *really* sure you don't want to know right now what I already know?"

"You just asked me that. But stay on the line, and we'll get your information so we can send out the prize you won as our tenth caller this morning."

"Well, it's your show, Liftoff. Nice speaking with you."

He pushed the hold button off-center, and it popped off. "Moneypenny, can you get this lady's contact information, please?" Chernin probably was the tipster, but it could be No-Time or Seven or Perishable or even Doc Leeds because they all were not-so-little big-ass birds too.

* * *

"Hey, Kim?" Lifton said as he breezed into the kitchen and found his sister sitting at the table hunched over some papers. "What's that?"

"Job application," she mumbled.

"Job application? Who's getting a job?"

"Why would I be filling out a job application for somebody else? Dumb question."

"You don't need to work. You already have a job taking care of your daughter."

Kimberly set the pen on the table and looked up at him. "You know what? I *really* need to move on. Demeka *really* needs to move on. I can't do what I need to do on a couple of hundred dollars a month child support, okay?"

"What the hell are you talking about?"

"I'll tell you what the hell I'm talking about, Ray. There's not going to be any miracle cure for Demeka, okay? That whole ridiculous mind trip we were on for awhile was bullshit. It's over."

"You don't know it's over."

"Oh, really? Well, then why don't you talk to the people in Gainesville like I did the other day?

"You didn't tell me anything."

She looked down and turned one of the pages of the job application. "Whatever."

"No, tell me. I want to know what happened."

"What happened is nothing happened. I called Dr. Feingold to see if there was any news. He was surprised I was calling, like news about what? The *'team,'*" Kimberly made the quotation-marks sign, "assumed I already had put Demeka in one of those special schools, you know, doing whatever kids like her are supposed to do in places like that."

"What the hell does that mean?"

"Just like it said in that report. Physical, occupational, and speech therapy. You don't remember what it said? The longer you wait, the less chance for improvement. I already waited too long expecting a miracle which never came. God only knows how much more damage I've caused by being such an idiot."

Lifton went over to the table and bent down. "Don't talk like that, Kim," he said, stroking the side of her cheek with the back of his hand as she wept. "You don't have to worry about anything, Kim. I'll keep taking care of everything for you and Demeka."

"That's the problem," she said, picking up the pen. "A problem I've got to fix *now*. I don't like being a charity case. I *refuse* to be a charity case anymore. And I *refuse* to have my child be a charity case. I'm getting a job, and I'm putting Demeka in a special school like I'm supposed to do."

"You need to finish college."

"*Yeah, right.* What I really need to finish is this Publix job application. I've made a lot of friends over there during our weekly shopping-trip adventures. They all love Demeka, including the manager. I went to see him this morning. He said I can have a job right now if I want. I can start off as a cashier. It's a great company, and it has great benefits. And there's an apartment building just a block away. I've already got a place lined up there starting next month."

"That old rundown building on Northeast Second Court? Are you *crazy*? You're not going to live there, Kim, not in that place, *no way*. It's a real rat trap. And the John Does run a drug hole right across the street. You know, the 'weed, base, and blow,' John Does?"

"*Really*? So why don't you or the feds go over there and bust them? Then I'll have a real nice safe place to live."

"You're *not* moving there, Kim. Your home is here with me. Maybe you could work part-time, but you need to finish college. I told you, I'll keep taking care of everything for you and Demeka."

She narrowed her eyes and shook her head. "Are you a broken record? You keep saying the same damn thing over and over again. From now on *I'm* taking care of everything for me and Demeka like I should have been doing before I ever moved in here. I'm working *wherever* I want, living *wherever* I want, and going to college *if I want to*, not because *you* tell me I have to." She grabbed the pen and job application, pushed back in the chair, and stood up. "I'm *tired* of your welfare program, Ray," she added and stormed out of the kitchen.

* * *

Joel Chernin stepped out of the elevator on the third-floor of the Metro Justice Building and spied Lifton to his right sitting on one of the dark-brown benches opposite the door to the grand jury room. He was leaning back with his head against the wall like he had dozed off. "Hey, general," Chernin said too loudly as he set his black satchel on the bench. "How's it hanging?"

"Thanks for being on time."

"You're kidding me, right? It's only 1:45. They're not gonna be ready for us for awhile. They have to take care of all their preliminary bullshit."

"It's been years since I've gone to a grand jury to charge a case. Well, at least there's a bunch of people in there doing something. So where's Medina?"

"Relax, general. Andy's on his way up."

A few minutes later Andy Medina stepped out of the elevator pulling a two-wheeler loaded with a bankers box. "It's a new grand jury, right?" He unhooked the bungee cord and slid the box off the cart. "So we're gonna be here awhile unless everybody decided to show up on American time instead of Cuban time. Anybody want some coffee?"

"I counted nineteen who got here before 1:30."

"It's a miracle! How many do we need so we can do our thing today?"

"Minimum is fifteen, maximum is twenty-one. So we should be good to go."

The muffled voices inside the grand jury room suddenly got much louder, and a few moments later the door opened. A silver-haired lady stepped out and closed the door.

"Mr. Lifton? My name is Helen Middlebrooks. I'm the one from the Clerk's Office who usually takes care of the new grand juries." She looked down at her clipboard. "We have enough people to empanel a new grand jury if they qualified. However, when I started going through the preliminary questions, it turns out some of these folks can't serve as grand jurors."

"Aren't the qualifications the same as for trial jurors?"

"You are correct, Mr. Lifton, but therein lies the problem. Convicted felons can't sit on any jury, and we've got three in there. Two state convictions and one federal."

"Why am I not surprised? And I'll bet they're all for drug crimes, right?"

The clerk looked over at Chernin and nodded.

"*Ay, mi madre,*" Medina said.

"That still leaves sixteen people. We only need fifteen."

"You are correct again, Mr. Lifton. However, any full-time federal, state, or local law enforcement officer *must* be excused unless he or she chooses to serve, and I've got a full-time DEA agent in there who won't agree to sit on this grand jury. He says he's got too much going on with the cocaine cowboys these days."

"That brings us down to fifteen which..."

"Which would be the minimum, Mr. Lifton, but there's another problem. It turns out two of these individuals are not U.S. citizens. That's the first question on the list."

"Why am I not surprised?" Chernin smacked his gum and rolled his head around.

"*Ay, mi madre,*" Medina said again, picked up the bankers box, set it back down on the two-wheeler, and reattached the bungee cord.

"I'm really sorry about this, Mr. Lifton," she said with a very embarrassed look. "We summon forty-five people, and generally about half show up. But it's the summer, and a lot of people are on vacation. Unfortunately, we still get the names of prospective jurors from the Department of Highway Safety and Motor Vehicles. I don't know if you heard, but the legislature passed a new law. Starting in January of next year the DMV has to start purging the names of drivers who are not U.S. citizens. Unfortunately, that whole process doesn't have to be completed until 1998 so it's still going to be something like six more years before we get jury lists with U.S. citizens only. Again, I'm really very sorry about this, Mr. Lifton, especially because our office screwed up on the original report date, and you've already lost a week."

"Do you need me here anymore?" Medina asked. "I've got something going on in the Gables this afternoon."

"No, you can take off, Andy. JC will be in touch with you."

"What I can do, Mr. Lifton, is make sure the ones who qualified today will be here for the next date. And then I'll try and track down the people who didn't show up today and read them the riot act. I'll mention they can be arrested for failing to respond to the summons. That usually gets their attention."

"We're talking about next Friday, right?"

"No, Mr. Lifton, that would be two weeks from today which is August 21. We have to give them at least ten-days notice."

"Why? The people who didn't show up already got notice to report today."

"Well, the thing is, Mr. Lifton, there's an administrative order which states any grand jury summons must provide at least ten-days notice to appear. I have to send out a new summons to everybody with the next report date even to the folks who qualified today. Three days are added for service of a summons by mail. That's why August 21 is the earliest lawful date even if I mailed out the new notices today. Once we've empaneled our grand jury, it's a whole new ball game. We put them on a schedule to meet every Friday unless there's a holiday or something like that."

"This is not good. I need you to make an exception. I need a grand jury next week."

"Well, I guess if the Chief Judge said it's okay, I could tell the people who qualified today, and the no-shows I reach by phone, they all have to be here next Friday."

"I'll go with you to present the request to the Chief Judge."

"I'd have you do that, Mr. Lifton, except Judge Furman is on vacation, a cruise in Alaska or some faraway place like that."

Lifton looked over at Chernin and rolled his eyes. "But there should be another judge standing in for him, right?"

"Yes, Mr. Lifton, that is correct. We do have an alternate judge to handle emergencies while Judge Furman is away."

"Helen, I need a grand jury next week. I'll go with you to see the alternate judge."

"That would be Judge Arthur Sobel. Unfortunately, it being Friday and all, he's probably already heading down to the Keys. That Judge Sobel *loves* to go fishing on the weekends. He's got a house on a canal in Islamorada, and he takes off early on Fridays. It's kind of a joke around here, but then you've got a bunch of judges who are golfers and do the same darn thing. Anyway, I was trying to reach the Judge just before noon on another matter and no luck. His judicial assistant didn't know where he was either. Maybe he just went out for an early lunch. I'll call chambers again as soon as I get back to my desk."

"Okay, Helen, let me know as soon as possible. Please."

"I will, Mr. Lifton," she said, smiling and nodding her head. "And I'll go ahead and tell those folks who qualified today that they have to be available next Friday." The clerk turned and went back inside the grand jury room.

"This case is jinxed," Chernin said as he kept pushing the elevator button.

"I thought we've been having some good luck. You know, like your Guardian friends asking *you* to kill Sanderson *and* getting it all on tape."

"That's not what I'm talking about." The elevator doors opened, and they stepped inside. "What I'm saying, boss, is I've got this feeling there's something out there in the cosmos that doesn't want this case to happen. This case is jinxed."

Cuqui Perez looked up as Lifton passed by her desk without saying anything. "What happened?" she asked Chernin. "No grand jury?"

"No grand jury," Chernin answered. "And your *jefe* is really pissed off."

"It's his latest thing," she said and returned to filing her nails.

Chernin went over to the window in Lifton's office and looked out. "So Plan B isn't looking so bad anymore, is it, chief?"

"Right now I'm not changing anything we're doing, okay?"

The detective turned and folded his arms. "Listen, boss, I didn't want to burst your bubble because I thought you were getting your precious little indictment today. But now that you're not, you need to know something. I haven't tried to get any more evidence on these fuckers because you got me all paranoid the other day about messing up the case and that early withdrawal thing. But I stopped by Skeeter's last night because I was starting to get very nervous about the situation. And I've gotta tell you, Swindall is really pissed about me not taking care of business yet. And he tells me they're gonna do this thing with or without me."

"I thought you had the situation under control. So what are you saying now?"

"What I'm saying now is me and Andy need to go out there and arrest these fuckers on an A-form."

"We're not doing that. You'll just have to find a way to keep them on a string for a few more days. Do whatever it takes except, of course, killing Sanderson."

"Of course." Chernin turned back to the window and looked out again. After a few moments, he said, "You know what, Lifton? Besides this case being jinxed, sometimes I think you really don't want it to happen."

"Do me a favor, will you, Chernin? Lose the editorials and just do your job, okay?"

"No problem, *mon capitaine*. But while you're here pissing in the wind for the next two weeks, I might as well go ahead and try and get some more evidence so we can make this case a lock."

"It's not two weeks. You heard what the lady said."

"*Yeah, right.* Good luck on another Friday in August." Chernin grabbed his satchel and started for the door. "So do I have a green light to get some more evidence or what?"

Lifton tore a sheet from his yellow legal pad and wadded it up. "That depends on whether I make this shot." Lifton closed one eye and launched the paper ball toward the mini basketball hoop hanging on the back of his office door.

"I'll take that as a yes anyway." Chernin picked up the paper ball which had fallen far short of its intended target and tossed it back to Lifton.

"Hey, JC!" Lifton called after the detective. "Please don't do anything crazy, okay?"

* * *

Valerie Witherspoon rolled over and sat on the edge of the bed. "Can you believe it's already seven something?" She reached down and picked up her wire-mesh bra.

"I knew you would change the subject." Lifton was on his back staring at the fan blades rotating slowly above him. "I'm really sorry, Val-er-ie."

"You've already said that enough." She hooked the bra, stood up, and twisted a few times. "A lot worse things could happen, you know."

"Really? I can't think of that many right now. I never should have started talking about the damn case last night."

"Don't tell me you had a bad dream about it too."

"No, but I'm having a nightmare right now."

"Oh, please, Ray," she yawned and shook her head. "You best forget about it."

"I can't. Last night *and* this morning? And you *and* hot-pink Victoria's Secret? I should be attacking you right now." He sat up, raised his hands, and whipped them back and forth like he was performing martial arts.

She giggled, got back into bed, and slid over next to him. "My, my," she said softly, pressing a thumb against his upper lip. "So what do you want me to tell you?"

"That I'm a bull of a man, of course."

"Of course. Okay, you're a bull of a man, Liftoff Lifton. No, you're a *big* bull," she added, her voice growing louder. "No, you're a *really* big bull!"

"Now that's more like it. What else?"

"What else?" she asked, propping herself on her elbows.

"Who's your daddy?"

"Oh, okay," she laughed. "You are, Liftoff Lifton. You're my daddy." She reached over, groped between his legs, and began massaging slowly. "So tell me, my really big bull daddy, is this gonna do the trick?" After a couple of minutes she released him and sat up. "Well, people, I have an announcement. I'm sorry to inform you all efforts to resuscitate the patient were unsuccessful."

"Damn, girl, you really know how to hurt a guy."

"Oh, *please*, Ray, will you just forget about it?" She turned, pushed off the bed, and started walking toward the bathroom. "There's always a first time for everything. Just try and make sure this doesn't happen too much *after* we're married. Oh, don't freak, baby," she added, when she looked back and noticed his startled expression. "A girl still can hope, can't she?"

CHAPTER SEVENTEEN

As he drove to Metro Justice Rayfield Lifton kept thinking about the latest fiasco. Yesterday afternoon Valerie had called to complain too many days had passed since they last were together, and so she invited him over to stay the night. After he got there he foolishly started venting his frustrations about the delays in getting a grand jury to return an indictment. Earlier in the day Helen Middlebrooks had stopped by his office to let him know she had good news and bad news. The good news was Judge Sobel had authorized her to call jurors and require them to report for duty this Friday. The bad news was out of the six August 7 no-shows she was able to contact, three didn't speak fluent English, two had state felony convictions, and one was a Metro-Dade police officer who exercised her right to decline jury service. "That means we'd still be short two grand jurors for this Friday so I went ahead and mailed out a notice to everybody for August twenty-one."

"Friday next week? I need a grand jury this week. And what if the people who show up the next time don't qualify? Then we're looking at a September date because of that ten-day notice thing."

"Well, I really don't think that's going to happen, Mr. Lifton. In addition to the thirteen people who already qualified last Friday, we've got a pretty big group coming in on the twenty-first so I'm sure we'll be swearing in a new grand jury then."

"From what I've seen so far the odds aren't that great."

"I certainly can appreciate your skepticism, Mr. Lifton, but you'll have your grand jury at the end of next week."

"Why am I not surprised?" Chernin said after Lifton had given him the bad news. "I told you this case is jinxed."

"So what else have you been doing out there?"

"I haven't done shit. I set up a meeting with Swindall at the undercover marina where me and Andy were going to try and get some audio and video, but then I cancelled at the last minute. You've still got me all paranoid about screwing up the case if I did anything else. But now you're telling me the end of next week to get the indictment. That's a long time. And I don't think my latest bullshit excuses are going over very well. So right now I'm starting to feel just as nervous about not doing something as doing something, if you know what I mean."

"I don't, JC, but it wouldn't be the first time. So just go ahead and do whatever you gotta do."

"Well, thanks for the vote of confidence, general, but I really don't know what the hell I'm gonna do."

Instead of going straight to Metro Justice Lifton had decided to stop by the house to see how his sister and Demeka were doing. Kimberly was still giving him the silent treatment. When she did speak with him, it usually was just a couple of words. She had signed a month-to-month lease for a one-bedroom apartment in the building down the street from a John Does drug hole and was planning to move there with Demeka next month. The manager from Publix had called the other day confirming she had been hired, and in two weeks she had an appointment in West Palm Beach at a school for special children to see about enrolling Demeka for the next term. Publix had agreed to a schedule where she didn't have to work most weekends. In a few months she was going to ask for a transfer to a store near Demeka's school, and then she would move to West Palm Beach so her daughter could live with her instead of in a dormitory. As he pulled up in front of his house

Lifton noticed his sister's faded-orange Gremlin in the driveway and next door Old Lady Muir on her porch rocking away and fanning herself, Mr. T sitting obediently at her side.

"And how are we doing today, Mrs. Muir?" Snoopy turned her head away and began fanning herself faster. "Have a nice day, Mrs. Muir." He checked to make sure Mr. T's chain was securely tied to the rocker, then lunged forward, provoking a fit of savage barking from the mongrel.

"Oh, hush up, Mr. T! Rayfield Lifton, why are you staying out all hours of the night? And why aren't you at work?"

"Why should I be at work?" he said as he unlocked the front door. "I've got a government job."

"He sure got a smart mouth on him, don't he, Mr. T?"

He expected to find his sister and niece there, but the house was deserted. On the kitchen table under the salt and pepper shakers, he found a note: "Ray, Demeka is with Valerie. Today I start my training at Publix and walked over there (to save gas money). Stop by and get in my line. Please? Kim. P.S. I love you!"

* * *

Joel Chernin entered the steel shed and looked up at the loft. "Hey, Andy! You ready for the next episode of *Candid Camera*?"

Detective Antelmo Medina craned his neck over the wood rail. "All set, Mr. Allen Funt. Just make sure I get a good view of you and your homeboys before you invite any of them into your truck. And let's do another sound check before Burl Ives and Three Dog Night get here."

Medina had set up a video camera on a tripod next to one of the peepholes in the loft. He also had taped a tiny transmitter to the bottom of the steering column of Chernin's pick-up. A cassette player in the loft would record anything said inside the truck.

Chernin went back outside and climbed into his truck. "Testing, testing, one, two! Hey, Andy, do you read me?!"

"Yeah, I read you," Medina called out through the peephole. "If it was just you, JC, I wouldn't need the fucking transmitter."

Chernin jerked his head to the side a couple of times to

indicate somebody was coming. Kenny Moser's pick-up crunched gravel and kicked up a thick cloud of dust as it made a wide turn into the lot next to the big steel shed. Swindall, Wendt, and Moser got out and walked over to where Chernin was standing.

"Hey, boys, how's it hanging?"

"It's hanging," Swindall said as he looked around. "Anybody else here?"

"The guy I work with is inside there."

"I don't wanna talk with nobody around."

"Well, you know what, Skeeter? I don't either so jump inside my truck."

"We gotta make damn sure this thing don't get fucked up," Swindall said as he pulled the passenger door shut.

"You are *such* a fucking pussy. Don't worry about nothing. Here, have a nice brewski." Chernin lifted the top off the small styrofoam cooler between him and Swindall and pulled out two cans of Budweiser. "They're *really* fucking cold, bro."

Swindall popped the top of his can, took a long swig, and wiped his mouth with the back of his hand. "We gotta make damn sure this thing don't get fucked up."

"Are you like fucking deaf or something? I just said don't worry about nothing. Only thing's gonna get fucked up is the nigger." Chernin gulped down half his beer and burped loudly. "I've already got all the shit I need to take care of business." He tilted his head toward the bed of the truck. "Turn around and see for yourself."

* * *

Cuqui Perez squeezed the top of the styrofoam container to form a spout, then carefully dispensed the *café cubano* into the plastic thimble and handed it to her boss. "Did you see the memo I left on your desk? And don't ask me what it says. You already know I stopped reading them years ago."

"But what if it's something important like I got appointed Dade State Attorney?"

"*Yeah, right.* Do you ever read the memos?"

"No, but I use them to make paper basketballs."

"I rest my case. The Big Girl called while you were out. It was long-distance. She'll call back."

"*She'll call back,*" he said with his Terminator imitation. He took the sheet of paper Cuqui had left on his desk, wadded it up, closed one eye, and launched it toward the mini basketball hoop.

"I'll get it." She slowly lowered her heavy frame so she could pick up the paper ball, which had bounced off the wall to the left of the hoop, and tossed it back to him. "I'm better than you."

"Better than me at what?"

"At basketball. What else am I talking about? When you're gone, sometimes I come in here and practice." She bent her knees slightly, put her hands together, and flicked her wrists like she was shooting a free-throw.

"You do what? Since when?"

"Since for a long time. It gets *very* boring around here. You should know, *jefe.*"

"Well, I'm sure our taxpayers would be delighted to hear how you spend your time around here." She shrugged and flicked her wrists again like she was shooting another free-throw. "Okay, Moneypenny, let's see what you've got." Lifton tossed the paper ball back to her, and she caught it with both hands. "But you're too close to make this fair."

She took a few steps back, bent her knees slightly, then rose and took her shot. "You see?" she said with a laugh, followed by a bout of raspy coughing, after the paper ball landed squarely in the net.

"Lucky shot, Moneypenny. And I'll bet you're the one who stole my nerf ball."

"I didn't steal your nerf ball. I always put it back in your desk. Maybe it was the *viejo* Vernon."

"He shoots hoops here too? Hey," he called after her, "I need to talk to Chernin."

A few minutes later the intercom buzzed loudly with its shrill, annoying game-show sound. "Helen somebody is calling you on line four."

"Mr. Lifton? This is Helen Middlebrooks from the Clerk's Office. It seems like every time we speak all I have for you is bad news. Judge Sobel decided to shut down the building tomorrow starting at noon."

"What? Shut down the building?"

"Yes, Mr. Lifton, starting tomorrow at noon. Everybody in your office should have gotten the memo by now."

"Hold on, Helen." Lifton went over to the mini basketball hoop, retrieved the paper ball, and went back to his desk. He straightened out the sheet and began reading. Judge Arthur Sobel had ordered all Dade County court buildings closed starting at noon tomorrow because The National Weather Service had issued a hurricane watch for Florida's southeast coast from Jupiter Inlet to the Upper Keys. "All Dade County court buildings shall reopen August 24 unless this order is extended. Please check local media for any further announcements." "Alright, Helen, I just read it."

"Mr. Lifton, the fact the court buildings are closing tomorrow at noon is going to be all over the news. The last notices I sent out told everybody to be here tomorrow at 1:30 p.m. So what I'm saying is nobody is going to show up tomorrow to report for grand jury duty."

The intercom buzzed again. "Give me a second, Helen." Lifton carefully pressed down on the hold button and then the intercom button. "Now what?"

"The *judio loco* is on line two."

"I'm sorry, Helen, but I have to take another call."

"No, I'm the one who's sorry, Mr. Lifton. I really shouldn't be doing this because it violates the administrative order but, just so you know, I'm sending out new summonses for August 28. That's fewer than ten days notice, but I really want you to get your grand jury as soon as possible. And, personally, I think closing the building early tomorrow is pretty darn silly. We haven't had a bad storm here since I can remember."

"Hey, good news, general. I met up with Skeeter and his

boys out here at the marina a little while ago, and we got some really good shit on audio and video."

"Well, JC, I've got some bad news. All court buildings are closing tomorrow at noon because there's a hurricane watch so we're not getting our indictment for another week."

"Well, strike three for the indictment. Anyway, here's the deal. These dudes believe we're gonna take some kind of a hit from that storm so they gave me my final marching orders a little while ago."

"And what the hell does that mean?"

"It means they see a big opportunity here. If we get this hurricane, they think I can take care of business and cover up my tracks real easy. And Swindall says if I don't take advantage of the situation, then for sure he and his people will."

Lifton sat up in his chair and tried to push back. "You know, it really hurts me to say this, Chernin, but I'm going to have to start agreeing with you."

"With everything I say and do?"

"No, JC, not with everything. People would question my mental competency if I did. But, number one, you're right about this case being jinxed. And number two, it's time to go to Plan B."

"Well, alright, praise God and hallelujah! Listen, boss man, I know how really paranoid you are about me screwing things up. But I've got a way to wrap things up real quick that will make this case a lock."

"Why does the sound of that worry me?"

"Listen, general, you just chill and let me get this thing done my way, okay?"

* * *

Aubrey Swindall tapped his right foot faster with each unanswered ring. After five of them his left knee buckled, and he lost his sweaty grip on the payphone receiver, pulling it back up by its metal-encased cord like it was a yo-yo fishing line.

"Aaron Tannenbaum," the boyish voice finally answered after three more rings.

Guardians Of The Faith

"Hey, Mr. Tannenbaum, this is Aubrey Swindall."

"Aubrey, the South Dade guy! You're supposed to call me Aaron, remember? So what can I do you for today, Aubrey?"

The lawyer's question was all wrong. He should have known *exactly* why he was calling. "Well, sir," Swindall bit his lower lip, "I was just checking in again to make sure I had the correct time for the closing tomorrow. It's at two, right?"

"What? Stewart Malman didn't call you? I told him to go ahead and call you himself because I was going to be tied up in a closing today. Are you sure he didn't try and call you? Maybe you don't have an answering machine. Stewart's such a responsible guy. Anyway, it's cancelled. The closing tomorrow is cancelled."

"What?! How can you cancel my closing?"

"Whoa, hold on to your horses there, pardner. I didn't cancel your closing, my friend, the Malmans did. I was ready to rock and roll tomorrow. Inspections and title work *done*. Closing statement, warranty deed, and all other paperwork *done*. And Stewart and Karen flew down here today with a check for the cash to close. Everything was good to go. Personally, I don't see why anybody would get all bent out of shape about these weather reports. I mean we haven't had a major hurricane here in years. According to the news yesterday they said this thing was history so for me it's been business as usual. I just did a closing in Key Biscayne. But Stewart said Karen got real jumpy when she heard about Andrew or whatever name they gave the storm. You see right there? It's the end of August, and we're just getting the first-named storm even though hurricane season started three months ago. I mean, come on, folks, more than half the hurricane season is over, and they're just naming our first storm? But Stewart said Karen got spooked and wanted to get the hell outta Dodge. Who knows? Maybe she's the one who wears the pants in that family. You wouldn't think so, Stewart being a military type of guy, right? You know, I really can't tell, but I can tell you this, Aubrey..."

"So Stewart's wife cancelled the closing?" Swindall had to cut off this loud-mouth lawyer because his head was about to explode from all his rambling. "Can she just do that without my permission after we signed the papers?"

"Well, unfortunately, Aubrey, yes, she can. She's one of the buyers. But, listen, Aubrey, remember, we're only talking about cancelling the closing tomorrow not the contract for the Malmans to buy your property. If you take a look at the purchase-sale agreement, it says right there in black and white the buyers have until September 4 to close. Remember when you were at my office, and I told you the September 4 date was like a deadline for the closing? Remember? And then when we last spoke I told you the Malmans were trying to do you a favor by scheduling the closing for an earlier date. Remember?"

Swindall let the receiver dangle from its metal cord and covered his face with his sweaty hands. He felt like he was going to start sobbing like a little kid. He could hear Tannenbaum's muffled voice keep asking if he was still there.

"I'm still here, and I've gotta tell you something. I am *not* a happy camper, Aaron."

"Yippie! You finally called me Aaron!"

If he had been within reach, Swindall would have grabbed this little fucker by his suspenders and then started wringing his neck. "I've gotta talk to Stewart right now."

"Sorry, but you're outta luck, big guy. By now the Malmans already are on a flight back to New York or at the airport waiting to get on one."

After the lawyer hung up, Swindall slammed the receiver against the cradle three times. "*No, no, no!*" he sobbed, pounding the wall with his left hand. "I was supposed to get my money tomorrow! *I was the one* who was supposed to get the hell outta Dodge! He snorted loudly and wiped his eyes and nose with the back of his hand. He shuffled over to the bar, pulled a Budweiser longneck out of the cooler, and gulped it down in a few seconds. He dropped the empty bottle into one of the trash barrels and burped loudly. He reached into the cooler, took out another bottle, and twisted off the cap. This one foamed up, a good part of it spilling on the concrete floor, so he put his mouth over the top as he headed to the back door.

Stepping out into the rear parking lot, Swindall noticed there wasn't a single cloud in sight, only a clear baby-blue sky and a pink-grapefruit fireball sun setting in the west. He looked down and realized he had spilled some beer on those real nice Timberland boots Emily had given him last Christmas. "Son of a bitch!" Aubrey Swindall squinted and looked at his watch, another gift from his wife who got the big employee discount on all K-Mart merchandise. He couldn't remember whether Emily already had told her boss she was quitting. They probably would let her come back anyway because she had been working there for so many years and always had been such a good employee. If things turned out bad, Emily was going to need that job at K-Mart, or maybe she'd just stay up there in The Panhandle with Kaye and Cecil. Swindall looked at his watch again and went around to the front of the building. It already was redneck happy hour, but the parking lot was still empty except for his own truck. It being the hottest part of the year and all the regulars should have been there looking to drink a few cold ones or at least to grab a couple of six-packs for take out. Swindall stepped up on the wooden porch and peered inside even though he knew nobody was in there. On that final stretch of US 1 at the far-south limit of Florida City there never had been any walk-in business.

"Where the hell is everybody?" He stepped off the porch and walked over to the edge of the road, shuddering as a cool breeze blowing across US 1 wrapped around him like he had just walked into an air-conditioned room. What was it they said about the weather before a hurricane? That a day or two before it hit you were going to have the best weather you could ever hope for that time of year. Maybe everybody was out doing something they hadn't done in years, or maybe never, buying hurricane supplies. As he entered the front door of his place, Aubrey Swindall decided he needed to sit down with a couple more beers and do some hard thinking before it was too late.

* * *

"Go home, Moneypenny," Lifton instructed his secretary. "It's late. You should have left at noon like everybody else. *Adios.*"

"You want to shoot some baskets before I leave? We could make a bet."

"Not with paper balls. You still owe me a nerf ball."

"I told you I didn't take your stupid nerf ball. But maybe I'll buy you a new one anyway when I go to the store later."

"You're buying hurricane supplies?"

"Are you kidding? Total waste of money." A few minutes later Cuqui buzzed him on the intercom. "It's your friend Alonzo Norris on three."

"My main man, Liftoff. You don't write, you don't call. Man, July the Fourth is long gone and no fireworks yet. So what's going on with your big case? Not even my inside sources have been getting back to me," Norris chuckled. "The only person who reached out to me was your lady, and she says you've been keeping your distance. Hold on a second." There was click, a brief silence, and then Norris was back on the line. "I've got this first-degree murder trial in Vero Beach. I've been up here three weeks now. I'm in my co-counsel's office, and another call came in, one of our defense witnesses who's going on the stand Monday."

"Take your call. It's a long story."

"No, that's alright. So, tell me, Liftoff, are you gonna make your big case happen soon, become rich and famous, and ride off into the sunset with your *be-you-tee-ful* lady, you know, like the things we talked about one cold December night on South Beach?"

"Well, No-Time, I wouldn't be betting the farm just yet."

"You still can't lose the negativity, can you, Ray? Well, you make your big case happen, my brother, and everything will fall into place. And *please* give that foxy girl of yours a shout, will you? I've got enough on my plate right now without having to play cupid too."

The intercom buzzed again, and Lifton put Norris on hold. "The Big Girl on two," Cuqui advised him. "Okay, I'm taking off now. *Hasta la vista, señor* Bond."

"No-Time, the boss is calling from out of town. Good luck with your murder trial."

"Yeah, I see The Big Girl all over the news with our boy Clinton. Okay, I'm gone."

"How are you, Rayfield Lifton?" Susan Purvis' deep voice with the distinctive twang greeted him. "I'm sorry I wasn't able to call you back yesterday," she added before he could answer, "but I had no idea what I was getting myself into when these folks asked me to go out on the national campaign trail. Well, of course, I've had to campaign a number of times over the years, but that was just around Dade County. I must tell you, this is a completely different world, and it's really quite fascinating. Well, anyway, I'm getting way off the subject. I was calling to see why we still don't have a case filed yet."

Lifton told her about the string of bad luck trying to empanel a new grand jury so they were going to proceed by way of information instead of indictment.

"Well, Judge Sobel probably jumped the gun on this one, but it was his call. Let's just hope the situation developing down there doesn't delay any further what you need to do. Ray, I really have been counting on a nice hate-crimes case to give me some good national publicity. You know, show the rest of the country the types of cutting-edge prosecutions we're willing to bring to protect the good people of Dade County. And, to tell you the truth, I am very disappointed about the way things have gone so far. So now just wrap things up as quickly as possible, okay? Can you believe there's only seventy-four days left until the election?"

"The polls I've seen show your man is ahead."

Susan Purvis laughed. "Wait until you have to run for office one day, Rayfield Lifton. You'll know you're ahead right after you get sworn in."

CHAPTER EIGHTEEN

Joel Chernin set his black satchel on the front passenger seat and started his truck. He lowered the driver's side window, and a rush of cool air flowed in, even though on an August afternoon at this hour it still should have been scalding hot. He peeked inside the satchel to make sure he had the A-Forms and his two firearms. He carried his Glock 9mm everywhere he went. His Smith & Wesson .357 magnum with the two-inch barrel was just a little extra insurance for special occasions, like when he was going out to make arrests. If the automatic jammed, like it had done a couple of times during his fifteen-year law enforcement career, then he would have a reliable revolver as back-up.

After he pulled out of the driveway, Chernin glanced over at his West Kendall three-bedroom cookie-cutter home, a carbon copy of most of the other houses on his block. Ellen was looking out of the living room window, but when he waved at her, she turned and disappeared. He was going to be in the doghouse for awhile, leaving his wife and kids alone when it was a certainty South Florida would be hit by a very bad hurricane. He had tried to explain the situation to her, but it didn't matter. She was the one who had to go out now with their rowdy kids and forage for food, water, and batteries in stores jam-packed with desperate shoppers.

Guardians Of The Faith

As he approached the intersection at Sunset Drive, Joel Chernin cursed himself for not planning ahead. He should have been paying more attention to the weather reports earlier in the day. There was a long line of cars backed up in the southbound lanes heading toward Kendall Drive where a Home Depot and countless strip malls and gasoline stations lined that major east-west street. "Dammit!" he shouted and slapped the steering wheel. He inched his way to the right to see whether there was enough space to squeeze through by mounting part of the sidewalk, but there was a bus bench and a fire hydrant not far ahead. "Dammit!" he shouted again.

Chernin popped open the glove compartment, felt around for a pack of Chiclets, and shook part of its contents into his mouth. The traffic light already had changed three times, but his truck hadn't advanced fifty feet. Somebody started honking, initiating a chain reaction of scores of blaring horns. Chernin turned on the radio and rolled up his windows to mute this irritating chorus. The last he had heard was the storm would hit South Florida in the late night or early morning hours. The fact they were going to take a direct hit had caught most people off guard. The majority of South Florida's inhabitants never had been through anything more than a tropical storm and knew nothing about getting ready for a major hurricane. In fact, over the years the idea of making storm preparations had become somewhat of a joke. The only thing most people did was buy enough booze for a "hurricane party." He pressed the button preset to the twenty-four-hour all-news station and turned up the volume.

"So that's pretty much where we're at right now, folks. Again, if you're just joining us, we have Hurricane Andrew, a Category Four hurricane, possibly becoming a Five, making a beeline for our neck of the woods. Let's go live now to Kara Mello from our tv partner, Channel 5. Kara."

"Don, I've been in the field for several hours now, and I could describe the situation pretty much as widespread panic. Don, what exactly should people be doing in the hours remaining before Andrew makes landfall?"

"Whew, Kara, that's a really tough one this late in the game. Unfortunately, too many years have gone by since a major storm hit South Florida. We've had our share of warnings during the past decade but no direct hits. While nobody would dispute that's a good thing, the flip side is after awhile people become complacent. So right now we've got a whole lot of folks out there who still haven't done anything. They haven't secured their property, and a lot don't have essential supplies, like flashlights, batteries, canned goods, and bottled water to see them through this event. There's definitely a trade off here so people are going to have to make some difficult decisions real quick as the storm makes its final approach. What I'm saying, Kara, the choice for a lot of folks is between leaving their homes to try and find supplies or just hunkering down and making do with what they've already got on hand."

"That really *is* a tough choice, Don. Being out on the street you see just how chaotic it is out here. We've got video from different parts of the County which your listeners can check out on Channel 5 which has suspended regular programming to cover the storm. Most supermarkets have sold out of bottled water, bread, and many canned goods. And a lot of other items also have been flying off the shelves. A few minutes ago we learned some home improvement stores have demanded a police presence to control unruly crowds fighting over whatever supplies are left, like plywood to board up windows."

"Well, Kara, it's a very unfortunate situation, but I must say I'm not the least surprised. In the last hour all of the computer models pretty much have merged into one track showing Andrew heading due west. It's being held in that trajectory by an extremely strong high-pressure ridge to the north. This puts central and south Dade County squarely in the path of this Category Four, possibly Category Five, hurricane. Again, a Category Four hurricane means it has sustained winds of 135 to 155 miles-per-hour which likely will result in complete roof structure failures on small residences, major erosion of beach areas, and dangerous inland flooding. And, unfortunately, there's not a whole lot of time left before we start feeling Andrew's effects. So, quite frankly, I don't recommend anybody venture out on the streets unless it's absolutely necessary. And there's one more thing, Kara. I know a lot of people out there still believe taping their windows is going to keep them from breaking, but that's another one of those myths we've been trying to debunk during our broadcasts."

"And there are quite a few of them to debunk. Don, I'm sure I speak for all of your listeners on news radio when I say thanks for what you're doing to keep us informed and to help us get through this major weather event."

Chernin turned down the volume, popped the glove compartment again, and took out his mobile phone. *"Oh, yeah, Kara Mello, I'd really love to get through a major event with you, baby."* He had talked to the reporter before leaving his house. *That voice!* Chernin pressed the on button, waited for a few moments, and then pressed another one to speed-dial. After ten rings someone finally picked up.

"Station 5. Officer Cabrera speaking."

"Hey, Freddy, it's me, JC. Listen, is Andy Medina there? We're supposed to go out and make some arrests. I'm running late because I'm stuck in traffic."

"You and a lot of other people around town. It's a zoo out there. Let me see if Andy's still around." Cabrera put Chernin on hold for a few moments. "Sorry, JC, he's already gone. Your boy pulled duty at the Home Depot on Kendall Drive."

"Home Depot? What the hell is he doing over there?"

"That's his special assignment. When you get here, JC, you'll find out what you drew."

Chernin turned up the volume on the radio. "So, again, just in case you haven't heard yet, earlier today Dade County Mayor Steve Clark and Miami Mayor Xavier Suarez declared a state of emergency and ordered all law enforcement personnel to report for special assignments to protect lives and property."

"Hey, Chernin, you're breaking up on me. You still there?"

"I'm here, Freddy. I've gotta go see Andy."

"Forget about Medina, JC. You need to haul ass over here like yesterday. My guess is you're pulling duty at MIA."

"The airport? That's not our district."

"That's what you get for being late. The early birds got all the good gigs around here, but Station 3 is short-handed. The Chief is using officers from other districts to help out at MIA. The Major had to chip in a dozen of our guys. Look, JC, I've got a bunch of calls. I'll see you when you get here."

"This is *not* good," Chernin mumbled. He had set his plan in motion when tropical storm Andrew had just become a minimal category-one hurricane with seventy-four mile-per-hour winds. Now Andrew had ramped up into a Category Four hurricane the likes of which South Florida hadn't seen in decades. He had kept the details of this plan from Lifton, telling him only he had "a way to wrap things up real quick" that would make "this case a lock." "Why does the sound of that worry me?" had been Lifton's response which now burned in Chernin's ears. And it was a really good plan, too, a way to ensure Swindall and company wouldn't be able to pull a fast one with that messed-up "withdrawal from the conspiracy" defense Lifton had been so concerned about. At least it had seemed like a really good plan when Chernin had made it, and Andy Medina had agreed to help him execute it.

* * *

Halfway up the steps to the porch Lifton could hear the television. It wasn't like Kimberly to have the volume so high. Her beat-up Gremlin was in the driveway so she had to be there unless Publix had called her in, and she had forgotten to turn the set off. As he entered the living room he saw the note taped to the screen.

"I'm over at Snoopy's. Demeka is alone!" Lifton tore the paper off and went to his niece's bedroom. She was sitting on the floor staring blankly ahead, a half-dozen *Sesame Street* figures spread out in front of her.

"Hey, champ," he said, crouching down and gently touching her cheek. "You know, he gathered her in his arms, "you sure are getting big. Pretty soon I won't be able to carry you anymore."

His sister was helping Old Lady Muir move slowly across her front porch. Mr. T was barking wildly from inside, and Lifton noticed a red stain on Kimberly's white jeans. He took Demeka back to her room and rushed outside again. In the meantime Valerie had arrived and was helping Kimberly maneuver Fredericka Muir's sizeable bulk off the porch and into the back seat of Valerie's car.

"Kim, you're bleeding."

"Mr. T nipped me while I was tying his leash to a chair. I don't know what's wrong with Mrs. Muir. She called the house and said she was dying. When I got there, she was having trouble breathing. I called 911, but they said it would be awhile because all the ambulances were busy transporting sick folks and pregnant women to the hospitals. My stupid car wouldn't start yesterday so when I couldn't reach you I called Val."

"Let me see your leg."

"I'm alright, Ray, and I'm going to the hospital anyway."

"Hey, baby." Valerie squeezed Lifton's bicep and gave him a peck on the cheek before climbing into her Honda Civic.

"You stay here with Demeka," Kimberly said as she opened the front passenger door. "We'll be coming back as soon as Mrs. Muir gets admitted."

Lifton lowered the volume on the tv and returned to his niece's bedroom. He sat down on the floor and picked up two of the figures, Cookie Monster and Big Bird, moving them around like they were playing basketball. "Check this out, Demeka. Big Bird, I mean Big *Larry* Bird, steals the ball from Cookie Monster a/k/a Michael Jordan. And then Big *Larry* Bird makes a fast break down the court! And then, with only three seconds left on the clock, Big *Larry* Bird makes a slam-dunk! And the University of Miami Hurricanes win the National Championship!" His niece continued to stare blankly ahead as if he wasn't even there. " Okay, then, *I'll be back*," he said, pushing up from the floor.

"So recapping where we're at right now," the weatherman

was saying as Lifton entered the living room, "the latest information we have is that Hurricane Andrew, a Category Four hurricane, and possibly reaching Category Five status, is expected to make landfall here sometime after midnight."

"Bryan, based on the flood of calls coming into our news center," the lady anchor said when the camera panned back to her, "there's a lot of people out there angry about getting caught off guard with this very powerful storm."

"Well, that's certainly understandable, Kelly. And I'm sure in the coming days this hurricane will be a case study about the lack of sophistication in our forecasting capabilities even though we've had satellite imagery for a few years now. We all need to keep in mind Andrew was named on August 17, but it developed extremely slowly as it tracked west-northwest. Most computer models had it breaking up when it encountered an unfavorable upper-level trough. And by August 20 Andrew almost had dissipated due to vertical wind shear. However, the next day, Andrew was midway between Bermuda and Puerto Rico right here," the weatherman pointed to a spot on the map behind him, "and then began a more westwardly path into an environment favorable for very rapid strengthening. Remember, it was only *yesterday* that Andrew became a Category One hurricane, meaning it had sustained winds of seventy-four miles-per-hour. And now, *today*, we've got a hurricane heading our way which may turn out to be a Category Five by the time it makes landfall later tonight."

"Bryan, a little while ago you mentioned one positive thing about this storm."

"Well, Kelly, I didn't mean to give the wrong impression. There really is nothing good about it. What I was saying was," he turned back to the map and pointed at the bright-red ball approaching the South Florida coastline, "Andrew is a fairly compact hurricane compared to most we've tracked over the years. Its gale-force winds, that is those around thirty-five miles-per-hour, extend outward only about ninety miles from its center, which makes it a much smaller storm than most."

"Does this mean we'll have less damage than a typical hurricane in this category?"

"Not if you have the misfortune of being in Andrew's path, especially *here* in the northeast quadrant, what we call the dirty side of the storm. While moving through the Bahamas, Andrew crossed Eleuthera, *here*, with winds of 160 miles-per-hour, and the Berry Islands at Great Harbour Cay, *here*, with winds of 150 miles-per-hour. And now the storm is in the Gulf Stream where it likely will regain strength."

"So, Bryan, in a worst-case scenario what kind of wind velocity are we looking at when Andrew finally makes landfall in South Florida?"

"Well, Kelly, if Andrew becomes a Cat Five, and you happen to be on the dirty side of the storm, you could experience sustained winds of around 160 miles-per-hour or possibly even a little stronger."

"That's a very scary thought, Bryan."

"It is, Kelly, but if everybody does those things we've been talking about, they should be fine. And I'll be staying hunkered down right here at our weather command center until this thing is over to make sure everybody gets through it okay."

"Bryan, thanks for everything you're doing to keep us safe. Okay, we'll be right back after..."

When the phone rang, Lifton picked up the remote and turned the television off.

"Ray, it was crazy over at Jackson," Kimberly told him. "All these old folks and pregnant women and ambulances pulling up every two seconds dropping people off. They couldn't see any more patients there or at Cedars so we had to bring Mrs. Muir all the way over here to North Shore. I don't know how much longer we're gonna be. We have to stay with Mrs. Muir until she gets admitted. How's my little girl doing?"

"She's doing fine. I hope you don't have to wait around there too long."

"Me and Val have been watching the news here in the ER.

I'm getting scared about this storm, Ray."

"Well, the real bad part looks like it's heading more for South Dade than us."

"You take care of my baby, alright? And don't go anywhere, you promise?"

"Hey, Kim, it's Sunday, and a very bad hurricane is coming our way, remember?"

"I know, Ray. Listen, other people need to use the phone now. Love ya," she said and hung up.

* * *

"Where the hell *are* you, Karl?" Aubrey Swindall stomped the ground hard a few times after he finished circling the big steel shed. The boat storage racks behind the building were still empty. "C'mon, Karl, where the hell *are* you?!" He grabbed the padlock and tugged on it, even though he could see it was secure, then placed his forearm on the sliding door and rested his head. "Why me, Lord?" he said, sniffling like a child, pounding the door weakly several times with his right fist. "Why me?" He straightened up, snorted, and wiped his nose with the back of his hand.

Karl had stopped by Skeeter's last night and said things were looking real good. The storm was turning out to be a lot worse than anybody had expected, and the worst part of it probably was going to hit right in the middle of the night. You couldn't ask for better than that. There was just one thing. He needed some help.

"But you said *you* were taking care of everything," Swindall reminded him. "We already agreed on that, Karl."

"Not to do nothing to the nigger, you pussy," Spitzer whined like a little kid. "I'm talking about helping me out with something else. The dude I work with had to go back to Ocala. I've got some customers bringing up boats from the Keys tomorrow afternoon, and I need help getting them out of the water and up on the racks. So you and your two little buddies gotta be at the marina tomorrow at five. And after we're done I'll swing by your place and pick up all my shit. You all gotta help me take care of my business, or I ain't taking care of yours."

Guardians Of The Faith

Bobby and Kenny hadn't shown up at Skeeter's this afternoon like they had agreed so they all could drive over to the marina in just one truck. And nobody had answered the phone at Moser's house when Swindall called. Should he wait until Karl showed up or leave now and try and find those two little peckerwoods? There was no way he could make the round-trip in under an hour even if Card Sound Road was wide open. If he wasn't there when the boats started coming in, Karl was gonna be real pissed. On the other hand, if the two of them couldn't get the boats out of the water and up in the racks fast enough before the weather got real bad, that crazy motherfucker might flip out and call the whole thing off. There was a helluva lot of money involved when you were talking major boat damage. He climbed into his truck, popped open the glove compartment, found a tiny green lottery pencil and began writing on the back of an old invoice from a liquor supplier. He got down from the truck, went over to the shed, rolled up the paper, and wedged it in a small hole in the sliding door next to the padlock. As he pulled up to the edge of Card Sound Road, Swindall gazed at the solid line of vehicles, many of them towing boats, making their way north to US 1 and Florida City.

* * *

"This is *not* good," Joel Chernin grumbled as he took in the frantic scene at the Home Depot. He had no choice but to move his pick-up over to the far-left lane and ease it up onto the median dividing the east-west lanes of Kendall Drive. He locked the truck, held up his right hand to stop traffic, and crossed the road to the Home Depot parking lot. Shoppers quickly were transferring the contents of their carts and dollies into their vehicles. But then they couldn't find a way out of the parking lot because several customers had left their cars in unauthorized places causing havoc with the traffic flow. Fifty feet ahead of Chernin two men were arguing in Spanish about who should get a shopping cart someone had just made available. After the bigger man shoved the smaller one hard, making him fall to the ground, Chernin grabbed the offender by the arm.

"Hey!" he shouted, shaking him like a rag doll. "Don't be an asshole!" He turned to the other man who was getting up. "Sir, take the cart and get the fuck out of here." After the second Latin male disappeared inside the store, Chernin released the first one who had been staring at the pair of swastika tattoos.

"*Hijo de puta,*" he mumbled loud enough for Chernin to hear who knew enough Spanish to understand the insult. When Chernin lunged forward to scare him, the man held up his hands. "Sorry, sorry!"

"Where the fuck *are* you, Andy?" Inside dozens of shoppers maneuvered dollies loaded with plywood for boarding up windows and patio doors while scores of others pushed shopping carts filled with flashlights, batteries, Sterno cooking fuel, and cases of bottled water. Chernin walked over to a young black female employee directing the traffic at the check-out lines. "Miss, I'm looking for a Metro-Dade police officer who..."

"Oh, they're back in lumber now." She frowned and shook her head. "Aisle eight."

"Sir, *sir!*" Chernin could hear Andy Medina's voice ramping up. "Now calm down, or we're gonna have to arrest you. Sir, *sir!*"

Medina and another officer had positioned themselves between two shoppers, a portly middle-aged man, his big beer belly spilling out from the bottom of his Miami Dolphins t-shirt, and a tiny old lady with silver-blue hair in a flowery housecoat.

"Alright. What's the story here?" Medina asked a young male store employee wearing a bright-orange apron.

"I saw that kid cutting these on the bench saw," he said, pointing at the wood sheets resting against a metal rack.

"That *kid* happens to be my grandson!"

"That's *my* damn plywood!"

"You're a big fat-ass and a liar!"

"And you're a *fucking* old bitch!" The man tripped when he took a step forward, pushing hard into the other officer who in turn almost knocked Medina down.

"Okay, that's it," said Medina. "Lenny, cuff this idiot."

"You've *gotta* be fucking *kidding* me! I've gotta get my house ready for the storm!"

"Shut up and put your hands behind your back," the other officer said. He rotated the man and quickly fastened a long white plastic band. "Alright, let's go."

"Hey, Lenny," Medina called out, "before you put Mr. Sunshine in the cruiser, parade him around the front of the store so everybody can see what happens to anyone who doesn't behave."

"Ma'am," the young store employee said, gathering up the plywood boards, "I'll help you take these up front."

"Hey, JC, you pulled duty here too? What a fucking zoo this place has been!"

"No, bro. Freddy Cabrera said I probably drew the airport."

"MIA? Well, that's very fucked up."

"Whatever. But right now you and me are going out to make those arrests. We're running late, but the Turnpike will be wide open heading south. We've got the transmitter in my truck, and the video equipment is set up. It's good you're not in uniform so I'll just tell Swindall and company that you're a friend helping out. You go up in the loft, shoot the next episode of *Candid Camera*, and then we take these guys down. Let's just hope we get there before they leave."

Medina looked at Chernin like he was crazy. "*Yeah, right,* JC. Why don't I just have Lenny come back here and arrest us too for violating orders during a state of emergency."

Chernin folded his arms, dropped his head, and smacked his gum a few times. "Maybe you're forgetting a little something like *the plan*?"

"I remember *the plan*. So what?"

"So what? So what?" Chernin raised his head and shook it like he had just received a blow to the head. "If I don't show up at the marina real quick, those fuckers might just go ahead and do what I was supposed to do."

"*The plan* was *you* would take care of Sanderson."

"Yeah, I *know* that. But what if I don't show up? Swindall told me they were gonna do this thing with or without me, remember, Andy?"

"Those losers aren't gonna do something big like that on their own, JC."

"We don't know that for sure, Andy. And I've got all that shit over at Skeeter's. We need to get the audio and video and take these guys down like we planned so we can make this case a lock."

"Well, I'm really sorry, JC, but there's *no fucking way* I'm leaving my special assignment during a state of emergency. That would be a career-ender. We've both got a lot of years in. You want to put your pension at risk after all this time? What you need to do, JC, is check in with the station *right now* and let the Major know about the situation. He'll notify one of our units out there in the area to go by and let Sanderson know what's going on, or he can get Homestead Police to do it."

"I need a land line, Andy. My mobile doesn't work in here."

"There's a phone over there in the middle of the store in kitchen design. Listen, I've gotta circulate. Good luck with the storm, JC."

"You too, Andy. Stay safe."

* * *

"Is that you, Chernin? What the hell is all that noise?"

"Yeah, it's me, boss. I'm at a Home Depot in Kendall, and it's a fucking zoo here."

"Tell me you already made the arrests."

"Well, no, not yet, chief."

"Then what the hell are you doing at Home Depot?"

"That's why I'm calling you."

"Talk to me."

"I came here looking for Andy Medina. He was supposed to go out with me this afternoon to make the arrests. But we have to report in for special assignments because a state of emergency was declared. Andy pulled duty at Home Depot. People are going nuts trying to buy stuff before the hurricane hits. Andy won't leave here because he doesn't want to get canned. We could lose our jobs and our pensions if we violate orders during a state of emergency."

"Hold on a second. You told me these guys said you had to do this thing now because the storm would make it easy for you to cover up your tracks. So what happens if you don't go out and make the arrests with the perfect storm heading our way? Well, on the other hand, I guess there's no way they would find out you didn't do anything to Sanderson until after the hurricane was over, right?" When Chernin didn't say anything, Lifton added slowly, "*Oh, boy.* The other day you told me you had a great idea how to wrap the case up quickly and make it a lock. And I said, 'why does the sound of that worry me?' And you told me to just chill and let you get it done your way. Well, let me take a wild guess. Your great idea is backfiring now, right?"

"See, captain, it's like this. Once I was sure we were gonna take a hit, I went by Skeeter's and told Swindall to meet me at the marina this afternoon. I told him some customers were bringing in their boats, and I needed help getting them out of the water and up into the storage racks. And I told him Wendt and Moser had to be there too. If they wanted me to take care of their business, then they'd have to help me take care of mine. Me and Andy would get them on audio and video showing they were in this thing, with full knowledge and intent, right up to the very end. That way they couldn't use that very messed-up withdrawal-from-the-conspiracy defense you've been so concerned about. And then we'd also have evidence to support an attempted murder charge."

"Evidence the Guardians had taken a substantial step so the murder of Sanderson in fact would be carried out."

"Bingo. They'd be right there helping me out at the eleventh hour to make sure the murder would go down."

"So what happens now if you're a no-show? With this hurricane as bad as they say, especially out there in South Dade, it's a great opportunity for them to try and get away with this murder without you. Your nice little plan to wrap this case up quickly and make it a lock just might end up getting Sanderson killed."

"Look, boss, me and Andy don't think these guys would do anything like that on their own."

"Are you willing to bet Sanderson's life on it after you're a no-show?"

"We've got people out south who can go by Sanderson's place and let him know what's going on, or we can get Homestead Police to do it."

"I hope you're right. And listen to me, JC. I need you to call me back as soon as you're able to confirm Sanderson is out of harm's way, okay?"

Chernin turned the steering wheel all the way to the right and eased the pick-up off the median. On the other side of the road the lanes were choked with vehicles heading west, a lot of people putting a lot of distance between themselves and the ferocious winds and big storm surge Hurricane Andrew would bring when it made landfall in a few more hours. He pressed the button to speed-dial Station 5. "We're sorry," a woman's voice answered, "all circuits are busy. Please try your call later. Message 5415. We're sorry," the recording began repeating, "all circuits are busy." It sounded like the woman had a severely stuffed-up nose. "This is *not* good," Chernin muttered. He cursed himself for not using one of the Home Depot land lines to try and call the Major before he left there.

"So everybody should be hunkering down very soon," the weatherman was saying. "You don't want to be outside when the winds start blowing harder later tonight. We're already getting reports of sustained winds of thirty-five miles-per-hour in the central and southern parts of the County and gusts up to fifty in Key Biscayne. MIA is reporting gusts of forty-five miles-per-hour. All inbound and outbound flights at South Florida airports are suspended as of five p.m."

At the next intersection Chernin noticed the Shell and Mobil stations on opposite sides of the street had huge lines of cars. Some drivers had gotten out of their vehicles to try and find out what was going on. "This is *not* good," Chernin muttered as he turned up the volume on the radio.

"So, Don, has there been any change in the direction or intensity of Andrew?"

"Jerry, the answers are 'no' and 'yes' in that order. Andrew's westerly track remains constant and is not expected to change except perhaps for a slight wobble or two before it makes landfall. As to the storm's intensity, it has picked up some additional strength over the warm open waters. If you just tuned in, a few minutes ago we had Dr. Bob Sheets with us. He's the Director of the National Hurricane Center in Coral Gables. Here's part of what he said."

"Hurricane Andrew remains on a due-west course locked in by a high-pressure ridge just off the central Florida coast. The latest report from one of our hurricane-hunter aircraft is that the storm's central pressure has dropped to around 922 millibars. That's the unit we use for measuring atmospheric pressure. If that central pressure doesn't rise before landfall, it would make Andrew the second most intense hurricane in United States history. Only Hurricane Camille was more intense at 909 millibars when it made landfall in Mississippi and Louisiana in August of 1969."

"Again, that was Dr. Bob Sheets from the National Hurricane Center in Coral Gables. We'll have another update from Dr. Sheets at the top of the hour."

"So, Don, is there *any* good news for our listeners?"

"Well, Jerry, what we're beginning to understand is this storm probably will not be a major event for us for more than a few hours as it travels rapidly west across the Florida Peninsula and out into the Gulf of Mexico."

"Which means less likelihood of flooding?"

"Exactly right. The biggest problem here is going to be the very intense sustained winds and even higher wind gusts."

"And where and when is it they're predicting Andrew will make landfall?

"Right now we're looking at the area of Homestead and Florida City in the extreme southern portion of the County sometime after midnight."

"So, Don, is it a fair statement what we've got in store for us is a relatively strong but compact storm which may clear out of Dade County sooner than we expected?"

"I'm sorry, Jerry, but that sounds way too optimistic. Hurricane Andrew is going to be more like a giant buzz-saw cutting across our area, and it's going to be a very devastating event for a lot of people."

CHAPTER NINETEEN

It took forty-five minutes for Aubrey Swindall to make it back to Homestead. And that was driving really crazy, weaving in and out of the tightly-packed line of cars and trucks heading toward US 1. Several times he had no choice but to forge ahead into the left lane of Card Sound Road for a very long stretch because nobody would let him merge back into the right lane. As he drove along North Krome Avenue into downtown Homestead, strong wind gusts tilted street signs and swung traffic signals like silent church bells. At the intersection of Northwest Sixth Street he turned left, and for the next mile had to swerve his truck violently a dozen times to avoid hitting the deep potholes. As he barreled down the last paved road at the town's western limit, he spotted Moser's truck, tailgate lowered, backed up close to the front door of the small concrete-block house.

"Hey, Lizbeth," Swindall called out to Moser's plain-jane wife as he climbed down from his truck. She was cradling a baby and leaning against the screen door to keep it open.

"Hey, Skeeter," she greeted him as he approached the house. "You ever seen my little one here?"

Just then Bobby Wendt walked out carrying a styrofoam cooler. His head shot back when he noticed Swindall standing there. "Hey, Kenny!" he turned around and shouted. "Skeeter's out front!"

"What the fuck?!" Moser appeared at the door with two fishing rods and a green plastic tackle box. "Oh, hey, Skeeter," he mumbled as he took a couple of steps forward and knocked into Wendt who hadn't moved an inch. "Dammit, Bobby, will you get your ass in gear? We've still got a lotta shit to take out."

"Where were you two peckerwoods? We were supposed to meet up at my place and go out to that marina."

"We were out buying some shit," Moser said. "We're leaving before the hurricane gets here."

"*Oh, really*? Well, you two can stop putting your shit in the truck because..."

"We ain't going to that damn marina now, Skeeter." Wendt walked past Swindall and set the cooler down on the tailgate of Moser's pick-up.

Swindall reached over and grabbed him by the upper arm and began leading him down the street like an angry teacher taking an unruly student to the principal's office. "You get your damn ass over here too, Kenny!"

Moser slid the tackle box into the truck bed and dropped the fishing rods. "This is such fucking bullshit."

"You two little shits are going with me now out to that marina, you hear?! We've got an agreement with Karl whatever the hell his name is."

"*You're* the one who's got the agreement with him, Skeeter," said Wendt, tearing away from Swindall's grip. "One of those conspiracy agreements."

Swindall moved toward Wendt, but Moser quickly stepped in between them.

"Now just hold on, Skeeter," Moser said, raising both hands defensively. "Will you just listen up? Me and Bobby went over to see Curtis today."

"*Oh, really*?" Swindall folded his arms and bobbled his head. "Please tell me he's either fucking dead or don't give a shit about

Guardians Of The Faith

the preacher anymore."

"Well, Curtis ain't dead," Moser said. "At least not yet."

"And just what the *hell* is that supposed to mean?"

"Well, see, Curtis still wants this thing done. And he wants it done *now* because the hurricane will be good for it and all. And he says if we don't do it, we're all gonna fry because he don't give a shit anymore about nothing or nobody, not even himself."

Swindall unfolded his arms and covered his eyes with his hands. "And so what did you two fuckers say?"

"We said, okay, Curtis, we're gonna take care of it."

"Then why weren't you two at my place like we agreed?"

"Well, now, just hold on a second, Skeeter," Moser said. "Metro-Dade police and some people from the County was over there at Curtis' building. And they were saying everybody had to get out and go to some big shelter in Miami at that university next to the Turnpike. They said the building wasn't safe anymore and had to be knocked down if the hurricane didn't do that itself. And they put up this sign the place was condemned and all. And they were gonna have buses at the Greyhound station and give people free rides to the shelter. They asked me and Bobby if we lived there, and we said no, but we were going up to see Curtis. And the dude from the County saw Curtis' name on some paper and asked us if we would make sure to tell him he had to leave right away and go to that shelter in Miami, and we said, sure, we'd be glad to do that."

"You're losing me, Kenny."

"See, what you don't get, Skeeter, is we went to see Curtis, but we never told him about having to leave the building."

"So, the thing is," Wendt said, still massaging the upper arm which Swindall had locked onto before, "the hurricane might end up taking care of Curtis so nobody has to take care of the old preacher man. And then we'd all be off the hook."

Swindall looked down and shook his head. "You know, you two are even fucking stupider than I thought. You're gonna count on something like that happening to make sure we don't end up in prison or worse?"

"Hey, Kenny!" Lizbeth shouted. "I can't stay out here with the baby like this!"

Moser and Wendt started walking back to the house, and Swindall followed them.

"Hey, Skeeter," Lizbeth said. "You know who's been calling over here?"

"I ain't talking to Curtis. If he calls again, you tell him..."

"It ain't Curtis who's been calling over here, Skeeter. It's Emily. Three times already. Says she can't find you anywhere. I got the number where she's at if you need it."

"I gotta use your phone. It's long distance. Is that okay?"

"Well, of course, Skeeter. Emily told me she's way up there in The Panhandle."

Swindall went to the kitchen, removed a scrap of paper from his wallet, and dialed Kaye's number. The line was making a sound like a big bowl of Rice Krispies. "Hey, honey," he said when he heard Emily pick up.

"Why didn't you call me today, Brey? *My gosh*. We've been watching the news up here, and it looks like it's gonna get real bad down there. Lizbeth said they're all leaving for Orlando where she's got her parents. I want you to leave too, Brey."

Swindall tugged on his chin-strip and bit his lower lip. "No, babe, I'll be fine. I really don't think it's gonna be that bad."

"Well, I don't care what you think. I want you to come up here. I miss you, Brey."

Swindall snorted and wiped his nose with the back of his hand. "I'd have to take care of stuff at the house and the business before I could leave."

"Well, you take care of all that stuff *right now,* and then you get on the road before it gets dark, okay? I love you, Brey."

"Okay, I love you too, honey," he said in a low voice and hung up.

Lizbeth strolled into the kitchen and came up close to Swindall. "We're just about ready to leave now, Skeeter." She peeled back the edge of the pink blanket so he could see the baby's face. "Isn't this a real cutie-pie?"

"Sure is, Lizbeth. What's his name?"

"You crazy, Skeeter?" Lizbeth slapped him gently on the arm. "It's a girl, silly. Boys don't have pink blankets." She raised the baby, took one of her tiny hands, and gently caressed Swindall's cheek. "Kenny wanted a little boy, but we got a little girl instead. So we have a little Jenny instead of a little Kenny."

As Swindall strode out of the house, he noticed Bobby and Kenny had positioned themselves on the right side of Moser's truck next to the front bumper. Their anxious expressions told him they were expecting another confrontation, but Swindall walked straight over to his F-150. He opened the driver's door, stepped up, and looked at them over the top of the cab. "You all have a safe trip, you hear?"

"Hey, Skeeter!" They both yelled out after he made a u-turn.

Swindall looked in the rear-view mirror. Wendt and Moser were in the middle of the street with their arms outstretched like how could he leave without telling them what he planned to do? But there was no reason to go back and tell them because he didn't have the answer to that question himself.

* * *

Sergeant Alfredo Cabrera swivelled in his chair at the reception desk and looked up at Joel Chernin. "Well, glad to see you finally decided to join us today. And I was right, JC. It's *el aeoropuerto* for you, brother."

"I tried to call you a few times on my mobile, Freddy, but I kept getting a recording."

"No kidding." Cabrera pointed at the twelve-line telephone console in front of him. "Do you hear any calls ringing off the hook? Do you see any lights flashing? The phone system in this part of the County crashed a little while ago."

"Freddy, I've gotta talk to the Major."

"The Major? Oh, you can forget about talking to him, JC. He's with all the head honchos out at the EOC. The Emergency

Operations Center," Cabrera added when he saw Chernin didn't know what he was talking about. "That scary-looking building with all the weird antennas on the southwest corner of Miller and Galloway. The one they spent all those millions on a few years ago but never have used." Chernin started to say something, but Cabrera cut him off. "Don't even think about it, JC. The Major's not gonna change your gig for nothing, bro. But I'll tell you what. You might be able to catch a ride out to MIA with R&B." Marvin Richards and Frankie Bennett, two black officers who rode together, were known as "R&B" because they serenaded their fellow officers with a vast repertoire of rhythm and blues songs. "Hey, JC, where are you going? R&B should be checking in any minute now."

"I'll be back."

"Okay, *Ah-nuld*," Cabrera said, "but don't expect me or R&B to go looking for you."

* * *

Rayfield Lifton pushed up from the carpet in his niece's room where he had been sitting cross-legged for nearly thirty minutes. He had tried get Demeka to react in some way to the figures spread out on the floor between them, but it was no use. It was as if she were just another one of those inanimate characters.

"What the hell is going on with Chernin?" Lifton thought as he went to his bedroom. The detective hadn't called him back like he had promised to do as soon as there was confirmation Reverend Sanderson was safe. He dialed Chernin's mobile number written on a piece of paper he had taped to the nightstand.

"We're sorry," a recorded message began, "all circuits are busy. Please try your call later. Message 5415." The woman on the recording had a nasally voice which made her sound like Ernestine the Telephone Operator on the old tv show *Laugh-In*. "We're sorry," the recording repeated, "all circuits are busy." Lifton dialed information to try and get the numbers for the Metro-Dade Police Department and The Reverend Wilkie P. Sanderson. Instead, he got the same recording as before, this time with bursts of static sounding like popcorn cooking in a microwave. He tried the number for Publix, also written on the paper taped to the nightstand, and the same message greeted him. He called the main number at the State Attorney's Office and then 911, but now the static was so loud it practically drowned out Message 5415. "Chernin was right," he thought. "This case *is* jinxed."

Lifton turned on the radio and learned the latest advisory still had the storm making landfall after midnight. What if Chernin hadn't been able to make sure Sanderson was out of harm's way? His sister was at a hospital far away in the wrong direction. There wasn't going to be much traffic now that everybody was "hunkering down." Lifton wrote a note to Kimberly, left it on the kitchen table, and went back to Demeka's room. "Okay, champ, let's go," he said as he scooped her up in his arms. "We've gotta make a little trip now out south."

* * *

The metal blades rotated slowly around the naked lightbulb flickering weakly in the center of the ceiling fan. The power already had gone out three times during the last hour but had come back on each time after only a couple of minutes. Thigpen guessed it wouldn't be much longer before it would be out for a good while. He leaned forward and tried to focus on the piece of paper stuck under the cracked glass. It didn't matter because the only number he needed right now he already knew real well.

"This is Reverend Sanderson. Well, Curtis," he added after a pause, "this is pretty early for you. Why so early today?"

"Cause you're a fucking boon."

"Well, I was wrong then," he chuckled. "I thought you might be calling me about the storm. You're lucky you got through. They've been saying on the news the phones are out just about everywhere now."

"Are you crazy, nigger?"

"I've been worried about you, Curtis, so I guess I am. Do you need some help?"

"I don't take help from niggers."

"They say the hurricane is going to be real bad out here."

"So maybe you'll die tonight."

"If The Lord says it's my time, I will. But first I'm gonna see if you need some help. I know you live in that old public housing building on West Mowry Drive."

"I told you I don't take help from niggers."

Thigpen wasn't sure if the line was crackling, or Sanderson was chuckling again. "You laughing at me, old nigger?"

"Yes, I am, but it's not the funny kind of laughing. It's the frustrating kind. Like when you're trying to figure somebody out, but you just can't no matter how hard you try. Do you know what I mean, Curtis?"

"I don't take help from no niggers. Are you still there, old nigger preacher? Hey, I just asked you something. Hey, are you still there?!"

* * *

It had taken Aubrey Swindall only twenty minutes to get back to the marina because nobody was heading down to Key Largo. He didn't even have to slow down at the tollbooth just beyond Alabama Jack's because the barrier arm was up, all tolls in Dade and Monroe Counties having been suspended. In the opposite lane there still was a long line of cars and trucks making their way to US 1, but it had thinned out some so Swindall knew his second return trip was going to be quicker which was good news. But then there was bad news because Karl, whatever the fuck was his name, wasn't at the marina. So now Swindall was driving back to Florida City like a bat out of hell. Although this time he didn't have to pass as many cars and trucks pulling trailers, it still was pretty dangerous because the stronger winds were making them swerve wildly.

As he turned right onto US 1, a strong gust shoved his truck across the dividing line, and he had to jerk the steering wheel hard to the right to get back in the northbound lane. *"What the hell?!"* he blurted out as he glanced over at the west side of the road. Through a small break in the vegetation Swindall could see there were lights on inside Skeeter's. He hit the brakes and made a wide u-turn. It had to be that dude Karl who somehow had gotten inside so he could pick up all of his shit. But then again it might be some thieves who had seen a golden opportunity to rip off his package store thinking the owner was home hunkering down for the big storm like everybody else. "Dammit!" He sure wished he had his Smith & Wesson .44 magnum with him, with its nice soft-rubber Pachmayr grips so when he fired it wouldn't fly out of his hand no matter how sweaty it was. But at the moment the most powerful handgun in the world was sitting on the ledge behind the bar. "Just fucking great," he mumbled. Maybe he'd end up getting shot with his own gun.

Instead of pulling into the parking lot Swindall left his truck on the side of the road just short of the entrance. Hidden behind the tall hedges he made his way to the rear of his property, catching sight of an old Caprice parked near the front door. The car looked familiar, but he couldn't place it right then. He walked across the lot and put his ear against the back door, but he couldn't hear anything. He started to pull out his keys but then realized the door wasn't locked. With all the bullshit going on he must have forgotten to do that last night. "So that's how these fuckers got in."

Swindall opened the door slowly and took a few cautious steps inside. He bent down and picked up the piece of rebar, the long metal rod he sometimes used to reinforce the back door against break-ins, wrapping his fingers tightly around its cold ridges. As he began inching forward, the only thing he heard was the sound of someone shifting position in one of the chairs. What the fuck was anybody doing sitting down at a table during a burglary? Unless the sons-of-bitches had *really* big balls and were taking a break to enjoy some free booze right there in his place. He crouched down before reaching the main room and then waddled forward to the edge of the big bar. He craned his neck so he could peer around its edge and made out two sets of feet at one of the tables near the window.

"So how much longer do you want to wait for your friend?"

Aubrey Swindall pushed up with the help of the rebar. "Reverend? Curtis?"

* * *

Joel Chernin couldn't stop replaying Andy Medina's words in his mind as he raced south on Florida's Turnpike. "That would be a career-ender." Yeah, that *might* be true if he *never* showed up for his special assignment at MIA during the state of emergency. But there might be something going down right now which would be a lot worse for his career than just being late for duty at MIA. That's why he decided he really had no choice except to book it out to Homestead, make sure no *human* disaster was going to happen there in addition to the *natural* one, and then get over to MIA as fast as possible. He just hoped Freddy Cabrera and R&B hadn't wasted any time looking for him around Station 5.

Chernin had been doing eighty-plus on the Florida Turnpike for the last ten miles. He had to jam on the brakes as he began descending the sharp curve of the Campbell Drive exit. It was a good thing the barrier arm was in the up position because he was still doing nearly forty as he approached the abandoned toll booth. After he turned left on Campbell Drive, Chernin checked the rearview mirror to make sure no Homestead Police were behind him, then pressed down hard the accelerator. Three minutes later he turned west off North Krome Avenue and screeched to a halt in front of a small concrete-block house on the church property. He started to knock on the front door but saw he could push it open. He stepped inside and looked around quickly, then walked over to the small red-brick church to see if it was open. The deadbolt securing the big double doors gave him his answer. He hadn't seen any signs of foul play in the house, but it was a bad thing the front door wasn't locked. "Well, isn't this just fucking great!" Now, instead of being able to start racing north to MIA, he was going to have to keep on going further south.

Back on North Krome Avenue he noticed a Homestead police cruiser in a Circle K parking lot and slowed down. But as soon as he crossed the railroad tracks on the other side of Mowry Drive,

Chernin hit the gas and sped along South Krome Avenue to where it merged with US 1. *"What the hell?"* A few hundred feet ahead he noticed Swindall's pick-up parked on the right shoulder just before the entrance to Skeeter's. It didn't make any sense for Swindall to leave his truck there. A sick feeling began welling up in the pit of his stomach as he pulled up and parked behind Swindall's truck. "This is *not* good." He fished his Glock out of the black satchel and checked the clip. Then he took out his revolver, opened the cylinder, gave it a spin, then snapped it shut with a flick of his wrist. Good thing there was all that vegetation on the north side of the property so he could make his way to the back of Skeeter's without anybody seeing him.

* * *

"Who's that out there?"

"It's me, Curtis," Swindall said as he approached the table. "Who the hell else do you think it is?"

"We've been waiting for you, son. Your friend refused to go anywhere unless we came here first."

Swindall started to say something, but no sound came out of his mouth. He stopped moving forward and cleared his throat a few times. "Well, Mr. Reverend, I didn't know you and Curtis were coming here or nothing. I was just checking up on my place."

"And I'll bet," Sanderson chuckled, "you thought somebody had broken in here."

"Well, sir, I actually did when I was driving by and saw the lights on, and..."

"Do it, Skeeter."

Swindall shrugged his shoulders and smiled sheepishly. Sanderson smiled back and shook his head like "I don't know what he's talking about either."

"Just do it!"

Swindall raised the metal rod and shook it a couple of times in jest like he was going to strike Curtis to try and shut him up. Sanderson raised his eyebrows and nodded like "not a bad idea."

Joel Chernin had walked quickly from the rear lot to the front of Skeeter's. Plastered against the building he had inched his way across the wooden porch to the front window. Something clicked in his mind about an old Caprice like the one parked in front. He shot a glance inside and quickly pulled back. "*Holy shit!*" Swindall was waving a crowbar at an old black man sitting at a table with someone who looked like Curtis Chance Thigpen. He slowly retraced his steps, jumped off the porch, and ran to the back of the building.

"Do it, Skeeter, or you know what."

Swindall lowered the metal rod and tried to lean on it like a cane. He winced in pain as the uneven end of the rebar dug into his palm. "Yeah, Curtis, I know what. I already been told enough by Bobby and Kenny." Swindall took a deep breath, then exhaled slowly. "And *you* know what, Curtis? You go ahead and do what you gotta do. I really don't give a shit anymore. Sorry, Reverend, sir," he added, biting his lower lip.

"Thank you, Lord," Joel Chernin whispered when he noticed the back door wasn't locked. He made a mental note to buy a couple of Lotto tickets and then pushed it open just enough to be able to slip inside.

"You do it, Skeeter." Thigpen's voice was flat and tired now.

Chernin crept past the alcove where the bathrooms and payphone were located and crouched down before entering the main room.

"Do it? Do it?" Swindall raised his voice in mock anger, winked at Sanderson, and lifted the rebar over his head with both hands. "I'm gonna bash *your* brains in is what I'm gonna do."

Chernin didn't know if Swindall and Thigpen were strapped, but after what he had just heard there was no time left to try and find out. He reached around with his left hand to make sure his back-up revolver was firmly tucked inside his waistband, raised the Glock above his head, and jumped up. "Hey, Skeeter!"

Swindall turned around and squinted at the bulky figure across the room. "*Oh, shit!*" he cursed under his breath. It was that dude Karl, and he had a handgun. "What are you doing here? I waited for you at your place."

"Who's that, Skeeter?"

"Nobody, Curtis. Just some asshole."

Chernin still couldn't tell whether these two pieces of shit were strapped. It sure would have been a lot better if Andy Medina had his back right now. When Swindall turned toward the table, Chernin knew he had to make his move except he hadn't noticed the big wet spot of spilled beer a foot in front of him. As he rushed forward Chernin slipped and fell backward. The Glock went off when he hit the concrete floor, making a huge thunderclap as if a bolt of lightning had sliced through the roof. As he lay there, Chernin felt a sharp pain in his lower back where the revolver was digging into it. Before he could sit up, he sensed Swindall's huge frame hovering over him. He turned on his side and reached out for the Glock, but Swindall kicked it away.

"This is my gig now. So you can just get the fuck out of here, okay, asshole?!"

Chernin didn't have time to wonder why Swindall didn't want him there. He got up slowly, brushed himself off, started to turn like he was leaving, then wheeled around and hit Swindall in the side of the head with his left fist. The metal rod fell from Swindall's grasp and pinged loudly as it struck the concrete floor. As Swindall stumbled backward, Chernin punched him two more times with a left-right combination to the jaw. His eyes bugging out with a look of amazement, Swindall crumpled to the ground like a giant sack of Florida grapefruit. Chernin glanced over at the table where the two other men were sitting calmly, then bent down to retrieve the Glock.

"Hey!" a voice called out.

Chernin looked up and saw the outline of a tall figure next to the payphone between the bathrooms. "And just who the fuck might you be?"

"I came by to help Aubrey."

"Oh, really?" Chernin cocked his head. "Well, as you can see, your friend just had a little accident."

"Didn't look much like an accident to me." The tall man stepped out from the shadows, revealing his ripped physique. "I saw you take him down." He shot a quick glance at the table near the window.

"So you came to help your buddy?"

"I just said that."

"Well, that was real sweet of you."

"I'm gonna need you to set that pistol back down on floor. Nice and easy."

"Oh, *tough* guy, huh?" Chernin chomped on his gum and nodded like it was no big deal. "Okay, sure." He bent down, released the gun, and stood back up with his hands raised. When the new arrival had advanced to within a few feet of him, Chernin reached back with his right hand and whipped out the .357 magnum. "Surprise!" He jerked the revolver twice, indicating for the new arrival to move toward the table near the window. "Come on in and join the party. You got any weapons I can't see?"

"Yeah, as a matter of fact, I do," the man said as he stared at the swastika tattoos. Before Chernin could blink the revolver was ripped out of his hand and flew across the room like it had been pulled over there by a giant magnet. The man grinned slightly as Chernin stared at him like a deer in headlights. "These," he said, holding up his hands. Chernin threw a punch, but his arm was only half-extended when the man made two more dizzying movements. Chernin felt his chest burn like it had been branded with a sizzling iron, and he folded like a jackknife and dropped to the floor right next to Swindall.

"It's like a game of human dominos, Curtis," Sanderson said, shaking his head. "Somebody comes in and knocks the next one down. And who might you be, son?"

"Stewart Malman," the new arrival said as he approached the table, "and I have no idea what's going on here, sir."

"Well, pleased to meet you, Stewart," Sanderson said as the two men shook hands. "My name is Wilkie." When Thigpen didn't react to the hand Malman had extended to him, he added,

"And this is Curtis, but he doesn't see so well."

"You here to kill the nigger preacher?"

Sanderson looked up with an expression filled with great disappointment, silently telling Malman, "don't pay any attention to what he just said."

"I came out here looking for Aubrey thinking he could use some help getting ready for the hurricane."

"Well, as you can see, Stewart, you got here a little too late to help your friend. You sure are one bad dude as the young folks say these days."

Malman turned back to check on the two men lying on the concrete floor. "I heard a gunshot as I was getting out of my car. What's going on here?"

"Well, you heard right then." Sanderson placed his hand gently on Thigpen's shoulder. "It's kind of a long story."

A flash of light pierced the room, and Malman stepped over to the window. "We've got company."

"Good. Maybe it's somebody who can help you move those two big bodies. We need to get out of here before the storm gets any closer, and I've got the safest place to be."

Malman opened the door, and a rush of cool air filled the room. "I'm looking for Joel Chernin," the new arrival said as he tentatively stepped inside and quickly scanned the main room. At a table near the window there was an old black man with his hand on the shoulder of someone who looked like it could be Curtis Chance Thigpen. There were a couple of loud groans behind him, and Lifton turned around and saw the two bodies in fetal position on the concrete floor.

"Is one of those two yours?" Sanderson asked. "They look like twins."

"The one with the swastika tattoos. He's a detective with Metro-Dade Police."

"*Ooops.* Just what the hell is going on around here?"

"You didn't know that guy was a police officer?"

"No, sir, I had no idea. I heard a gunshot as I was getting out of my car so I came in through the back door to see what was going on. I took him down when it looked like he might want to harm these folks. By the way, I'm Stewart Malman."

"Rayfield Lifton, Assistant State Attorney."

"He's a pretty big fellow like you, Stewart, this new one," Sanderson said. "Alright, people, let's focus. Son, we're gonna need your help moving those two big oafs. We need to get over to the church while the getting is still good."

"Reverend? Are you The Reverend Wilkie P. Sanderson?"

"That's me, Liftoff Lifton."

"You know I'm Liftoff Lifton?"

"Well, you looked a little familiar, and then you said your name was Rayfield Lifton. I remember how much I used to love to watch you play, Liftoff Lifton."

CHAPTER TWENTY

Rayfield Lifton silently cursed his very bad decision as he set Demeka down in the right front pew. "You stay here, champ," he said softly and then walked quickly to the rear of the church. Bringing his niece with him on this ill-fated road trip confirmed he was a chronic fool. He had placed his niece squarely in the middle of harm's way, the worst part of the hurricane on a track to slice and dice South Dade right where they were "hunkering down." Lifton had listened to the weather reports as he followed Sanderson's Caprice to the church. The storm's central pressure had dropped to 922 millibars which made Andrew the third most intense hurricane ever to hit the United States. The measuring instruments on one offshore automated station already had been destroyed after registering sustained winds of 142 miles-per-hour and gusts up to 177. But the biggest fear wasn't damage from the hurricane's straight-line winds but from "vortexes," tornadoes embedded in the storm, and there were going to be *thousands* of them capable of destroying every structure in their path.

Lifton had to lean hard against one of the church's double doors because the strong wind was like a hulking football lineman pushing from the other side. He shielded his eyes from the blowing dust and spied Sanderson hunched over next to his

Caprice, trying to move forward like an old ox pulling a heavy plow. "Reverend, what are you doing?!" He untangled Thigpen's arms from around Sanderson's neck and eased him down off his back. Lifton grabbed Thigpen under the knees, picked him up, and carried him inside the church while Sanderson held open one of the double doors.

"He sure seems a lot heavier now than before."

"You could have hurt yourself really bad, Reverend. Why didn't you wait for me?"

"Well, I already carried him like a cross twice today and made it okay."

Lifton deposited Thigpen at the far end of the left front pew. "He's a real bad guy this Thigpen. I don't think you know what's been going on around here."

"Well, I'd be pretty surprised about that, Liftoff, because I've lived right here my whole life. Anyway, I'd sure love to hear what you've got to say sometime, but right now I need you to go back outside and help Stewart with those other fellows."

"Hold on, Stewart," Lifton said, grabbing one of Swindall's meaty arms as he teetered from side to side, still woozy from the blows Chernin had inflicted on him.

Swindall was too big to lie down on one of the wooden benches so they took him to the front of the church and got him up on the pulpit. Swindall rolled over on his back and started snoring.

"I'm okay," Chernin muttered when he felt a hand nudging him. "I'm okay."

"We need to get you inside, JC."

"Lifton?" Chernin opened an eye and craned his neck. "And who the fuck is that?"

"I'm sorry I had to hurt you, Detective. I didn't know who you were."

"Yeah, yeah, whatever." Chernin sat up slowly and groaned, then began wriggling his way across the back seat of the Lincoln Continental. "*I'm okay*," he whined, waving off any assistance. He placed his feet on the ground, pushed up, and took a couple of small steps. A strong wind gust propelled him forward, and Malman and Lifton had to grab his arms and prop him up, steering him inside the church where they set him down in the last row of pews. Malman went to the front of the church and asked Sanderson to drive him and Lifton back to Skeeter's so they could retrieve the trucks Swindall and Chernin had left on the shoulder of US 1. Lifton asked Chernin if he was feeling good enough to keep an eye on everybody while they were gone.

"I'm okay. I see that piece of shit Swindall lying up there," Chernin nodded toward the pulpit, "but I don't see Thigpen."

"Now you don't need to be swearing here inside the church."

"I'm sorry, sir, but there's things you don't know about yet. That Thigpen dude wanted to kill you, and I was trying to stop him." He noticed Sanderson was smiling like he was laughing to himself. "Is that funny what I just said?" A very sharp pain shot through Chernin's chest. He placed his right arm on the back of the bench in front of him, leaned forward, and rested his head.

"Are you sure you're okay, son?"

Chernin raised his left hand and waved it weakly. "That big fat dude up there was taking care of all the arrangements." Chernin turned his head toward the aisle and saw Sanderson was still smiling as he walked away. "The old man must be deaf."

When they returned from their trip to Skeeter's, Lifton sat down next to his niece and began stroking her head gently.

Sanderson walked up to the front pew, put his hands on his knees, and leaned forward. "Hello, young lady. My name is Wilkie." He searched Demeka's face intently before standing back up. "You started to tell me how you ended up in this mess," he said, turning to Lifton, "but so far I'm not sure I understand any of it. Well, we've got a long night ahead of us so I'm sure you'll have plenty of time to explain things to me. But just for starters I'd like to know why this little lady is so quiet?"

"Demeka has something wrong with her, Reverend. We just call it 'the thing.'" Lifton related how out of the blue his niece had developed this condition, the hopes he and his sister had held out for her to get better, the bad news from the medical team in Gainesville, and how his sister had reacted to it. "So next month Kimberly's moving out and sending Demeka to a special school in West Palm Beach."

"Okay, all vehicles are secured behind the church." Malman handed back the keys he had borrowed from Sanderson and Lifton.

"Good idea to park them in the back there. Most of those old trees out front look like they're coming down in this storm. Now, Stewart, if you could give me a hand, I've got some things to bring over from the house."

Chernin's mobile phone still wasn't working so Lifton asked Sanderson to check and see if his land line was back in service.

"I'll sure do that, Liftoff." The Reverend stooped down again, reached out, and gently squeezed Demeka's arm.

A few minutes later Sanderson and Malman returned with a case of bottled water and two brown-paper grocery bags and began emptying their contents, a radio, flashlight, candles, matches, a jar of peanut butter, a package of cheese slices, a box of saltine crackers, paper cups and plates, plastic knives and forks, and a roll of paper towels.

"I'm sorry, Liftoff, but my phone still isn't working."

"I'm gonna look around for Everly a little more."

"No, Stewart. I'm sure she'll make her way back soon."

"Who's Everly?" Lifton asked.

"Oh, she's my old dog. I guess I didn't shut the door good when I left the house to go out and get Curtis."

Lifton could see Sanderson was hurting as he thought about his dog. "You named her after the Everly Brothers?"

"Don and Phil? No," Sanderson chuckled. "I'll bet when you meet Everly," his expression brightened, "you just might figure out why I gave her that name." He pulled out the last item from the bag. "Anybody know if this stuff is any good?"

"It's a lot better than good, Reverend," Lifton said. "That's Johnny Walker Blue Label."

"My sister gave it to me when I turned eighty."

Guardians Of The Faith

"Well, it's not quite as old as you, Reverend, but it's aged something like sixty years and costs around one-fifty a bottle."

"Well, then, I'll bet somebody gave it to my sister, and she didn't know how much it was worth, so she passed it on to me. I don't have any ice over here."

"You won't need ice for that stuff, Reverend," Malman said. "You just sip it like a fine liqueur a little at a time. It's like honey."

"Actually, it's more like anesthesia."

"You got that right, Ray," Malman agreed.

Some of the small stained-glass windows on the left side of the church began vibrating, buzzing like a row of giant kazoos.

"I think we should try and find out what's going on with the storm." Sanderson picked up the radio and fumbled with the dials.

"I know you're all getting really tired of hearing this, but this is going to be the most intense hurricane to hit our area in nearly six decades. A few minutes ago I was able to speak with County Administrator Jack Osterholt, and here's what he told me."

"Kara, in 1935 a storm similar to Andrew leveled portions of the Keys and killed nearly four-hundred people. Right now we're in the bottom of the ninth, and we still don't have a large turnout at the shelters. For whatever reasons most people aren't taking this situation seriously enough. And I..."

"Kara, this is Don. I'm sorry, but I've got to interrupt you. Let's go live now to the National Hurricane Center where Director Bob Sheets is about to make an announcement."

"We're going to be seeing something here that I hoped we'd never experience," Sheets began. "The Center is now predicting Hurricane Andrew will be a Category Five hurricane by the time it makes landfall in South Florida sometime in the early morning. A Cat Five hurricane is one with sustained winds of 155 miles-per-hour or more. Our latest information tells us Andrew could have sustained winds up to 165 miles-per-hour. We anticipate after the hurricane passes through our area it will surge across the Florida Peninsula, exit somewhere around Fort Myers, then move into the Gulf of Mexico. Tropical storm force winds and strong gusts already have been felt in parts of Dade County. Hurricane force winds are still a few hours away. At this time we're predicting the eye will pass over the extreme southern portion of the County sometime between three and six a.m. But let me emphasize again this is a compact storm which is moving unusually fast so it could be here earlier. All I can say is I hope the advance warnings and evacuation of low-lying coastal areas will keep Andrew's death toll low, no worse than the experience we had when Hugo smashed into the Carolinas back in 1989."

"Mr. Sheets! Mr. Sheets!" a number of voices called out.

"I'll take your questions in a few moments, but right now I want to turn the floor over to Paul Herbert from the National Weather Service in Miami."

"What we have here is very close to a worst-case scenario. Wherever the eye hits, that part of Dade County will be leveled."

"My ass is grass," Chernin mumbled as he sat down in the second row of pews.

Lifton looked back at him. "Well, that makes two of us, JC." Right now Kimberly probably was deciding on which method she would employ to torture and kill him as soon as he got back home.

"Maybe I should cuff that dude," Chernin said, "before the weather gets worse." Swindall was lying on his back now, eyes open, staring at the ceiling. "Once I tell him he's under arrest and read him his rights, he might try and take off."

Sanderson cocked his head and listened as a howl rose over the buzz of the vibrating windows. "I thought for a moment that might be Everly."

"I'll go out and check."

"No, Stewart, I'm sure it was just the wind."

"Now *that* sounds like a dog to me," Malman said after the howling started again, rising from a guttural low to a shrill whine. "I'm checking it out."

"Be careful out there with things blowing around."

"Reverend," he smiled, "I've been in a lot worse than this."

"What a group we've got here!" Lifton said. "Two rednecks,

two blacks, and..."

"Three rednecks," Swindall interrupted. "I heard that guy Karl out there. Where the hell am I anyway?"

"Why you're in my church, Aubrey. You've never been here before?" Sanderson glanced over at Lifton and winked.

"Hey, Swindall," Lifton said, "did you know that guy Karl really is Metro-Dade Detective Joel Chernin?"

"You gotta be shitting me," Swindall sputtered. "Sorry, Reverend, sir."

"Oh, that's okay, Aubrey. I'm starting to get used to all this bad language."

"That's right," Chernin said as he approached the pulpit. "And I'm a Jew too."

"You gotta be kidding." Swindall wanted to laugh at this additional revelation, but he was hurting too bad so all he could manage was a painful cough. "With those tattoos?" He coughed a few more times. "Stewart's a Hebe too."

"I stand corrected," Lifton said. "That makes two rednecks, two blacks, and two Hebes, and we'll just leave my niece out of the whole thing."

"Okay, then it's two by two by two," Sanderson chuckled. "And a real bad storm on the way. It's starting to sound very Biblical around here."

One of the back doors suddenly flew open and a blast of cool air rushed into the church. A very obese black-and-brown dog waddled down the aisle with its big tongue hanging out. Sanderson crouched down and hugged the Rotweiler mix. "She's real old like me," he said, his voice cracking with emotion. "Maybe now you'll see why I named her Everly," he looked up, his eyes moist. "You see, Liftoff, Everly rhymes with..." Lifton's smile confirmed he had gotten the inside joke. "Can you believe my sister still hasn't figured it out after all these years?"

There was a big commotion at the rear of the church. Malman had latched both doors open, and some birds flew in followed by a parade of stray animals. Lifton raised his forearm to shield his eyes as he made his way back there.

"We've got another visitor!" Malman beckoned for Lifton to follow him outside. "He's not sure yet what he wants to do, but he's a goner if he stays out here. I just hope he doesn't decide to take a crap."

"Any ideas, Reverend?!" Malman shouted over the sharp clip-clopping which was echoing through the church as he and Lifton led the horse inside.

Sanderson's eyes widened, and he scratched his chin. "Now what would Noah do?"

* * *

"*Oh, yeah.* We've got a real nice cold cell waiting for Mr. Thigpen at the Dade County Jail, don't we, chief?"

"Are you really planning on doing that, Joel?"

"*Oh, yeah,* we really are, Reverend. He's gonna be charged with conspiracy murder. Same for that big fat-ass lying up there on your pulpit."

"I'm supposed to be the victim, right?"

"You *are* the victim, sir. I worked up the whole case myself."

"Weren't you supposed to talk to the victim?"

"I didn't have to. I got everything I needed from the bad guys. Matter of fact, it was *me* who was gonna kill you."

"Then I guess *you* should get charged too, right?"

Chernin turned to Lifton with a quizzical look like "what's his problem?"

"Reverend, your sister was the initial source of information in this case. She told us what's been going on around here."

"Oh, I see, Liftoff," Sanderson said, nodding thoughtfully, "my *sister* told you. Well, as the victim, I still have some say in this thing, right? So then let *me* tell you a few things about what's been going on around here."

* * *

Last week Sanderson went for his annual physical at Deering Hospital. As he was about to enter the building, the automatic sliding glass doors parted, and an orderly wheeled Curtis Chance

Thigpen outside. When the hospital worker returned to the lobby with the empty wheelchair, Sanderson asked if he knew what was going on with that patient. The orderly had no idea, but he had picked him up in the endocrinology department. Sanderson went to that department to see if he could find out what was wrong with Thigpen. Nobody was at the front desk, but he noticed Thigpen's chart was on the counter and decided to take a look at it. When he got home, Sanderson called a physician in Miami who was the son of old friends.

"Well, it's not my specialty," the doctor told him, "but I'll try and find out a few things for you." A few hours later the doctor called back. "Diabetic nephropathy is a complication of long-term diabetes," the doctor explained, "and develops in stages over many years. You see, the kidneys are the body's filter, and bundles of capillaries there make up the filtering system. And when those capillaries lose their efficiency as a result of long-term diabetes, some pretty bad things can start to happen. You get high blood pressure, retain fluid, suffer from fatigue, and feel sick all the time. I hope I'm not going too fast for you."

"No, I understand. Those are some pretty bad things."

"And it can get a lot worse than that, Reverend. Diabetes can harm the eyes. It can damage the lens and the retina. Some people lose their sight if blood vessels rupture and form scar tissue. If that scar tissue pulls tight enough, it will detach the retina from the back of the eye." When Sanderson didn't say anything, the doctor added, "Sounds like this might be a family member or a close friend. If you give me the patient's name and treating physician, I could try and find out more specifics about this particular case."

"That won't be necessary, Doc. Just tell me, can there be any other problems when somebody has this condition?"

"Unfortunately, yes. Ulcers in the legs and feet which cause a loss of sensation. If injuries in those areas go untreated, they can become infected. There's a decrease in circulation to the legs and feet which slows healing. Nourishment doesn't get to damaged tissue so the infected material is not destroyed. The smallest injury may end up becoming ulcerous. There also can be bladder dysfunction where urine remains there and becomes stagnant, allowing bacteria to grow which travel up to the kidneys and cause infection. And then there's vascular diseases, macrovascular, peripheral, cerebral, and also coronary artery disease. You want me to explain those to you?"

"No, Doc, I think I've heard enough for right now. So how do you treat such a big mess like that?"

"Well, you've probably heard about dialysis. After the amount of kidney damage is determined, the patient might go on hemiodialysis which is done at the hospital three times a week. Then there's peritoneal dialysis three or four times a day at home. In some cases there's the possibility of a kidney transplant."

"And what happens if somebody's got this diabetic whatever you call it and doesn't take care of it?"

"Well, Reverend, that wouldn't be good. You're talking about loss of vision and, if there's a badly infected limb, you could be talking about amputation."

For awhile now Sanderson had known Thigpen was ill with something. That was obvious from the way he looked when Sanderson would see him around town. But now he had learned about the nature of Thigpen's medical problems and just how bad things could be for him. When Thigpen called this afternoon, instead of at night like he usually did, Sanderson asked him if he needed any help.

"Curtis said he didn't take help from nobody, especially those people he likes to call boons or niggers. But with this bad storm coming I decided to go over to his place anyway."

"To help that piece of...crap? You're crazy."

"I'm crazy, right? You know, Liftoff, that's exactly what Thigpen told me too."

"So why did you do it?"

Wilkie Sanderson smiled and reflected for a few moments before he spoke. "Well, in my job description, I'm pretty sure it says I'm supposed to help people. I *think* about helping people a lot. And I sure *talk* about it a lot, mostly when I'm preaching on that pulpit right up there. Remember that fellow Gandhi from India? He said something pretty interesting once. 'Happiness is when what you think, what you say, *and* what you do are in harmony.'" He fixed his gaze on Chernin and Lifton. "And a long time ago I decided I wanted to live happy." They looked over at Thigpen who, from the moment he had arrived at the church, had been sitting silently, slumped down at the end of the left front pew. "So, gentlemen, let me ask you again. Do you really want to put Curtis in that cold jail cell you were talking about?"

* * *

Sanderson passed out small styrofoam cups to Malman, Chernin, and Lifton, then picked up the bottle of Johnny Walker Blue Label and unscrewed the cap.

"Can I have some of that stuff too?" Swindall asked after he had rolled over on his side. From what he had just overheard, he was praying Curtis was so sick he wouldn't feel like saying anything about that mixed couple from New York. In fact, maybe he was so messed up he couldn't even remember what had happened out there on Card Sound Road a few years back.

"Here, Stewart. You seem like the one who knows the most about this stuff."

Malman took the bottle from Sanderson and poured shots for each of them. "A few drops at a time is the way to drink this stuff."

Strong wind gusts rattled the stained-glass windows, making them sound more like a swarm of killer bees now than a chorus of kazoos. In the back of the church the horse snorted, one of the dogs started barking, and two cats sprang down the center aisle.

"Sounds like the bad part of the storm is getting closer." Sanderson held out a styrofoam cup, "Well, I might as well have some too, Stewart. So what shall we toast?" When nobody said anything, Sanderson added, "Alright, how about toasting me? I'm the one who brought the good whiskey to this shindig."

"To The Reverend," they each said and raised their cups.

After he took a small sip, Sanderson smacked his lips.

"Wow! This stuff really is something else. So what kind of music do you all like?" When nobody volunteered, he shook his head. "Well, you people sure aren't much fun. Okay, then, I'll be back."

"*I'll be back,*" Lifton and Chernin blurted out at the same time.

"No, it's more like this." Swindall's deep voice had returned after a few sips of Blue Label. "*I'll be back!*"

Sanderson climbed the stairs to the pulpit and disappeared through a door on the right side. There was another big blast of strong wind, the lights flickered, and then the power went out.

"Hold on everybody." Malman grabbed the flashlight and directed its beam to guide Sanderson down from the pulpit.

"Well, we all knew that was going to happen sooner or later. Can one of you gentlemen light up some of those candles?" Sanderson held up the object he had retrieved. "I keep this cassette player in my office so I can listen to music sometimes when I'm working in there. I hope the batteries are still good." He pressed a button, a lid popped up, and he took out the cassette. "Stewart, can you read the label on this tape?"

"It says 'Sam Cooke.'"

"That's the one I was hoping was in there. You all know Sam Cooke, right?" When there was no response, he added, "Well, I'm sure you'll recognize some of his songs." Sanderson slipped the tape back in the machine, pushed the lid down, and pressed the rewind button. When the whirring sound stopped, he pressed the play button.

"Darling, you ooo-ooo-ooo, send me," the singer crooned, his honey-combed voice filling the church. "I know you ooo-ooo-ooo, send me."

"Now I'm sure you all recognize that golden oldie. Well, that's Sam Cooke." The Reverend turned up the volume. "You Send Me" was followed by "Wonderful World" and "Bring It On Home." "The next one should be 'Chain Gang,' Sanderson said." He pressed the stop button and held out his styrofoam cup.

"Are you sure you want another one, Reverend?"

"Oh, I'm sure, Stewart. That stuff is real good." After

Guardians Of The Faith

Malman poured him another shot, Sanderson took a sip and set the cup down on the edge of the pulpit. "Sam Cooke left us too early, almost thirty years ago. But, before he did, I actually got to meet him one time."

In 1957 Martin Luther King, Jr. and other black ministers founded the Southern Christian Leadership Conference. The next year The Reverend Wilkie P. Sanderson went to Atlanta to attend its second convention. The main objective of the Conference was to use the power and organization of black churches from across the nation to conduct non-violent protests in the fight for civil rights reform. It was there Sanderson met the singer's father, The Reverend Charles Cooke, a Pentecostal minister from Chicago. By that time Sam Cooke already had two major hits, "You Send Me" and "I'll Come Running Back To You." In fact, "You Send Me" had made it to the number one spot in the Top Tens.

"Sam Cooke showed up one night in Atlanta, and I told his father I wanted to meet him. I *had* to because he was my favorite singer back then. We must have talked a good hour, me and Sam, mostly about music and civil rights. Sam Cooke believed music moved people more than speeches. I had a friendly argument with him about that, and I noticed he changed his mind some after he heard Dr. King speak that night. But, you know, Sam was mostly right. Motown went uptown and changed a generation. For the first time, in large numbers anyway, white folks started enjoying something together with black folks because of people like Sam Cooke, James Brown, Marvin Gaye, and all the other greats. They were just as important, maybe even more important, to the cause of civil rights as anything else that was going on. But back then nobody ever thought about it like that."

Sam Cooke died when he was just thirty-three, shot to death by a motel manager. A coroner's jury believed the manager's explanation about what had happened and determined it was a case of justifiable homicide. "It's a real shame he left us so young." Sanderson seemed lost in thought for a few moments. "You know, Sam Cooke never forgot about the friendly argument we had that night in Atlanta. A few years later he called me out of the blue and said he had written a song about it. He named it 'A Change Is Gonna Come.' I guess it was one of the earliest civil rights protest songs. `It's been a long, a long time coming,'" Sanderson sang softly, "'but I know a change is gonna come, oh yes, it will.' Well, now you all can see I can't carry a tune," he shook his head and chuckled. "But you know what? That change finally did come. Anyway, next up is 'Chain Gang.'" He pressed the play button, and Sam Cooke's silky-smooth voice again filled the church. A few seconds after the song ended, the tape stopped, and the play button popped up. The stained-glass windows were constantly buzzing now, and the church itself seemed to tremble.

Lifton sat down next to his niece, put his arm around her, and pulled her close. "You think we're gonna be okay in here?"

"Oh, we'll be just fine." Sanderson turned toward the others. "Alright, everybody. I've done my part. Now you all have to keep this party going." He took another sip of his drink. "For one thing, I'd like to hear how Joel was planning to do me in."

* * *

"Hey, boss man." Joel Chernin jerked his head to the side, motioning for Lifton to follow him down the center aisle out of earshot of the others. "This is *not* good."

"You mean the hurricane or everybody getting plastered?"

"C'mon, boss, can you be serious for a minute? Sanderson is messing with our case."

"Looks to me like he doesn't think we have a case."

"Well, chief, you need to tell him to get with the program. Our asses are on the line here. I'm already in deep shit for not showing up for my special assignment at MIA. And there's gonna be hell to pay for both of us if we screw up this case."

"Hey!" Swindall called out from the pulpit, "Can I say something to you people?"

Chernin walked back down the aisle to the edge of the pulpit and held up his hand. "No, you can't, Swindall. You're drunk. Anything you *shay*..." He stopped abruptly after slurring his last word. "I must be friggin drunk too."

"Why don't you let the man speak?" Sanderson asked Chernin. "It sounds like he wants to get something off his chest."

"Thank you, Reverend. You see, sir," he pointed at Chernin, "I was trying to stop this dude from..."

"That's bullshit. You had that metal club. I saw you through the front window and went around back and got inside. I stopped *you*, dude, before you could hurt The Reverend. Now don't say anything else."

"No! You got it all wrong. I stopped *you*, bro."

"I'm sorry, Joel, but I think Aubrey's right. He's was just fooling around."

"*Oh, really*, Reverend? Just fooling around, huh? I heard him. He said he was going to bash your brains in."

"Not *The Reverend*, man. Curtis. I was joking with The Reverend like I was going to smack Curtis to shut *Curtis* up."

"That's bullshit, Swindall! You said it was your gig now. You told me to get the fuck out of there. You don't remember? You were standing over me, getting ready to hit me with that big piece of rebar."

"*No, dude*! You don't remember? You pulled a gun on us, but then you fell down. I had to stop *you*, bro. You were gonna kill The Reverend. I still got all your stuff stored over at my place. You were gonna use that shit to..."

"I wasn't going to use that shit to do anything! I'm an undercover cop, you fucking idiot! I was trying to get *you* to get *me* to kill The Reverend!"

"*Ooops!*" Sanderson blurted out.

"*Dammit*! You all know what I mean."

"Yes, Detective, I believe we do," Sanderson chuckled. "It's called entrapment."

"Why don't you just drop it for now, JC," Lifton said.

"Let the man talk, Ray," Sanderson held up his hand. "This is getting pretty good."

"Thank you, sir. So then this bad ass shows up," Chernin

pointed over at Malman, "and says he's there to help fat ass up there. So then I had to stop *him* too."

"Wait a minute." Malman tapped his chest a couple of times and then burped. "I had to stop *you* because *you* were going to kill The Reverend."

"*No, I was not!*" Chernin whined like a spoiled child, triggering a huge burst of laughter from the others. "You know what? Just screw all of you and give me another drink, dammit!"

Malman held up the bottle of Blue Label. "Anybody else want another hit?"

"I'll take one, Stewart," Swindall said. "So you came out to my place to help me?"

"Yeah, to help you board up or whatever it is you all do to secure your property. Karen was freaking about the hurricane so she decided to get the hell outta Dodge." Malman lowered his voice as he poured Swindall another shot. "Looks like you got yourself into some kinda bad trouble, huh, Aubrey?"

"Well, I didn't do nothing wrong." Swindall looked over at Lifton. "You see, sir, Stewart here and his wife bought my bar and package store. We were supposed to have the closing last week, but this damn hurricane came along and messed up everything. We're gonna close as soon as this is over, right, Stewart?"

"Oh, I have no doubt." Malman poured the others another round, followed by another until the bottle gave up its last drop. "Alright, folks, that's all she wrote."

"You know, Reverend," Chernin was swaying from the effects of the booze, "to fat pig up here on your pulpit, and that piece of crap sitting over there, African-Americans are just a bunch of niggers." He turned around and looked up at Swindall. "Am I right, or am I right?"

Lifton leaned toward Chernin. "Why don't you just let it go for awhile?"

"Now hold on everybody." Sanderson raised his hand as Chernin and Swindall started to say something at the same time. "Yes, Joel, folks like them do talk like that. But they sure aren't the only ones. You're with the police so you know what's going on in the streets. And you know that's how a lot of young black men talk these days. They call each other 'nigger' and 'dog.' It seems like every other word that comes out their mouths is 'nigger' or 'dog.' And I'm sure you've heard their music. Glorifying drugs and easy money and even guns and killing. The other day I was at the music store and saw some magazines. One was called *Thug Life* and another one *Killer Dog*. *Thug Life* and *Killer Dog*! I couldn't believe it! All these years of struggle for that?!" Sanderson crouched down and began stroking Everly's neck for a few moments, then looked up at Chernin. "Let me you tell you something, son. I'm not so worried about Aubrey Swindall and his type anymore. I'm a lot more concerned these days about our own young black folks. Too many of them are going down the ladder instead of up."

"And what's that supposed to mean?"

"Well, Joel, I'll tell you. But before I forget, you don't need to be calling me African-American. I know it's the new thing, politically correct they call it, but it doesn't make me feel good. It makes me feel bad. We've been fighting a long time to be accepted as just plain old Americans, just like you or anybody else whose people came here from some other place. And I don't think you'd like it very much if you were known as Joel, the Eastern-European Jewish American, or wherever it is your people came from. Am I right, or am I right?"

"Aw, just forget about it," Chernin grumbled.

"Now about that ladder. I got that from your people, Joel. Going up means getting closer to God by doing the right thing. And it doesn't matter how high up on the ladder you are right now. What matters is whether you're going up or going down."

There was a stir in the back of the church as the horse snorted a few times, and a dog began howling.

"What's that all about, Everly?" The Reverend's dog barked three times. "Animals hear better than us. I think she just said something big is out there." A few seconds later it sounded like a freight train was approaching. "There's some railroad tracks a few blocks away," Sanderson added, as he gently stroked his dog's back, "but we all know there's no trains out there tonight. So I'd say most likely it's a tornado."

That was the last thing anybody said before the building began shaking violently, and the candles blew out.

CHAPTER TWENTY-ONE

Rayfield Lifton wriggled out from under the first-row pew and had to shield his eyes with his forearm. Bright sunlight was streaming into the church from a gaping hole above. The last thing he remembered was wedging himself and Demeka beneath the pew and wrapping his arms tightly around her. A few moments before he did that, it had sounded like a runaway locomotive was about to roll right through the middle of the church while the roof groaned like an angry Chewbacca

"Up here, Ray." Malman was on the pulpit. "Aubrey got banged up pretty good. Part of the roof came down on him. Your niece is fine. She's right over there. And watch your step. There's stuff from the roof all over the floor."

Demeka was sitting next to Thigpen at the far end of the left front pew. Lifton latched onto her arm and pulled her up, but she slid right back down. "C'mon, champ."

"Hold on, Ray. Here, Stewart." Sanderson handed a plastic sack up to Malman. "Well, Liftoff," he said as he walked over to him, "I guess you drank too much whiskey last night like the rest of us. Remember that freight train sound coming right at us? The walls started shaking so hard it was like being at the Battle of Jericho. I got under one of the pews just like you and your little niece did. A beam fell on Aubrey's legs, and he's got some cuts and bruises and maybe even some broken bones. I brought over some antiseptic and bandages. We let the animals out and tied up the horse behind the house. They were saying on the radio it's a lot worse out there than anybody expected, and they just hope there's not a lot of dead."

"I gotta go over and see what happened to my place."

"You're in no shape to go anywhere, Aubrey," Malman said. "I'll check on your place when I go out and take a look around."

"Well, there won't be any power for awhile so I'm going back to the house to get some things out of the icebox. Ray, I could use some help." When Lifton reached down and grabbed Demeka by the arm again, Sanderson said, "You can leave her there for right now. She's been doing just fine."

"Don't worry, Ray," Malman said. "I'll keep an eye on her."

As they walked out of the church Lifton said, "I don't like Demeka being next to Thigpen. I don't even like her being on the same planet with that piece of crap."

Sanderson ignored his comments. "So, Liftoff," he asked with a sweep of his hand, "what do you think about what Andrew did to us?"

It looked like a giant weed whacker had sliced through everything in sight. Only a few towering royal palms were left standing. On the street in front of the church a power line hidden under a pile of brush was sizzling like bacon in a frying pan. To the right the rows of modest houses on both sides of the street all had major roof damage. To the left the intersection at Krome Avenue was littered with all kinds of debris, a partially-crushed bus shelter, utility poles, and signs which had blown off businesses.

"Hey!" Chernin yelled from behind them. "Don't go in the street! There's power lines down and all kinds of snakes and other critters crawling around out there." He came up behind Lifton and grabbed his shoulder. "So, how's it hanging, sleeping beauty? That Blue Label really did a number on you, huh?"

"Well, you sure are all wound up, JC. Did you already find

a place to get some Cuban coffee?"

"Man, I sure could use some of that rocket fuel right now."

"Well, I might be able to make you all some instant coffee if I can find the Sterno. We're going over to the house right now to get some things."

"You're lucky, Reverend. Your house survived except for the gutters and a bunch of roof shingles. Stewart's in the church there with Thigpen and Swindall, right?"

"Yes, that's right. Why don't you go back and relieve him, Joel? He wants to get outside and take a look around too."

Chernin tugged on his chin-strip, then tilted his head, gesturing for Lifton to follow him. "You realize what that old fart is trying to do, don't you? He wants to brainwash you about the case. You heard the shit he was talking last night, right?" Chernin stopped abruptly, looked at Lifton, and shook his head. "You know, I'm starting to get a really bad vibe here so let me tell you something, boss man. Everything will be getting back to normal real soon. And then you and me are gonna have hell to pay if we've screwed up this case. And you know what else? I am *not* going down just because you happen to have some kind of a personal problem with success."

"Let's go, Ray!" Sanderson called out from the front door of his house.

"Hey, chief," Chernin said as Lifton began walking away. "I'm sorry, but you and me and everybody else know it's the damned truth."

* * *

Wallace Thigpen became the butt of one too many jokes around Homestead and Florida City after his infamous encounter with The Reverend Wilkie P. Sanderson. He couldn't show his face anywhere without someone making a comment about what had happened that Sunday morning. Every day he suffered the loud snickering of men and the muffled giggling of women even if they had the common decency not to say anything to his face. And anybody who knew the story had no doubt that's why not too long after the incident Wallace Thigpen got into a knife fight in the parking lot outside a bar in the Redlands over something which was nothing and picked up an aggravated assault and battery charge. Nor was anybody surprised when he couldn't stay out of trouble while serving his nine-month sentence at the Everglades Correctional Institution. Wallace Thigpen was out of control from day one at the Everglades CI and got into it, not just with the other inmates, but with the guards and even once with the warden himself. So it really wasn't that much of a shock when after only two months into his confinement there, somebody from the Florida Department of Corrections called to advise Mary Thigpen her husband had gone missing. The man with the husky voice warned her it was a serious crime to harbor a fugitive, and the best thing she could do for herself and her children was to immediately report any information she had as to the whereabouts of Wallace Thigpen.

It turned out Mary Thigpen never was presented with the dilemma of having to assist the authorities. A few days later two licensed hunters on a swamp buggy ten miles west of Krome Avenue took down a twelve-foot nine-hundred-pound alligator using harpoons and a specially-fitted crossbow. Back at their camp they started to process the gator for head, hide, and meat when they discovered some undigested material, including half of a rubber work boot, pieces of bright orange-colored fabric, and parts of a human skull. The next day someone from the Everglades CI delivered an ice chest containing several plastic bags to the Dade Medical Examiner who was charged with investigating unnatural deaths in the County. Nobody ever figured out why Wallace Thigpen had decided to venture into Everglades National Park after escaping from the prison camp instead of heading north toward the Tamiami Trail, nor how he could have gotten so far west, seeing as how it was nearly impossible to slog your way on foot through Florida's river of grass. But the truth of it was nobody cared that much about what really happened to Wallace Thigpen so the inquiry into his death officially ended a few days later when Mary Thigpen signed papers in downtown Miami releasing and discharging forever the State of Florida and Dade County from any potential liability.

When she returned from her trip to Miami, Mary Thigpen paid a visit to The Reverend Wilkie P. Sanderson. Before he could say he was sorry to hear about her husband's untimely passing, she reached for his hand and thanked him for that day when he put Wallace Thigpen down on the ground where he belonged, squirming around with all the other lowly creatures on this earth. He asked her how she planned on getting by now that her husband was gone. "A lot better," she replied, except for the extra money he used to bring in because she didn't make enough cleaning houses part-time to support her three boys. A few days later a Negro woman came by the house and gave Mary Thigpen a piece of paper with a name and telephone number and told her she could call to see about a job. Within a week Mary Thigpen had been hired as a supervisor at Langford-Hall Fresh, the biggest produce shipper in South Florida, even though she had no experience in that kind of business and should have started out as one of the line packers who mostly were Negro women.

Mary Thigpen never would forget January 28, 1956, the day she got hired at Langford-Hall Fresh, because that night she saw a singer named Elvis Aaron Presley who was making his first television appearance. Her oldest son, Walter, had started to unplug the television when he found out his mother was going to watch Elvis on the Dorsey Brothers' show because his father had said Presley was a queer and a communist. For the first time in her life, Mary Thigpen threatened one of her children, screaming at Walter he was welcome to leave the house and come back in an hour if he had a problem with her seeing the program. So Walter decided to stay put and ended up watching the show too. In fact, he tried imitating the singer's straight-legged pounding and pendulous gyrations, clutching a broom handle just like Elvis was doing with the microphone stand. And Elvis Presley appeared five more times that year on The Dorsey Brothers' *Stage Show* and on other television programs like *Milton Berle, Steve Allen* and, most importantly, *The Ed Sullivan Show*. Mary Thigpen never missed one of those shows and bought every Elvis record which came out that year, including "Heartbreak Hotel," "Don't Be Cruel," and "Hound Dog." When *Love Me Tender* was released on November 16, 1956, she gathered up her children and took a bus to The Miracle cinema in Coral Gables, a three-hour round-trip, because it was the closest theater playing that movie.

On her supervisor's salary from Langford-Hall Fresh Mary Thigpen was able to pay her bills, raise her three boys in modest comfort, and see her two oldest, Walter and Chester, graduate South Dade Senior High School. Walter decided to join the Navy after trying a year of community college and ended up stationed in San Diego for awhile before he left the service for some unknown reason. He moved to San Francisco where he landed a job in the music business. Chester planned on going to college, but he wanted to see a little bit of the world first and traveled out west to visit Walter. After a month he called home and told his mother San Francisco was such an incredible place, and he wouldn't be returning to South Florida. Walter had been able to pull some strings and had gotten him a job in the entertainment business.

Mary Thigpen seemed happy for her two older sons, but within a few months after Chester said he wasn't coming back, Curtis noticed her mood had changed. At first he thought she was just sad about the house being so quiet now, but soon he figured out what really was going on. One afternoon Curtis got home early from school and went through his mother's dresser. In the middle drawer at the bottom of a pile of undergarments, Curtis found an envelope with a San Francisco return address containing a letter and photograph. The picture was of his two brothers, now sporting bleach-blond surfer hairstyles, their arms slung around a young muscle-bound boon. It had to be a fag party because they were all wearing glittery party hats and were naked from the waist up except for the bow-ties.

"Walter and Chet are a couple of queers, aren't they?" Curtis asked his mother the moment she walked through the front door.

Guardians Of The Faith

Mary Thigpen never answered that question. She took time off from work and traveled to California to see her two sons, leaving Curtis behind with Roy Wendt and his family. When his mother returned, she looked very tired and much sadder than before. Never again did she smile that sweet special way Curtis had loved so much since he was a little kid, head tilted, eyes almost-shut. The only time Mary Thigpen ever looked at peace again was a few years later lying in an open casket in the funeral home.

Curtis Thigpen never graduated high school because for him learning most of what they taught there was a big waste of time. And activities like musicals and plays, things his two older brothers had gotten into which their father never would have allowed, most likely would turn you into a fruitcake. He thought his mother would kick him out of the house when he told her he was dropping out of high school, but she didn't seem to mind at all. And Curtis couldn't figure out why because she was always saying education was by far the most important thing there was for young people. Maybe she had heard enough by then about how other kids constantly made fun of her youngest, taking after his father and looking like a cover from *Mad* magazine, instead of taking after her like Walter and Chet who were carbon copies of Dennis and Brian Wilson of The Beach Boys. So instead of starting his junior year at South Dade Senior High School, at age sixteen Curtis went to work at Wendt's Engine Repair where he learned how to rebuild motors for cars, trucks, and agricultural machinery. He felt good going there every day, like he was part of their family. And he enjoyed it when Roy and Jimmy reminisced about Wallace Thigpen and the things he had stood up for, trying to keep the country from turning into a bigger shit-hole than it already was. What with all the hippies and niggers running around wild burning down buildings and causing all kinds of other problems, and his two older brothers turning into a couple of big-time California queers, Curtis figured his father must have been right about a lot of things.

One afternoon after work, while they were sitting around polishing off a six-pack, Roy said, "Jimmy, tonight we're taking

Curtis with us." They drove down Card Sound Road until it ended at State Road 905. A mile south they turned and made their way a few hundred yards down a dark gravel road until they reached a wooden gate. A giant man with a shaved head and full beard, wearing bib overalls, a shotgun resting on his shoulder, shielded his eyes from the headlights. He walked up to the driver's side of the pick-up, Roy muttered something, and the man went back and swung open the gate. "That's Gus," Roy said. "He makes sure we ain't got no intruders." A short distance ahead a dozen vehicles were parked in a small clearing where a group of men were standing around a campfire drinking beer and talking loudly.

"So who you got there, Roy?" one of the men asked.

When he answered "this here's Wallace's boy," the rest of them turned and regarded Curtis like he was some type of royalty instead of the freak he had been made to believe he was. Each one of the men shook his hand vigorously, and some patted him on the back. They said things like "your father was a great man," and "we sure miss him," and "we're still fighting for what he believed in," and nobody seemed to care at all he could have been the identical twin of Alfred E. Neuman. That night Curtis learned a whole new vocabulary. He was at a "Klonvocation," the big man at the gate was a "Night Hawk," Roy was one of the "Klabees" who collected money for beer and other things, and Bob Robb, a minister from Key Largo, was the "Kludd," the chaplain who led them in prayer at the beginning of their meetings.

Curtis eagerly took in everything that night. He learned that not so long ago a whole lot of adult white males around the United States had been members of the Ku Klux Klan. However, as a result of the underhanded tactics the federal government had been using over the years, like infiltration and wiretaps, their ranks had greatly thinned. It was all part of the big conspiracy to lock up patriotic white Americans who weren't afraid to tell the truth about what *really* was going on in the country.

After his third beer Curtis suddenly found himself making a speech. He was surprised to find words flying out of his mouth fast and furious, like a preacher speaking at a tent revival, seeing as how he never had done anything like that before. Everybody else looked damned surprised too, especially Roy and Jimmy, their jaws dropping halfway down. After thirty-minutes of non-stop ranting and raving, Curtis Chance Thigpen pretty much had covered everything gone wrong with the world and the reasons why. It seemed like nobody stirred for at least a whole minute, and then they all began shouting at the top of their lungs. Gus and Roy walked over to an aluminum shed, pulled out a six-foot high wooden cross, and dragged it over to the campfire. Curtis had never seen a cross-lighting before. As he stood there, the bright orange flames making the wood snap, crackle, and pop, Curtis couldn't take his eyes off the beauty of the tiny bright-blue border dancing clockwise along the edge of the wood. And all the bad memories about his father, which had haunted him since he was a small child, were consumed in that magnificent blaze.

Word soon got around about this odd-looking boy with the silver tongue. The South Dade Klavern tripled its membership the first year Curtis became the main attraction at its Klonvocations. They joined up in droves because they wanted to see and hear this young charismatic figure spew out his venom against those types they openly or, more likely, secretly despised. They came to hear somebody who had the guts to tell the truth about what *really* was going on, how people of color and others were taking over the whole country, and how they had better stand up and do something about it before it was too late. For the first time in his life Curtis Chance Thigpen experienced what it felt like being looked up to instead of being an object of ridicule. Within a few years their group counted more than five-hundred members, including several who worked in law enforcement.

The South Dade Klavern continued to operate below the community's radar screen, a vow of secrecy still in place because nobody wanted to end up in prison. Whenever they spoke on the telephone or met with someone they didn't know, they would have to identify themselves by exchanging acronym greetings, like

"AYAK" for "Are you a Klansman?" and "AKIA" for "A Klansman I am." In the early eighties things definitely started looking up. For one thing most white hippie types by then had turned into fairly respectable citizens enjoying the good life so it wasn't a concern anymore that segment of society would bring the country down. And a lot of their sons and daughters had started waking up to what *really* was going on, mostly because they often ended up being the victims of the wrong turn the country had taken in the sixties. In high schools where the federal courts had forced integration, they got threatened and beaten up. They didn't get accepted at the best universities because a certain number of minority applicants were guaranteed admittance. They were passed over for good jobs because, at the end of the day, it was the dark color of your skin, not your intelligence, skills, or accomplishments, which mattered most. And to add insult to injury, these sons and daughters of the hippie generation didn't feel safe walking their neighborhoods or even sleeping in their houses.

For the first time in memory it looked like America was starting to take a hard turn to the right. And the demographic of the South Dade Klavern started reflecting this shift, the average age of its membership plummeting from fifty-seven to twenty-five. But they should have anticipated things were going too good to last for very long. Back in 1971 a couple of agitators in Atlanta started something called The Southern Poverty Law Center whose purpose was to provide free legal services to victims of hate crimes. After awhile its mission expanded, and the SPLC became proactive and began monitoring and tracking the activities of the KKK all around the country in a project it named "Klanwatch." In 1981 the SPLC won a lawsuit against the Klan, a federal judge enjoining it from any further racial harassment and intimidation against Vietnamese fishermen in Galveston Bay. That same year the SPLC forced an Alabama county to pay salaries to the staff of its first Negro probate judge. The Klan was not about to take this full frontal assault lying down. In 1983 it burned down the SPLC's 6,000 square-foot office and destroyed its records. But the federal government had a lot of resources, and soon they were able to charge and convict three men of conspiring to threaten, oppress, and intimidate members of black organizations the SPLC represented. Not much long after that more than thirty persons associated with the Klan and other white supremacy groups ended up getting charged, convicted, and jailed for all types of crimes, including several plots to kill Morris Dees, one of the SPLC's founders.

A few years later the worst news would come. Back in 1981 a black man named Josephus Andersonan had gone on trial in Mobile, Alabama for the murder of a white policeman, but the trial ended with a hung jury. Some of the locals believed the jury failed to reach a unanimous guilty verdict because several of the jurors were black. At a Klan meeting after the mistrial, Bennie Hays, number two in rank in the Alabama Klan, said, "If a black man can get away with killing a white man, we ought to be able to get away with killing a black man." That was followed by a cross-lighting on the Mobile County courthouse lawn, and later that night two white men snatched a black teenager named Michael Donald off the street. He was beaten, his throat cut, and then hung from a tree right across the street from where he lived. In 1984 James Knowles, one of the members of Klavern 900, and Henry Hays, Bennie Hays' son, were convicted of Michael Donald's murder. In 1987 Morris Dees obtained a seven-million dollar verdict on behalf of Beulah Mae Donald, the victim's mother, in a wrongful death lawsuit the SPLC had filed against the United Klans of America. Because it wasn't able to pay the multi-million-dollar award, the UKA was forced into bankruptcy and had to deed over its Tuscaloosa County meeting hall to Beulah Mae Donald. She used the proceeds from the sale of that building to buy her first home and then passed away a few months later.

By the end of the eighties the Michael Donald case, and a number of other criminal and civil cases around the country, effectively had chased away just about everybody who used to be associated with the Ku Klux Klan. Even before that Curtis Chance Thigpen and his South Dade Klavern had begun feeling the heat of this oppression. In 1985 investigators from the Internal Revenue Service and the Florida Department of Revenue paid a surprise visit to Wendt's Engine Repair. It turned out Roy Wendt hadn't filed any federal income tax statements for the previous twelve years. Nor had he turned over to the State of Florida thousands of dollars in sales taxes he was required to collect during that same period. Jimmy Wendt was in just as much trouble because his father had put the business in his name three years before. Their lawyers finally convinced them they needed to plead out instead of going to trial after the judge denied their pretrial motion to dismiss. The judge had ruled the law didn't recognize refusing to pay taxes was a legitimate exercise of free speech guaranteed by the First Amendment to the United States Constitution. So Roy and Jimmy ended up accepting a plea bargain whereby their three-year state prison sentences would be served concurrently with four years of federal time. As part of their written plea agreements, they had to forfeit Wendt's Engine Repair to the federal government which would sell it at public auction, applying the proceeds to pay back taxes, fines, and penalties.

By the time Roy and Jimmy Wendt self-surrendered at the federal prison camp at Eglin Air Force Base near Pensacola, the South Dade Klavern counted only a handful of members. Everybody else had been scared off as a result of what was going on between the feds and the Klan. So Curtis Thigpen decided to do the same things other Klan leaders were doing around the country. He changed the name of their group to the Guardians Of The Race, a name suggested by the speech he gave that night Roy Wendt had introduced him to the South Dade Klavern. And instead of using the Klan acronym greetings "AYAK" and "AKIA," he replaced them with "Guardian" and "In Guard's name." Next, he dispensed with secret cross-lightings and organized public marches and rallies instead, always securing the proper permits. At these events they brought a large banner, the American flag, with a swastika in the canton where fifty white five-pointed stars should have been, and the motto "In Guard We Trust." This makeover seemed to be working but, just as people started having the guts again to find out what *really* was going on with the country, something started going very wrong with Curtis Thigpen's health.

It didn't really matter Curtis Thigpen was out of a job after the Marshals padlocked Wendt's Engine Repair and planted a big U.S. Department of Justice for-sale sign on the property. By then he no longer was able to tear down and rebuild an engine anyway. In fact, he couldn't even do simple things anymore, like unscrew a light bulb, without it feeling like needles were being jammed into the tips of his fingers. And then things took another bad turn because he received written notice that in forty-five days on the steps of the Dade County courthouse the Sheriff was going to sell his mother's house. He hadn't paid the property taxes on it for the past four years. And he already knew the courts didn't recognize the First Amendment as a legitimate defense to non-payment of taxes so he allowed the sale go forward without a fight.

Curtis Chance Thigpen had no place to live and no income. He stayed a few weeks at Skeeter's Bar and Package Liquors, sleeping on a cot in the storage room, but he could tell Skeeter didn't like him being there so he finally agreed to go to Deering Hospital to find out what was wrong with him. It turned out he was suffering from a very severe form of diabetes and could apply to the government for total disability. Skeeter found him a place to live in Homestead, a tiny apartment in a rundown two-storey building on West Mowry Drive, subsidized low-income housing he could afford with the monthly checks he began receiving. For a time Skeeter and Jimmy Wendt's son, Bobby, used to come by and take him around town so he could buy things he needed. But that didn't last for long, and he had to start calling them to complain nobody was helping him out. His struggle to show white America what *really* was going on came to an end, a new one taking its place, trying to get through each day alone in a world which slowly was fading away before him.

CHAPTER TWENTY-TWO

As Lifton approached the pulpit Joel Chernin was grinning wide like the proud father of a newborn. "Okay, JC, what the hell happened while I was gone?"

"Step into my office." Lifton followed the detective to the rear of the church. "Want some gum?" Chernin unwrapped the band on the thin red-and-yellow box and shook it until three peppermint Chiclets had dropped into Lifton's hand. "Alright, I'll tell you what happened. While you were taking your sweet time over there at The Reverend's house, I had a nice little conversation with Mr. Piggy up there." Chenin tilted his head toward the pulpit. "*Oh, yeah*, and what a nice little conversation it was, general."

"Well, I see I'm back to general status now so let me take a wild guess. You told Swindall if he gave you a statement and agreed to cooperate, then you'd make sure he got a great deal, maybe even no jail time. But if he didn't, he'd be looking at a lot of time and, *voilá*, a miracle, he gave you a full confession! And then you thought, *damn*, 'I forgot to read him his *Miranda* rights *before* he confessed.' So then you gave him *Miranda* and told him he needed to repeat what he told you before, which he did, of course, because he's thinking the cat's already out of the bag anyway. Am I right, or am I right?"

"Are you finished now?" Chernin chomped on his gum and regarded Lifton with a look of disdain. "You're wrong, bro. I read the fat bastard his rights before he confessed."

"Well, I guess miracles do happen. But you know what? Sanderson and I just had a nice little conversation too."

Chernin leaned forward. "Why am I not surprised?"

"He thinks this case is a lot of bullshit. Well, he used the word 'hooey' instead of 'bullshit.' He says the case really isn't about him, it's something his sister wants, and he won't be part of it. And there's more. If we try and go forward with it, we'll end up looking like a bunch of fools." When Chernin pursed his lips and bobbled his head like he wasn't the least bit fazed, Lifton added, "And you need to know something else. He's taking Thigpen in."

"And just what the hell is that supposed to mean?"

"It means Thigpen is real sick and doesn't have anybody else to take care of him."

"Well, I'm all choked up. And you need to know something else too. Maybe we don't have to give a rat's ass anymore about what Sanderson wants. See, boss, Swindall just gave me a confession about something else that went down. And it's a bigger and better case. We're talking homicide now. A *double homicide*. And we don't need Sanderson for one damn thing on this other one. See, fat bastard up there thought he was horse trading with me. We drop him from The Reverend's case, and he gives us this other one. Of course, he wanted a promise of immunity from prosecution in the other case before he would start talking." Chernin grinned wider and smacked his gum louder.

"Of course. And, of course, you told him you couldn't make that promise because only the prosecutor has the power to do that."

"Of course I didn't tell him that. Don't get all religious on me now because you happen to be in a church. You know damn well how we do things. And I don't hear anybody from your office ever complaining because you all just *love* it when we get confessions. They make your job *so* much easier. So I said to him he was gonna *fry* in Old Sparky if he didn't come completely clean on this new case. Yeah, that's right, while we were having our little chat I just happened to mention he could be looking at the chair. And then, *voilá*, a miracle! He suddenly decides he wants to cooperate fully on this other case. *Oh, yeah*, this dude *really* wants to cooperate on this other case, and he tells me the whole story. And you know what, Lifton? I like you so I'm gonna take the time to tell you about it." Chernin recounted the events of that stormy night a few years ago when Curtis Chance Thigpen bashed in the heads of the mixed couple from New York because they had committed race treason. "So you decide if you want in on this one. If you do, fine. If not, I'll find another prosecutor, and it will be your career on the line not mine."

* * *

Alonzo Norris knocked loudly a few more times, shrugged his shoulders, and turned back toward the street.

"No-Time!" Kimberly Singletary flung open the front door, wrapped her arms around Alonzo Norris, and began sobbing. "Ray left this note saying something urgent came up about a case, and he had to take Demeka with him, and..."

"Now, girl, will you just stop? See? I already rounded up The Posse."

She loosened her grip just enough so she could peer around him. Wayne Parrish, Reginald Crawford, and Donald Leeds were advancing toward the house.

The front door opened again, and Valerie Witherspoon stepped outside. "Well, it's about *time* you all got here."

"*Um-um*," Crawford groaned. "She's still got *atti-tude*."

Valerie took a step forward and shoved him hard, almost making him fall backward, and they all laughed.

"We don't have any power here," Kimberly said, "but the phone started working again so I told Val to give you a call. We've got a little battery radio, but we can't tell what's really going on."

"We've been watching tv in the limo, and South Dade looks like it got nuked."

"Damn, Perishable," Norris mumbled after Kimberly started

sobbing again. "Now listen up, Kim. You don't even know if your brother went down south."

"Oh, no? He left a note saying something urgent came up about a case. And the only case he'd do something as crazy as put my little girl's life in danger is the one you all got him into. And everything about that damn case is out there where the hurricane hit worst. We looked up the numbers for Homestead and Florida City police, but you can't get them to ring. The radio says all lines south of Kendall Drive are dead. And I can't get an operator or even 911 to answer."

Norris put his arms around her again. "Val-er-ie told me all about your situation. That's why I rounded up The Posse. And we decided to come by and personally let you know we're going out south to look for your people."

"But they said nobody's supposed to be driving around. You could get arrested."

"South of Kendall Drive, Kim," Crawford said. "And there's a seven p.m. curfew everywhere in the County. Mayor Clark has declared martial law, but His Majesty No-Time here," he patted Norris on the shoulder, "has declared *nobody* has the legal authority to suspend *his* civil rights."

"Well, you all know I can talk my way out of anything. Now you two ladies just sit tight right here. Let's roll, my Posse. We've got a long drive ahead of us. Good thing my man Carlos stocked up on the Black Label before this damn storm hit."

* * *

The Mercedes limousine slowed to a stop, and the smoked-glass panel descended. "Señor Norris, I can't see no more where is the road."

A thick carpet of tree limbs, palm fronds, and other severed vegetation lay directly ahead of them covering up most of Old Cutler Road.

"Keep on going, Carlos," Norris instructed him. "Just make sure you don't run into the mangroves on the left over there."

The chauffeur inched the limousine forward, and it rocked

gently as the tires crunched piles of debris. A quarter mile ahead
two odd-looking camouflage-painted military vehicles blocked
their way. Three National Guardsmen jumped out of one of them,
slung their M-16 assault rifles over their shoulders, and advanced
quickly toward the limousine. One of the soldiers gestured for
Carlos to get out. A few seconds later the rear doors flew open,
and the other two soldiers stuck their heads inside. "Everybody
out!" they barked at the same time. The soldier standing next to
Carlos pulled off his sunglasses and squinted. "No-Time? Is that
you? You remember me? Darnell Rozier. You handled my
cousin's rape charge a couple of years ago."

"Is your cousin Cleveland Rozier?"

"Yes, sir," the black soldier chuckled. "Guys, this here's No-
Time Norris, the best damn criminal attorney in the whole world.
The jury walked my cousin in under twenty minutes." He went
over to Norris, and they hugged. "How are you, No-Time?"

"I'm good, Darnell. How's Cleveland doing?"

"He and the family are doing real good, No-Time. He got his
old job back too."

"Well, that's just great. You be sure and give him my best
regards, Darnell, alright?"

"I will, No-Time. I sure will. Listen," the soldier continued,
his tone becoming serious, "you know we've got martial law going
on in Dade County. Nobody is supposed to be driving around
south of Kendall Drive unless they're trying to get back home.
We've got orders to take any violators into custody."

Norris turned to the two white soldiers. "Well, we can dig
that, but we've got a real situation here."

A few minutes later, after the three soldiers had conferred
privately about what Norris had told them, Darnell Rozier returned
and said, "Look, we can appreciate your situation. We know you
need to find your people, but it's just too damn dangerous right
now. There's a lot of looters out that way, and you all might get
shot by mistake. Our orders are zero tolerance."

"Darnell, let me ask you something. Do we look like we

Guardians Of The Faith

could be looters driving around in a Mercedes limo, or do we look more like we'd be the *lootees*?"

"Now, hold on, No-Time. I've got good news. You all just earned yourselves a military escort."

"And you all just earned yourself some Johnny Walker. Carlos, give these soldiers a bottle of Johnny Walker Black. So what the hell are those crazy-ass vehicles you boys got over there?"

"Oh, those damn things? Follow me," Rozier said with a sweep of his hand. "Go ahead and take a look inside. They delivered a whole fleet of these Humvees last month. They're replacing our jeeps and other light tactical vehicles."

"I can see it now," Norris made a circular motion with his right hand like he was filming a scene. "The Posse cruising down Ocean Drive in a big black Humvee limo."

"I'm not down with that," Parrish said. "You give me your Mercedes limo, No-Time. These things are so damn ugly the ladies would be running away even from you."

"You think so, Perishable? You stretch out one of these babies, slap on some nice rims, put in a good sound system, and you've got one *bad* ride."

"Well, you rich lawyers don't have to be troubling yourselves about all that," Rozier said as he climbed into one of the Humvees. "These are strictly military vehicles. So unless any of you are planning on joining up with the Florida National Guard, you're never gonna be riding around in one of these babies anyway."

"Never say never." Norris pulled open the passenger door. "I'm gonna ride with you Darnell, alright?"

Rozier looked over at the other two soldiers who nodded their approval. "Well, alright, but just you, No-Time. And tell your driver to make sure he follows us real close. If we don't find your people soon, I'm putting your big black asses on the Turnpike so you all can make it home before the seven p.m. curfew."

* * *

The faint whirring of the rotors turned into a deafening roar as the police helicopter approached the church. It hovered briefly over the gaping hole in the roof before setting down in the big open field behind Sanderson's house.

"The cavalry has arrived!" Stewart Malman called out as he entered the church. "Ray, there's somebody out there looking for you and The Reverend."

"Major Kevin Trawick," the burly uniformed Metro-Dade officer introduced himself. "Well, you can see it's one royal mess we've got on our hands. But trust me. From a bird's-eye view, it looks a thousand times worse than what you're able to see on the ground. The other guy said you've got one injured but nothing life-threatening. Chief Taylor ordered me to take the chopper to try and locate you. Detective Chernin made some arrests out here on one of your cases, right? I'm supposed to bring you and the victim back reference a six p.m. press conference at the State Attorney's Office. That's all I know about the situation. Does Chernin need me to call for a unit to help with transport of the defendants?"

"Well, thanks for checking up on us, young man," Sanderson said, holding out his hand. "You have a safe trip back," he added, then turned and walked away.

"I guess the big shots downtown are in some kind of hurry to go public with your case. Personally, with all that's going on right now, I think it's a pretty damned stupid thing to be doing. I'm supposed to be at the EOC right now dealing with the biggest natural disaster this County has ever seen. So please go and get the old man, and let's get the hell outta here, okay?"

"I'm really sorry, Major," Lifton said shaking his head, "but we won't be going back with you."

Before Trawick could say anything a camouflage-painted military vehicle roared onto the church property, a black Mercedes limousine following in its wake.

"My main man, Liftoff!" Alonzo Norris jumped down from the Humvee. "Your magnificent Posse has arrived!"

Lifton grabbed Norris' hand and twisted it, and they gave each other a hard back-slapping hug. "You're starting to sound a lot like Don King."

"Now that's alright as long as I don't start *looking* a lot like him," Norris chuckled. "Are you okay, my brother?"

"Have you talked to Kimberly?"

"Did I talk to her? Man, I rounded up the whole Posse, and we went by your place to personally tell her we were coming out here looking for you. Your lady, Val-er-ie, was there too. And they're both fine except for being worried sick about you and your niece. I'd try and call your sister right now, but my mobile isn't working out here."

"Thanks for doing this, No-Time. So how the hell did you swing a military escort? Wait, hold on." Lifton went back to where Trawick was waiting and asked him to call for an ambulance and to try and notify his sister that Demeka was doing fine. After Trawick jotted down his home number, Lifton shepherded the protesting police major over to the open door, pumped his hand, and sprinted away from the helicopter. The rotors began whirling, the chopper rose straight up two-hundred feet, then tilted north and thundered away. Norris had been joined now by Crawford, Leeds, and Parrish.

"Damn, Liftoff," Parrish muttered. "We were supposed to be first to your rescue. The Posse *never* finishes in second place."

"Well, you made it here fast enough. Don't go in the street. Power lines are down, and there's other dangers lurking out there."

"Everybody okay, Ray?" Leeds asked.

"We're all fine, Doc, except for one."

"Part of the church roof fell on him," Sanderson said as he joined the group. "He might have some broken bones."

"This is The Reverend Wilkie P. Sanderson."

The new arrivals introduced themselves and shook hands with Sanderson.

"Please tell me it was that Thigpen dude who got hurt."

"No, Perishable, it was Swindall, the one they call Skeeter."

"You all holed up inside the church during the storm?"

"That's right, Seven. Me, Demeka, The Reverend, Chernin, a guy named Stewart from up north, and two of the targets,

Swindall and Thigpen. We also had a bunch of cats and dogs and birds and even a horse in there with us."

"Well, I better go take a look at the guy who got hurt."

"I'll go with you, Doc," Sanderson said as Leeds started toward the church. "What did you say your name was again?"

Norris regarded Lifton curiously. "Did I hear you right? I could swear you just said 'targets.' Once you arrest somebody, he's not a target anymore, he's a defendant. Am I right, or am I right?"

Crawford reached over and slapped Lifton on the back. "Did you know, Ray, you're the number two news story today? You gave people something to feel good about in the middle of this big bad mess."

Parrish made fists and crouched down, twisting from side to side, then lunging back and forth like he was punching Lifton. "And number two ain't too shabby considering the number one story is about one of the biggest natural disasters ever to hit the United States of America. Our man Liftoff is about to be crowned the new heavyweight champion of prosecutors."

"Wait up, Wayne." Norris' smile was gone. "I'm picking up a bad vibe. You all should know what I'm talking about." He folded his arms and narrowed his eyes. "Please tell me you already arrested those Guardian dudes."

"Nobody got arrested, No-Time. It turns out that Reverend Sanderson doesn't want to prosecute."

"Oh, that's funny, Ray." Parrish stood up and wagged a finger at Lifton. "That's *very* funny."

"He's not joking, Wayne."

"Yeah, *right*, No-Time. It wasn't Liftoff who got knocked in the head when the roof came down."

"Man, Ray, you *cannot* be serious."

"Hold on, Seven." Norris held up his hands. "Let's say Sanderson told you that, Ray. *So what*? He's just the victim. Your office makes the decision whether to prosecute. Sure, you all care a little bit about what the victim wants, but the victim can't force you to drop a case. You boys in the State Attorney's Office remind me about that shit all the time. Like when you charge some dude with domestic violence, but the wife doesn't want to press charges because the couple made up. And then one of your hotshot prosecutors right out of law school tells me the case isn't going away because he's got a picture the cops took when they responded to the wife's 911, some tiny little bruise on the wife's hand. Except the wife forgot to mention she got it when *she* smacked her husband. So you know damn well, when you've got evidence of a crime, it doesn't matter what the hell the victim wants. You all still do whatever you all damn well please."

"Ray, everybody assumed things had gone according to plan. There's a press conference about the case at six."

"I already heard about it from the guy in the helicopter, Seven. Don't you think it would have been a whole lot smarter to make sure first there was gonna be a damn case?"

"I *can't* believe this shit," Parrish said. "Yesterday Chernin called and said everything was going according to plan."

Doc Leeds stepped outside when he heard the wail of a siren. A few seconds later a lime-green Dade County fire-rescue truck pulled up in front of the church and two paramedics jumped down. They opened the rear doors and pulled out a stretcher. A few minutes later they were wheeling Swindall over to the truck and, with Malman's help, hoisted the stretcher up and pushed it inside. The truck's bank of red-and-white emergency lights activated, and a foghorn erupted with ear-splitting blasts.

"He'll be okay," Leeds said, "but it does look like he's got a couple of broken bones."

"Is Chernin inside the church there?" Parrish asked. "I say we go and get him and have this thing out right now. After all we did, are we just..."

"You can save your breath, Wayne," Norris interrupted. "I know this dude. C'mon, let's roll." He turned and started walking over to the limousine.

"Take care, Ray." Lifton could tell from his expression Doc Leeds knew what was going on. After all he had just spent the last few minutes inside the church with Sanderson.

Crawford grabbed Lifton's arm. "Ray, some advice from an old friend. If you don't show your face at your office today, it's gonna be a real bad thing."

"I know, Seven. So, tell me, how is it out there?"

"Well, we came down US 1 and then got on Red Road. Things didn't start looking all that bad until we crossed Kendall Drive. It's like some kind of freaky dividing line. The streets south of there are covered up with trees and all kinds of shit. It's damn total destruction south of Kendall Drive. You all take the Turnpike back, and you'll be okay."

"Anything happen to your properties?"

Reginald Crawford smiled and slapped Liston's shoulder. "No damage at all. Can you believe it? My good luck streak is still going strong."

* * *

Kimberly Singletary started down the porch too quickly when she saw the faded-blue Volvo coming down the street. She tumbled to the ground at the bottom of the steps, picked herself up, raced to the curb, and tore open the right rear door. "My baby!"

"You okay, sis?"

"Now that I see my baby I am."

He found Valerie in the kitchen and crept up silently behind her. "Bernice Valerie Witherspoon." He wrapped his arms around her waist and squeezed hard. "I'm happy to see you too," he added after she turned and pushed him away.

"You're not funny anymore, Ray."

"Look, Val-er-ie, I know you all probably want to kill me for taking Demeka out south. It's a long story."

"Oh, we already know your long story, Ray. Some police major called here, and then your friends did too."

"You already knew Demeka was okay? So what's the damn problem then?"

She leaned back against the counter and crossed her arms, shaking her head like he had just said something very stupid.

"You're the damn problem, Ray. A lot of people did a lot of things for you, and this is how you thank them?" He started to say something, but she cut him off. "Remember our first date? I told you what *my* thing was, and then I asked you what was *yours*? And you said you didn't have one. Well, you really did, and now I know what it is. For sure now I know what it is. *Your* thing is you never got to make it big as a pro player so you do everything in your power to make sure you never make it big as *anything* else. That's *your* thing. And it's so damn stupid and childish."

"You don't know what's going on."

"*Oh, really*?! You got a big second chance with that hate-crimes case. You were gonna be the next Dade State Attorney, and then after that anything would be possible. Whatever you could dream, Mayor Lifton, Senator Lifton, President Lifton. But now it's never gonna happen, *never*, because as soon as you start moving up, *you* always find a way to bring yourself down."

"*Black* President Lifton? I don't think so."

"You're not funny anymore, Ray."

Kimberly had been eavesdropping on their conversation and stepped into the kitchen. "You put Demeka in danger, Ray! And for what? To sabotage your own future?"

Valerie picked up the big canvas handbag sitting on one of the kitchen chairs and shook it violently a few times trying to locate her keys. "You're not funny *or* interesting anymore," she muttered as she walked out of the kitchen. Before she slammed the front door, she shouted back, "Take care, Kim!"

"I can't believe this."

"Believe it, Ray. You just tore up your ticket to ride." His sister turned to leave. "Somebody called and said you've gotta be at The Big Girl's office at five-thirty."

* * *

Lifton entered the four-number code on the keypad, there was a loud groan, and the motorized chain-link door began ascending. The underground parking lot was pitch-black except for the area near the elevators where a handful of cars were parked.

Guardians Of The Faith

A pair of 2000 kilowatt Caterpillar generators perched atop giant cement slabs were humming loudly nearby, providing standby power for the Metro Justice Building. The receptionist ignored him as Lifton stepped into the Office of the Dade State Attorney. She picked up the phone and pressed a button. "He's here."

"Send him in. And, Nancy, see if there's anybody in the press room."

"Hello, Ray." Madeline Menendez rose from behind Susan Purvis' massive desk and leaned across it to shake his hand. The Cuban-American Chief Deputy had a look very different from that of The Big Girl, the extra-large t-shirt and baggy sweat pants unable to hide her shapely figure. She had thick shoulder-length brown hair and brilliant green eyes and looked more like a soap-opera star than a prosecutor. "You were expecting Susan, huh? Right now she's a thousand miles away doing the campaign thing. Lucky her, huh? Well, the presidential election is only two months away so I can understand that, but it means I have to deal with all the bad shit Andrew has dropped on us. Unlucky me, huh? Do you know how many arrests there have been since daybreak for looting and other crimes? And then we've got the nice folks streaming down from Broward and Palm Beach selling ice at twenty dollars a bag. Carpetbaggers from the North! And can you believe people are actually paying that much so their food won't spoil? It's Civil War *déjà vu*. We should thank the Lord downtown Miami didn't take the bad hit. Could you imagine what that would have been like? Glass everywhere and stores and office buildings ransacked. But I'm going way off on a tangent. I didn't bring you in here to listen to me complain about this disaster I've inherited. You're here to give the people of Dade County some good news about your hate-crimes case. You know about the press conference at six, right?"

She sat back down in the big oxblood leather chair. "Have a seat. You know, Joel Chernin called here a little while ago and spoke with the Duty Assistant. That crazy detective told him something weird, but we all know Chernin *is* weird. He said something like you were dropping the case." After Lifton gave her a brief account of what had transpired, she reflected for a moment. "Well, that is a pretty strange story. Anyway, have you seen the teaser hyping the case on tv today? 'Good news for South Florida, star prosecutor announces arrests under new hate-crimes law,' and a clip of you making a slam-dunk when you played for the Canes.'"

"So who was the genius who gave the press the story before there was a story?"

"Who cares? What you need to do now is get together with Beverly Sanderson as soon as possible. She'll straighten out her brother, and the case will go forward."

"Actually, she's the last person in the world he would listen to. In fact, he blames her for starting this whole mess. And there's one more thing you need to know."

"*Mess*? What mess? Look, Ray, I hardly know anything about your case except for what you just told me. I've had my hands full here ever since Susan headed out on the Clinton campaign trail. But the bad guys are Klan types, and the victim is an elderly African-American minister and the brother of a very popular Dade County politician. That's a case made in prosecutor heaven. And I can tell you this, Ray. If Bill Clinton wins the election, Susan very well might be asked to join the new administration. At least that's the buzz going around. And she's been counting on you to raise her political capital with a high-profile case under the new hate-crimes law. And you, my friend, would be looking at some very good vertical movement in this Office. Do you understand what I'm saying?"

"There's one more thing you need to know. The Reverend is taking in..."

"I already know what I need to know," she cut him off and stood up.

The intercom buzzed. "Madeline, the press room is pretty much full."

"Okay, Nancy, thanks. Look, I'll take care of this today. I'll talk about Hurricane Andrew and all the arrests we made so far and warn people they better not become looters or carpetbaggers. I'll even try and delay this thing for awhile until I get some people over here." She breezed past him. "Nancy, call the EOC. I need to speak to somebody high up with Mayor Clark, same for Chief Taylor. Tell them I'm doing a press conference about the current situation, and we need some of their people down here in thirty minutes. Tell them it's about how we're throwing everybody's ass in jail who violates the curfew or price gouges, you know, stuff like that." She turned back to Lifton. "No matter how much I talk about Andrew, somebody will be asking me about your case. I'll just say we're focusing on Andrew right now, and all other matters have to take a backseat. Okay, I need to change my clothes, fix my hair, put on some makeup, and get ready for my appearance on *Meet The Press*."

As he waited for the one elevator in service, Lifton noticed a tall figure with a big shoulder bag strutting down the dimly-lit hallway like a runway model. "Rayfield Lifton, I presume," she said. "When they told us this thing was going to be delayed, I took a peek outside and caught you trying to make your getaway."

"Kara Mello, I presume." Her creamy-white complexion contrasted starkly with her raven Cleopatra-style hair, bangs halfway down her forehead, the rest falling to her shoulders. Lifton pressed the call button a few more times.

"Anybody ever tell you doing that doesn't make the elevator come faster?"

"You really *can* learn something new every day." He made sure she saw his smirk.

"My reporter instincts and your sunny disposition tell me your big case has taken a bad turn. Oh, Lord, I *am* right," she added after he gave her a dirty look. "Well, at least I got one good story today. You heard President Bush flew into town, right? I interviewed him. I had assumed he came down here so fast because he's been dropping in the polls like a lead balloon, and the election is just around the corner. But I've gotta tell you. After I met the guy, I think he genuinely is concerned about this disaster."

There was a loud ding, and the elevator doors opened.

"Where are you going?"

"Where do you think? A reporter is supposed to follow the next big story. I need to find out what happened to your case because so far you're still the next big story."

He extended his right arm to prevent the doors from closing, and they abruptly jerked back open.

"Liftoff Lifton," she sighed. "So your hate-crimes case has a problem. That doesn't necessarily mean it's the end of the story." She pulled his arm back. When he didn't reach out again, she pressed the close-door button. "Now that's a good boy. You don't know this yet, but I'm partly responsible for your problems. So we need to talk."

"Fine." He scowled and folded his arms. "But don't call me boy again, okay?"

She giggled and pushed the button a few more times.

"Anybody ever tell you doing that doesn't make the doors close faster?"

* * *

They found shade near the main entrance to the Metro Justice building. The sun had descended to just above the horizon, but the temperature and humidity were still both in the nineties.

"Can you believe no breeze?" Kara Mello lit a cigarette and dropped the lighter back in her bag. "Not too many hours ago the wind was clocked at one-hundred something around here."

"So how are you responsible for my problem?"

"I'm getting there, Liftoff Lifton. Believe me, I don't want to be out here too long. My hair will frizz up."

"You said you were responsible for my problem."

"*Wow*, so serious, you! I said *partly* responsible." She took a long drag on her cigarette then tapped it so the ash would fall off. "Your detective has been keeping me in the loop for awhile now. But there were things which didn't sound right to me. Anyway, a few days ago when he told me you were close to wrapping up the case, against my better judgment I dug out the archival footage, pulled some newspaper articles, and whipped up a fifteen-second teaser for the story. Then Chernin called yesterday and said he was on his way out to make the arrests. So even though it's all about Andrew today I got my people to run the teaser. That way everybody would be looking for the story at eleven. And the audio portion has been running all day on our AM affiliate. You know, why not give the public some good news to balance out the bad? We'd get the rest of what we needed for the story at today's press conference. Everybody who's got their power back will be glued to the tv tonight about Andrew, and a lot of them will be expecting to find out about your case too."

Kara Mello took another long drag on her cigarette. "The teaser went something like this. 'Tonight at eleven on TV 5 an exclusive report. Can there be any good news for South Florida after Hurricane Andrew? The State Attorney's Office announces arrests in a major hate-crimes case. What is the alleged hate-crime? Who was its intended victim? And who is the *star* prosecutor trying to *slam-dunk* the alleged perpetrators under the new hate-crimes law? The surprising answers to these questions tonight at eleven *only* on TV 5.' There were a couple of video clips, Thigpen at a Guardians rally, a pan of Sanderson's little church and, of course, the legendary Liftoff Lifton making one of his famous slam-dunks. I think the footage was from a Gators game. You and Sanderson would have a press conference today, we'd get that in the can, and then we'd be good to go with the full story at eleven. I had you all packaged up as a big black knight in shining armor." She dropped her cigarette and stubbed it out with the toe of her left stiletto-heel shoe. "And don't give me another one of your dirty looks. I hate people who litter too, but you can see they took all the trash containers inside before the storm hit."

"That's not the reason for the dirty look."

"Oh, I see. It's because I said you were a big *black* knight in shining armor? Well, I couldn't very well say you were a big *white* knight in shining armor now could I? And I assume you're joking anyway. If you're not, it's because you don't know me, and that would be your own fault."

"My fault? How am I supposed to know you?"

"Bad memory, counselor. You don't remember when I reached out to you? I said a not-so-little bird told me you had a big case for me to scoop. You didn't want to talk to me. You said there were timing issues. I mentioned your colleagues try and get me into the mix early on because they know I put together a nice package. And then you made that cute little remark about your own package. I asked you *twice* if you wanted to know what I already knew, but you weren't interested. I even told you how much I used to love watching you play basketball."

"I remember talking to you, and it wasn't the right time back then to get you into the mix. And it turns out there never was a right time because there is no case."

"But, see, you're forgetting something important. You said it wasn't the right time because things hadn't happened yet. And then I said 'maybe that's the best reason why you should talk to me now.' *But, no,*" she batted her eyelashes dramatically, "you weren't interested in what I already knew."

"Which was?"

"*Which was,*" the reporter continued with a trace of sarcasm in her voice, "Thigpen and his Guardians weren't doing anything anymore. After the couple of pieces I did on them, I asked our investigators to follow up a few times. I wanted to know what they were up to. And guess what they found out? For the past three years no marches, no rallies, no nothing. And that's what the Guardians Of The Race have been up to. A whole lot of nothing. And that's what we would have talked about, you and me, but you never gave me the chance."

"I think you wanted to scoop what you thought was going to be a good story about a case under a controversial new law, and it didn't make any difference if..."

"You know," she interrupted, "I think I'm already starting to frizz up." She pulled a tissue from her bag and dabbed at her forehead. "Of course I always want to scoop a good story. That's why they pay me the big bucks. But that doesn't mean I'm a pooper scooper. Crap is crap. So when I heard you were going after Thigpen and his band of fools, the right thing to do was to have a sit down with you and share my information. You know, before you stuck your neck out there too far where it might get cut off. Why? Because when you played for the University of Miami, you gave us all something to cheer about. And in this world into which we're born, that's a rare commodity. I really didn't want to see you get hurt. So call me crazy. I said I'm *partly* responsible for your problem because I went ahead with the teaser anyway when something didn't feel right. And that's just not me. Hurricane Andrew made us all a little crazy, but I'm not saying that's an excuse. I should have talked to you first." She picked up the crushed cigarette with the tissue and rolled it into a little ball. "Listen, I'm going back to the press room. You can wait around for me if you like. We could have that long talk we never had, that is, if you still want to."

"What about the curfew? You're not supposed to be on the street after seven."

"The press is exempt. So where are you going to be hanging out in a little while?"

"My office on the ninth floor. If the lights are working, we can shoot some baskets."

Kara Mello dropped the tissue into her big bag and snapped it shut. "Well, I'm not sure what you mean by that, Liftoff Lifton, but it sounds intriguing. And you know what? Don't worry about the lights. I went to night school."

CHAPTER TWENTY-THREE

Aubrey Swindall gently set down his third cup of piping hot coffee, pulled a paper napkin from the silver dispenser, and pressed it against his forehead. It soaked up a pool of sweat which had been accumulating there for a couple of minutes after his visitor slid into the booth across from him. "Son of a bitch," he cursed silently as the napkin broke apart. He balled it up, brought it under the table, and let it drop to the floor. He couldn't tell if Malman knew he was shitting bricks. All the fucking delays from the fucking hurricane! He needed to close the deal before these New Yorkers found out about the insurance situation. Otherwise, they would try and jew him down big time.

"So what are you ordering, Aubrey?" Malman asked without looking up.

"Hell, I don't even know yet, Stewart."

Malman continued flipping through the laminated pages of the menu so Swindall grabbed a thick wad of napkins, folded them once, and dabbed lightly at his wet cheeks. Dammit! That strange feeling was welling up inside him again. *Bad luck!* Now he had to erase "jew him down" on his mind's blackboard and in its place write "beat him down." If he didn't go through this ritual, Swindall was certain something terrible was going to happen to Emily or him or both of them. He really wasn't worried about himself anymore after getting the biggest pass of his life with those criminal cases behind him now. But his wife never had done anything bad to anybody. He needed to get *paid* so he could give her a better life even if it was to be one without him. He had turned out to be such a worthless piece of shit. He couldn't even give her a child to share her life with as she grew older.

The waitress spied the big oaf dropping napkins on the floor *again*. "I should make that asshole pick up his own trash," she grumbled as she began trekking toward the kissing booth. "Well, then again, maybe not." That good-looking military guy was there now, the big tipper who always called her by her first name. "Oh, my Lord," she winced as she got closer. "The fat slob is sweating like a pig." This odd couple's relationship had to be on the rocks, she concluded, but she still hoped cutie-pie would be in a generous mood like the last time she had waited on him.

Swindall noticed the waitress approaching and flicked his wrist, shooing her away. She raised her pen and pad like "you don't want to order?" "No," he mouthed and shook his head so she turned around and sauntered back to the main dining room.

"Oh, this *really* is messed up." Malman was torturing him, continuing to review the menu without looking up. Swindall grasped the handle of the coffee cup, but he didn't dare lift it to his mouth. His hand started trembling as he relived his recent meeting with Charlie Newcastle.

"I'm buying the donuts this time, Jolly Green," Charlie beamed as Swindall stormed through the front door of The Newcastle Insurance Agency.

"Cut the damn bullshit, Charlie," Swindall snorted, "and just give me the bottom line. Tell me when I'm getting my damn insurance check."

"Sit down, Aubrey, if you would please, and let me try and explain the situation." Newcastle was wearing a white short-sleeve dress shirt with a button-down collar and a wide burgundy tie which fell only halfway to his waist.

"I don't need any explanation about any situation, Charlie.

I just need my damn insurance money, Charlie."

"But, Aubrey, like I told you over the phone, if you already sold your place, it's the new owners who would be entitled to any insurance proceeds."

Swindall lowered himself into one of the guest chairs and leaned so far forward his chin almost touched the desk. "I *didn't* sell my place yet," he hissed. "The *closing* got *cancelled* because of fucking Hurricane Andrew."

Newcastle folded his hands on his lap and tossed his head back. "I see. So that fellow from up north, Milton, Mellon, the guy who called me awhile back to verify your coverages, he never..."

"Listen, Charlie, I gotta get outta Dodge like right now. I haven't seen Emily since before Andrew. She's been staying up in The Panhandle with her sister. It's already been a month since I called you the first time and said I needed my money!"

Newcastle put his arms behind his head and leaned back too far, causing his feet to leave the floor, his arms flailing wildly to prevent himself from tipping over backwards. He pulled open a desk drawer, took out some Kleenex, and blew his nose. "Wow, that was a close one."

"I need my money, Charlie."

"Aubrey, if you would, please." Newcastle gestured for Swindall to move back a little. "Thanks." The insurance agent opened a manilla folder, flipped through a few pages, closed it, and cleared his throat. "Okay, here's the situation. The claims adjusters have been out to your place several times now, and they have recommended your claims be denied. Hold on! I know what you're gonna say, but let me finish. The commercial carrier takes the position the high winds were the *direct* cause of your losses. Your place got hit with a Cat Five storm and probably one or more tornados. There were hundreds of tornados embedded in that hurricane, and they were twisting around at two-hundred plus. I'm not making that up. It's right there in the reports." Newcastle tapped on the manilla folder a few times. "I know what you're gonna say. Your commercial package covered fire losses. But that's not what the carrier is saying. It's saying the fire got started when all those gasoline containers you were storing blew around and somehow ignited. There were initial breaches of some type, broken windows or holes in the roof, which allowed the high winds to start swirling around inside your building. And then, as all that gasoline was fueling the fire, the propane tanks exploded, causing severe structural damage. You see, the thing is you got hit with a double whammy. If Andrew would have been a normal hurricane, it would have brought torrential rains, putting out the fire long before your building burned to the ground, or those propane tanks would have exploded. The driving rains would have acted like giant fire hoses. But this wasn't your typical hurricane. It was unusually dry because it moved across the Florida Peninsula so fast. Hell, we get more rain with just a garden-variety August thunderstorm than we got with Andrew." Newcastle paused for a moment to let Swindall think about everything he had said.

"And, Aubrey, there's one last thing you need to understand. The commercial carrier has made a reservation of rights to declare the policy void if you decide to fight the denial of coverage. They say you lied on your application because you never disclosed you stored gasoline and propane on the premises, and you had no legitimate business purpose to have all those highly-combustible items there. If an insured lies on his application, under Florida law, the insurer can declare the policy void for fraud. And if you bring a lawsuit, and the insurance company wins, you'll get socked for some big attorney's fees. But hold on! There's a lot of people in the same boat as you. The insurance companies are facing twenty-five *billion* in claims so they're pretty desperate, blaming everything they can on the windstorm."

"But, see, that's what I can't understand, Charlie. What the hell *is* a hurricane *except* a big fucking windstorm?! My place was there before this big fucking windstorm, and now it ain't there after, and I was supposed to have insurance so I could get paid. To me everything else is just a lot of mumbo-jumbo and bullshit. You guaranteed me I had the best insurance, Charlie! I was supposed to get $750,000! So tell me why the fuck I'm totally screwed now!"

Before he answered, Newcastle rubbed his hands and blew into them a few times like it was freezing-cold inside his office. "You do have great insurance, and you always get the best rates. It's just you don't have *every* type of coverage. A lot of people are in the same boat as you, Aubrey. See, hurricanes always cause a lot of damage from heavy rains and flooding so most people assume they'll collect under their flood, homeowners, or commercial policies which also pay for losses of personal property, you know, furniture, appliances, clothing, stuff like that. But what the insurance companies are saying in your case is hurricane-force *winds* were the *direct* cause of your losses."

"Well, then I must be pretty fucking stupid because I still don't understand. Are you saying nobody around here is getting any insurance money? That don't sound right, Charlie, no sir, that don't sound right. There's gotta be something missing in all this mumbo-jumbo and bullshit you're telling me."

"Well, quite frankly, Aubrey, there is." Newcastle turned beet red as he continued in a low voice. "There are folks who have something called windstorm insurance. A lender requires it when it gives a mortgage, and it's named as an additional insured on the policy. Now in your particular case you didn't have that type of coverage but, then again, there are a lot of people who are in the same boat as..."

"Wait!" Swindall held up a hand and pushed back in his chair. "Are you telling me there was some other insurance I should have had? Is that what you're telling me now, Charlie?"

"Listen to me, Aubrey. In all the years I've been in business most people who own their property outright, like you do, don't want to pay for a windstorm policy because it's so damn expensive. The premiums cost like three times more than homeowners or flood. So people figure it's a good deal to roll the dice on roof damage and such and just pay for it out-of-pocket. I mean, hell, for an average house you're only talking fifteen thousand for a brand-new roof. So if we don't get a bad hurricane for ten years, and the

Guardians Of The Faith

windstorm premium is three-thousand a year, you've saved twice what a whole damn new roof would cost. And the State of Florida doesn't make windstorm coverage mandatory like they do with PIP for your vehicles. Look, Aubrey, we haven't had a bad hurricane in Monroe or Dade in nearly sixty years. People got to feeling too lucky, I guess."

"You never told me about windstorm coverage, Charlie. I don't know jack-shit about insurance. I trusted you, Charlie!"

"Look, I know you're real upset," Newcastle said sheepishly, "but the fact is I tell *all* my new clients about the availability of windstorm coverage and give them the option to purchase it. And I'm sure I did the same with you way back when for both your house *and* your business. That's my standard operating procedure. You took out the flood policy because your business is located in Zone A, a Special Flood Hazard Area. You decided to purchase the commercial package to protect yourself mainly from slip-and-fall and other types of negligence lawsuits and fires started by people leaving burning cigarettes around. I've always prided myself on what I do here. Never had an unhappy client as far back as I can remember, but I guess that's about to change now. Look over there, Aubrey." He pointed across the room to a table piled high with manilla folders. "Yeah, all those folks are in the same boat as you. By the way, Aubrey, didn't you tell me there wasn't any damage to your house? That's pretty amazing for *any* property out there in Florida City."

Swindall covered his eyes with his right hand and rocked back and forth. "Charlie, this can't be happening. What am I gonna tell Emily?"

"Hey, get a grip on it, big guy," Newcastle said firmly. "You know, I'm really glad you finally came over here. I could tell you haven't been paying attention to me on the phone because you've been so upset. Listen to me! You've still got a signed agreement. The hurricane didn't destroy that! You can *force* those buyers to go through with the purchase. Don't let those New Yorkers try and wiggle out of your deal because of what happened to your place.

The law is on your side, my friend. Remember when I gave you that power-of-attorney? You didn't have to pay a lawyer for that document, it allowed you to sign the papers for your wife, and that made the whole deal legal. You tell those buyers if they don't close on your property and pay up this is going to litigation. And make sure they understand it's not just about handing over the earnest money. You tell them you're taking them to court to get the *whole* damn purchase price."

"I've got a meeting with Stewart Malman tomorrow," Swindall said weakly.

"Why the long face, then? Would he be making that trip all the way down here if he thought he could weasel his way out of the deal? I don't think so. He'd just call and tell you to take a hike."

"But what if they don't end up buying my place? I don't get the $750,000 from them, and I don't get it from the insurance. I need that money, Charlie. I need a house for me and Emily up there in The Panhandle. And I need that money so I can get into the real-estate business with my brother-in-law. Otherwise, I'm gonna be totally screwed!"

Charlie Newcastle stood up, went around his desk, and held out his hand. "You just remember I'm always here for you, my friend. You go and have your meeting tomorrow and let me know what happened. Remember, if the buyers try and pull a fast one, I know a couple of pretty good lawyers, real pit-bulls. One way or the other this is all going to work out, believe me." Newcastle guided Swindall to the front door. "Hang tough, Jolly Green!" he shouted as Swindall climbed into his pickup.

"Aubrey?" The sound of Stewart Malman's voice startled Swindall, bringing him back from his daydream. "Aubrey?" He picked up the mug at an angle, his hand trembling violently, and a big pool of coffee spilled across the table. Malman scooted out of the booth to avoid getting soaked and went to the main dining room. He returned a minute later smiling and chatting with their waitress, his arm around her. She gave Swindall a dirty look as she mopped up the table with a big white rag.

"I'll be right back with your coffee, sir," she said to Malman, not even bothering to ask Swindall if he wanted another refill.

"So, Stewart, you came down here to close the deal, right?"

"Well, that depends." Malman grinned that special way someone does when he has the other person by the balls. He waited until the waitress had returned with his coffee before saying anything else. "Thanks, Frances." Malman picked up the mug and took a cautious sip. "What I mean, Aubrey, is Karen and I still are willing to go forward with the purchase, but the price will have to be adjusted to fit the current situation."

"The current situation?" Swindall felt a wave of intense heat as blood rushed to his head, and he started getting a little dizzy. "Look, *dude*, I already talked to my people. This is going to litigation if you try and pull any shit!"

"*Really*?" Malman said calmly. "Well, I don't know who your people are, Aubrey, but they're dead wrong. You want litigation? Knock yourself out. You'll spend a ton of money and end up with nothing." He stared at Swindall as he took another small sip of coffee. "On the other hand, if you still want to sell your place, well, then..."

Swindall fidgeted with the napkin dispenser until it fell over. "So then what are we talking about here?"

"What we're talking about here is seventy-five, seeing as how you turned out to be such a racist fucking piece of shit. You know, *dude*, I've lost more than a few good friends overseas. I've even seen a couple of them get their heads blown clean off. And for what? To keep the world safe for fucking assholes like you? But, anyway, we thought..."

"Look, sir, I'm not into that bullshit anymore," Swindall choked on his words.

"Well, what I was going to say was Karen and I thought about it a little more. And we still like you some, Aubrey, we're not sure why, so we're willing to go up to one-hundred."

"One-hundred-thousand dollars? Are you fucking shitting me? For my bar and package store and the land too?"

"You mean the little that's left of your bar and package store. I've been out there, and I've seen the warning signs the County posted. 'Dangerous Conditions.' And you've only got a few more days left to correct them. And if you don't, you're looking at a fine of a thousand dollars a day which will add up to a small fortune very quickly. So, quite frankly, Aubrey, what you've got left to bring to the table is much worse than just bare land because serious money has to be spent right away for demolition and removal."

"I'll be back." Swindall squeezed out of the booth and started lumbering toward the main dining room.

"*I'll be back!*"

"Fuck!" Swindall barked under his breath, Malman making fun of him now with a Terminator imitation. "Pick up, Charlie, dammit! Hello, Charlie? Yeah, it's me. I'm using the pay phone over here at Denny's where I'm having that meeting with Stewart fucking Malman. He's dropping the price to one-hundred. What? From seven-hundred-fifty-thousand, that's what! Okay. Alright. Are you gonna be there for a few minutes? Please, Charlie, stay by the phone, okay?"

"I just talked to my attorney," Swindall huffed as he wedged his way back into the booth. "He says there's no way you can try and change the price. He says you're gonna be in default if you refuse to close, seeing as how there's a written contract and all."

Malman stood up, stretched, and signaled the waitress who was taking care of some customers a couple of booths away. "No problem," he smiled. "I guess we'll just have to wait for your crack legal team to file suit and see how it goes after that."

"Not now!" Swindall waved away the approaching waitress, but she didn't stop.

"Okay, Frances, what's the damage?"

"Lady, can you just give us a damn minute here?"

The waitress raised her eyebrows and rolled her eyes. "It's just gonna be two-fifty for the coffees," she answered as if Swindall didn't exist.

Malman pulled out some bills, flipped through them, and

gave her a twenty. "You keep the change, young lady. I'm sure business around here still isn't back to normal yet."

"That would be true, sir." She tucked the bill into a front pocket of her uniform. "Thank you very much for the generous tip. And thank you for the 'young lady' too."

"Stewart, can you just give me a minute here? I need to call my attorney again. Listen, if you got something in particular I can tell him, then..."

"Well, yeah, Aubrey, I do have something in particular. You can tell him you've got a copy of the contract." Malman picked up the manilla folder he had brought with him, took out several sheets of paper, and handed them to Swindall. "And you can read him what's highlighted in yellow."

"Charlie, it's me again," Swindall said as he leaned against the wall between the two bathrooms. "I've got the contract right here with me so listen up. 'Seller shall keep in force sufficient hazard insurance on the property,'" he began reading slowly, "'to protect all interests until this sale is closed and the deed delivered.' What? No shit because you fucked up, right? It also says here, 'If the property is destroyed or materially damaged between the date hereof and the closing, and seller is unable or unwilling to restore it to its previous condition prior to closing, purchaser shall have the option of canceling the contract and receiving back the earnest money.' What? No, I can't fucking restore the property. *Why*? Because I don't have any fucking insurance money, that's why! It also says here, 'Seller warrants seller has not received notification from any lawful authority regarding any repairs to said premises that have not been satisfactorily made.' What? The County posted signs all over my fucking property it's got dangerous conditions so I guess they've got me by the *cojones* on that one too, right? And what about this? 'Said contract shall only be renegotiable upon a major defect with an individual repair cost in excess of $500.' What? Well, Charlie, since practically the entire fucking building burned to the fucking ground, would you say *that* might be a major defect which is gonna cost more than $500 to fix?!"

Guardians Of The Faith

"Okay, Stewart, I'll go ahead and take the deal," Swindall said as soon as he returned. "So when can I get my money?"

The waitress almost felt sorry for the big fat slob, the way he left the restaurant so sad. "Boy," she thought, "cutie-pie must have given him some very bad news. Well, like the song goes, 'breaking up is hard to do.'"

As he drove away from the restaurant, Swindall began weeping convulsively. "Hang tough," Charlie Newcastle told him yesterday. *Hang tough*?! I just got screwed real bad! As he pulled into his driveway, Swindall gazed up at the little dollhouse he hated so much, the only structure for miles around which had no damage from one of the worst hurricanes of all time. He went straight to the refrigerator and pulled out a six-pack of Budweiser longnecks. He slumped down on the sofa, stared blankly ahead like a zombie, and drank the beers in rapid succession. As the large quantity of alcohol coursed through his body, his rage began subsiding. He had to be very thankful for at least one thing. Not only would he never have a date with Old Sparky, he never would have to see the inside of a prison, not even for a single day.

CHAPTER TWENTY-FOUR

"Good evening, and welcome to the first of three debates among the candidates for President of the United States. The candidates are independent candidate Ross Perot, Governor Bill Clinton, the Democratic nominee, and President George Bush, the Republican nominee. I am Jim Lehrer of *The MacNeil/Lehrer News Hour* on PBS, and I will be the moderator for this ninety-minute event which is taking place before an audience here in the Athletic Complex at Washington University in St. Louis, Missouri."

Kimberly Singletary got up from the couch for the tenth time and went to the front window. She parted the curtains and looked out on the street just as the faded-blue Volvo pulled up to the curb.

"Do you see what time it is?!" she yelled from the porch.

The right rear passenger door opened by itself, and Demeka stepped out and closed the door. Kimberly's eyes opened wide as her daughter began strolling up the driveway, her arms swinging playfully at her side. When she reached the porch steps, she stared up at her mother, then turned back to her uncle and shrugged her shoulders. Lifton smiled and shrugged his shoulders too. As the little girl began to climb the steps, Kimberly rushed down and swept her up in her arms.

"One small step for mankind," Lifton said to himself.

* * *

"You know, I was really mad at you today." Kimberly gave him a shove, and he slid over to the other side of the couch.

"You couldn't have been that mad because you made me microwave popcorn."

"You promised we'd watch the first debate together, and then you weren't back when it started."

"I'm sorry, sis. We ended up staying longer than usual at our Sunday get-together."

She tore a paper towel off the roll next to the bowl of popcorn and began dabbing at her eyes. "You know I really didn't like you going out there with Demeka, but..."

"Let's don't talk about it, Kim. You know how we're both a little superstitious."

"A little?" She glanced over at him and tried her best to smile through her tears.

"We are all in this together." Ross Perot was responding to a question about the importance of racial harmony. "We ought to love one another, because united teams win and divided teams lose. If we can't love one another, we ought to get along with one another. If you can't get there, just recognize we're all stuck with one another, because nobody's going anywhere. Right?"

"Look how the people are laughing, Kim. But, you know, what? They're laughing with him and not at him. That Perot is such a character."

They sat in silence for awhile as the candidates fielded more questions and then were asked to give closing statements. Kimberly began sobbing quietly when Ross Perot said, "When you go to bed tonight, look at your children. Think of their dreams. Think of your dreams as a child. And ask yourself, 'Isn't it time to stop talking about it?'"

Lifton scooted over and put his arm around his sister. "Look, Kim, there's Susan. She's sitting next to Bill Clinton's wife and daughter over there on the left, see?"

"I liked what Clinton said a minute ago. 'We don't have a

person to waste in this country.' I'm voting for him, but it really doesn't matter anymore for you if he wins and The Big Girl goes to Washington, does it?"

"You mean now that I'm not 'moving on up' like George Jefferson? Yeah, nothing has changed. I managed to single-handedly piss off a whole lot of important people. Word around the office is I'll be lucky if I still have a job next year." He stood up and held out his arms dramatically. "Now wait just a darned second, Saunders," he said, imitating Jimmy Stewart in *Mr. Smith Goes To Washington*. "I don't get it. First you're crying, and now you're laughing. Now just what is so darned funny, Saunders, about me losing my job in Congress?"

"I'll tell you in a minute, Senator. Now can we please watch the rest of the debate? It looks like it's almost over. President Bush is giving his closing statement."

"I've admitted it when I make a mistake, but then I go on and help try to solve the problems. I hope I've earned your trust, because a lot of being President is about trust and character. And I ask for your support for four more years to finish the job."

The debate was over, and Jim Lehrer thanked the three panelists. "The Presidential candidates will appear again together on October the fifteenth and again on October nineteenth," he said. "Next Tuesday there will be a debate among the three candidates for Vice President. And for now, from Washington University in St. Louis, Missouri, I'm Jim Lehrer. Thank you and good night."

"Ray, I've been wanting to ask you something. You've been out to see The Reverend like five Sundays in a row now, and you always go there in the afternoon. He hasn't tried to get you to go to church?"

"Never. Not once. In fact, today I brought up the subject myself because I thought it was strange he never asked me. He said that would be like giving advice, and he only gives advice in two situations. If somebody asks him for it, or he sees danger. I never asked him about church so he never said anything about it. And if I wasn't attending church, that didn't qualify as a dangerous situation. So I started talking religion with him and told him what I thought about it, that it was just a bunch of fairy tales. And he laughed and asked me what I thought about fairy tales. And I told him I liked Hans Christian Andersen, 'The Emperor's New Clothes' and 'The Ugly Duckling,' and *Aesop's Fables*, 'The Boy Who Cried Wolf' and 'The Tortoise And The Hare.' They teach important lessons about life, and each has a moral of the story. Then he asked me why I believed in the law, and I said because society needs rules so people know what they can and can't do. 'So let me see if I've got this right,' he says. 'With fairy tales you get taught important lessons about life, and each one has a moral of the story, but fairy tales don't give you laws. And with laws you're told what you can and can't do, but that's all. Well,' he says, 'the Bible is full of laws too, what you can and can't do, and it also has stories you say are fairy tales. But those Bible stories teach important lessons about life too, and each has a moral of the story, just like the ones you like from Hans Christian Andersen and *Aesop's Fables*. So if you really think about it, with the Bible you get *two* things you think are good for the price of one.' And then he says, 'Not such a bad deal if you ask me.'" Lifton grabbed the remote and turned off the tv. "Okay, sis," he folded his arms. "I haven't forgotten about what I asked you which you never answered. Now, what was so damn funny a little while ago?"

"It just struck me," she burst out laughing. "Well, it's really not funny, but it just struck me that way tonight, the fact that we're back exactly like we were before."

"Exactly like we were before? What does that mean?"

"It means like we were before you had your big case, your beautiful girlfriend, and all that talk about you being the next Dade State Attorney. Now we're back exactly like we were before, sitting here on the sofa, you and me, watching tv or a movie and eating microwave popcorn."

* * *

Rayfield Lifton already had jogged more than four miles from downtown Miami to Miami Beach before the endorphins finally kicked in. It had taken longer than usual for this welcome rush of natural painkillers to begin coursing through his body. But then again it was a breezy sixty-five-degrees when Lifton left the house over Kimberly's complaint he was breaking his promise to stay home and watch tv with her. When her protest failed, she warned him about getting hit by a car on the narrow shoulder of the MacArthur Causeway because too many drivers were distracted by the blazing lights of towering cruise ships to their right and glittering mansions to their left.

Traffic was always heavy on Collins Avenue and Ocean Drive, the two streets closest to the beach which boasted the most popular bars and restaurants. Lifton turned right and headed down the five blocks to South Pointe Park. He came up to Joe's Stone Crab with its big blue-and-red neon sign at the southern end of Washington Avenue. There was a long line of people waiting to get into the landmark eatery. Parking valets were scrambling to meet the new arrivals, tearing off ticket stubs and handing them to drivers before jumping into their vehicles and pulling away. One of the bartenders was outside taking drink orders to ensure people wouldn't get angry or bored while they waited for a table.

As he came alongside the main entrance, Lifton stopped to look at the busy scene inside. There were a lot of customers at the bar, many of them gazing up at wall-mounted televisions. He moved closer to one of the bay windows so he could get a better view. Waiters hoisting trays piled high with plates of stone crab claws were gliding through the restaurant, others were pointing at menus, explaining to diners how to order the right size and number of this pricey delicacy. Lifton realized heads were starting to turn his way so he bent down and tightened the laces on his shoes.

"Don't worry, I'm leaving," Lifton said after feeling a tap on his shoulder, followed by a harder one, and then a shove. He stood up and whirled around. "Hey!"

"You don't know my tap?"

"Damn, Seven! I was ready to get into it with you."

"Until you saw what a big bad dude I am." They slapped

hands and locked in a fierce handshake. "I saw you looking inside like one of the hungry homeless. So you're out jogging tonight? I thought you'd be home watching the election. The first results are starting to come in. Clinton's ahead, but it's way too early to tell who's gonna win."

"I'll take a look when I get back home. You know it doesn't matter for me anymore. If Clinton loses, and The Big Girl stays, she'll probably fire me. If Clinton wins and asks Susan to join his administration, and Madeline doesn't move out to Wyoming, then she'll be the next Dade State Attorney, and she'll kick my ass out."

"I'm sorry about the way things turned out, Ray. But you sure made a lot of enemies these last few months. Well, then," Reginald Crawford said after a few beats, "I better get back inside. I'm here with No-Time and Perishable."

"And Val-er-ie too I see."

"Yeah, her too. She came by for the second half of our game. You know, fall league at the DSC. When she heard we were going to Joe's, she just decided to invite herself."

"Can't say I blame her." As if she knew they were talking about her at that moment, Bernice Valerie Witherspoon looked up from her plate and gazed over at them, then turned and whispered something to Norris. They laughed at whatever she had told him and then returned to the serious business of cracking open another giant stone crab claw. "So who are those other two at your table? They look familiar, but I can't place them right now."

"*Damn*, Liftoff."

"Wait, hold on. You know, they look a lot like those two City of Miami cops who rousted us at The Little Store last year."

"Yeah, those two there have been friends of No-Time and Perishable for years." Crawford reached out, grabbed Lifton's arm, and pulled him back before he could go anywhere. "You don't need that, Ray. You've gotta understand we were thinking about your best interests when we put on that little show back then."

"So you were in on it too? For what, Seven? So I would feel the pain of an educated black man from the hood being put down by white cops? And then I would do whatever you all had in mind for me? *Damn*, Seven. Maybe No-Time and Perishable, but I never would have expected something like that from you." Lifton jerked his arm back, freeing himself from Crawford's grip, and flipped over the hood of his sweatshirt.

"It was for a good cause, Ray. To give you a chance to be a real player again."

"A real player again? Yeah, one who would help you all fix your problems, right? Like if No-Time or Perishable had a tough case and needed the State Attorney himself to approve a favorable plea bargain? Or if Crawford Holdings had some big-time legal issue with the County? Who better than the Dade State Attorney to use the influence of his Office, except maybe the Mayor or County Manager?"

"Think whatever you want, Ray. We've always been friends and always will be."

"Yeah, I sure can see that. No-Time and Perishable are tripping all over themselves trying to get outside here to see me." He reached down and grabbed the heels of his shoes for a few seconds to stretch his back. "You take care, Seven," Lifton said as he stood back up, inhaled deeply, and took off running down Washington Avenue.

CHAPTER TWENTY-FIVE

"Are you sure about that, Ray? I'd really like it if you, your little niece, and Doc, the rest of the Sunday Supper Club, were up there on the stage too." The Reverend Wilkie P. Sanderson smiled warmly and squeezed Lifton's arm. "Okay, then."

Sanderson climbed the stairs and eased himself down into the last metal folding chair on the left side of the front row. Also seated to the left of the lectern were Dade County Mayor Steve Clark, United States Senators Bob Graham and Connie Mack, and Congressman Lincoln Diaz-Balart. To the right were Judge Gerald Rice, City of Miami Mayor Xavier Suarez, Congresswoman Ileana Ros-Lehtinen, State Attorney Susan Purvis, and Commissioner Beverly Sanderson. Behind them were two more rows filled with local clergy, civil rights leaders, and other figures from all walks of life. Lifton turned around and scoured the Bayside Marketplace open-air theater which had filled to capacity. He finally spied Kimberly waving at him from one of the last rows, and he bolted up the concrete steps.

Judge Rice came to the lectern and introduced everyone on stage, and then The Reverend Keith Blakely of the Central Baptist Church gave the invocation. Senators Graham and Mack read portions of a statement from President Bush officially proclaiming

Guardians Of The Faith

Monday, January 18, 1993, as the Martin Luther King, Jr. Federal Holiday. There were brief remarks from a few others before Judge Rice introduced the keynote speaker.

"When I was asked to officiate at this year's ceremony nearly a year ago, I was very honored and immediately accepted. As part of my duties I was responsible for finding somebody to give the main address. But it turned out I didn't have to think about whom I would choose for very long because, you see, he found *me* a few days later. For those of you who don't already know him, let me mention a couple of things. Like Dr. King, he is a man of the cloth. He has been a life-long resident of the South Florida community, a distinguished member of the clergy for more than a half-century, and the leader of his congregation in Homestead for nearly that long. *And* he has a sister right here on this stage." Judge Rice glanced to his left at Beverly Sanderson who had crossed her arms and was shaking her head like she wasn't pleased at all about the family connection. "Ladies and gentlemen, honored guests. The Reverend Wilkie P. Sanderson."

Before he headed for the lectern, Sanderson said something to the man in the wheelchair next to him and straightened the blanket covering his lower body.

"Thank you, Gerald. I should tell you all first that to get this gig I had to bribe your newest federal judge." Sanderson turned toward Judge Rice. "I said to him, 'If you give me this opportunity, I'll go back and change your Bible class grades from D to A.'" There was laughter and applause as Judge Rice covered his face and shook his head.

"Someone once told me a good speech should be like a good dress. Long enough to cover all the important points but short enough to still be interesting. I'll try and follow that principle today, but I realize I'm up against some pretty stiff competition." He turned around and looked up at the image which filled the giant screen behind him, The Reverend Dr. Martin Luther King, Jr., on the steps of the Lincoln Memorial delivering his "I Have A Dream" speech to a quarter million people. There were shouts of "that's right!" and "amen!" and another round of applause.

"I was there that day nearly three decades ago, August 28, 1963. You don't see me on the screen, but I was there with the likes of Harry Belafonte, Sammy Davis, Jr., Marlon Brando, Bob Dylan, and Sam Cooke. Some of you younger folks may not know who all those people are, especially the last one. Let me tell you about Sam Cooke. He was one of the greatest singers and songwriters of all time at least in my book. I met him in Atlanta in 1958 at the second convention of the Southern Christian Leadership Conference, the organization Dr. King had founded the year before with other members of the clergy. Someone told me a Pentecostal minister from Chicago attending that convention had a celebrity son. When I found out his son was Sam Cooke, I went looking for The Reverend Charles Cooke. And then when Sam showed up there, I invited myself to meet him, just like I invited myself to be a speaker here today. I *had* to because he was my favorite singer back then. That one hour I spent talking with Sam Cooke is one of the greatest memories I'll take to the grave. Sadly, like Dr. King, a bullet took young Sam's life a few years later. He was only thirty-three years old. But before he left us, he gave us some great songs like "You Send Me," "Chain Gang," "Wonderful World," and "A Change Is Gonna Come." That last one Sam Cooke wrote in 1964 shortly before his death. Diana Ross and Tina Turner and many others have recorded that same song. And I'd like to think I had something to do with Sam Cooke writing it. But that's a story for another day.

"It's been thirty-five years since 1958, when I went to that convention, and twenty-five years since 1968, when Dr. King was snatched from us by an assassin's bullet. That same tragic year Representative John Conyers asked Congress to set aside a federal holiday commemorating Dr. King. Nothing happened for fifteen years until Congress finally passed legislation creating Martin Luther King, Jr. Day, and President Ronald Reagan signed it into law. So this year is the tenth anniversary of this federal holiday. And there's something else important about this year. It's the first one where *all* fifty states are celebrating this holiday in some form."

Sanderson waited until the cheers and thunderous applause had subsided. "But I didn't want to be up here today just to speak about these milestones. I invited myself to this gathering because of a principle I always try and stick to. And that is I don't give advice unless somebody asks me for it, or someone might be in danger. Otherwise, as far as I'm concerned, you're on your own. Now nobody here has asked me for any advice. But I'm still going to give some so that means somebody here might be in danger."

There was an awkward silence until The Reverend broke it. "That somebody is *us*, people. You see, life is like a ladder. When you're going up, it means you're going in the right direction, and that's good. But when you're going down, it means you're not, and that's bad. The danger these days is too many of us are going down. Many brave souls have fought long and hard for civil rights, and some, like Dr. King, have even given their lives. And because they did, they made it a lot easier for the rest of us to go up the ladder. They sure did. In the sixties and seventies new laws were passed to end discrimination. Opportunities started opening up. We got elected to Congress and state legislatures. We became mayors and police chiefs and movie stars, and some of us even got our own television shows. Like Sam Cooke had predicted in his song, a change did come. A *big* change. And it was a new world. One I never had expected to see in my lifetime."

Sanderson paused and surveyed the crowd for a few moments. "I'm sure you all must be wondering, 'Where is he going with this?' The speakers who went before me kept saying 'African-American, African-American.' 'Dr. King, the greatest African-American.' 'Gerald Rice, first African-American federal judge in Florida.' Well, just in case you don't know, Dr. King was born in Atlanta, Georgia, not somewhere on the dark continent of Africa. His father, Martin Luther King, Sr., and his mother, Alberta Williams King, didn't come from Africa either. Neither did Gerald Rice behind me here who was born in Homestead, Florida. And if Gerald applied himself in geography class like he did in Sunday

school, he would have a hard time finding Africa on the map."
Sanderson's last comment provoked only scattered laughter.

"You know, when I was preparing this speech, I couldn't find
that word 'African-American' in my dictionary. That's probably
because the one I've got is pretty old, and this word only became
popular not too long ago. Dr. King never would have said he was
an African-American even if that word had existed while he was
still alive. It just wouldn't have been part of his vocabulary. Dr.
King wasn't fighting for some *new* way to describe us as being
different from other Americans, some type of separate class. But
now you have to say African-American to be what they call
'politically correct.' Well, do you need me to tell you politically
correct and Dr. King don't mix? He sacrificed his life *for us* because
he *refused* to be politically correct. 'I have a dream that my four
little children will one day live in a nation where they will not be
judged by the color of their skin but by the content of their
character.' Anybody happen to remember when Dr. King said
that? 'With this *faith*, we will be able to work together, to pray
together, to struggle together, to go to jail together, to stand up for
freedom together.' How about those words? He said them right
there." Sanderson half-turned and pointed at the giant screen.
"I'm *not* African-American. Never have been, never will be. The
day I buy into this whole politically-correct thing is the day I will
dishonor Dr. King, and I will *never* do that. Some of our young
people have begun subscribing to a new culture glorifying drugs
and guns and violence. Too many of our kids freely use the word
'nigger' and 'dog' to describe each other. And unless we start
doing something about it, people, much of the progress we've
made so far at such great sacrifice will be lost. Dr. King surely
must be turning over in his grave."

There were rumblings of discontent in the audience, and a
few dozen people stood up and began making their way toward
the exits. "Don't like the message much, I guess," Sanderson said,
then waited until the aisles had cleared, and there was silence
again. "Dr. King gave his life so you and me would be accepted as

just plain old Americans, *period*."

"Next speaker, please!" someone yelled from the middle of the amphitheater, and there was a round of applause and shouts of approval. Judge Rice got up from his seat, went to the lectern, and said something to Sanderson.

"That's fine, Gerald. I'm almost done, but I'm going to introduce somebody first." Sanderson went over to the far left of the stage, grabbed the handles of the wheelchair, and pushed it over next to the lectern. "This is Curtis Chance Thigpen."

"He's that KKK dude!" someone shouted, and there was loud booing. Another group of people got up to leave, but when Sanderson placed the microphone in Thigpen's hands, out of curiosity most of them decided to remain. Beverly Sanderson called Judge Rice over to confer with her, and it was obvious she was very agitated.

"I couldn't hardly see or get around no more," Thigpen began. "And people I knew didn't care. I mostly just wanted to die. But The Reverend here brought me over to his church the night Andrew hit, and I've been living out there ever since. He got me a doctor who tried to save my legs, Doc Leeds is his name, but it was too late. I didn't know before, but a long time ago The Reverend helped my mother get work after my father went to prison. All these years I caused so much hurt to The Reverend and his family, but he just kept it to himself how he helped my mother. He saved my life so I could have another chance, just like my middle name, to try and finish my life in a better way." Thigpen hesitated while he thought about his next words. "When I lost my sight is when I began to see. To see people for what they do instead of what they look like. So that's about it," he said, raising the microphone so Sanderson could take it back.

The amphitheater was dead silent for a few moments as Sanderson slipped the microphone back into its metal clip on the lectern. Everybody who had gotten up to leave had returned to their seats.

"Forty years ago," Sanderson continued, "on a Sunday

morning in the streets of Homestead, Florida, Curtis' father, Wallace Thigpen, tried to beat me with a baseball bat. He was the head of the Ku Klux Klan in South Dade back then, and Curtis ended up following in his footsteps much of his life. He tried to make my life miserable, but I never let it get to me because I remembered. I remembered the face of a very frightened little five-year-old white boy who, on that particular Sunday morning forty years ago, witnessed the horrors of racial hatred. And, on the other side of the street that morning, there was another little boy about the same age, a little black boy from my congregation. And he saw what Wallace Thigpen was about to do to me and, scared out of his wits, kept yelling 'Somebody call the police!' What Curtis did for so many years I never let get to me because I believed one day these two little boys would sit together at the table of brotherhood. And, you know, it actually happened. Forty years later these two little boys sit near each other here on this stage, the little black boy now a federal judge."

Like he had done during Sanderson's opening remarks, Judge Rice leaned forward and covered his face. But this time it wasn't to hide embarrassment about his low grades in Bible class but rather to soak up the tears streaming from his eyes. Gerald Rice's legs buckled as he rose from his chair. He took a couple of weak steps forward and crouched down next to Thigpen.

"My sister thinks I've lost my mind." The Reverend glanced to his left, but the Commissioner's chair now was empty. "She thinks Curtis should spend the rest of his life in prison, just like his father, instead of living in my house like he was part of my family. The Vietnam War took my only child, and my wife passed away ten years ago. So my house had been empty for a long time before I went and got Curtis right before Hurricane Andrew. And, yes, at the time Curtis was about as low as you can go on that ladder I keep talking about but, you know, he's been moving up some. You see, people, it's not about *where* you are on the ladder at any particular moment, it's about whether you're going up or down." Sanderson reached inside his pocket, pulled out a sheet of paper, and adjusted his glasses. "Let me read you something Dr. King said. 'The family is the main educational agency of mankind, and it is within the family that we must first teach lessons about love and fairness, decency and kindness, and the difference between right and wrong.' So I leave you with those words and this advice. When you get back home, you should ask yourselves, 'Am I teaching my children these things Dr. King said must come from the family?' When more of us can answer that question with a 'yes,' more of our young people will start heading in the right direction on that ladder."

The amphitheater was dead silent as The Reverend Wilkie P. Sanderson followed Gerald Rice, who was pushing Thigpen's wheelchair, back to the left side of the stage. Mayor Suarez stood up and looked over at Judge Rice who signaled him to take over.

"Thank you all. This concludes today's program."

The scene at the Lincoln Memorial suddenly came to life on the giant screen, and Dr. Martin Luther King's resonant voice boomed out the final words of his most famous oration. "And when this happens, when we allow freedom to ring, when we let it ring from every village and every hamlet, from every state and city, we will be able to speed up that day when all of God's children, black men and white men, Jews and Gentiles, Protestants and Catholics, will be able to join hands and sing in the words of the old Negro spiritual, 'Free at last! Free at last! Thank God Almighty, we are free at last!'"

* * *

"The Big Girl," Cuqui Perez' raspy voice cracked, "wants to see you."

"First I'm going for some coffee, Moneypenny, and then I'll meet up with SP."

His secretary always smiled when he did his pretty good Sean Connery imitation, but this time she looked up at him with only sad eyes. "You think she tells you today?"

Lifton folded his arms. "Who tells me what?"

"Por favor, jefe." She was not in a joking mood this morning.

"If you go, I go too."

"Don't worry, Moneypenny. SP doesn't fire her double-o agents on Wednesdays. So tell me, do you want some plain old rocket fuel or a *cortadito*?"

As Lifton stood at the end of the long line in the Pickle Barrel, a familiar guttural voice erupted behind him. "Hey, boss man. You don't recognize me?"

Lifton half-turned and regarded the beefy figure. "Is that you, JC? You've got hair."

Joel Chernin shook his head, and his long, light-brown hair fluttered like a flag in a breeze. "Yeah, I need to keep changing my undercover look."

"And a big change it is, Chernin. So what happened to the swastika tattoos?"

"Oh, those damn things weren't *real* tattoos. There's this special thing they do, but it's a long story." Chernin folded his arms and looked down. "You know, I was thinking about taking off when I saw you in line. You probably want to kill me."

"No, JC. You wanted to make a case against the Guardians, and you didn't want to lose your job. And see? I'm still here."

"Yeah, I'm glad they didn't fire your ass over that shit."

"Well, not yet anyway. So what finally happened with the other case, that double homicide Swindall told you about? It sounded pretty good. You had a confession."

"Oh, yeah, the mixed couple murder." Chernin nodded and scratched his beard. "Well, remember Kara Mello, that really hot reporter from Channel 5? She showed me how it was all bullshit before I even had a chance to start investigating the damn case."

It turned out that Thigpen hadn't killed the black man and white lady who had wandered into Skeeter's on their way to Key West that dark and stormy night. There was an incident report on file in the Key West Police Department, dated December 30, 1989, describing an assault and battery on a couple from New York. It had occurred north of Key Largo on State Road 905 approximately five miles from the entrance to Ocean Reef. The male victim had multiple contusions resulting from the attack which allegedly had been perpetrated by three subjects who had followed their rental car on Card Sound Road after they left a Florida City bar. When questioned why they hadn't reported the incident to Florida City or Key Largo police, and why the male hadn't sought medical treatment as soon as possible, the victims were unable to provide a credible explanation. The intake officer also noted "the victims appear to be under the influence." A consensual search of the female's purse yielded a clear-plastic baggy with marijuana and quaaludes. At that point the victims were administered the *Miranda* warnings and declined to speak further without the assistance of counsel. The incident report had been forwarded to the State Attorney's Office for "review and decision re: controlled substances cannabis and methaqualone." "With that couple in possession of weed and ludes the case sucked, and it was already four-years old anyway. I tracked down Swindall and let him know he wasn't going to be prosecuted for anything and, *boy*, was he relieved. He sold Skeeter's to that Malman dude and moved up to The Panhandle."

"I know. Stewart has stopped by Sanderson's place a couple of times. The Reverend really did take Thigpen in, you know."

"Yeah, I know. You didn't see me, but I was at Bayside at that Martin Luther King thing. Pretty strange story. By the way, how's your little niece doing?"

Lifton smiled and patted Chernin's shoulder. "She's doing good, JC. You ought to stop by The Reverend's place one of these Sunday afternoons. Demeka goes out there with me. We all have a good time."

On his way out of the cafeteria Lifton noticed the two interns turn away so he wouldn't see them. "Too late," he said, sitting down at their table. "So what are you legal eagles up to these days? You're graduating this semester, right?"

"That's right, Mr. Lifton." Jennifer Trazenfeld's face flushed. "Both of us."

"I never heard back from you two. I thought you wanted me

to recommend you for jobs here. I'm *just* messing with you. My recommendation probably would get you both blackballed. So whatever happened to those two big hate-crimes cases?"

"You mean *R.A.V. v. City of St. Paul* and *Wisconsin v. Mitchell*?" Melton asked. "Well, just like me and Jen thought. Scalia ended up writing the opinion in *R.A.V.*, and he held the city ordinance was facially invalid, saying it imposed unconstitutional prohibitions for just expressing views on disfavored subjects like race, creed, and religion."

"That was at the end of June last year," Trazenfeld said, "but *Mitchell* is still out there. Oral argument is scheduled for April 21. The smart money is betting the Court will find enhanced penalties for hate crimes *are* constitutional. Some say it might even be a unanimous decision. Of course, there's a big difference with the *Mitchell* case because there was an actual crime against somebody, not like just talk or holding up a sign or..."

"Burning a cross on somebody's front lawn like in *R.A.V.*? Okay, I get it."

"We saw you talking with that detective."

"You know Joel Chernin?"

"Well, yeah," Melton admitted, "he knew we were doing legal research for you on your hate-crimes case, and he wanted information about any potential defenses to a conspiracy charge."

"And if I remember correctly," Trazenfeld said, "he was especially interested in the defense of 'early withdrawal.' He also wanted to know whether the enhanced penalties under the hate-crimes law could be applied to something which happened a few years ago. I told him no, no way, because retroactive application of aggravated penalties would present an *ex post facto* problem."

"Article I, Section 9, and *Calder v. Bull*," Melton added.

"You know, you guys are *so* good I *really* feel obligated to go and see Susan Purvis right now and tell her she *better* hire you two. I'm just *messing* with you again," he added quickly when he saw the panic spread across their faces.

After he and Cuqui had polished off the entire *colada*, Lifton

descended the fire stairwell to the sixth floor. The Dade State
Attorney's secretary didn't bother to look up when he checked in.
"Yes, Nancy, you can send him in," Susan Purvis' deep voice with
the distinctive South Florida twang responded over the intercom.
She was sitting at her huge semi-circular desk, but it no longer was
covered with stacks of papers like the last time Lifton was there.
Instead, there were only a few dark-brown accordion files and a
small television. "Sit, sit, Rayfield Lifton. I was just checking to see
if the ceremony had begun. Yeah, the presidential inauguration
should be starting up anytime now."

Purvis turned up the volume on the tv. "Can you believe it?
That damn concert has been going on for two hours. Look," she
said turning the television screen toward him. The images were
shifting between different views of the two-hundred thousand
people congregated on the Capitol Mall. The "Call For Reunion"
concert was taking place at the Lincoln Memorial. Joined in hands
and taking bows were Diana Ross, Aretha Franklin, L-L Cool J,
Tony Bennett, Bob Dylan, and Michael Bolton.

"It looks like it's just about over now."

"Oh, really?" Purvis turned the tv back to her. "Well,
finally." She settled back into her chair and folded her hands.
"Have you heard about what's going on? Well, maybe not.
Everybody thought I was a shoe-in for Attorney General. All that
campaigning I did. And it's not a gender issue because they say
everybody being considered for the position is a woman. But the
scuttlebutt now is I'm running third. One of those ahead of me is
a corporate lawyer from Connecticut, and the other one is a federal
judge, but district court, not even Court of Appeals. Can you
believe this? I guess being one of the first top female prosecutors
in one of the largest counties in the entire country isn't as good as
being just a plain old lawyer or a trial court judge." Purvis stared
at him looking for some feedback.

"Anyway," she continued after he didn't say anything, "I
wanted to get you in here and personally tell you a couple of things
so you won't have to keep wondering about your future like I am

about mine. First, to set your mind at ease, I don't think your hate-crimes case which turned into one royal mess has anything to do with me being in third place right now. That incredible fiasco remained pretty much a local story although it did make this office look like we're a big bunch of fools over here. The media can be *so* very cruel the way they spin things. 'Prosecutor bungles hate-crimes case against white supremacists who plotted to kill elderly black minister.' 'Murder conspiracy victim takes leader of neo-Klan group into his home after prosecutor flubs case against him.' 'Prosecutor chose wrong career, should try coaching little-league basketball.' Some people had a good laugh, but I'm sure it wasn't very funny for you."

Purvis glanced over at the television. "You know, it looks like this thing is about ready to start so here's the deal. Everybody who had been pulling for you, well, none of them are with the program anymore, including Leander Baldwin, your man in Tallahassee. Once Alonzo Norris jumped ship everybody else followed, and then your ship sank real fast, if you know what I mean. Now if I don't end up going to Washington, then I really don't have a problem with you staying on here. I was at Bayside on Monday. And I can tell you I was very touched by what I saw. Now if I do end up going to Washington, then Madeline most likely will be taking over as long as her hubby drops that crazy idea of moving to where the buffalo roam. And then it will be up to her if she wants to make any changes here. So there you have it. Oh, look, there's Chief Justice Rehnquist now." She leaned forward and turned up the volume. When Lifton stood up, she added, "You're welcome to stay here and watch this shindig if you want."

Lifton declined the offer and climbed the stairs back to the ninth floor. As he pulled open the heavy door, he noticed Vernon Castleberry pushing a squeaky metal cart down the hallway. As Lifton neared the conference room the maintenance man had gone into, he heard echoes of Bill Clinton's voice.

"I've got the inauguration on, Mr. Lifton," Castleberry said when he noticed Lifton at the door. "Come on in and watch it with me if you like."

It was a cold but sunny day in Washington as Bill Clinton stood alone at the lectern on a platform jutting out from the west steps of the Capitol Building. Huge Stars-and-Stripes banners hung from the platform on each side.

"Our founders saw themselves in the light of posterity," Clinton said after the last round of applause. "We can do no less. Anyone who has ever watched a child's eyes wander into sleep knows what posterity is. Posterity is the world to come, the world for whom we hold our ideals, from whom we have borrowed our planet, and to whom we bear sacred responsibility."

"Everybody loves them when they first start, don't they? But by the time they're gone, they've usually left behind a big damn mess for the next one to try and fix."

"You're talking about the prosecutors over here at Metro Justice, right?"

"Well, some of you people do make a mess of things around here I end up having to fix, but I was talking about politicians."

After they had listened to a few more minutes of the speech, Castleberry was paged. He used the conference room phone to call back the number displayed on his pager. "Another damn water leak on the fourth floor," he muttered.

Toward the end of his speech the new President challenged his listeners to act on their idealism through service to others. "In serving, we recognize a simple but powerful truth. We need each other. And we must care for one another." He reminded everyone that, "but for fate, we, the fortunate and the unfortunate, might have been each other. An idea ennobled by the *faith* that our Nation can summon from its myriad diversity the deepest measure of unity. An idea infused with the conviction that America's long, heroic journey must go forever upward." Bill Clinton looked out at the enormous gathering and paused for a few moments before saying the final words of his inaugural address. "From this joyful mountaintop of celebration, we hear a call to service in the valley. We have heard the trumpets. We have changed the guard. And now, each in our way, and with God's help, we must answer the call. Thank you, and God bless you all."

As he walked slowly back to his office at the other end of the hallway, Rayfield Lifton thought about the new President's words and the events of the past year. About his niece. About Aubrey Swindall and Curtis Chance Thigpen. And about The Reverend Wilkie P. Sanderson and that damn ladder he kept talking about.

CHAPTER TWENTY-SIX

"Ray, you said you were coming early," Kimberly whined. "I made a big dinner."

"Kim, give me a chance. We're not at The Reverend's place. We're over here at Deering Hospital."

"Is Demeka alright? And what about Dennis and Emily?!"

"Demeka's fine. It's The Reverend who got sick. And who are Dennis and Emily?"

"Those two damn hurricanes out there!"

"Calm down. There's no warnings or anything like that yet."

"I'm sorry, Ray, but it's only been one year since Andrew, and you know how I get. So what happened to The Reverend?"

"We were sitting around at his place, catching up on things like we always do on Sunday afternoons, and Doc Leeds saw something was wrong with him. He realized it was serious so he called rescue."

"Is Reverend Sanderson gonna be okay?"

"Kim, hold on. Doc is waving at me from down the hall. I'll call you back."

After an hour had passed without any word from her brother, Kimberly Singletary called Deering Hospital. The operator was unable to connect her to Sanderson's room because there wasn't any information in the system yet about his admission. Kimberly glanced at the clock on the stove, turned off the gas burners, and covered the two steaming pots. Even if they left South Dade right now, they wouldn't get home until after eight. She turned on the tv and found a station giving an update on the two most recent tropical storms which had formed in the mid-Atlantic. Bryan-Norcross, Chief Meteorologist for the NBC affiliate, and a local hero for his twenty-three-hour marathon broadcast during Hurricane Andrew, was predicting both storms soon would take a sharp turn northwest and would not pose a threat to the Florida Peninsula. So far this year no hurricane had made landfall in Florida, and Kimberly silently prayed it would stay that way for the rest of the season. South Florida still had a long way to go to recover both physically and emotionally from the trauma Hurricane Andrew had caused exactly one year ago that day.

A big racket outside startled Kimberly out of the deep slumber into which she had fallen on the living room sofa. It was pitch-black except for the image on the tv screen. Mr. T was barking unrelentingly which most likely meant her brother and Demeka had just arrived. She turned the knob on an end-table lamp, rubbed her eyes, went to the front door, and turned on the porch light.

"I said hush-up, Mr. T!" Old Lady Muir steadied herself with her cane, her other hand just above her brow to help her see what was going on in the dimly-lit street.

Lifton popped the trunk, took out the folded wheelchair, opened it up, and set it down on the sidewalk.

"Demeka, get up here right now!" Kimberly shouted as her daughter slid out of the front passenger seat.

Instead of complying, Demeka defiantly shook her head "no" several times and opened the right rear passenger door. Lifton closed the trunk, reached into the back seat, and pulled out what appeared to be a big package. But when he turned around and set it down on the wheelchair, Kimberly realized the package was really a person. Lifton reached into the rear seat again and dragged out a heavy dark object and set it on the ground. He went back to the wheelchair, spun it around, and began pushing it up the driveway. Demeka followed, holding a leash connected to a large black-and-brown dog who wheezed heavily as it waddled up the driveway behind her.

"No way," Kimberly Singletary whispered. "No way."

"Who's that you got there? Who's that you're bringing into your house? Fredricka Muir's loud questioning had triggered another round of ferocious barking from Mr. T, and then he picked up the scent of Sanderson's old dog and lunged forward, knocking into Snoopy's meaty calves. Her legs buckled, and she landed on her ample rear, her legs entangled in Mr. T's long metal-chain leash. But instead of asking for help, Old Lady Muir continued her interrogation. "Are you bringing a white man into your house, Mr. Prosecutor? Hey, I'm talking to you, Rayfield Lifton!"

Kimberly grabbed one of the wrought-iron chairs and used it to prop open the front door. "Hurry, Ray! We've got to help her get up."

Lifton swivelled the wheelchair and pulled it inside. "Stay clear of Mr. T!"

"I don't need no help from you all!"

"Oh, yes you do, Mrs. Muir." Kimberly stood at the bottom step of her neighbor's porch. "But first you need to calm down your dog."

Fredricka Muir soon realized there was no way she could get out of her predicament without assistance. "Hush-up, Mr. T." She began fumbling with the clip which connected the leash to the dog's choke collar.

"No, don't let him loose, Mrs. Muir!" Lifton shouted out as he came up behind Kimberly, grabbing her arm in case they needed to bolt back to the house.

"Well, that's the only way you can get close to me, fool. He won't do nothing. Now go over there," she said, turning the dog and giving him a shove. Mr. T went to the other end of the porch and laid down. "See what I mean, fool?"

Guardians Of The Faith

They stepped up on the porch, and Kimberly untangled the leash from around Snoopy's legs. As they latched onto Old Lady Muir's arms and began lifting her up, Mr. T started growling, but he didn't move. They guided Fredricka Muir into her living room and eased her down into an old recliner.

"Are you going to be okay, Mrs. Muir?"

"I'll be all right, young lady. But why is he bringing a sick old white man and a big dog into your house?"

"It's a long story."

"A long story? A long story? You only arrest black people, Mr. Prosecutor, and now you're bringing white people and their big dogs over to your house too?"

"Let's go, Ray. We left Demeka alone with Thigpen."

"You just say Thigpen? That KKK dude? He's bringing the KKK into your house? We got the KKK in our neighborhood? I'm gonna sue your black ass!"

"Let me see if the coast is clear." Lifton cracked open the screen door to make sure Mr. T was still lying down at the far-left side of the porch. "He's gone!"

"What?! Well, you better go find him, or I'm gonna sue your black ass for that too!"

Kimberly pushed him through the threshold and took off for the house.

"I'll go look for your dog, Mrs. Muir," he said, as he picked up the leash.

Lifton jumped up onto his porch but had to stop because Kimberly was blocking the front door. She turned around and looked up at him with tears in her eyes. Curtis Thigpen was in the same place Lifton had left him. Everly was lying on the floor to his left, Mr. T sitting obediently to his right. And in between Thigpen and Mr. T stood Demeka, one hand on the man's back, the other gently caressing the dog's massive square head.

* * *

"I have to say this latest tropical depression you see here pretty much caught us by surprise." The weatherman made a sweeping counter-clockwise motion with his left hand as he stood next to the green-screen which displayed satellite imagery of Florida's Gulf Coast. "It formed off The Panhandle right around here just about eight hours ago."

"*Oh, yeah,* another tropical depression." Aubrey Swindall couldn't help but chuckle at the thought. "Yeah, that's exactly what I got." He leaned forward so he could slip the empty bottle back into the six-pack on the coffee table and grab another Budweiser longneck. He twisted off the cap and tossed it over to the other end of the small efficiency. Instead of landing in the Publix bag filled with garbage, it bounced off the wall and rolled across the floor to the middle of the small room. Swindall leaned back and chug-a-lugged this last beer just like he had done with the other five. The old cloth sofa, which still had a faint musty smell from getting wet during the move from Florida City, sagged noticeably under his considerable weight. He let his head fall back and stared up at several dark-grey moldy splotches on the white plaster ceiling. They had been expanding steadily over the past few days due to all the rain coming through a leak in the roof. "Lordy, Lordy, I got me another one of those tropical depressions."

"Now, folks, I know you all get very concerned every time you hear about a tropical system approaching our neck of the woods," the weatherman was saying. "And rightly so. Most of us still have in our minds those images of Hurricane Andrew devastating South Florida two years ago. And let's not forget just a month ago we had Alberto which made landfall near Destin over here. And although it never quite reached Category One strength, thirty deaths, all the result of inland flooding, as well as millions of dollars of damage, are attributed to Tropical Storm Alberto. So, viewers, what do you need to know right now? Well, this new storm likely will intensify further and have maximum sustained winds of sixty miles-per-hour by the time it makes landfall about four hours from now right over here in the area of Panama City."

There was a sound like somebody was drumming his fingers on the small window pane next to the refrigerator. Swindall snorted, pushed himself off the couch, and wobbled over to the kitchen area. The wind had picked up and was slapping thick sheets of rain against the glass. His head started to spin so he reached down and steadied himself against the small gas stove. On a clear day you could see a tiny sliver of sand and water from their third-floor unit on the east side of Mountain Drive a couple of blocks from the beach. What a really stupid name for a road in Florida, *Mountain Drive*, where the only thing remotely akin to a mountain was a landfill piled high with tons of solid waste. "That describes me pretty damn good, doesn't it?" He had to laugh out loud. "One big pile of solid waste."

There was no point in leaning further to the right to try and see two blocks away. Instead, Swindall looked down at the broken concrete driveway to make sure Emily hadn't pulled in. If she came home early for some reason, it would screw up everything. Aubrey Swindall had made his decision, and now he needed to take care of business. That damn nightmare! It had been wrecking his sleep for too long, making him jerk up suddenly in the middle of the night, his t-shirt and shorts soaking in sweat. After Emily kissed him on the cheek, told him she loved him, and smiled sweetly as she left for work this morning, he realized it never was going to stop. That dream was the sign, telling him the time had come to fish or cut bait. The white wine and beer had filled him with the courage to just do it. The State of Florida never tried to strap him down and fry him in Old Sparky. But now, two years later, how crazy was it he was headed for the same fate?! He had become his own judge and jury, pronouncing sentence which would be carried out momentarily.

Aubrey Swindall wiped his mouth with the back of his hand and swung open the refrigerator door. Every Death Row inmate had the right to make one last request, and his was to just polish off the rest of that bottle of Chardonnay. If you want to get a woman crazy drunk, give her a few tall glasses of real cold white wine. That's what he had learned from all those years in the liquor business. And that formula worked pretty good on a man too if he also drank a large quantity of another alcoholic beverage along with it. So Swindall had gulped down nearly two-thirds of that bottle of Chardonnay right before he started on the six-pack, and that explosive mixture now made him stagger toward the front door. After the rest of the white wine was in his gut, he was confident he would be ready to take care of business.

He took a big swig from the bottle, opened the door of the efficiency, and turned to get one more look at his last residence on this earth. "*Hasta la vista*, baby!" he said, giving it the finger, so ashamed this clammy little dark cave was all he was able to give Emily after so many years. Just the thought this place was ten-times worse than their stupid little dollhouse back in Florida City made him want to blow his brains out right then and there, but he had pawned his guns months ago. He pushed the lock button on the inside knob and pulled the door shut. The rain pelted him relentlessly as he slowly descended the slippery stairs, one hand grasping the handrail, the other clutching the bottle of Chardonnay, his t-shirt and shorts getting completely soaked through. When he reached the last step, he had no choice but to step into a big pool of water, his flip-flops sinking deeply into the mud.

How things had changed! It no longer was about getting outta Dodge to live his dream. Now, because he no longer had one, it was just about getting out of this world. As he slogged his way across the muck, he paused every few feet to take a swig from the bottle. That damn dream kept popping into his head even when he was awake! He tried to pick up his pace, but wind-driven sheets of rain restrained his advance like a hulking offensive guard. He finally reached Highway 98 where he had asphalt under his feet to make his trek easier. He didn't bother to look for traffic before crossing the road because safety no longer was a concern. There were loud sustained honks from both directions, and he raised the bottle with one hand and flipped everybody the bird with the other. As he stepped onto the curb on the other side of road, Swindall tossed his head back and made sure he emptied the bottle of any remaining drops. When he opened his eyes, he realized the sky had merged with the earth into one indistinguishable big gray mess. The rain was so heavy now he couldn't tell how far it was to the water's edge. He was *really* drunk, his massive body swaying heavily from side to side as he stumbled forward, the bottle slipping out of his hand.

Swindall turned around to take one last look at the two-storey beachfront house on concrete stilts, beneath it a shiny new cherry-red-sparkle pick-up and a twenty-one-foot Boston Whaler perched atop its trailer. But, of course, they existed only in his imagination. All his big plans had gone up in smoke after his incredibly bad run of luck. Hurricane Andrew had destroyed his business, forcing him to sell out to those New York sharpies for a hundred-thousand dollars. His brother-in-law told him not to worry about the rest of the big money he should have gotten. "Don't even *think* about it anymore, old buddy," Cecil had said with a hearty slap on the back. "Turns out to go partners with me you won't have to invest as much as I originally thought. And you know what else? You're gonna make back all that money you never got real fast." Because the hurricane had left their stupid little dollhouse untouched, they had been able to sell it quickly for a very good price in the seller's market Andrew had left in its wake. A few days after he arrived in The Panhandle, Aubrey Swindall handed over to Cecil Hornby nearly all the proceeds from the sale of their two properties.

Emily already was working in a K-Mart near Cinco Bayou seven miles west of Destin. They would have to live in a small rental apartment, but only for a short time, because it wouldn't be long before the big bucks would start rolling in from the deals he and Cecil would be making in the red-hot local real-estate market. But then Cecil started acting a little strange, telling him stuff like he needed to get his real-estate license before he could work in the business with him, which was something he never had bothered to mention to Swindall until after he had taken their money. Cecil got him a thick book to study so he could take the state exam, and Swindall stayed in the tiny efficiency reading it a few hours each day after Emily went off to work. One afternoon he decided to head over to Cecil's office to find out how things were going with the business. The tiny strip mall on the Emerald Coast Parkway near the Mid-Bay Bridge had a Farm Store, a Chinese restaurant, a locksmith, and vacant office space with an address corresponding to the one on Cecil's business card for "Hornby Investments, Ltd." When Swindall asked the Farm Store clerk how long that office space had been empty, the man said as long as he had been working there which was close to six months now. Swindall raced back to Destin to hunt down his brother-in-law, but he was nowhere to be found, having abandoned his wife and children the night before and taken off for parts unknown. Within a few days the big story around Destin was that Cecil Hornby had bilked dozens of victims out of more than two million dollars.

After suffering through a couple of weeks of deep depression, which included heavy drinking, Swindall took a job bartending at the marina down the street for minimum wage plus tips which always were so small he would have preferred just plain old insults. He never fully recovered from his severe bout of depression, something obvious to his customers because they kept asking him, "So what's wrong, buddy?" And that same question a hundred times a day finally became too much to suffer so he quit. Emily never mentioned he should get another job even though they were living day-to-day on her modest paycheck, and he was buying booze with her hard-earned money. "Oh, stop worrying about what Cecil did, babe," she would keep telling him with her big sweet smile. "We're doing just fine." But he knew better because his wife had been feeling bad these past few weeks, and it looked like it might be something serious. She promised to go and see a doctor soon, but he already knew what was wrong. He had made her deathly sick by ruining her life too. But now he was about to give her the cure. He had to be the biggest loser of all time! Another tropical depression!

Without warning he felt the cold tide rush all the way up to his knees, and his legs started buckling. He thought he was going

to fall backwards so he lurched forward to maintain his balance
and plunged into the rough surf. His mouth filled with salty water,
and he started choking as he swallowed some of it. He had been
out fishing a thousand times in the Keys, but he never had learned
how to swim and always had been scared shitless of drowning if he
fell overboard. At first his arms shot out and flapped wildly like
big bird wings. But then something started pulling him away from
the shore, as if he had latched onto one of those underwater
scooters in a James Bond movie. He decided right then to stop
struggling against the fate he had chosen. A few feet below the
churning water his body began rotating slowly and gracefully on
a journey out to sea. His body was flush with a warm and peaceful
feeling, and he even welcomed that damn nightmare as it played
in his mind for the last time.

He was sitting in a big shopping cart as it rolled along the
supermarket aisles. He didn't recognize the store, but how many
dreams happened in familiar places? As he traveled along a giant
hand would reach out and take items from the shelves and place
them in the cart. All of a sudden the cart started rattling loudly as
it raced along the wide part at the front of the store. Reverend
Sanderson stood next to the last cash register with his arms crossed.
"It's time to check out, son." The Reverend regarded him with sad
eyes. "Are you sure you got everything you wanted?" From his
perch on the cart Swindall took inventory of the things which had
filled the basket. There were tiny replicas of the bar and package
store and their stupid little dollhouse. And in front of these
miniature structures a large group of people had gathered. His
mother and father and brother and sister, the skinhead detective
with the swastika tattoos and Stewart Malman, and Curtis Chance
Thigpen and those two little peckerwoods, Bobby Wendt and
Kenny Moser. And in front of all of them, Emily was standing
there with her sweet smile. They were all gazing up at him
anxiously waiting for his answer. "No, sir." This was the first time
he had answered The Reverend's question because the dream
never had gone that far before. Sanderson smiled kindly and

leaned forward slightly, "Then, son, you need to go back." Had he been lying in his bed back at the tiny efficiency apartment, Aubrey Swindall knew this time he wouldn't have jerked up soaking in sweat. Instead, he would have finished off the most peaceful rest of his entire life.

"No! No!" He felt the panic overtaking him as he tried to free himself from the iron grip of the rip current dragging him out to sea, but he was sick drunk and completely drained of strength. "No! No! I need to go back!" This couldn't be happening because he had just granted himself a stay of execution!

"Brey! Brey! Are you okay?!"

Swindall thought he must have passed on because he heard Emily's voice calling out to him. But when his head rolled to the side and his mouth dropped open, instead of salty water rushing in, he tasted sand and began coughing uncontrollably as he sucked in air. He cracked open one eye and saw two pairs of black rubber boots a few inches away.

"You want us to call rescue, ma'am?"

"Are you okay, Brey?" Emily was kneeling next to him, stroking his head. "These two men from the power company stopped to help. You weren't looking when you crossed the road. A bunch of cars almost hit you."

"Took both of us to drag you back to shore, big guy. A little further out, and you would have been a goner. Don't you know you can't go in the water when there's rip currents like that?"

"Next time you get caught in one, you gotta swim parallel to the shore."

"Oh, my husband doesn't even know how to swim," Emily giggled as she squeezed his cheek hard.

"Well, that's not good a thing when you live in Florida because there's water just about everywhere."

"He looks like he's gonna be okay, ma'am. You still want us to call rescue?"

"Do you want rescue, Brey?"

Swindall coughed out a big wad of yellow and green sputum

which trickled down his chin as he shook his head.

"No? He says no. Thanks so much for your help."

"You all should get inside. We've got this tropical storm coming our way."

"Are you drunk again, Brey?" Emily scolded him after the black boots were gone. "You damn well nearly got yourself killed! I brought home two big steaks just like you like. This was supposed to be a special night for us, and instead I'm out here getting drenched."

"Special night?" Swindall said weakly. When Emily didn't answer, he opened his eye wider. The thick rain almost completely blurred his vision, but he was able to make out her big sweet smile. "Special night, babe?"

"Beryl is on the way."

"I know about the damn storm," he grumbled, closing his eye and letting his head flop to the side.

"No, silly. That's what we're gonna call our son."

This time Swindall cracked open both eyes and was pelted by blasts of sand gusting across the beach.

"Did you hear what I just said?" Emily tugged hard on his ear lobe. "You're gonna have a son! Well, the doctor said most likely it's a boy. And I decided we're gonna name him after this storm. Beryl Swindall. Are you listening to me, Brey? Turns out I've been sick the last few weeks because I'm pregnant. Can you believe that?" She waited for a moment so he could think about what she had just told him. "After all these years you've given me the greatest gift I could ever hope for, a child, Brey, a child. And that's a gift so much greater than any million dollars or big house or anything else."

CHAPTER TWENTY-SEVEN

The billboard at the end of the gravel parking lot no longer displayed the American flag with a plea to southbound motorists: "Will The Last American To Leave Miami Please Bring The Flag?" Now it was filled with the dark-blue flag of "The Conch Republic" of Key West, with ten stars and a blazing sun and conch shell in its center and the motto: "We Seceded Where Others Failed." And, instead of announcing "Skeeter's Bar And Package Liquors Last Chance For Booze Before The Florida Keys," it now read: "Manatee Malman's Last Chance For Food, Drink, And Souvenirs Before The Florida Keys." The lime-green one-storey cement-block building had a v-shaped thatched roof woven from sable palm fronds just like a Seminole Indian chickee. A half-dozen people were sitting in white resin wicker rockers scattered along the wooden porch. Speakers at each end of the porch were blasting out "a-wimoweh a-wimoweh" from the last chorus of the Tokens 1962 hit "The Lion Sleeps Tonight," followed by Jimmy Buffet's "Margaritaville," the unofficial national anthem of The Conch Republic.

"Welcome to Manatee Malman's," said the man who greeted Rayfield Lifton just inside the store. He had long hair and a full beard, and Lifton almost didn't recognize him.

"I need to speak with Mr. Manatee Malman, please."

"You're looking at him."

Guardians Of The Faith

Lifton scratched his chin after they shook hands. "Sir, I'm with the State Attorney's Office, and we're investigating your operation. It appears you've been engaging in deceptive trade practices here. For example, take that billboard you've got out there. First, people who don't know this area are going to believe they're leaving the United States and entering another country. Alright, so Key West *is* another country, but it's still about a hundred-twenty miles from here. And, second, that sign implies this is the *last* chance for people to buy this kind of stuff when, in fact, Key Largo is just ten minutes down the road, *and* the Keys are jam-packed with places like yours all the way to Key West."

"Key Largo is at least another twenty minutes from here." Stewart Malman laughed and slapped Lifton's shoulder. "You should take a look at the other side of the billboard. It also has the flag of the Conch Republic, but it says: 'Leaving The Conch Republic. Manatee Malman's Last Chance For Food, Drink, And Keys Souvenirs.' A lot of people don't buy everything they need until they've already left the Keys, and we've got it all right here," Malman said with a sweep of his hands. "T-shirts, hats, postcards, shells, key chains, plastic sharks, lime and coconut drinks, baked goods, Jimmy Buffet and Bob Marley music. You name it."

"This is serious. You get them coming and going."

"That's the whole idea, brother. You may know this already, but back in 1982 the Border Patrol set up a roadblock and inspection point just a couple hundred feet south of here to intercept narcotics and illegal aliens. The feds picked that spot because it's where US 1 and Card Sound Road merge, the only two ways to get in and out of the Keys by land. But tourists started complaining about the long delays it was causing, and tourism in the Keys went down. In protest Key West seceded from the United States and declared itself the Conch Republic. The Mayor became its Prime Minister, and he immediately declared war against the United States, surrendered one minute later, and applied for one billion in foreign aid. So prosecute away because I've got some good defenses to your allegations of deceptive trade practices."

"Alright, case closed. You know, Stewart, you've got a really cool place here."

"Thanks, Ray. Things are going well. We knocked down Skeeter's all the way to the cement slab and rebuilt this place from scratch. We learned a big lesson from Andrew so underneath the palm thatch up there we've got a roof of poured concrete which isn't going anywhere no matter how bad a storm we get. No more wood trusses or asphalt shingles for us, my friend."

"You look pretty busy here today. Are you sure you still want to go out there and do this thing with us?"

"Wouldn't miss it for the world. Karen will stay here and mind the store. In fact, yesterday we were making some potpourri tapes for our place, and we decided to put together one for the trip out there today."

Stewart Malman followed the bright-yellow Hummer in his vintage milk-chocolate Mercedes 450SL convertible. They crossed over the railroad tracks into Homestead and turned west at the town's north end, lime and avocado groves straddling each side of the narrow road. They had to navigate carefully to avoid dozens of potholes until they reached their destination. After they all had gathered near the granite markers, Malman pressed the play button on the small boom box.

"It sure is a beautiful day." Kimberly Singletary put her arm around her daughter and drew her close as Sam Cooke began crooning "What A Wonderful World."

"Cloudless blue skies and seventy degrees in November. Now I know why I moved to South Florida."

"Yeah, right, Stewart. I thought it was so you could get them coming and going."

"You better be careful, Ray," Reginald Crawford warned. "That foxy lady you brought along might just decide to do a story about your stupid jokes."

"Alright, people, let's focus, as The Reverend used to say." Donald Leeds stepped forward, pulled a pair of sunflowers out of the white plastic bucket he was holding, and knelt on the grass between the two salt-and-pepper granite slabs. He placed one on the final resting place of The Reverend Wilkie P. Sanderson, the other one on the slab bearing the name of Curtis Chance Thigpen.

They remained at the cemetery until the cassette tape had played the full set of Sam Cooke songs, the last one being "A Change Is Gonna Come." Before he walked over to Crawford's Hummer, Lifton took another look at the inscriptions on the gravestones. "When We Do Good, We Become God's Autograph On His Masterpiece," read the one for The Reverend Wilkie P. Sanderson. And for Curtis Chance Thigpen the inscription was a quote from The Reverend Martin Luther King, Jr. "Faith Is Taking The First Step Even If You Don't See The Whole Staircase."

* * *

The intercom buzzed as Rayfield Lifton was removing the miniature basketball hoop hanging on the inside of his office door. He returned to his desk and pressed the button to extinguish the shrill, annoying game-show sound. The button popped off and fell on the floor. Cuqui Perez announced a visitor, and he told her to send him in as he bent down to search for the button. Vernon Castleberry pushed a squeaky metal cart into his office.

"I'll be right with you, Vernon, as soon as I find the intercom button which..."

"Well, you can go ahead and just toss it in the trash along with the whole damn phone because I've got a present for you." Lifton turned around and saw the wiry maintenance man holding a brown box. "The new system is going in today. But don't ask me how to use this new contraption. It's got a control panel something like a jet plane."

Lifton located the plastic square under his desk and stood up. "I won't be needing that new equipment, Vernon. This is my last day here."

"You really ought to take a look. This is some contraption." Castleberry set the box on the cart and scratched his head. "I heard you were leaving, Mr. Lifton, but I don't get why you're doing that. You're the nicest damn prosecutor out of the whole sorry lot here."

"Thanks, Vernon." Lifton reached out to shake his hand.

"I was talking to your secretary, and we both thought we should just up and quit because of what they did to you."

"Nobody did anything to me, Vernon. I could stay here if I wanted to. And you should keep working here if you still enjoy it. This building would come crashing down if you weren't around to fix things up."

"Oh, they'd get along just fine without me around. But if I quit right now, the truth is I wouldn't know what the heck to do with myself with all the free time."

Lifton picked up the bankers box and miniature basketball hoop and walked out of his office for the last time. "Well, Moneypenny, this time I *won't* be back." When she didn't say anything, he moved closer to her desk. She was dabbing at her eyes with a big wad of tissues.

"I said I was going to quit if you were not here anymore. I want to quit, but I need the money. Maybe I'll quit when Castro is gone, and I can go back to my country."

Lifton set the bankers box down and took her hand. "Cuqui Perez," he said, guiding her up from the chair, "you're better than any Moneypenny James Bond could ever have." She tried to laugh as he hugged her warmly but, instead, she made a sound more like she was gasping for air. He lifted her chin. "You know how to find me, Moneypenny. Stay in touch, okay?"

* * *

"Hey, big brother." Kimberly was out of breath, hugging and rocking the ball like it was a baby. "Somebody's looking for you over there." She leaned to her left and looked past him.

"No way I'm falling for *that* one, Kim." He lunged forward and tried to steal the ball, but it was too late because she already had passed it off to her right.

Lifton half-turned and glanced over at Northwest 17th Street where he spied the exotic black vehicle. Alonzo Norris' Cuban chauffeur, Carlos, was yelling and waving his arms. "I need a time out," Lifton said and took off jogging across Williams Park, marveling at the first Hummer limousine he had ever laid eyes on. As he got close the right rear window began slowly descending.

"You all thought I was kidding about doing a Hummer limo. You like it, Liftoff?"

"It's something else. But you know what, No-Time? I'd be real happy if I could just have your old Mercedes limo."

Alonzo Norris stepped out. "Too late. I sold it to Wayne when I got this. But listen, Liftoff, fame and fortune can still be yours. So why don't you jump inside here, my brother, and we can do some *serious* talking."

"Sorry, No-Time, but I've got a game going on over there."

Norris shook his head disapprovingly. "See, that's *exactly* my point, Liftoff. You're *still* in the same damn place you were twenty years ago. Now listen up. The new league starts next week over at the DSC, and half my damn Posse has gone missing."

"You mean the half that's over there?" Lifton tilted his head toward the basketball court on the other side of Williams Park.

Norris shielded his eyes so he could see better. "Damn, Liftoff! You're playing pick-up ball with Doc and Seven?"

Valerie slid across the back seat of the limo and poked her head out of the window.

Wayne Parrish emerged from the other side of the limo. "I see his sister and two other girls over there. And one of them is as white as a sheet!"

"Wait! Let me see!" The right rear door opened, and Valerie stepped out. "That's his sister, Kim, and that lady reporter, what's-her-name, and..." Bernice Valerie Witherspoon looked like she had just seen a ghost. "Wait, that can't be..."

"Yeah, Val-er-ie. That's my little niece. Well, I guess she's not so little anymore."

"Damn, look at her playing ball. What the *hell* happened to that *thing* she had?"

"Nobody knows, Perishable. Reverend Sanderson used to like to say something happened the night Andrew hit. Some kind of connection between her and Thigpen. And the connection kept getting stronger, and things started changing. We gave up a long time ago trying to figure it out."

"The victory of light over darkness!" Norris bellowed, like he was trying to rally a jury to his side in closing argument. "*That, my friends, is* the cosmic megadrama!"

"Hey, Liftoff!" Crawford shouted from the edge of the court as he twirled the basketball on his index finger. "Will you please get your sorry ass over here!"

"Now, look here, Ray," Norris continued, "I heard you finally lost your gig over at Metro Justice. But what we talked about a long time ago that cold winter night over on South Beach, that's still on the table. You can come work for me, my brother, and we'll reset the clock and start things fresh."

"My brother," Lifton said, putting his hand on Norris' shoulder, "I didn't finally lose my gig over at Metro Justice. Like George Jefferson, I just decided to move on up to the east side. Brickell Avenue is east of Metro Justice, right? You're looking at Crawford Holdings' new corporate counsel."

Norris stepped back and folded his arms. "Now I *heard* it through the grapevine Seven and your sister were an item, but I didn't know you were gonna go work for him."

"Yeah, Kim and Seven are getting hitched, and I'll be working the civil side of law for a change. You know, the other day I was listening to the radio, and I heard that song 'No Time.'"

"What song?"

"No, 'No Time' is the name of the song by Guess Who."

"Who? Oh, yeah," Norris chuckled, "that's the name of the group, right?"

"Right. The lyrics go, 'No time left for you. No time left for you. On my way to better things. I found myself some wings.' So, Val-er-ie, how's the acting thing going?"

Bernice Valerie Witherspoon didn't answer the question because she never heard it. Instead, she continued staring across Williams Park with her mouth wide open.

There was a chorus of yelling now from across Williams Park

for Lifton to return.

"Well, it's just a pick-up game with a bunch of girls, but we're having some fun. And, No-Time, thanks but no thanks for the offer."

Norris shouted out something, but Lifton never looked back as he sprinted across Williams Park.

"So whose ball is it anyway?"

"You know who, Uncle Ray." She tossed the ball inbounds to Reginald Crawford who immediately passed it back to her. Demeka Singletary shifted up and down and side to side, deciding on an escape route to take to the basket as Lifton picked his spot to try and block her advance. She began dribbling the ball faster and faster until it sounded like a small jackhammer.

"Kara and Doc, you be careful. These people play real dirty."

"You're so funny, Uncle Ray," Demeka giggled and shook her head. "I remember all the things you used to say. Like Big *Larry* Bird," she giggled again. "Hey, look over there!" She jerked her head, and he fell victim to the ploy. She shoved the ball between his legs and recovered it behind him before he could turn around. Demeka Singletary cocked her arms and launched a fifteen-foot jump shot. And it was nothing but net.

Guardians Of The Faith

About the Author

Martin Alan Feigenbaum grew up in Kansas City, Missouri and resides in South Florida. He is the co-author of the non-fiction work *The Inner Ring: The Set-Up Of Mike Tyson And The Uncrowning Of Don King*.

He invites your questions and comments which can be forwarded to him at: marty@surfsidesixpublishing.com.

Guardians Of The Faith

Guardians Of The Faith

CPSIA information can be obtained
at www.ICGtesting.com
Printed in the USA
LVHW011448150720
660769LV00017B/1145